Praise for The Beekeeper's Daughter . . .

In *The Beekeeper's Daughter*, Jessica Stilling deftly intertwines the stories of Lorelei (a writer and teacher recovering from a deep betrayal), her difficult and compelling mother, the poet Sylvia Plath, and a mysterious manuscript, showing how secrets, sorrow, pain, and love in its multiplicity of guises can echo and reverberate. Stilling's insightful connections, imagery-rich prose, and compassionate exploration of her characters will stay with you long after this novel ends. — Kate Angus, author of *So Late to the Party*

"An elegantly-crafted and brave tale of the struggle of the artist against betrayal, madness, and myth. Haunted throughout by the legacy of Sylvia Plath, The Beekeeper's Daughter mingles fact and fiction, past and present, into a story that you won't want to put down." — Danny Goldberg, author of *Serving the Servant: Remembering Kurt Cobain*

The
Beekeeper's
Daughter

Hi Tim!
Thanks so much for
coming to the launch!
12/13/19

Santa Stilling

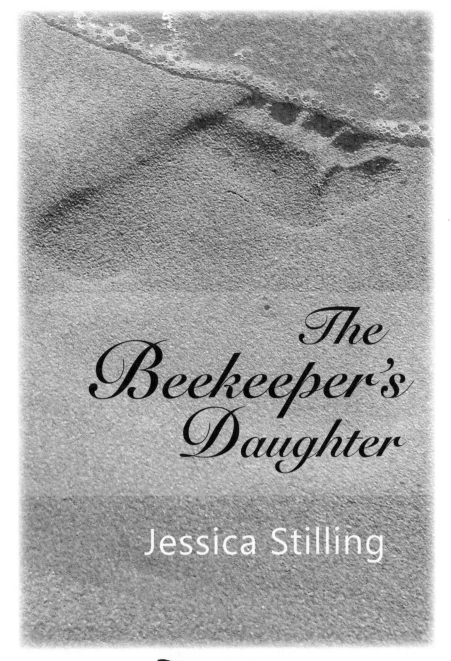

The Beekeeper's Daughter

Jessica Stilling

BInk *Bink Books*
Bedazzled Ink Publishing Company • Fairfield, California

978-1-949290-19-6 paperback

Cover Design
by

Bink Books
a division of
Bedazzled Ink Publishing Company
Fairfield, California
http://www.bedazzledink.com

For Adam

Because You Are My Leonard

Lorelei

"IT IS NO night to drown in:/A full moon, river lapsing/Black beneath bland mirror-sheen." I hear Plath again. That poem my mother used to half sing before bed, at the dinner table, any time her mind wandered. I hear it in the back of my mind as I watch the ocean off of Cape Cod and consider swimming too far out. Slipping further, there's always a moment when I might just drown, just . . . let it happen.

They let Barry Larsen out of prison last week. It took a while for the letter, an official-looking piece of paper stamped with the crest of the Commonwealth of Massachusetts, to come but I knew he might get parole. It's only some-of-my-business, maybe, in some circumstances, it's none-of-my-business and I have tried to keep my distance since we're still basically strangers.

I remember the day I learned his daughter, Heather, had been killed. It was a week after I'd found out about her affair with my husband. In that time I'd kicked Theo out of our home. I'd tried to ignore Heather, who was one of my English 201: Introduction to Modernism students at the college where I teach. I'd tried to stick my head in the sand I was so angry at the two of them and then I'd found out Heather had died, her cousin had beaten her to death and her father had given him the keys to the warehouse where he did it. After that there was no room for my anger. No room for anything but sorrow and guilt and I kept my distance from Heather and her family, knowing that was what they'd want.

Tonight all I can hear as I stare out at the ocean, at Cape Cod, is this damned Sylvia Plath poetry my mother used to whisper to me when I couldn't sleep. I look out at the ocean just past the waves breaking. When they're breaking they might bring you in. It's when they stop, when they remain calm a long way out, that's when you know you've gone too far. That's when to worry.

"The blue water-mists dropping/Scrim after scrim like fishnets/Though fishermen are sleeping." The Lorelei, "Lorelei," a Sylvia Plath poem I loved as a child because we shared the name. My mother loved the poem as well. She'd been one of those post seventies feminists in the early eighties and my father always said she used to walk around the house on Cape Cod, her belly a great round mound, "like the moon, she used to say, but I think she got that from somewhere," my father once told me. She'd walk around singing this Plath poem to me. "Lorelei, The Lorelei," she'd say. "A woman who could control

men with a single gaze. She'd just look at them and they'd fall in love with her. Such raw power. A woman needs that." She was older when she had me, in her late thirties. She was not supposed to be able to get pregnant, she used to say. I was her little miracle, she'd continue on her good days. On her bad days all her words were poison and she'd spit them with such vitriol that it took me into my adulthood to truly come to turns with the things she said.

I used to swim when I was younger. A little girl growing up in Waltham, Massachusetts I was on the swim team. The breaststroke was my favorite, not that it wasn't everyone's, it really is very simple, just what you think when you think about swimming up and down, up and down, none of this crawling, this butterflying. As a child I always wondered if I swam fast enough could I fool the gods. Would they let me see that spot between time and space, where the sky and the ocean meet?

Once my mother went too far out. We were swimming together at the beach near nightfall. We shouldn't have been out. The lifeguards had already told us to come in but we stayed a few minutes longer bobbing in the water together. "Watch this," she said and she just started swimming, doing the crawl along the tiny waves until I couldn't see her anymore. I treaded water as long as I could, waiting for her to come back. I was twelve years old, I felt like I was in the middle of the ocean out there and she just kept going. She went under, I didn't see her come back up. By then I knew my mother's antics. Sometimes she'd run and hide in the house and wouldn't come out even when I called for her for an hour, even when I started crying. Sometimes she wouldn't get out of bed for days. Losing her in the ocean, another perfectly fine place to hide, was not beyond my mother, and at twelve I already knew this. Yet I called out to her as the water lapped over my head and I went under. The current had its great fist at my ankle and I barely pulled myself up. I crawled to shore, stroke after stroke waves beating over my head, and I felt like I was falling. My mother didn't come back. I sat on the beach and waited for her. If I were older I would have run for help but I just sat there stunned. It wasn't that I didn't know what to do it's that just then I couldn't move. Eventually she came out covered in seaweed. She'd crawled out a few feet back and I hadn't seen her in the dark. But she came up to me looking like some Creature From the Black Lagoon, put her hand on my shoulder and motioned toward the house.

It was time to go back.

My mother did things like that. As a child I did not question them.

No night to drown . . . Oh Sylvia! She was so much like my mother.

We used to visit Cape Cod every summer and stay at my grandparents' little bungalow on the ocean. The house has been in the family for three generations, my great-grandfather, a speakeasy owner in Boston, bought it back when a house on the Cape did not require three diversified portfolios and a CEO position in a city like Boston or New York. The house is falling apart and hopeless looking, the clapboard walls dingy with disrepair, two, maybe three shutters are about to fall off, but it's worth a fortune now. I wonder sometimes why my father, who inherited it once my grandfather passed, doesn't sell it.

It's been years since my mother and I used to swim. It's been a single year since she finally went too far, not in the ocean but in a bathtub. There were also pills involved.

There are no lifeguards tonight, no people, just a few bonfires up the beach, probably six, seven city blocks away. I strain to hear voices, the gentle murmur of nightcaps on the beach, before heading back. The light over the house betrays an expected but uninvited guest and I shake my head at how predictable my life has become. My white cotton dress snags for a second on the small wooden stake in the ground that denotes the barrier between our property and the property belonging to another rich Bostonian who never comes to visit. The cotton is warm and rustic on my skin and I feel it over my shoulders before marching to the house and this visitor.

The outline of his body comes into focus, the way he stands, hips slightly shifted, his hair longer than it was last week. He is the kind of man who always puts off the next haircut. I walk nearer and his trimmed beard skews my impression of his face. "Eamon," I call and he smiles and waves like I'm expecting him. This relationship has progressed in the last few months and now I'm always expecting him at least in the back of my mind. Someday soon I should just give him a key.

"I saw your light was on and thought I'd come over," he says as I reach the porch. A single light shines over its shabby boards and I grab a towel near the Adirondack chairs and attempt to dry the spray of the sea off my arms. "I just wanted to see if you were okay, I'm sorry about the . . . I don't know, the father getting out."

"I never met him. He didn't kill his daughter, he just let her killer take her away."

"And things got out of hand," Eamon mutters, shaking his head. He didn't know me when this happened. He never met Heather or her father and still this upsets him.

"I just wonder, you know. If her cousin never found out. If he wasn't a possessive little shit who thought it was okay to beat a girl to death for having an affair. It's the what-ifs, right? What if the affair had been quietly handled instead of all this?"

"You can't think like that. Are you all right? What were you doing out there?" he asks, his eyes big, like he's looking out to sea and all he can see is my face.

"I'm fine, just water watching."

"And what does the water do when you watch it, my dear?"

"I should say something deep here," I ponder instead of saying anything deep. "It does tricks, I guess. So how was Liar's? What time is it?" I reach up and kiss his cheek. He pulls me close and I smell the bar where he works on his clothes, smoky cigarettes and the bitter bite of spilled whiskey. He breathes deeply and I take him in. Eamon is very big. He's tall and broad and at another time one might mistake him for a Viking.

He works at a bar called Liar's, a seedy joint of a place for locals only. Those old-fashioned Massachusetts's fishermen who still carry lobster crates into the water, the men who wear rubber overalls, boast about the Red Sox, and use the word "wicked" not in reference to a witch. It's a place where bar fights are prevalent and nothing is high end. It's also the kind of bar that doesn't close until well after one a.m.

"I didn't stay the whole night, left at ten and thought I'd stop by. Some guy came in all happy about Trump, you know? He said he can't wait until we deport all the slimy foreigners and when I asked him if he thought I was a foreigner, you know, because of the accent, he laughed and said, 'White foreigners are okay. White foreigners don't leach money.' Got a little heated for a while, another guy threatened to beat him up if he didn't take that red hat off and he left on his own. People were a little on edge after that but it was fine by the time I got off. Left a bad taste in my mouth though."

"I can imagine. Being an Irish guy in Boston you must not get many sideways glances."

"County Kerry. People eat up the accent," Eamon says as he takes a seat.

"It's a lovely accent," I tell him, sitting on the side of his Adirondack chair I drape an arm around him. Water still clings to me in tiny salt crystals and the light flickers for a second.

"Not as lovely as your accent, Lorelei." He gives me those eyes, big and blue, bottomless eyes. "So I got some more wood from that worksite over in Dennis. I'm going to start fusing it with metal scraps, see what comes out of it."

"Sounds very blue collar," I tell him and he laughs.

"All artists are blue collar, especially sculptors. I don't care how much money they make or where they live. They work with their hands, they have to create something. There's wood and clay and metal—workman's materials. As blue collar as it comes."

"True."

Despite the fancy graduate degree in Studio Art he barely uses, Eamon fits the blue-collar description to a T. Apparently art degrees are only good for tending bar. He lives in a two-room apartment above a liquor store in Wellfleet. He works at a bar, takes odd jobs, sometimes carpentry and painting, one time he spent a month subbing in for a guy at a bookstore. He usually adjuncts a couple of classes at Cape Cod Community College. But he shows regularly at galleries in Provincetown, Bar Harbor, and Yarmouth, once a summer he has work up in the Hamptons, every three or four years he lucks into a gallery show in New York City. One time he did a show in Sausalito, California. He straddles that line of successful and unsuccessful very well.

Headlights run across the porch for a second and the sound of tires on gravel crunches over the sound of sifting waves. And why my father never bothered to pave the driveway after all these years I will never understand. I remember the rocks in the drive, they used to cut my feet when I ran in the yard as a child. You'd think a child would learn but children never learn when they're distracted.

"Who could that be parking next to my pickup?" Eamon muses.

The sound of feet shuffling over rocks and soft cries of "shit, shit, shit," replaces the sound of tires crunching as a new presence enters. I do not move from my spot and Eamon doesn't appear too interested. "You know, you really should pave your freaking driveway, Lorelei," a voice that is both tough and amused comes out of the darkness of the netherworld my porch light cannot reach.

"It's not my house. Call my father in Florida, tell him to take care of it," I reply as my friend Amelia appears.

She looks as if she's come out of the water. Her hair is stringy and wet, her dress clings to her and she does not wear, but carries, her black Christian Loubiton heels dangling from one finger as if they're some kind of red-soled accessory. "What happened?" I ask and Amelia leans against the weather worn post of the porch.

"Fell in the pool. Maybe I jumped. It was hard to tell. Took my shoes off first—got an Uber home."

"That kind of party, eh?" Eamon asks, placing one hand on my shoulder. It feels like the paw of some kind of bear.

"I don't remember." Amelia shakes her head. "There were a few too many cocktails. I really thought it would be more sophisticated, a party for *Maude Magazine*, but it got out of hand. I guess what happens on the Cape stays on the Cape."

"Is that what they say?" I ask, eyeing her fuchsia pink Diane von Furstenberg dress. It was a find at a thrift store, sixteen dollars, but it fits Amelia's ample curves perfectly and clashes with her auburn hair in such a way that seems intentional.

"I don't know. But tomorrow night there's this *hors d'oeuvres* thing—much more classy. You said you'd come, right, Lorelei, you're still coming? I promise it won't be jump-in-the-pool crazy."

I nod calmly and look out at the ocean. The thought of a party makes me want to dive back into it. "I'm coming. My aunt Sarah is in from New York. She's going to be there."

"Great, I love Sarah. And I just think. I mean, you wanted to get away. Out of the city, away from that . . . I know it's nice with all this privacy, but you need to see people. You need to network. There will be people there who might end up getting advance copies of your next book." Amelia is the kind of woman who constantly tells other people to network.

"The book I have yet to write."

"The book you *will* write," Amelia urges. "This is what happens, the story's been told a thousand times. Author has big first book, author has emotional trauma in her personal life brought on by a cheating husband—"

"It was more than that," I add, picturing Heather. "Much more."

"I know," Amelia acknowledges and I wonder if she knows about Mr. Larsen getting out. "Then, author has more trouble writing second book. Author's best friend brings her out of it and saves her by being awesome."

"Something like that." I can't help but laugh at Amelia, wondering how much she's had to drink. At the very least she hasn't fallen over.

The waves rock, like they're sighing us to sleep, and I watch the gentle pull as Eamon lifts his hand from my shoulder and places it on my knee. General background noise comes from the bonfires up the beach but it is silent, the kind that calls to mind awkward glances and crickets, when I hear the ping of metal falling and the heavy crack of something shattering at the other side of the house.

"What was that?" Eamon asks first, getting to his feet. He moves in staggers, feet apart like he doesn't know what they're for and I wonder how many he had after leaving his shift at the bar.

"It's probably a rabbit, maybe a raccoon. Do they have raccoons on Cape Cod?" Amelia asks.

"I don't know. Maybe I should check it out," I say, and Eamon puts one hand up.

"I'll look into it," he says. He speaks just like a knight in shining armor, or like he's mocking one, I can't quite tell. Maybe it's the alcohol or the ocean, maybe it's just that he's here with two women or the racist guy at the bar earlier who really seemed to piss him off, but he wants to handle this and I'm too tired not to let him. "Let me just see." He grabs a long pole that usually goes with my beach umbrella as a weapon. It's yellow and made of flimsy metal, but at the very least it has a big spike at the end that, if given a chance, could probably do some damage. He stays up on unsteady feet and then nearly tumbles into the side of the pole he meant to defend us with.

"You ok?" Amelia half laughs at him and he turns back.

"I have this firmly in hand I'll have you know."

He walks toward the side of the house as if on tiptoes, but a man like Eamon, he's big, of good Irish stock, all muscle and bone, the kind of body that has two sizes on just about anyone, and tiptoeing doesn't quite work for him. Amelia still laughs as I watch him carefully round the corner as if bats might fly at him.

"Are you okay?" I finally ask as he stands there, just staring at the side of my father's eighty-five-year-old bungalow.

He turns his head and then slips on something. His arms flail out and the pole flies away, down the bank and into the sand. I'll have to retrieve it later. He yells something, or maybe he just yells, inaudible words, a great rumbling like a bear, and falls on the ground.

"Eamon, you okay?" I call, rushing toward him. He is not so proud that he does not lift his hand, allowing me to help him. I pull and he pushes as he finally gets to his feet.

"Fine, perfectly fine. But it appears there's something," Eamon says, and I turn to the space by the window in the living room that he'd been eyeing.

"What is that?"

A ceramic planter has been turned over, part of it is broken but I never cared for plants or planters, my thumbs being entirely black. I walk the few paces to the spot where the living room light shines on the sandy ground and pick up a long, red and black scarf. I stop for a second. I think I remember that scarf but I can't place it. The other object lying there is almost too small to be seen in the dark. It's a tube of lipstick in a pinkish case. I open it up and look at the lipstick, it appears to have been used, but infrequently.

"What is it?" Eamon asks. He does not come close and so I return to the porch where Amelia stands in her wet dress.

"I don't know. A scarf. Amelia do you know who this might belong to? It's really nice, looks expensive. If someone lost this don't you think they'd come back for it?"

"I've never seen it," Amelia replies. "Whose is it?"

"And this lipstick," I say, opening it up and showing it to her like a lipstick is a completely alien object I must identify to this writer at a fashion magazine. "It's red . . . really, really red."

"This is like Lady of the Evening red. You know Sylvia Plath used to love red lipstick. I read about it once in a biography about her time at *Mademoiselle*, she always wore these deep, cherry red lipsticks. Very 1950s."

"That's great, so Sylvia Plath came here and left a very nice scarf and her lipstick behind," Eamon counters. "What was that noise? Aren't either of you nervous? Should I call someone?" Knight in Shining Armor take two.

"Someone broke a planter. Or something. I'm betting it was a raccoon." But I look at the window ledge to see that not only is a mud colored planter shattered but a piece of the windowsill, one of the white painted boards, has come off. This is an old house and stuff like this is bound to happen. Still, someone must have been pulling on it.

"A raccoon with a penchant for nice scarves and red lipstick?" Eamon asks. "Aren't you just a little concerned? I know your father doesn't have much in the way of valuables, but maybe someone was staking out the place. And what if it's concerning—"

"It's not," I counter quickly. "It can't be. We have an alarm system."

"I just think we should call someone. The day you get a letter saying the father was let out of prison this happens. I just think we should call and—"

"And say what? That a man who has just been let out of jail might have come to my house and left some makeup? I don't have any proof but, you know, he has a criminal record. Is that what you want me to say to the police? All because I found a scarf and a lipstick. Anyone could have done this. Maybe one of my other students . . . I don't know, I'm sure word got out about Heather's father and a few of them wrote me some nasty emails after everything. Some of them blamed me. I was her professor."

"All the more reason to call the police," Eamon argues.

"They'll only bother him. I don't want that on my conscience, the man was just put on parole and all he needs is this kind of trouble."

"If you say so," Eamon acquiesces.

"Thank you," I reply, smiling sheepishly to let him know that I do realize that calling the police is not the worst idea here but I appreciate his willingness to let me be unwise. I look at the scarf in my hand. It's familiar, like seeing something from your childhood and not being able to quite place it. "I wonder if . . . Heather used to have a scarf like this but I remember hers, it had this flower pattern, not so much splashes of color."

"You think it could be hers? Really? And you don't want me to call the police?" Eamon asks.

"No, I remember, one of my students told me they buried her with her scarf."

"Maybe it's just a popular scarf," Amelia interjects and I can tell that this is her being practical.

I walk closer to the window to see if anything else is damaged. The wood isn't rotting, that's good. I don't want my father to have to worry about anything like termites, but there's a hole, an indent under the sill, and I see something white, not natural wood. Something is pushed in there like it was buried. "What is this?" It doesn't appear Eamon or Amelia can hear me. I reach in and pull out a hardcover book with moldy blackened pages that look more soft than wet. "I found something. In the window."

"Something in the window? You sure it's safe?" Eamon says as Amelia wanders over wordlessly.

"I don't know." I open the book and read the inscription, *Property of Magdalene Bauer—Personal Journal 1968*. "It's my mother's. Her journal." I flip through it and only a few pages, maybe twenty, are covered with her flowing, rushed script, the kind she had used to write notes to my teachers at school. "It starts well before I was born. She was in high school in 1968. It was a tough year for her. I remember my aunt telling me about it. That was the year her best friend died. And she had a run-in with some boy she was dating that just made her so depressed. I never got the details. I think that was the year her mental health started to become an issue."

"Wow that's heavy. You think that's the start of her mental issues . . . not that there's ever a concrete start," Eamon says. "Are you going to read it?"

"I don't know. It's not as though she was very forthright when she was alive. I wonder if it would be okay to read a woman's private thoughts like that."

"She's dead," Amelia says and I can hear the alcohol slurring her voice like a record skipping. "I'm sure she'd want her daughter to understand her."

"Maybe," I say, closing the book. "Amelia, don't you need to change? I'll leave this other stuff on the table and deal with it tomorrow. We should all head to bed." I keep the journal but leave the scarf and lipstick out. I'm not afraid to go to bed tonight, not with an alarm but still I say, "Eamon, you can stay, right?"

"Always," he replies, draping an arm around me.

"Bed, right," Amelia says as if it's an afterthought. "I need to be rested for that party tomorrow. Lorelei, you're going . . . you're just, I won't take no . . . you're going."

"Of course." I place my hand on Amelia's back as she turns toward the house. "It's open," I call and she lets herself in.

"We should follow her," I tell Eamon and he ushers me inside.

He walks over to the couch, he always does, and I pull him by the hand and bring him upstairs. We met last summer when I paid a visit to the seedy bar where he works. It was just after my mother had passed, a year after the fiasco with my husband's affair and Heather's death. I wasn't in the mood for shiny happy people and so I'd ended up at Liar's. We didn't do much those first few weeks, just sat together and hung out until we were comfortable enough to go out, to talk all night, to stay over. It was supposed to be a just-started-the-divorce-proceedings fling but we stayed in touch much better than I thought we would after I returned to Boston to teach during the year.

Nothing has been decided as far as our relationship goes, not yet. The baggage we carry into our adult years, after the world has run us over a few times, accumulates on our backs. But when I'm with Eamon I feel like he lifts the baggage, takes a couple of suitcases, and gives me room to breathe.

"You still need to come to the Kraft Gallery, my piece is up in the window. Tomorrow, before the party?"

"I can't very well miss a showing of the next great Irish Ex-Pat."

"You cannot," he replies, giving me a gentleman's bow before I head toward the soft light of the bedroom with the journal in hand.

I'll wait until Eamon's asleep. He can't help it; he always falls asleep before me. With the insanity of the last two years came a bout of insomnia that lets up about every third evening. I'll wait until I cannot hear Amelia showering in the next room, perhaps until the waves have quieted, but the waves never quiet, that's the beauty of them. I'll open the journal and read it. It says *Property of Magdalena Bauer*, property of my mother when she was in high school. I'll flip through the pages and maybe they'll mean nothing, like when I pass the time with a magazine before heading to work or those piles of Freshmen Comp papers I never get enough time for. Then again maybe this journal will be like reading *The Bell Jar* for the first time, or *The Old Man and the Sea* or *The Waves*. Maybe these words will be as life changing as the time I ran off on the beach with Theo, my ex, only to marry him six months later, as life altering as my first novel or the time my mother read me *Good Night Moon* as a child and I couldn't sleep for a week. I don't know why those words were so haunting but they terrified me.

Sylvia
1962

IT WAS A row house Sylvia had moved into, one of many on these blocks. Except this part of London, so far from the hustle and bustle of Piccadilly and Trafalgar, had a calm quiet to it even with the houses right on top of each other. Just like out in the country but not so desolate, so alone. Row houses one after another and a pub here or there, a grocery up the block. There was a little park, not really a park but a piece of untamed wilderness, weeds and trees all tussled together a few blocks away. Sylvia wondered if she might take the children there when winter was over and it was not so cold. The house was painted a lightish green on bottom with brick on top, a kind of calico brick like the old houses in Boston. And she wondered, really, since the blitz, if London wasn't just as old a city as Boston, with so many structures going up, or going back up, after the war. After the war, after the war, and Daddy used to say that so much of the world had to be rebuilt "after the war." Sylvia had been very young when the fighting had started and though boys from the neighborhood had gone off to fight, and there was that anti-German sentiment, most of the war had been stories and pictures in newsreels when she was growing up. But in London she could really see the scars of the war. Hotels that had lasted hundreds of years reduced to rubble, rows of houses, established businesses, all gone in the dust of the German air raids. This made her wonder what it would have been like to live in the old London that had not been destroyed by the war.

Sylvia watched the house and remembered part of the advertisement, "Room to Let. Yeats' house." She'd looked it up just to be sure and the address, 23 Fitzroy Square, had belonged to the famed Irish poet when he'd lived in London. And to think—Yeats' house! Really, Yeats' house, how wonderful. It was the house William Butler Yeats had lived in—that's when she knew she had to take it.

That's what had brought Sylvia back to Primrose Gardens in Camden town, a neighborhood in Central London. If she was going to return to the city, from the house in the country, this was the place to go. Past the shops a few blocks away, places where hardened mothers of five and six came to do the weekly shopping, where cars backfired on the poorly paved roads and the pubs . . . the English and their pubs, but it was a friendly enough neighborhood all the same. It was the house of William Butler Yeats and Sylvia knew the moment it came on the market that it was hers, she needed to take it and make it her new home in London. Now that she and the children were on their own, since Ted had left with That Woman, she needed a sign to say that everything would be all right and there it was in the advertisement. "Yeats' House to Let 23 Fitzroy Square," and here she was.

It had been hard getting the place. True to form everything in her life recently had been a fight, and Sylvia knew that despite her long hair, her delicate limbs, that she could fight, would have to fight the rest of her life since that day she answered the telephone and a woman trying to disguise her voice like a man's started talking. Ted had been so queer about that call and she knew. She knew then to put up her dukes, clench her fists. It wasn't the same kind of fight like when he slapped her or pushed her so hard that she fell down on the bed. And the one time she'd miscarried there had been a fight that night too. Ted had pushed her and then there was no baby. The world would hand her nothing but she would take what she needed. And now it was just herself and the children and Sylvia had marched to the estate agent's office and asked to let the property. "You're the first to arrive," they'd said. But later she'd learned that the neighbor, the man renting the flat downstairs, had also asked about taking more rooms at the property. And Sylvia needed two floors with her two children and no other arrangement would do. She'd already lived once in a cramped London flat not four blocks away. She and Ted and little baby Frieda had had no room to move and there had been screaming matches that seemed to grow into pushing, into boxing, matches and then the miscarriage and it had been hell trying to write poetry in such a cramped space. She couldn't do it again not with two children.

And so she had argued with the estate agent. She'd paid cash, cash up front not just for the first month but for the entire first year, paid in full. She took nearly all of her money, some made from writing poetry, some even from Ted, gifts from her mother she'd been saving over the years to buy something nice. But when you are a woman in her situation something nice is no longer an option, even if you write poetry.

Her friends had told her she was mad, handing over all that money all at once. But London was in the midst of a housing shortage and there was no guarantee she'd find anything suitable at all. And it was Yeats' house. His poetry ran through her. She could remember in Ireland with Ted, the way those great rolling hills fell before her, and she felt the poet speaking to her like a revelation. Even when Ted stood next to her, a huge shadow of a figure, already brooding, the poetry of Yeats had been hers, countering her husband's darkness.

She walked in, the children were already inside with her friend Jillian and her husband. She could hear them. The stairway was tight just like the old flat.

Sylvia carried up the stairs a cumbersome floor lamp with a long stem and a wide base, the last of the furniture she'd taken from the house in Devon. She had to twist it, maneuvering her body up the short, constricted stairway. There were no windows in the hall and just a tiny bulb of sickly yellow light above her and the stairs. The walls and the ceiling were all dark wood like entering through the mouth of a cave.

"Mummy!" Frieda cried, running at Sylvia even though she was still carrying that unwieldy lamp. She threw her arms around Sylvia, who shifted and set the lamp down before she softly touched the top of Frieda's head.

"Frieda, my darling. Do you like the new flat? Does it feel like home?"

Frieda looked up at her with very big eyes. She was nearly three now and her short straight hair had been cut to frame her face. She was still a little boyish in the face and she liked to play out in the garden while Sylvia tended to her baby brother. And when they'd kept bees, or had tried to keep them, Sylvia had always been terrified that one would sting little Frieda. But her father had been a beekeeper and she had such fond memories of those fuzzy, fat creatures as a child. What will it be like for a little girl, living now in London, in a new flat? A flat where there can never be bees? Sylvia wondered. So unlike her childhood in Wellesley. And even a new flat that had once belonged to a great poet couldn't really make up for the fact that Frieda was now living without her father.

"Nicholas doesn't like the new carpet," Frieda tattled, pointing to her baby brother, who could now sit up on his own and look out at the world. He watched them dumbly (all babies watch dumbly) and Sylvia laughed.

"I see, Nicholas doesn't like the carpet. I'll see if we can't have it changed, make it a little brighter in here."

Frieda ran off at that, away from Sylvia and toward the window, where she stood watching the street at dusk as the cars drove by. "Mummy, look at the cars! And the people!" she'd cried out the other day when they came to visit the new flat after Sylvia had properly secured the place and needed only to grab a few more things from Devon before moving in.

The flat was cramped and not in the best repair. The wooden bookshelves were empty but Sylvia had taken her books, mostly poetry and biography and the postmodern novels she'd started reading in Boston, with her. The walls were dark wood, not very bright and incredibly Victorian, and though there was only a red carpet here, a green dash there, the entire flat seemed to pulse with color, like a stained glass window in a church. She could picture Yeats here among Tiffany lampshades reading in a green upholstered chair before retiring to bed to wake up in the morning and write such glorious poetry.

The blue water-mists dropping/Scrim after scrim like fishnets/Though fishermen are sleeping. "Lorelei," the Lorelei, Sylvia thought. She had written it for her last collection, *The Colossus.* "Lorelei," and That Woman it seemed had taken the poem to heart and become her—stealing men—stealing husbands. As a child Sylvia had read stories about The Lorelei, a mystical woman who could force men to fall in love with her, simply by laying eyes on her. She had such charms, such powers, and Sylvia, she'd always felt like The Lorelei, with Dick and Richard and so many others, she'd had so many boyfriends once, and then there had been Ted and he'd married her. But she feared she was not The Lorelei anymore, someone else had taken her place, her title, someone else had become who she was supposed to be and who was she now?

And the poetry, it had been coming for weeks now, since Ted left. All this insanity with Ted meant the poetry had been coming and she could feel it pulsing as if through her veins in this flat. She knew she was home away from Devon and the prying neighbors and their daughter who kept coming around to see Ted, the way the women were always fussing, wanting to sit in their garden or come and have tea with Ted while she minded Frieda. Ted had taken her away from London for two years while he trained back and forth for "literary functions" seeing That Woman every time. And Sylvia too was a poet. It wasn't only Ted who deserved to go to those functions. He didn't even like the parties and galas everyone was always inviting him to and yet he had been invited because he was Ted Hughes, The Great English Poet. He had gone because he had a new poem out in *The Guardian* or *The Observer* or his book had just been reviewed and there at those parties all the trouble had started. There at those parties was where he kept seeing That Woman. But now, now she and Ted were in the same city. Now she was back in civilization like Lazarus (ah, but Sylvia had been hearing Lazarus lately, *A sort of walking miracle, my skin/ Bright as a Nazi lampshade,/ My right foot,/ A paperweight . . .*) rising from the dead and even in these cramped rooms where the estate agents had told her that there was a chance the pipes might freeze if winter grew too cold, she would write and publish again.

"I've put the kettle on," Jillian said, coming out of the kitchen with a red and white checkered dishcloth in her hand. Sylvia could just hear the little silver kettle her mother had sent as a gift when she'd found out Sylvia and Ted were moving back to England many years ago. "The children have eaten. Nicholas has had his bath."

"Thank you so much," Sylvia said, smiling at Jillian as her husband Gerald came from down the hall.

He was a thin round-faced man who had been a friend of Ted's before everything. Perhaps in some secret way he was still a friend of Ted's. Everyone had remained friends with Ted even if they were also kind to Sylvia. Ted was the kind of man who made and kept friends so easily.

"All in working order in the bedrooms. You just have to put a few coins in the slot and the heat goes on."

"Thank you, Gerry, for taking a look," Sylvia said.

"Are you sure you're going to be okay over here? Primrose Gardens, it might be London but it's still far from everything?" Gerry asked and Sylvia nodded effusively.

"Everything is lovely. I'm living in Yeats' house, the poet will energize me. I can't wait to get the children to bed, to put everything in order. I can't wait to start living here."

"A new chapter," Jillian said as Frieda came over and grasped at Sylvia's dress.

"Milk, mummy. I want milk," she said rather sadly and Sylvia looked down at her.

"Of course, love, just let me . . ." Sylvia fumbled as she walked toward the cupboards. And where were the cups, the ones for the children? Had she unpacked them? Frantically she opened one cabinet and then another.

"Here, let me help you," Gerald mumbled as Jillian stood on tiptoes, looking in the opposite cupboards in the tiny kitchen.

It really was ridiculous that they couldn't find something in such a small space, and if she couldn't even find a cup on her own how was she going to function with two small children? As Sylvia walked back she brushed past the oven and her hip hit the gas.

"Just a second, honey, just a second," Sylvia said. "I can't believe . . ." She went on as Frieda stood calmly in the kitchen waiting for milk and still all Sylvia wanted to do was put her head in her hands and cry at this mishap. "In the country at least I knew where everything was." She felt that pang. Only a few months ago things had been normal. She had been happy or at least oblivious to Ted's affair and now . . . now this darkness was coming in and it was so easy to get frazzled.

"Here we go, the cups for the children, right here. I must've unpacked them with the dishes. I'm sorry," Jillian said, coming to the rescue she handed Sylvia one of Frieda's small plastic cups, the ones she'd gotten in Devon from a shop in town. They had little pictures of cows and chickens on them. They'd lived on a farm out in the country and Sylvia wondered if there was a way to buy the children new cups with city pictures on them. Maybe some of those red London buses or the tower of Big Ben.

Sylvia took the glass jug of milk and poured a little for her daughter. There was hardly any left and she'd like to save at least a little for her tea and there was the baby. Nicholas took formula made with water now but just in case it was always nice to have milk in the house and new milk wouldn't come until six tomorrow morning and she couldn't very well send Ted out . . .

"It's fine, here you are, Frieda. It's going to be time for bed soon. Drink your milk and then we'll say good night," Sylvia said, handing her daughter her plastic cup.

Frieda smiled and ran back to the living room and her little brother, who cooed and gurgled as the girl started to talk to him about the cars going by the window. "And in that car is a man who works for the queen. And the little red car, a movie star is driving that one." Children and the stories they tell.

"I think I smell . . ." Gerry said, looking about the kitchen. "What is that?" He faced the stove and turned off the gas. "That's what it was, the gas was on. Sylvia you're going to have to be careful with this oven, the gas was on. You could poison yourself and the children if this were left on all night. You might even poison the entire block, the way gas spreads I read about it, some report from the BBC. It's very dangerous."

"Of course," Sylvia replied, rushing to the oven to see what she'd done. "I must have brushed it, I felt something but I didn't even think to check. I'm going to have to be more careful."

"Careful, yes. Alone with two children, Sylvia. I really do hope you're okay. And if you need anything, you can call," Jillian said, wiping the last of the dishes as Gerald left the kitchen to visit the children before they left. "Or you can always call Ted."

"I don't need Ted. I've been taking care of these children on my own for months now. Ted barely ever gives me a penny and when he visits the children he's so cold to me and it's all fun and games with them. He just plays and plays and lets Mummy do the hard stuff. I don't know what kind of figure Ted will cut when it's time for school or Heaven forbid there's a discipline problem." These are things you don't think of when you have children. At first it's only the thought of a baby and a big happy family and pushing a pram down wide streets. You don't think about what might happen if that pram were to get stuck on a shoddy London sidewalk, or how are you going to pay for the child's milk or schooling and what happens when the baby has a fit and you have a two-year-old daughter kicking and screaming for attention right out in Piccadilly. But there it was and Ted hadn't thought of that either, which was one of the reasons why Ted was not here now.

"I'll be fine." Sylvia placed a soft hand on Jillian's shoulder as she walked her out of the kitchen. Gerry was already at the door, putting his scarf on over his coat. He picked up his wife's coat and held it out to her a second later as Jillian waved good-bye to the children.

"Good-bye," she said, smiling sadly as she moved to go. "Sylvia, take care of yourself and watch that oven."

"I'll watch the oven," Sylvia replied. She waited until her friends were gone, until she heard the door close and their footsteps and voices on the stairs, before turning to the children. "Time for bed."

Frieda made a pooh-pooh face but did not argue as Nicholas looked up at her with such wide, innocent eyes. She scoped the little boy up and held him close to her chest, his wiggling warmth was such a comfort as she followed Frieda to the back bedrooms.

Bedtime did not take long. Frieda had become adept at changing her own clothes and brushing her own teeth as Sylvia fed Nicholas and lulled him to sleep. Once the baby was down she sat on her daughter's bed, telling her a story about a mouse and a cow that made friends even though one was very big and the other very small. "So you see, Frieda," Sylvia coaxed her daughter as she lay back, her eyes closed as if she was about to fall asleep, "friendship is a very big thing, even among very small animals and you must learn to feed it so it can grow."

"Where's Daddy?" Frieda asked. He had been gone a while and Frieda hadn't asked after him in weeks. "Is he going to live in the new house with us?"

"No," Sylvia replied. "Daddy lives somewhere else now. But this flat, isn't it nice?" She smiled brightly, so brightly, she could feel the sides of her mouth about to crack. "Don't you think you'll like living in London?"

"There aren't cows," Frieda countered, still lying back. "But I like all the cars out my window."

"Wonderful," Sylvia said, turning off the light as Frieda settled into bed.

Once the children were asleep and the noise in the house, the light even, had died down, it was like a fire going out and slowing to bitter embers. First Sylvia closed the kitchen, she turned off the light and checked the gas. And really, she thought, I'll have to always check the gas, every morning and every night, just to make sure it's not left on. She folded a few blankets and put the pillows back on the long brown couch that had come with the flat. It was dark, even with the light on it was so dark in here, with Jillian and Gerald gone and the children in bed.

Sylvia moved through the living room as Yeats must have done. It was through the walls and beyond the new carpet Frieda had said Nicholas hated, that's where she would find her poetry. And the poems had been coming so fast and with such fury it was as if once she lost Ted and the great colossal weight of him, her mind was free and she could finally write.

Sylvia walked toward the window and stared out, as Frieda had done. "And in that car is a man who hates his job," Sylvia said aloud. "And in that car is a woman who wishes she had married a wealthier man." Lamplight shone every few feet. The streets were slick, probably wet from a simple London shower, and the light was on in the house across the way. She saw a man sitting in a chair and a woman in the kitchen. No children were awake but perhaps they had them in bed already. And here was this couple as they went about their little domestic life, which was really very big, the cornerstone of all civilization as far as Sylvia knew. And I destroyed my book, she thought. We were sitting on the porch, Mother and I, and I ripped page after page out and put it in the fire. I burnt it to ashes right in front of my mother and she had such a horrified look on her face as if I'd just harmed one of the children. But that was Ted's fault. The book was about him and then he cheated on me and I couldn't even stand to look at it anymore. I'll have to write another one. I cannot let him burn me up like that.

Sylvia wanted to leave the window but she couldn't. There wasn't much movement at this time of night in this part of London but she could not move as she stared out. One day she'd see Ted. He would have to come, if only to see the children, and she just kept staring . . . looking out for the longest time.

A horn beeped outside and she heard the streets. The way rain pitter-pattered all over London, the constant fog and the way shop girls would look at her now that she was a mother brandishing two clinging children. But in the shops they couldn't know better, women, married women, came all the time to shops on their own with their children these days. It was only here, alone in her flat, that people would notice, that the whole world would see as if they were looking into her home through a magic mirror. Sylvia Plath, the spurned woman. Sylvia who had been left for another woman, another Lorelei, who'd been better at trapping her man.

Here she was, a grown woman, almost thirty, with two children and a husband (technically she still did have a husband) and she was moving not to a house in the country, like most people did, but back to the city, to a small flat that barely fit herself and the children. This was not the way life worked. Families were supposed to get bigger, not smaller. Houses were supposed to get larger, they were not supposed to shrink. Women who live in the country were not supposed to go traipsing back to the city. But that's where life was, where the poetry, would come from. She would go to parties and galas, the kinds she could not attend before (though Ted never missed them), the kind where she would meet critics and poets and they'd ask her about her book. They'd want to know what she was working on. She would find a life here and she would write poetry again as she'd been doing in a frenzy since Ted left. Poetry, this time in her life had given her so much poetry and it wouldn't stop. She couldn't make it stop. She wouldn't.

Sylvia looked up, tears now in her eyes. Her books were not on the shelves yet. She had packed them and brought them in. She would unpack tomorrow and put them on the shelves, the wooden bookshelves that covered half the walls of the living room. She would put them in and this place would be home. It was only that her books were not up and when her books were up this place would be better.

Lorelei

AFTER EAMON FALLS asleep I find the journal. I consider calling my father in Florida, or putting the journal away and reading a book instead, but I pick it up. There's no use spending an hour, spending five minutes or thirty seconds, wrestling with the moral implications of reading this. I know I'm going to give in. It's my mother's journal and I remember her struggles. There was the time I found her in the bathtub crying, the time I found her standing next to a chair near a poorly constructed noose made of loose sheets hanging from the ceiling fan. She was just staring at it, staring so vacantly. Do I really want to read this? Do I want to know what's inside her head? Won't it open up more wounds than it heals?

Maybe the answer is no. Maybe this will hurt me. But she's been gone a year and I need to know.

The phone rings. It's late, telemarketers don't call past nine and so I pick up the phone worried it's my father who might be ill or a cousin with sad news. What news, but bad news, comes at night?

"It's Sarah, Aunt Sarah," the voice replies when I answer. "Nothing's wrong."

"Hi, Sarah, I wasn't sure. It's late."

"Sorry, sorry, I just wanted to tell you I missed my flight out. It was delayed and I still missed the damn thing. Completely my mistake, you know the saying about heads being screwed on? But I won't be coming out until tomorrow night. I might as well get some work done here in the morning and the new flight was cheaper if I went later. Anyway, I won't be at the *Maude* party tomorrow. Which is too bad, I was going to meet my old friend Joanne, do you remember her?"

I search my memory and shake my head. "No, I don't."

"You were really little when we were friends. Joanne used to work in New York before she moved to Boston. She's been a magazine writer there for years, though she does more freelance, works on and off—long story. But she Facebook friended me a little while ago, I think she just got on. She's a woman of that generation and they're a little slow on the social media uptake. But she contacted me, we've talked a few times and I thought since she has a place on the Cape and I was going to be there, I'd meet her at the party. But now I'm going to miss seeing you and seeing her, I'm so sorry."

"It's okay. We'll have dinner later. And you can still stay with me. I mean, Amelia has the guest room but you can take the hide-a-bed in my study." I look over at Eamon, true to form this call hasn't phased his sound sleep.

"You know I don't sleep on hide-a-beds, a hotel is fine. And thanks for humoring your kooky old aunt. No one there needs me at the party, but it would have been nice to see you and Joanne. You sure it's not too late to call? I'm in a cab now."

"Not a problem. Thanks for thinking to call." I want to hang up but I pause, looking over at the journal. "It's just I found something today . . . did Mom keep a journal when she was in high school?"

I hear the hesitation and the silence inside her cab pummeling down the bright-lighted streets of New York City. My aunt Sarah was always the type of woman to make rushed phone calls from cabs flying through the city.

"From when?" she asks. "What year?"

"She was in high school. It says 1968."

"I don't know," she says but I can tell her mind is not on the conversation anymore. She's mulling over what I just said. "Look, Lorelei, I know, your mother was tough to handle. She had her demons. If she had a journal from that time I wouldn't . . . I mean, I don't know if I'd want to know what it said."

"I think I have to know. I don't think I can *not* read it."

"Okay. I get it. Just be careful. Can we talk about it later. When I get to the Cape? Over dinner?"

"Yes, of course."

My aunt Sarah is the only one of my mother's sisters who ever got along with her. My mother had seven sisters and most of them came to the funeral but I hadn't seen them in years. One of them flew out from Ohio. She wore a muted blue dress, her hair frosted tastefully blond. She had the bloated features of a Midwestern housewife and never once smiled, not because she was too sad about losing a sister she never saw. One of them lived in Boston but I hadn't seen her in years. I hadn't seen her three daughters, my cousins, who had not bothered to come, something about "the little ones at home." Aunt Sarah was the only one who cried, really cried. She'd been there when my mother first tried to do it, really tried to do it, seven years before she succeeded. She was there for Thanksgiving when my mother bought a batch of tofu, and only a batch of tofu, and said we were going "green" that year. She insisted on making dinner all by herself and then didn't even bother to cook the tofu. We ended up ordering fast food. She was there when my mother slept through my thirteenth birthday, she wouldn't get out of bed and Aunt Sarah took me into New York. We had tea at The Russian Tea Room and dinner at Tavern on the Green. We went shopping at Macys and I wanted to see The Met and so we wandered those halls all afternoon. We went to the ballet that night and I slept at her apartment in Greenwich Village.

"Aunt Sarah, thanks for calling," I say again as the call winds down. I hear a horn honking extra loud and long in New York and picture my aunt in a cab with dark upholstery, the driver listening to a foreign news station on the radio. "I just . . . do you remember Mom, you know, before I was born, in the late sixties? What was she like? Did anything happen to her then? Anything you can warn me about."

"The late sixties? She was in high school. Her best friend died her junior year, she took that pretty hard but other than that I don't know," Aunt Sarah replies.

"I wonder sometimes what she would have been like."

"Thinking of writing about your mother? I think it's a great idea. You two have quite a story to tell."

"Yeah, maybe," I don't bother to disagree. "Did anything happen?" I ask carefully.

"I'm sorry, Lorelei, but the cabbie's about to turn onto Houston. I have to go. I'll see you probably not tomorrow, but in a couple of days. I'm so sorry I missed my flight. I'm getting worse in my old age."

I take her silence on my question to mean that she's not going to tell me. But there's no affirmative that I don't have to be careful. "No problem, and you're not old," I add and she laughs before hanging up.

I put the phone down. It's a cream colored contraption with a corded receiver, a remnant from the nineties, when I lived here as a child with my family. My father would always make breakfast in the mornings when we went to the Cape. He'd serve it for my mother, even when she didn't get out of bed. Even when she'd sit at the table, mascara running down her face as if she'd spent the entire night crying and hadn't bothered to wipe her eyes. I pick up the journal. *Property of Magdalene Bauer—Personal Journal 1968.* Personal . . . but is anything personal once we're in the ground? I remember reading Plath's journals in college or the letters of Virginia Woolf published so many years after her death. The lives of great writers picked and pulled apart after they've stuck their heads in ovens or walked into rivers with rocks in their pockets.

I look over at Eamon, sleeping peacefully curled to the side of the bed. This room used to belong to my grandparents when I was very little and my parents came for one or two weekends a year. Then, after grandpa died and grandma moved into a home, we took over here in the summer. Dad still worked in Boston but I stayed all week with my mother. Sometimes I'd sleep in this room with her, cuddled in the same bed, especially when there was a summer storm. We'd listen to the waves outside, lightning flashing, an electrical episode right on the walls and sometimes my mother would start reciting poetry. *"God's lioness/How one we grow/Pivot of heels and knees!—The furrow."* The memories of my mother weren't all bad.

I hold the journal in my hand and start to read. Some of the front pages are torn out. I wonder where they went and what they said. These pages of my mother's life were ripped from this and I'll never read them. No one will ever know what happened then.

April 2nd 1968

Allison and I had a swim meet today. I was really excited. Last meet against Central I placed third in the crawl and Allison got a first for butterfly. She's so good at the butterfly. Today though, she sat off to the side. I tried to talk to her but she wouldn't look at me. Alley's boyfriend Brian was there but he barely talked to her. I thought maybe they were in a fight but when I asked Alley she barked at me that everything was fine and I should mind my own business. I brought her a hot dog from the food cart and she ate it silently. Then she started gagging and ran to the bathroom. I don't know if she threw up but she swam today. Came in fourth which was a surprise because most of the time she's first, maybe second. Coach Martins looked upset and confused with Alley's performance but Alley didn't look like she cared at all. I called her house just now, before I started writing, and her mother sounded worried or something when she said Alley couldn't come to the phone.

There are more torn out pages before I land here.

May 14th 1968

School is almost out for the summer and I haven't seen Allison in over a week. Allison gave me Sylvia Plath's The Bell Jar *and I've been reading it just to feel closer to her. Alley never misses school. I've known her since first grade. We used to swim together all the time and who am I going to go swimming with if Allison is sick all summer or away on some trip? I remember in junior high one time she went to school with a fever of 102 just so she could do the butterfly in the relay at the swim meet that day. She was so good at that, so strong. She still has those muscles in her shoulders, the ones my grandmother says are unlady-like. She was going for perfect attendance this year and ever since she and Brian have been going steady it's like she's a totally different person. Right before she stopped coming to school she was so quiet. She acted all annoyed with everything and when I asked her what was wrong she just yelled at me to shut up and stop butting in. But she wasn't always like that. We used to hang out together, Allison, Brian and I. Sometimes I'd bring a date but I can't commit to one guy. Maybe when I get older I'll settle and get married. But this summer we were going to do so much. We live so close to Boston that we thought about getting jobs there this year. Now I don't know where she is.*

But I called Allison's house today and her mother said she wasn't there. Mrs. Morrison is usually so friendly but today it was like she just wanted me off the phone. It's so weird but if Allison weren't okay her mother would say something. Maybe she's in trouble. Maybe she got a D on one of her math tests, which would be crazy because Allison is the smartest girl in the school and has been since she won the Scholar's Competition freshman year. But if she got a D on a test I know her mother she'd be so grounded and not allowed to come to the phone.

May 19th 1968

I still haven't seen Alley. She hasn't been in school. She hasn't missed this many days ever. I asked Mr. Turner if he could give me her assignments and he just looked at me like I'd fallen off some kind of truck. I asked Mrs. Caldwell if I could get her homework for English class and she was nicer about it. "That poor thing," she said. But I've been Allison's best friend forever and she hasn't told me anything. I called her house again last night and this time her father picked up. "Allison has gone on a trip," he said. That was it. But Allison never told me about any trip. And he usually calls her Alley. Is he mad at her? We've been best friends since first grade. She would've told me about a trip.

But I saw Alley's boyfriend, Brian, today. He was throwing a football around with Carl and Tommy. Then Susan Hiller came up and wrapped her arm around Brian like they'd been going steady forever. I just stared gawking at him. I asked if he was worried about Allison. I yelled at him actually I was so mad about how Susan was acting. He just laughed at me and walked away.

"You know what's going on with Alley, right?" Tommy asked once Brian left. I said I didn't know but maybe she was on a trip or something. Tommy just shook his head.

I went home and kept reading The Bell Jar *because it makes me feel close to my friend. But all the stuff poor Esther, the main character, went through. She had all those issues with boys and school and the other girls in her internship program. I can totally relate to that Esther girl. I feel like her all the time, left out, not like them, but also like I want so much to be liked, to be popular, to do well and I always feel like I'm failing. Just like Esther.*

May 27ᵗʰ 1968

My mother called me to the breakfast table early today. She sat me down and told my sisters to go away. Sarah was visiting from New York. She's working at a magazine there and I told Mom Sarah could stay at least. I was a little nervous. Did one of my teachers call and say I wasn't doing well? I thought my grades were okay but I might have bombed my Civics test. But Sarah is the only one of my sisters I can stand so if I was going to get in trouble, it should be with Sarah nearby. But Mom told her to leave too. Mom looked at me like she pitied me and I didn't understand it at first and then she said that she had some bad news.

I wondered why she was only telling me and not my sisters. If that bad news were about grandpa or someone in the family she would have had dad here. But dad was at work. She would have let all my sisters stay. Something fell in my gut. I swear I could just feel my whole body go numb because I knew something very bad had happened and it was close to me. Only me.

"It's not Alley," I said desperately. I wanted my mother to shake her head no. I wanted her to say that it was only that Alley wouldn't be back for the end of the year because she was on some amazing trip she forgot to tell me about. Or maybe Mrs. Caldwell, my favorite teacher, was leaving at the end of the year. Sometimes when only medium bad things happen I take it too far. I feel like it's my fault and I feel so sad about them that Mom has to be careful with me. She needs to be more careful than she'd have to be with Sarah or Samantha or Cecelia.

My mom said that Alley had an operation. Her parents sent her away because she was sick and she had an operation and she died during the operation. I said I didn't even know she was sick and then Mom said that she wasn't even sick that wasn't it. She was going to have a baby. A baby, my best friend was pregnant and I didn't even know. She didn't even tell me. Her parents had sent her away to a little place in the woods where the nuns took care of her and other girls like her, young, unmarried girls who were going to have babies. The nuns were going to make sure the baby was put up for adoption. Then Alley would be able to go back to school next year, she'd start her school year off fresh.

I ran out of the room and cried. Later, I tried calling Alley's parents but they didn't answer. I called Brian but he wouldn't talk to me. He told me to buzz off because he didn't have to explain anything to me. I locked myself in my room reading The Bell Jar *until Sarah came in to talk to me but even Sarah couldn't make me listen. Esther is getting sick, in the book, she's staying in bed all day and losing weight and now showering. I wish I could do all that.*

May 30th 1968

I went to Allison's funeral today with Sarah and my mother. My other sisters wanted to go but it was going to be crowded. I wore black and sat on my bed before the funeral, wondering how I was supposed to act. I'd only been to Grandma Baine's funeral when I was fourteen. I've never seen a friend in a casket before. And she looked so dead. They say the dead look like they're sleeping but you know what, they don't look like they're sleeping, they look like they're dead. Just cold and solid like concrete.

Brian was there with Susan. She actually started crying and he put his arm around her. I wanted to scream at them. I wanted to tear her hair out but I knew that would only upset Alley's family. At the funeral I just stood there staring. The church was draughty and breezy and I remember looking up at the stained glass windows and thinking how sad, but how colorful, they were. How can something so colorful be so sad? Then they put up a picture of Alley, her long strawberry blond hair, her big, toothy smile. She was so happy in that picture but I couldn't help wondering what her last moments were like.

Then we walked over to the cemetery for the burial. They lowered her casket into the ground in this great big cemetery and I just remembered Alley when she was alive. She was my best friend and now she's gone. We used to run around in the grass together by her house. We used to swim at the pool, at the lake, sometimes we'd go out to Cape Cod and swim in the ocean. She used to swim and do laps around the block in the neighborhood. She wanted to be a scientist. It didn't matter that she was a girl she was the best in all her classes. She could have discovered a new element but instead Brian got her pregnant and then started dating Susan. Instead they sent her away and then there was a problem and now she's in the ground.

After the burial, when everyone left, and it was just a few of us, I walked up to Brian, who was still with Susan. I screamed at them about how Alley was dead and it was all their fault. Susan is a slut and she stole Alley's boyfriend after he got her pregnant. Susan yelled back at me that I was crazy and started swooning all over Brian like he's some kind of Greek god.

I ran at her and Tommy held me back. Brian looked mad, like he would have said something, he would have done something, if we'd been any other place. But there, at Alley's funeral, when she died because she was pregnant with his baby, he stayed quiet. He just walked away. I screamed after them but they just kept walking. Tommy brought me back to my sister Sarah, who drove me home.

When I got home I locked myself in my room and just started screaming. It was only then that I really felt it, that I knew it. Alley is gone. She's dead. She must have been so scared. I threw myself on my bed, buried my head in my pillow and just cried. Then I threw my pillow against the wall. I started punching it, beating it like it was Brian and Susan. I punched it just picturing them and then I took out my scissors. I cut into my pillow until the stuffing came out. It flew around my bed like snow and I didn't care. I just wanted it out. I wanted it to suffer. When I finally stopped I just stared at it all, my unmade bed, my beat up pillow. Then I took the stuffing and shoved it into my mouth. I stuffed more and more inside until it was thick and scratchy. When I tried to swallow it the cotton almost choked me. I started gagging and that's when Sarah came in. That's when she put her arms around me. She forced my mouth open. I wanted to keep the stuffing in even as it was choking me but she forced my mouth open and started pulling it out until I heaved into the wastebasket. Nothing came out and I just sat there heaving and heaving.

Sarah came in and said it would be okay. But how can it be okay when my best friend is dead? It's three in the morning now and I'm writing this because I cannot get the picture of Alley out of my mind. There was the big picture they put up, a school picture, she looked so nice in her argyle sweater and then I see her in the casket. Just lying there. She looked cold and pale and just a raw piece of meat and I hated everyone then. I hated her parents and Brian and Susan and myself because none of us helped her.

June 22nd 1968

I sat down with Sarah today. She went back to New York after Alley's funeral but came home to visit today. I'm out of school for the summer but I have no plans. Alley and I were going to work behind the counter at Carrols but I can't face that job by myself. I've been out *a few times but mostly all I do is mope around the house. That's why Sarah came to see us. She has some time off from the magazine and train tickets to the suburbs of Boston are cheap now. My other sisters are nice to me. They walk on eggshells, that's what mom calls it, but only Sarah seems to care. Only Sarah called every day when she was back in New York. Now Cecelia is talking about getting married. She's not even engaged yet but she and Alex have been dating for three years and it's about time. I've been seeing a guy named Steve, who started calling after the funeral. He was at the get together at Alley's parents' house after her funeral. Apparently his father knows Alley's dad from work. Steve and I talked for a while and he took down my number. He goes to B.U. but his family lives in Waltham and he's home for the summer. We talk a lot these days. Sarah thinks it's a good idea, me having a guy to get my mind off all this. The first week I wouldn't take his calls but after that Mom said I needed to get out of the house and I've seen him twice, once we saw a movie and another time he took me bowling.*

But today Sarah told me what happened to Alley. I didn't know. No one told me. I thought there was a problem with the baby, that's why she died. Women die like that all the time, they've been dying because of childbirth complications since the dawn of time, why should Alley be any different?

Sarah said that Alley snuck out of the home they put her in. She called a guy she met who arranged for her to have an abortion at the home of a doctor. She paid the guy a lot of money. I guess she took all of her savings and paid him. It was like $600. He picked her up in a van and took her to the doctor's home. Actually, I don't even know if he was a doctor. But something went wrong. There was a lot of bleeding. From what the doctor at the ER said there was blood just . . . everywhere. The man who did the procedure though, he didn't help at all. He just let her bleed for a while and then told the guy with the van to get rid of her. The guy brought her back to the home and she snuck into the showers and just sort of stayed under the water all night. When the nuns found her they were shocked. They tried to help her. They really did. First they wrapped her up. They called a real doctor, who told them to get her to a hospital. They tried to help her there but she had already bled too much. It was too late. She died that morning.

I still don't know why she would have an abortion. It's illegal and the only way to do it is to do it somewhere dirty and scary. She was smart enough to know that. She was going to give the baby up for adoption. She could go back to school after it was over. She could make up the class work, get back on the swim team.

Sarah said that Mom told her, and I think Alley's mom told Mom, that Brian first told her he'd stand by her. He said he'd wait for her. Then when she called him once he said he was dating some other girl. He said he was in love with this other girl and then he said he couldn't be with her because she was pregnant and he couldn't deal with that. Maybe she thought he'd like her again if she got rid of it, maybe that's what she was thinking. But she just bled out. They let her bleed to death.

I still don't know how they can just do that. I know Alley had an illegal procedure but they killed my friend. They let her die! Aren't the police going to do anything?

Sarah said that they found the guy with the van and he's got some fines or something, but not much. And we can't find the doctor. The cops tried the address the guy with the van gave but of course the doctor is gone now. There's nothing we can do.

Allison is dead. She's gone forever and everyone is just obsessed with hiding everything. Alley's parents won't talk about it and neither will my teachers. There are whispers around town from the kids at school but that's it. I'm glad Sarah is in journalism, maybe she'll tell Allison's story someday. Maybe she'll find the doctor and uncover the truth. But I don't know who to be mad at, at the world, the doctor, at Brian, at Alley. I just feel so helpless. But at least I have Steve to talk to. He's been a great guy through all this. I'm glad he's here. I told him about that scene in The Bell Jar *where Esther looked down at a body during a surgery. Her boyfriend was in medical school and he let her watch. She felt so cold, so violated, watching the surgery, the way doctors just open people's bodies up and go poking around. It reminds me of Alley and what happened. Steve said it was all made up in* The Bell Jar *but I think I read somewhere that it wasn't. That Sylvia Plath actually had a boyfriend in medical school who took her to watch a surgery once.*

July 27th 1968

I went out with Steve again last night. We've been going out a lot lately. I don't know why he just keeps calling me and calling me and I need something to take my mind off of Allison. I went by her house today and talked to her brother Kyle. He's been sitting in his room and writing a lot of poetry. He's only an eighth grader, he doesn't know what happened. He just knew Alley was sick and then she died.

I wanted to tell him but that's not my place and I don't want Mrs. Morrison to tell me not to come over anymore.

But Steve is a really nice guy and we went out to a pizza place and then there was a double feature showing in town. We saw Five Card Stud *and then* For the Love of Ivy. *They were both pretty good. Then I went back to Steve's house. His mother let me go up to his room and we made out for a little bit. Steve read me some of the poetry he wrote. Steve is such a poet, such a good writer, that's what people say about him. Even Sarah thinks he'll be the next Ginsberg or something. But after the poetry Steve showed me these awful pictures. He said he got them from a friend of his. These pictures were of a woman who had died after having an abortion. There was blood everywhere. The blanket, the mattress she was lying on, were all soaked in blood and then there was this close up shot between her legs and all you could see were massive cuts and blood. I don't know what they did to her but it looked so painful, so horrifying. And I said, "Is that what they did to Allison?" And Steve just nodded yes. Then I fell into his arms and cried and cried until he took me home.*

August 3ʳᵈ 1968

I just got home. It's two a.m. and I just got home. I had to sneak back in, using the back door, but Mom and Dad weren't up and no one saw me. Steve took me out again today. We saw another movie. For the Love of Ivy *again I don't know why he likes that movie so much. Then we grabbed a soda at this place and saw some of his friends. Then we drove out of town. Steve just kept driving and driving until there weren't houses anymore and it was just woods. I asked him where we were going but he was really quiet. He didn't tell me anything and I thought maybe he had some kind of surprise because he's going back to college soon and things have been going well.*

But then we parked in this spot in the woods and we started making out and it got really heavy. And I liked it, I really did, I like it when I'm that close to him and he just keeps kissing me. But then he started to take my shirt off and I told him, "No, not that." But he wouldn't listen. He just kind of ripped it and pulled it off of me. I told him to stop again and he said that he wouldn't drive me home, he'd just leave me here in the woods if I didn't do what he said. I tried to get out of the car. And really I don't know what I would have done if I had gotten out of the car because it was the woods. We'd driven on a long, lonely road to get there and I hadn't seen any houses and I don't think it was the kind of place with a lot of payphones. I don't even know if there were telephone lines. But it didn't matter because he grabbed me and held me down. He pulled my pants off and got on top of me and that's when I just stopped struggling. I just kind of stopped. I put my mind somewhere else and let it happen because I couldn't push him off and every time I tried he just hit me. I closed my eyes and prayed for it to be over.

And it hurt so much. This was my first time and I wanted to cry out but after a while I just shut down and stared at the ceiling of the car. And when he was finished there was all this blood. And he gave me a towel and told me to get in the back and then he drove off while I was still trying to clean myself. He was quiet on the way home and then he stopped at my house and just said, "Well, you can get out now." He started to drive away before I even shut the door.

When I came home I called Sarah in New York and told her what happened and she told me to tell Mom. To tell the police. But how the hell can I do that? How can I just do that to them? What will they think of me? Somehow this has to be my fault. And Sarah said Steve was a nice guy. She said seeing him would be good for me and look what happened. I started crying, almost screaming, that I can't, I can't and finally Sarah stopped asking me to tell someone. Sarah has so much work. She's so busy. I was worried she wouldn't even talk to me. But she said she'd take a train up in two days. Two days! I have to wait two days. But for now, I can't sleep. Every time I close my eyes I see Allison and the blood between her legs. I see what happened to her and I'm sure it'll happen to me too. I'm not clean anymore and it'll happen to me.

August 7th 1968

I haven't been sleeping. Mom keeps asking me to sit at the kitchen table and talk to her but I can't even look at her. I can't look at myself. Every time I glance in the mirror I see this ugly defiled creature and I want to throw up. Sometimes I even do throw up. She asked me about Steve. "Why haven't you talked to that nice boy, Steve? Didn't he write poetry?" A nice boy! She actually called him a nice boy! And I run out of the room every time she asks about him you'd think she'd take the hint. He hasn't called again. I haven't tried to reach him. I haven't slept in so many nights, I just stay up pacing, or I sit on my bed with my knees pulled to my chest and just rock. I swear I can hear Allison at night. My mother said that her own mother used to hear voices. She used to not be able to sleep and maybe I'm like her. Maybe it's happening again. But last night I swear to god I was staring at the walls and I saw Allison. She was holding a rag in her hand and it was full of blood and I screamed at her to go away, just go away. Then Mom and Carmen came in and tried to hold my arms back because I was punching the walls. They say they don't know what to do with me but they don't know the half of it. Then I spent all this morning throwing up and Mom is sure I have the flu.

August 12th 1968

School is going to start soon. I went for my physical with Doctor Thompson and that's how I found out. I was alone and he asked me if I was okay and I said I hadn't been sleeping. I wasn't well and I needed to rest but I couldn't sleep. He took some tests and then called me into his office three days later and told me I was pregnant. "Do you want me to tell your mother?" he asked like there was a choice. I've heard before that Doctor Thompson is a strange doctor, much too loose, too free. One of his patients called him a hippie and maybe he is because when I said "no" he just nodded and said he'd leave it to me. But I went to the pharmacy two towns away so no one would know me and took another test. The man looked at me funny but he gave me the test. I gave them my sample and three days later I returned to the pharmacy and he told me that yes, I was pregnant. I just looked at him with big, big eyes and ran away from the counter.

That night at the dinner table Mom and Dad were talking about senior year. Saying that I have all this stuff I could do and I need to think about junior college next year and wouldn't it be great if I could make first doubles on the tennis team? And I just stared at them and then ran away to throw up. What am I supposed to tell them? How am I supposed to have a baby now? I didn't tell them when it happened and Mom and Dad, my sisters, everyone at school, will just think I'm a slut. Just like they call Allison a slut now because they all know she was pregnant, they all know what she did. It got out during the summer I don't even know how and I can't take it. She's dead and they're calling her names, I can't take it. Then I called Sarah and told her everything.

September 20th 1968

I'm still not sleeping. School has already started and I got sick twice during P.E. Mom and Dad keep talking about the tennis team and going to junior college next year. I hear voices at night now. Alley is talking to me. She's telling me not to go through with it. "You can't have this baby. I will drown it in the swimming pool. It will come out of the water like the creature from the black lagoon." Allison's voice keeps telling me this and I'm sure she's right. I have to get rid of it. I have to make this go away. I can't have this baby, this baby will kill me. I'm already hearing voices.

I called Sarah and she said she didn't know about helping me get rid of it but I told her that the other night I took half a bottle of aspirin and then made myself throw up before anything happened. And the day before that I was at the pool and I wondered what would happen if I put rocks in my pockets and just let myself drown. That's where I am. I need to get rid of this before Allison comes and kills me. And so Sarah said that she would set something up. She'd call someone.

She said she's going to pick me up at the bus station in a few days, maybe a week, and we're going to stay with a friend of her's on Cape Cod. It's a long weekend and I don't have anything to do yet at school and so when I told Mom and Dad I'm going on a trip with Sarah, they just thought it was nice. Mom thinks maybe it will get my head out of the clouds. And I can't believe Mom doesn't see it. She still doesn't see it. But it's better this way. She doesn't have to know. But I can't do this. I hear too many voices. I can't sleep at night. I know what Alley was feeling now. I know why she did it. I'm going crazy like this and I'm scared every night and if the kids at school find out they'll call me a slut. But it's the voices, they keep telling me how terrible I am.

September 29th 1968

I read somewhere that Edna Saint Vincent Millay used herbs to do it. Her mother was a nurse and knew how to get rid of unwanted pregnancies. And just like her that's what I had to do. I thought I could be strong but I'm not. I pace the halls of the school like a crazy person. I've been sent home twice. I could tell Mom and Dad and go away to a home like Alley. But I can't. I keep hearing voices, voices that say they'll go away once I get rid of it. I don't sleep. I can't go to a hospital and so I did it alone in a house where no one else was staying.

Only it wasn't that simple, Sarah and I didn't just do it. We'd been planning it for over a week. I had a dream the other night about Allison. She came to me and told me not to have it. She said if I did she'd come to me at night, while I was in labor, and slit my throat. And I know Alley, she'll do it. She never went back on her word. I

*don't want any of this and why do they make me take it? I could give
it away like Alley was going to but then I'd be cursing another family
and I can't do that.*

*Sarah called a man and he did it in the bathtub. We went to the
house of a friend of Sarah's, someone much more successful in magazine
publishing than even my sister. He said she could borrow his place for
the week. I don't think Sarah told him what we were going to do there.
But she picked me up at the bus station and drove me to the house. We
stayed over night and then the doctor came in the morning.*

*He did it in the tub. Sarah cleaned the place up, she did something
called sterilizing first. It was cold when he did it. It felt medical and
professional and it hurt but it wasn't like with Allison. It hurt but I
didn't die. He numbed me first. Not much, but he gave me pills, shot
me through with something that made me feel almost numb down
there. Then he stuck that metal something in and there was blood, so
much blood. I didn't think there would be so much blood, though why
I didn't think that I don't know . . . I saw the pictures. I know what
happened to Alley.*

*He stayed with me. I cried. Even before the numbing agent wore
off I felt pain and it's only gotten worse. Worse.*

*And then there were the remains. I hadn't thought of that. If I had
just been able to do it in a clinic there wouldn't have been remains. I
could have just paid them to dispose of them. I mean, my sister had the
money, she paid the "doctor" or I don't even know what he was. But no
. . . no . . . We had to take the remains. He wouldn't dispose of them,
he said, not even for a higher fee. So my sister scooped up the blood
and other goop. It didn't look like anything but blood but we had to
be careful. I tried to see what was there but Sarah wouldn't let me see
and I couldn't make anything out.*

*Sarah said they'd find it if we just threw the remains in the
garbage and so we took them outside. She wanted to just throw them
in the ocean. No one would notice. No one would find out. There
would be no fingerprints; no way to tell . . . would there? I don't
think so. Why couldn't I have just gone to the doctor for this? Why
wouldn't they let me? It seems so unfair and now I have to dispose
of the remains.*

*But I wanted to bury it. Even so close to shore I wanted to risk it
and so we left the house. I think Alley would have wanted it that way.
I wish Alley could have buried what happened to her. Sarah drove
me to the other side of the Cape, over near Wellfleet. It was late. It*

was desolate. I was still bleeding. I put on an old pair of pants and a million maxi pads but I still bled through. By the end of the night I looked like someone had stabbed me there. And really . . . they had.

We walked out to sea. I didn't do it right at the beach. I leaned down and dug a hole. I dug and dug and I realized that it wasn't going to work, you can't dig a hole in the sand in the ocean, the water just fills it in. And so we walked over to some rocks. We dug and dug. We dug with our hands, Sarah and I, until we hit dirt and then we dug some more, mud right in our fingernails and we just kept digging. I was crying. I don't even know why. Something was shattered. Something had ended. I had ended it. I cried and cried and finally Sarah said, "All right, all right, give it to me." And she put it in, she covered it up while I sat on the beach.

I just sat there. I could feel the smear of blood on my face.

But I'm fine now. I'm fine. It's buried by the ocean. It's finished. It's done and I can rest now. I don't think Alley will come to my room anymore and try to talk to me.

I put the journal down shaking. There are many more pages but they're all blank after that. I guess my mother stopped journaling. But she saved this. She knew to hide it. All these things my mother went through when she was seventeen years old. No wonder she acted the way she did. She must have been so haunted by a past she never spoke about.

I might have had a brother or sister? I see a sister as if all my mother could birth were women. I was born in 1988, my mother was older, thirty-seven, this child would have been more like an aunt or uncle to me since we'd be so many years apart. Still, we'd share a mother, we'd share blood and that means something. That always means something. But my mother was in high school. Her best friend had just died in a horrific way. She was raped by some man . . . Steve, I've never even heard of him. He just got to fade into the background without ever facing what he'd done. She struggled with mental illness her whole life but just now it's like it all started there. This summer destroyed her.

I wonder at the young girl who wrote that journal. I hear my mother in the voice. Who is she? Was she? Or were these just the ramblings of a crazy woman? This might not have happened at all. My mother was prone to telling stories. Maybe in high school she told more elaborate stories. But why shouldn't I believe her? She's my mother and she was wounded, by the loss of her friend, by society, by this Steve. Was she writing a novel? Am I allowed to think that because the alternative, that this is real, feels so much worse? My mother suffered so much and I didn't even know.

I pick up my phone and dial my aunt's number. She could have warned me. Her name is all over so much of my mother's journal and I was just on the phone with her. Her phone rings and rings and no one answers. It's only been a half hour or so. Is she home already? Is she in bed? I call again and get her voicemail before I give up.

I look at the journal and know there will be no sleep, not for a while, maybe not tonight. I kiss Eamon's cheek and he shifts in his sleep. If he had woken up I might have snuggled into him. I might have asked him to hold me, but he only shifts, still breathing heavily and so I get up, put on a robe, and walk out to the ocean. The chill in the air, the way it whispers across my face reminds me of the woman who was my mother on her good days. There were days we'd come out and just look at the water together. She'd sip coffee and I'd have a soda and we'd just quietly watch the sea.

Lorelei

THE NEXT DAY I find myself at Amelia's *Maude* party. But I don't find myself there, not exactly, I knew where I was going. I got dressed, sat in a car with my friend, she gave me directions, I drove, parked, walked in perfectly happy, or at least content, to be there. My mother's journal still rings in my mind. I tried calling my aunt again today but she didn't pick up and this is nothing to leave a message about. I reread the journal this afternoon after Eamon left for work. But I had to put it down. I can't keep worrying about it. Even if it's true my mother is gone. I can't help her now.

This party for *Maude Magazine* is held on the ocean. Not inside the kind of ramshackle shack my father owns but something newer with carpet and chandeliers, with white walls and pristine wood floors, more a five-star hotel than a place people live. I can see a maid coming twice a week to clean this house that is probably only occupied three or four times a year. Even at this party, with so many people, high heels, nice suits, the smell of perfume mingling with aftershave, it feels empty.

"You know I was thinking." Amelia comes up on my elbow with a drink in hand. I'm not holding a drink but a waiter comes and hands me a white wine as if my outfit is incomplete without it. Amelia looks at me, but there are two other people, people I've been introduced to, Harold, who works in finance and Matilda, the Lifestyle Editor, at my side and I'm sure she's really talking to them. "We should start a new mentor program," Amelia says to her colleagues. "Like the one *Mademoiselle* used to have in the fifties and sixties. We should bring in the best and brightest college girls, ones who want to be writers and editors, fly them to New York, and have them intern for the magazine for a summer."

"You can get interns without doing a nationwide search," Harold counters. "And putting them up, paying them, being responsible for the girls, that's not what internships are anymore. You take who's in town and pay them next to nothing, work them to death and hope they're good enough to hire in a couple of years, if they haven't gotten too burnt out."

"That's the thing, internships like that are starting to look really bad. An internship like this, one that's more encompassing, not only would it create a better talent pool, one that's maybe not burnt out in six months, but it would be really good publicity. We could use the girls as models for the magazine, they could write content like *Mademoiselle* had them do. We could really give them useful experience and I don't think it would cost that much. A couple of suites in Brooklyn, maybe put them in Queens, Long Island City is in right now. We'd pay them something, but not much. It would be worth the publicity. We could call it a fellowship."

"I remember reading about the *Mademoiselle* internship program," I jump in and Harold and Matilda look over at me as if they've just noticed my existence. "Sylvia Plath based *The Bell Jar* on her experience there."

"Oh I knew her." A woman who'd been walking through the room stops at the mention of Plath. "Such a great poet, she really was. A troubled, troubled soul." This woman is tall with thick dark grey hair. Her eyes are large and entirely made up with dark shadow and thick mascara. Her skin is rubbery and wrinkled as if she's spent too much time in the Florida sun but the way she holds herself, the way she speaks, belies a certain natural beauty. "I was there in New York. I wasn't working at *Mademoiselle*, but a friend of mine knew one of her roommates. She told me the story of the caviar, when Sylvia ate an entire bowl of caviar herself as if it were nothing, just ate it right up. I don't know if she was embarrassed or not, but she acted as if she had every right to do it, even when a couple of girls commented on it."

"I did my senior thesis on *Colossus* and *Ariel* in college," I comment as Amelia turns back to Harold and Matilda and the elderly woman faces me. Cliques are forming even at this one-off party. "The way she was so into great big things . . . larger than life . . . like the world was a fairy tale."

"She was a colossus herself, that woman, don't ever let her husband, who was more famous in their time, eclipse her. A disturbed woman, a great poet, but aren't all great women, dare I say great people, disturbed?"

"I've heard that saying before," I reply. "I think it was my mother who said it. It's so refreshing to hear someone say it again."

"Your mother was a wise woman. And you, what do you do? Do you write for *Maude*?" The elderly woman places her hand on my arm like we're old friends.

"No. My friend Amelia works there. I write novels, which means I mostly teach English." I laugh at myself but this large eyed woman only shakes her head.

"It's a sad thing, what's happened to writers. It's either a bestseller or the poor house. In my time, as a writer, you could live in New York and no one could have heard of you and you could still afford a vacation. Times have changed but not for the better."

"I'm in a bit of a writing funk now, but I'm hoping to change that."

This woman's eyes dart away from mine, she's seen someone else in this room and she smiles once politely, ending the conversation, and moves on. "I just have to head . . . But good luck with your novel, maybe it'll be that bestseller." I smile politely, aware she's about to go. I guess when you're that old, at a party like this, pretence is over, you're finished impressing colleagues. You do what you want, politeness be damned.

As this strange woman walks away from the group I've found myself in, I turn to Amelia, who's already engaged in more conversation with her colleagues. I know on some level it is a privilege coming to this party for *Maude,* such a prestigious magazine, and I should be grateful to Amelia for forcing me to go but a part of me, much of me, just wants to curl up in my pajamas and binge something on Netflix. Some days I think I should just get a cat when I return to Boston.

The walls of people, of slight conversations, too-bright smiles, jargon and water cooler talk make me want to run to the ocean. It's there, only a few feet away, I could walk out the door and be upon it. If I only dipped my toes in it would be enough. Instead I down the rest of my wine and wander over to a table that looks as if it's been set up as a bar. A young man in a nicely fitting suit nods to me. "White?" he asks and I nod "yes." "Sauvignon Blanc or Pinot?"

"Pinot." He hands me a glass, and I wander over to the window and look out. I can't hear the ocean against the gentle hum of this party, but I sense the ebb and flow of the waves and wonder what Theo, my ex, is doing back in Boston. Where is Eamon and would it be okay to call him? Would he come to this party, pick me up like another knight in shining armor and whisk me away to . . . where?

I place my wine on the edge of the windowsill and feel inside my purse for the scarf. I brought it, I don't know why. I don't know whose it is. I asked Amelia again if she knew where it came from, thinking a night of sleep might have helped stave off the empty headedness of a night of so much drinking, and she still didn't know.

I take the lipstick out for a second and look at it. It's red, so very red, do people still wear lipstick this red? Amelia was right, as a young woman Sylvia Plath had loved red lipstick and would wear no other color. But she was so different, that young Smith girl, going wide-eyed to New York City, so different from the somber faced poet who traveled Europe, who moved to England and married a large, domineering fellow poet with a wandering eye, who tried so hard to eclipse her. And that scarf we found reminds me of something Heather used to wear almost every day. I remember sometimes she'd toss it up in her thick blond hair or she'd tie it around her neck in a little bow or just wear it loose around her shoulders. I remember that scarf so well but this one isn't quite the same, there's a different pattern, more flowers than splashes of color. But it can't be hers. She loved that scarf. She was buried in it.

My phone buzzes. I feel it through the leather straps of my purse as if my phone is a kind of telegraph device. I pull my phone from my bag. I know it's rude but Amelia has dragged me to this party full of people and I feel lost in the crowd.

I do not get to my phone in time and a missed call and voicemail wait for me. It's Barry Larsen, that's the name, and a number for a Wellesley, MA area code. "Heather's father," I say out loud and no one seems to hear me. And I know, it says her father but it could just as easily be her mother who called. Her father is just out of prison why would they reach out? "Why is he calling me?" I ask no one in particular.

My phone buzzes again, alerting me to my voicemail. "What could he want?" I decide to ignore it for now.

"They usually want your first born son," a woman answers my question and I wonder how long I've been standing in the middle of a party with my mind on this. It's a sea of people, all with wine glasses or sherry, some sipping martinis or bright red cosmos, lots of expertly applied makeup, laughs a little too high pitched. But this woman stands out. She's not wearing any makeup and her long grey hair comes down well past her shoulders. It's washed, styled enough, but nothing like the other aging women at this party, the ones whose faces have been lifted, the ones who have dyed their hair so many times their natural color is as much a mystery to them as what life on a distant planet might be like. She wears a long skirt, a nice white peasant's blouse, and three or four silver necklaces that look like they have been crafted in the woods by aging artisans.

"I can't help them with that," I reply good-naturedly putting my time-to-socialize-at-this-shindig face on.

"I'm Joanne Henricks," the woman replies, holding out her hand.

"Joanne, do you know a woman named Sarah Moretti? She's my aunt."

"Lorelei! You're Lorelei." Joanne reaches around me she hugs me close for a second like we're old friends. "I remember you came to see your aunt at her office a couple times. You were just a little girl. My hair was much shorter and I was much thinner in the nineties."

I remember the office where my aunt used to take me. There were metal cubicles and a big picture window looking out on those grand New York City skyscrapers, the peak of the Empire State Building surrounded by towering boxes of apartment complexes. There were people at my aunt's office, mostly women in nicely fitting suits or professional skirt and blouse numbers. I remember wanting to be that powerful, that professional, that busy with what looked like important work, whenever I looked at them. But I do not recall a face, not a single one, but this Joanne, twenty-something years later, might have been one of them. "I'm sorry, I don't remember anyone specifically. I was five or six when my aunt took me to her office."

"That's all right, I remember you as a little girl, you certainly have grown up, but you still look young, how old are you, thirty-one, thirty-two?" she asks as if we've known each other forever. I only nod and smile demurely at that. "My wife dragged me to this party and then left halfway through with a cold." This Joanne is a lesbian, I could have seen it a mile away, but I wasn't going to make an assumption. I've always found myself gravitating toward aging lesbians at parties. I don't know what it is about them, they're so blunt, they know just what to say. Their particular brand of no frills-conversation draws me in every time.

"Why did you stay if your wife got sick?" I ask.

"She wanted me to stay, thinks it'll be good for my career. Not that I need to worry so much about my career at my age."

"That's what my aunt says," I reply casually. "Then she spends six months on a story like the world will end if it's not perfect."

"Give her my love. Sarah just emailed and said she wasn't coming in last night, I guess her plans changed. I'll have to see her sometime."

"She used to spend more time at the Cape, especially when my mother was here." "Was here," that's what I tell her. I wonder if she knows what that means. But the way this Joanne eyes me, like she knows and doesn't want to say, I can tell she's been privy to my life, to my mother's life, even if I don't really know who she is. My aunt must have told her about us.

"Magdalena, correct? Your mother?" she asks. Her voice softens and we both know why. "I'm really sorry about your mother, Lorelei." She grasps my arm for a second. With suicides one always treads on careful ground. "They called her Maggie?"

"Yes," I say just as softly. It's been a year but it still stings.

"I'm sorry. I used to know her. I mean, we used to hang out sometimes, when Sarah was in town. Your aunt and I met in New York, worked at *Cosmopolitan* together and somehow we both ended up with ties to the Cape. I settled in Boston, I work for a smaller magazine there, but your aunt stormed New York City, she was the It Girl, Ms. Female Journalist for a while."

"My aunt Sarah was always savvy. She's the reason I decided to become a writer."

"Oh, you write?" And here it is. What have you written? Have I heard of you? When is your next novel coming out?

"I published a novel a few years ago. I'm kind of stuck on my next one."

"Aw, well, you'll be okay, you'll find it. Novels are found, they're not constructed. That's what Sylvia Plath used to say."

"I love Plath," I reply almost silently.

"I met her a few years before I met my partner. It was the late fifties."

"Wow, that's a long time ago. When did you meet your partner?" I ask. Once years are mentioned the subject always seems just a tad touchier.

"Tammy and I have been together since 1982, if you can believe that."

"That's a long time."

"We almost didn't get married when they made it legal. We thought it was silly, after all the time we'd been together, why let a law change our lives, but then we thought . . . we should do it. We can, if it had been legal when we'd first met we would have done it, why not just do it?"

"Good for you," I reply as we move toward a back door. I find myself walking with this Joanne as if she's the only person here. The party has kept itself completely indoors and I never would have violated that unsaid order on my own, but Joanne opens the door to the empty patio that wraps around the living room and I follow. We take a seat on one of the high back bar stools that look out at the ocean and I wonder why no one follows. Is the talk of interns and celebrities, the alcohol, really that compelling? Does it keep people so tied to such tight spaces when out here there is the ocean and on the other side . . . what is it, Brazil, all the way to Brazil and they're stuck indoors?

"So you met Mimi," Joanne starts. She leans against her seat and her ample body pushes the chair outward a bit.

"Yes, I did." I glance back through the large glass windows.

"She's a nice woman. She's obsessed with the fact that she once knew a woman who knew a woman who knew Sylvia Plath."

"I wish I had known her," I tell Joanne. "I wrote my thesis on her in college, mostly on her transition from the *Colossus* to the *Ariel* poems. Some people said I have her bone structure . . . I think it was just because we're both five nine."

"Ah, yes. I can see it a little in your eyes, the make up of your face, the same tiny features . . . like a ballerina. I think if she had not been so tall Sylvia might have been a dancer. I knew her briefly when she lived in New England before she left for Europe and married Ted."

"That's amazing."

"She spent some time on the Cape when she was at Smith, the summer before *Mademoiselle*. I used to see her on the weekends. We weren't close, but she came to my cabin a couple times. We listened to records together. Mostly she talked about boys. I didn't have the heart to tell her I was only into girls. She was very prim and proper that one, a real do-gooder, but there was something of the bohemian in her, something dark waiting to come out. You can see it in her diaries." I remember my mother's diary, the one I read the other night.

"I can see that," I reply, trying to picture Sylvia Plath. She lived inside my bones in college, her poetry spoke to me as if she were whispering in my ear. My mother loved her so much, she'd read me her poetry on her good days. There was so much anger in Plath's work, so much soul searching, as if she were trying to piece together through poetry the disparate folds of her life as it was falling apart.

"She sent me a manuscript before she died," Joanne goes on, leaning in and whispering, her hand over my ear like we're pre-teen girls giggling at a birthday party. "It's not really novel length, more like a novella, but I'm sure she would have edited it, made it longer, had she lived.."

"Is it like *The Bell Jar*?"

"It is. The Manuscript, which is untitled, is the continuation of Esther's story. They say Ted destroyed her last book but Sylvia must have been working on another because she sent this one to me. She said it was an original and she wanted me to have it because I had always been so nice to her. But I think she knew Ted was going to destroy her work and she wanted a safety net. She sent it to me because we were friends but not close, no one would go looking at me after she died."

"She sent it before she died? Wow."

"Yes." Joanne nods carefully. "I didn't know that was her plan. I got the manuscript and a week later I heard she'd committed suicide. It was really terrible. I wanted to publish it after I found out about her death, but I knew by the way the papers said Ted was acting about her work, censoring it, only publishing what was old and therefore not critical of him, that I couldn't take the chance. So I held onto it and now I don't know what to do with it. I still don't think it's time to let the world see it."

"Really? You've never had it published? You've never shown it to anyone? How do you know she wrote it?" I fire questions and wish I were not a writer of fiction but a journalist like Amelia who might be able to get at the truth of this story.

"She and I corresponded for years, not much, we weren't friends, just a letter here or there. But yes, I have the manuscript at home. I can't have it published, Ted is dead but the estate would have a field day and so it sits in my study, in a safe . . . maybe when I'm dead someone will let it see the light of day. I think it's a shame though that it just sits in my study."

"She was the reason I started writing. I knew I could never be a poet. I couldn't write like that, but the way she could capture emotion, the way she could say so simply all the complicated intricacies of human thought, human emotion. When I read *The Bell Jar* it was like she was talking about my mother. I know it's over the top but art—"

"It makes you feel over the top, yes." Joanne takes a sip of her white wine. In the summer on the Cape all anyone drinks is white wine but I have a feeling this woman might be more comfortable downing shots of something stronger. "So you write, you said, what are you working on?"

"I published a novel a few years ago." It's a familiar story. Published first novel, did fairly well, good reviews, got contract for second novel and a teaching job at a state university that gives me a steady income. It's not The Lives of the Rich and Famous but it's good as far as authors go these days. Still, the second novel, personal issues, writers block. I could sum it up in a sentence at this point but I don't think Joanne needs to know all this and so I move on. "The second one is hard coming. It's about a woman going through a divorce after her husband cheats on her. She also has some father issues."

"Ah, father issues, cheating husband, I think you are channeling Plath."

"It wasn't my intention, but perhaps. My own husband . . ." I start, wondering why I'm so okay telling her this. Then again maybe I'm not so okay because I don't go on.

"I'm sorry to hear that, I think your aunt said something," Joanne says, laying a hand on my arm.

"And the girl, what happened to her. I can't even be angry because a week after her family found out her cousin took her to a warehouse with the intention of 'talking some sense into her.' Then they said he got so angry he started beating her up. It turned out she had an undiagnosed heart condition and the beating triggered a massive heart attack and she died." I close my eyes and flinch. I hate telling this story but I feel like I must. It's my penance. "Her father went to prison for a year for giving the cousin the keys to the warehouse. They thought he might have been in on the beating even if he didn't think it would go so far. I don't think that's true but he didn't defend himself at the trial."

"Lorelei, that is awful. Just awful."

"And she was a really young girl, one of my college students. Not under age, nineteen, but still, she was from a very traditional, very Christian family and there had been some issues with the cousin. Apparently he had a thing for her. He used to follow her around when she was in high school. It came out that Heather had told her friends she was still afraid of him."

"Wow. I was going to say, you shouldn't feel bad, if the girl got her heart broken, that's on her. But that. No one deserves *that*, Lorelei," Joanne says. "I'm sorry. A husband cheating with one of your students is bad enough but to carry that around."

"We were all shocked. It put everything into perspective."

The party continues as Joanne and I sit outside. I don't need to stay with her, I don't even need to stay at this party, but I do. Amelia will come out in a few minutes to get me, she'll pull my hand, I'll feel her clammy fingers in mine and I'll be happy to go. Joanne does not look at me again, not until I tell her, "I'm going to give you my number, maybe when my aunt is in town we can all meet up."

"Of course, I'd like that," she replies. She pulls her phone from a pocket in her purse and prepares to receive the digits.

I give them to her and we are quiet, as if now that we've made contact the pretense is up and we just want to look out at the waves. I remind myself to call my aunt. I still haven't gotten a hold of her and we need to talk. She'll be in town soon and my mother's high school journal still rings in my head, mingling with the story I've just told Joanne, as she and I look out at the ocean. I wonder what she feels, what's on this stranger's mind.

"You know, Sylvia Plath," Joanne starts after a few seconds. "She loved the sea. I remember I used to sit out with her, a bonfire raging. It was really nice. She was a really compelling woman. I have a feeling you would have liked her."

Sylvia
1962

FIVE IN THE morning is a perfectly natural time to wake up, Sylvia thought as she sat at her writing desk. People who wake at five are early risers, get up and go people who want a fresh start on the day. Four in the morning is a different story. Four a.m. is for crazy people pacing the halls because they can't relax enough to sleep. It's that one hour of sleeplessness that separated her from the good industrious people of the world. When the sleeping pills wore off too early Sylvia sank straight back into the crazies she'd been in ten years prior, when her brother Warren had found her in the crawlspace after taking nearly a bottle of pills. But five, five a.m. was different, at five she was merely a poet at work, writing alone at her desk, in the house William Butler Yeats used to occupy, for three gloriously quiet hours before the children woke up.

It had been a good writing session today. She'd been having so many great writing sessions since Ted left. There had been "Daddy" and "Lady Lazarus" and all the Bee poems. She would publish them all eventually in *The New Yorker*, they would want the lot of them, Sylvia was sure. They hadn't been taking much of her stuff lately but they still paid her for a first look and if not *The New Yorker* then *The Observer* or *The Atlantic*. Maybe even *Mademoiselle* would be interested. The rhyme schemes of some of these would definitely be better for popular consumption. Her "Daddy" poem, she was sure they would take that.

And where was Daddy anyway? Sylvia thought and first she pictured that strong German man her mother had married, the one who loved the outdoors and his oldest daughter, Sylvia, the man who'd taught her to keep bees. Then she remembered another Daddy who would be on his way today. Frieda and Nicholas would need to get up soon if they wanted to meet their father on time.

Just as Sylvia thought this, she heard the children in their rooms, Nicholas crying to be fed, Frieda jumping on her bed. And really, how anyone could get anything done with children in the house was beyond her. Life seemed to stop dead in its tracks the second she heard them in their room. The pushing and prodding just to get Frieda to walk down the sidewalk and having to take the pram everywhere because Nicholas got so heavy when she carried him.

Then Frieda got jealous that Nicholas was pushed and she didn't get a ride and an errand that would have taken ten minutes became an hour-long trek into barren country. And then of course there was the noise. When they were not dead asleep there was always noise and how on earth could a woman write poetry with so much screeching, needy noise?

Ted used to mind the children in the morning; he kept Frieda and then Nicholas completely out of her hair until noon at least. Even when Nicholas nursed constantly, Ted had quietly taken the boy in and pulled him right back out when he was fed. Neither of her children had been very fussy babies. She'd not had to be a mother really until lunchtime when the family ate their meal together and then Ted retired to write all afternoon. It had been glorious, everything she wanted, a beautiful home, a wonderful husband and children, and poetry. No, they hadn't been rich but they had been supporting themselves with their writing and so few writers, especially poets, could boast of that.

"Mummy," Frieda said when Sylvia entered the white painted bedroom she shared with the baby. "Mummy, Daddy is coming today, Daddy is coming!" The girl jumped on the bed and Sylvia closed her eyes, wincing as she turned to grab the baby from his crib.

"Don't do that!" she cried, sounding sharper than she meant it to. "Don't," she nearly seethed but she caught herself at the last second. "You'll ruin the bed. Let's get dressed and have breakfast and then Daddy will be here."

"We're going to the zoo," Frieda informed her as Sylvia handed her a blouse and a plaid skirt, something her mother had sent over from Boston when Frieda turned two She took a pair of leggings out as well. It was cold this winter and the children needed to be properly dressed.

"You'll see lots of animals. Make sure to say hello to the pandas."

"I like panda bears," Frieda said. "When I grow up I want to be one."

Sylvia laughed as the baby cooed on her shoulder. Her body slackened and she felt a certain release. If Ted took the children at least she'd have some time to work in the afternoon, maybe do the shopping and prepare a nice dinner, before they came home. "Mummy is just going to the kitchen, are you almost finished dressing, Frieda?"

"Yes," Frieda said as Sylvia headed out to fix breakfast.

A few minutes later little Frieda came into the kitchen where Sylvia had been readying oatmeal and warm milk. "I'm done," Frieda said, standing before Sylvia in her blouse and skirt and leggings. She could just see the girl grown up, her forehead a little too high but she had such beautiful, big, blue eyes, so like her father.

"Lovely darling," Sylvia replied, plastering that sugar candy smile she reserved for the children. "Now, I have to fix breakfast and then Daddy will be here. We'll have oatmeal today, okay? I'll make it the way my mummy did in Boston with milk and just a little honey."

"Ok, Mummy," Frieda cried, her plump little hands raised as Nicholas fussed in his high chair.

Usually the children were not interested in what they called "American food." It was too rich, too heavy, and they preferred English potatoes or lamb stew to the cow meat Sylvia sometimes insisted they have for dinner. But oatmeal was a good staple for breakfast, better than the cold baked beans the British served.

Sylvia got to work on breakfast, boiling milk and measuring Frieda's oats. She made sure to put in just a little honey so it didn't get too sweet. The girl always got just a little too wild when she had too much sugar. She fed Nicholas his formula as the milk boiled. She'd become so adept at maneuvering, even with a baby in her arms, that she was able to turn the kettle off without interrupting the baby's meal. When he was finished, she put Nicholas back in his chair and set to work on her own coffee. She liked tea, living with the English had given her a taste for it, but in the morning good, strong coffee really hit the spot.

"Frieda," she called as the coffee percolated on the stove. The baby fussed in his chair, reaching for Frieda's bowl as Frieda ran into the kitchen, shaking the walls. I wonder if Yeats ever had to deal with children in his house, Sylvia pondered as she watched Frieda greedily gulp her breakfast.

"So, are you excited to see Daddy today?" Sylvia asked, taking a seat across from her daughter and talking to her as if they were old friends. "Do you think he'd like to see Mummy in her new green dress?"

"Her new green dress?" Frieda repeated as if this were not her concern. "He wants to see the fishies. He likes fishies, remember, at the stream near the house?"

"Yes, your daddy and the fishies," Sylvia said and Nicholas gurgled just as the coffee started to boil.

Sylvia put a little cream and sugar in her coffee and stirred it carefully, with her thin hands that had started to shake just a few days ago. Her doctor had said maybe she needed new medication. He wanted her on antidepressants; monoamine-oxidase based medications, he'd said, because they would start to work more quickly. It had helped to calm her nerves and she could sleep more easily at night, but her hands shook more and still she didn't feel as if they were really helping. The old darkness was creeping back. She did not see the point in the things she did, the washing, the cooking, shopping in this crowded London neighborhood. Even writing poetry felt passionless sometimes. But there were times, like ten years ago, when she did not want to get out of bed, even if she was only lying there awake. It was just that nothing was sometimes preferable to everyday life. These days it was really only the children and the fact that someone had to care for them that kept her going. They would be helpless without her.

As Sylvia drank her coffee Frieda placed the bowl of oatmeal she'd just finished near Nicholas' high chair. The wooden chair scraped across the floor as Frieda pushed it in. Sylvia winced and almost snapped at Frieda as the girl ran into the living room to look out for Daddy.

"You like coffee don't you, little man?" Sylvia teased. Ted had never been great with the baby, not like he'd been with Frieda. While he used to happily hold their little girl in his arms all morning, he only reticently started picking up Nicholas, and Sylvia used to worry that they'd never get along. Now more than ever, when she couldn't be around to protect her son, she worried.

Nicholas reached for the bowl Frieda had left near his high chair and knocked it over. The china bowl came crashing to the floor and Sylvia stared at the mess, the little pieces of porcelain, the shards of splattered oatmeal. She didn't move for a second, it was too much, just too much. When you're a mother, it's not only the inconvenience, the mess, when something breaks, when a child cries, when anything goes wrong. It's also that nagging feeling that it's your fault. No matter how far you are from the fallen object it's always your fault. Even if you scold the children and they say they're sorry, they're your children, you're responsible for them and it's your fault. You shouldn't have left the glass something out, you shouldn't have left the child for a moment to step over by the sink, you should have smiled more . . . she'd felt, she'd heard, it all. That's what it was being a mother, especially without a father around to help. Everything, everything is your, your, your fault.

She felt the darkness again, a red fervor building up in her. She felt it, that old . . . the old . . . what was it . . . nothing, just nothing. The nothing would eat her up and tear her to shreds until she was invisible. Now it flashed white-hot, this anger, this exasperation. She had just cleaned the floor and Ted would be here soon and all she wanted was a second to herself. Sylvia let out an exasperated sigh and then stopped herself.

"What's wrong, what's wrong?" Frieda asked, running in.

"You left this on the table," Sylvia cried. She couldn't help it. She knew she should be calm when this happened but it all built up, it was so exasperating and she couldn't help it. She felt herself starting to seethe as she looked down at the saucer eyes of her little girl. Frieda wasn't about to cry at her mother's outburst, she had more steel in her than that, but she was hurt and Sylvia fell to her knees, holding her little girl close. "I can clean it later, it's okay, darling, it's okay, Mummy is sorry." Frieda grasped Sylvia for a second and then pulled away. This too, her own outburst, the fact that her daughter was upset, was her fault.

"I'm going to clean this up and then I'm going to put on my new green dress. What do you think? Some red lipstick and a new green dress. It's time Mummy start looking nice again."

"Okay," was all Frieda said as she stood watching Sylvia clean the floor with a rag before sweeping the shards of porcelain away with a broom.

After the room was clean, Sylvia put the baby on the floor in the living room and went to change. It really had been a long time since she'd worn her green dress. And how new was it? She'd worn it once many months ago to some gala or other that Ted had taken her to. It was more an evening dress than something to wear on a chilly London morning but the ruffles at the sleeves were really very becoming and she always liked how this dress flattered her figure, not that her figure needed much flattering since she'd lost so much weight. Sylvia pulled her long light brown hair, the kind of past-the-waist hair a lady has to wear up, into an elaborate bun like she'd seen Swedish women do when she was at Cambridge. She put a little shadow on her eyes, smoky blue, like the models were all wearing now. Even during the day these days, girls wore so much makeup. It really wasn't too much, highlighting the eyes and her lips needed red lipstick. Even so early red was her color. Women wore makeup in the morning now, even mothers.

She'd always worn red lipstick when she'd lived in New York. And when she had been with Richard in Paris . . . ah Richard . . . and Paris. If only Richard and Paris had continued, if only he hadn't run off to the Navy. But what was it about Richard? Was it only that he was the last one, the final great love affair before Ted, and so if it had worked out she wouldn't be in this mess? But Richard was slight and smart and he would have loved her so much and they would have talked about art and poetry for days on end. And would it have mattered so much that he was Jewish? Was that all in her head, her German family, his Jewishness? Yet he'd come from a good family and he'd taken her around New York. She used to sit up with him and talk about Yeats and Hemmingway and it made her happy, those hot nights in New York and the dinners they would have, the theater tickets and walks in Central Park. What would have happened if she'd stayed with Richard?

But, she needed to get ready. She needed Ted to see that she would not lay down and die as he wanted her to. He could gallivant around London with models, that mistress always waiting in the wings, but she would have her life and when he took the children out she would wear her nice green dress and red lipstick.

"You look pretty, Mummy," Frieda commented when Sylvia entered the living room. She said it as if it were a surprise that her mother could ever look pretty. Sylvia wanted to change that. Mothers could look just as pretty as shoddy mistresses.

"Thank you, my dear, your father will be here soon."

Just then Frieda jumped up and down. "Daddy! Daddy! I saw Daddy!"

Nicholas reached his fat little baby arms out toward his sister as she ran around the room as if the walls could not contain her. Ted had always done that to her. They had a special bond, the kind Sylvia had had with her own father, until he'd died when she was ten years old. Ten years old and Frieda was only two and already she was losing her father.

After several seconds there was a knock at the door. Since her bell had not rung, Sylvia could only assume that Trevor, the downstairs neighbor, must have been leaving. He must have let Ted in, an accident on the stairs, as sometimes happens sharing a flat. Sylvia cringed as she heard the knock. She thought there would be a warning, the bell would ring, she would buzz him up, but he'd taken that power away from her.

Sylvia froze and Frieda continued running around.

"Mummy, it's Daddy, it's Daddy knocking, answer the door," Frieda cried and Nicholas gurgled.

Sylvia turned and looked in the mirror, patting her hair and puckering her lips together. "Do you think my eye makeup looks pretty?" she asked Frieda who only gazed up at her as another knock sounded.

"Mummy, it's Daddy, its Daddy! Open the door!" she cried.

Sylvia stood frozen for a moment. She hadn't seen Ted in weeks and here he was at her door in London to see the children.

"Mummy!" Frieda cried and Sylvia shook her head and gazed at the door.

"Yes, of course, Daddy is here," she said, smiling sweetly. It felt like eons as she crossed the living room. Was the flat small, would Ted notice that so little of the furniture was theirs? The books! She still had not put the books up and the dishes had not been done from breakfast. The baby was on the floor. Was it really okay for a baby to play on the floor like that?

Sylvia opened the door and there he was. It was Ted, just as she'd remembered him. Things had changed so utterly in the past few months that she had not expected the same person. Ted was so inconceivably tall and it was his bigness, like she'd married a giant, which had first attracted her. At five-nine she really did need a giant. He was fit and broad-chested, his hair was always short but shaggy and it didn't matter what he could afford he was always wearing scruffy suits that looked so becoming on him though they really shouldn't. Ted's fashion defied all logic. Ted was a very big thing the way he filled up the doorframe as he stood towering over her once more so she could barely speak.

"Ted," she said and he mustered a smile, which grew bigger as Frieda ran to him.

"Daddy!" Frieda cried and Sylvia stood back. She swooped away, picked up Nicholas, and held him tight as if this were a competition.

"I'll have them back after lunch," Ted said, not coldly, but professionally. She had been his wife. They had borne these children together, they'd vacationed in Spain and shopped in Paris and married in a little English church and that he should talk to her like this, as if she were a shop girl he were giving directions to, was inconceivable.

"After lunch?" Sylvia asked. "I thought you'd keep them until at least tea time."

"I have a meeting with Bates and I really need to be on my best game," Ted explained, again, as if she were only a shop girl.

She handed Ted the baby after Frieda had finally removed herself from her father's leg. He took Nicholas carefully; as if the baby were made of glass and he might break him. He held him not close to his chest, but away, and it was as if she'd handed her son to a total stranger. "I really should be going. I'll be back by one. You know how this London weather is you never know when it might rain."

"When it might rain?" Sylvia asked. "But you said you'd keep them until tea and how am I supposed to get anything done? How am I supposed to write when you're out all the time?" she started but stopped herself as the eyes of her little girl gazed up at her.

Ted looked at the door as if it were salvation. He shook his head and his shaggy hair fell into his face. *Also of high windows. Worse/Even than your maddening/Song, your silence. At the source.* Ted glanced outside then and Sylvia pounced.

"She's here, isn't she? She's here? You knew better than to bring her up. I never said she could see the children and you brought her to my home. She was jealous I'm living in such a glamorous place, Yeats' house, and she's here isn't she?"

"Sylvia relax," Ted said, annoyed. "She's not here. No one is here. But I should take the children, let me give you some time." He put the baby down and walked closer to her. Sylvia could feel his largeness descend upon her and she wanted to cower away.

"She's here, you brought her to my house. I didn't want her to see it. I didn't want her to," Sylvia cried and before she knew what she was doing she was out the door, running down the stairs. She had not put on shoes. She hadn't thought of that when she was putting on her nice green dress and what was a nice green dress without glamorous shoes? She felt the wood of the stairs on her bare feet and then the freezing cold concrete outside. Even in the chill she ran. Cars passed, boxy brown and reddish Peugeots and tiny Volkswagens, they didn't breeze by but stammered slowly up the block, most of them looking for parking. Sylvia peered around the houses, at the grass coming up through the cracks in the sidewalks. She peeked in the alley to see if That Woman were hiding there. She called her name, that miserable woman's name, but no one came out. At the very least she should have come out of hiding.

Sylvia marched up the block, looking in every corner, every alley, she almost started to open the neighbors' rubbish bins to see if That Woman had been so cunning as to hide in there, but thought better of it as a couple walked by. It would have been silly seeing a woman so dressed up going through a metal rubbish bin. Finally, satisfied that That Woman was not in fact with Ted, Sylvia walked back to the house. She opened the front door, it had been left unlocked, and walked up the stairs. She reached the door to her flat and felt a little cut on her foot. She wouldn't let Ted know. She would tend to it later.

"Satisfied?" Ted asked, more exasperated than angry. He came very close and grasped her arm, she felt the weight of his fingers and wondered if he'd leave a bruise. "No mystery woman, see? Just a father who would like to take his children to the zoo." He laughed as if those words were not for her and gazed down at little Frieda before letting go of her arm.

Sylvia looked at herself in the mirror. Her red lipstick had faded, how had that happened? And her hair was disheveled. Was that all it took now, running out in the street and her hair, which she'd spent at least twenty minutes on, fell to wrack and ruin? There had been a time when there were not so many punishments for being so impulsive. In college Sylvia had been able to drink all night and roll out of bed in the morning looking just as fresh as the sunshine outside.

Ted turned back to the children. Frieda showed him one of Nicholas' toy cars. He looked at it with such amazement it was as if Frieda had shown him the eighth wonder of the world.

"Ah, such a lovely toy," Ted said. "And little Nicholas, will you drive a car like that someday?" Frieda laughed at that and Sylvia took a deep breath. Taking another glance at herself in the mirror, she smiled and felt the corners of her mouth curl, her eyes wrinkle.

"Ted, before you go, would you like some tea? I just made coffee but I can put the kettle back on? I know Englishmen and their tea."

"No, that's all right. I'm just going to take the children and be off. I'll be back by lunchtime, Sylvia, is that okay?"

Her stomach sank as she thought of the writing she would not get done. With the prospect of getting the children two hours earlier she could count all the things she would miss today. And there was the washing still and the shopping and it was so much easier to clean the house without the children in it. But she had wanted to write this afternoon and now there would be no time for that. "Of course," she replied, still turning up her smile. There was nothing else she could do but smile. "By lunchtime of course, but really, why don't you have a cup of tea before you go?"

"That's all right, Frieda, put your jacket on," Ted said. He picked the baby up and marched toward the pram. "I'll just take this. It'll be hard getting it down the steps but I'll manage. Frieda, you'll be my magic helper."

"I will, Daddy!" Frieda cried, following her father out the door as he maneuvered the cumbersome pram.

Sylvia turned to her kitchen. She still had not cleaned up the mess from breakfast and so she got her rag. In her green dress, the one with all that taffeta, she started to work. She heard Ted in the street playing with the children, their voices mixing with the sound of the cars Frieda loved so much.

Lorelei

THE WELLFLEET DINER is made of metal. It's one of those by-the-ocean contraptions that comes right out of the 1950s. I wonder when it ceased to be a relic, something ugly and behind the times, like see-through phones and butterfly chairs left over from the 1990s, to an antique rarity that tourists must visit to get a taste of the good old days. I wonder if Sylvia Plath, a fifties girl if ever there was one, would have eaten here. The plaque above the door reads *Established 1952* and so there's a chance. I know she used to spend time on Cape Cod but I'm not sure if Wellfleet, a more commercial section of the Cape that boasts its share of blue collar fisherman, would have been her style. In college she only dated the Harvard and Yale boys.

"You know, I just don't think he can step in like that, especially with all the money he makes," Eamon says, taking a great big bite of his toast and then wincing.

"You sure you're okay? Not hung over?" I ask and he shrugs only half playfully. "You need to drink water."

"I'm fine. But I mean, your book sold but not so damn well that he has to go probing into its finances. You know what, if you don't want to be on top of how well your book is doing, if you don't want to go probing to make sure your publisher is paying you your fair share of royalties, that's none of his business."

"Not only does Theo hiring a lawyer like this piss off the publisher but it makes me look bad. I don't even know what he's looking for. He makes three times what I make teaching. This book was a one shot deal. I have a contract on my next book and I don't think he should be able to touch that, since he was messing around with a nineteen-year-old girl the entire time I was working on it."

"I can't believe you tore half of it up."

"I needed to. It wasn't working. I couldn't have written any more if I hadn't. It needed to go. To be purged."

"You artists are a wee bit crazy." Eamon takes another bite of toast and I note that he hasn't touched his eggs. Eggs were never great hangover food for me either.

"Speaking of crazy artists, what were you up to last night? You look like you got run over by a freight train."

"Just a lively bar fight with a man named Craig who seemed to think those limey English should have stayed in Ireland. Can't have people saying that, not in Boston."

"Here, here," I call, lifting my glass of orange juice over my head like it's a beer stein. Eamon winces like I've just shouted though my voice barely reached an extra decibel.

"But, I had this flash, while we were tangled on the floor fighting—"

"You were actually on the floor. You were actually fighting?"

"Did you not believe me? Did you think I was making it look worse than it was? Oh, Lorelei, my love, you need to learn that an Irishman does not over embellish when it comes to a fight. He tells you exactly what happened. You'll get no tall tales from me."

"I see." I smile playfully.

"But I saw this painting, you know how it works, as an artist, the entire piece just falls into your head and sure there are details, technical stuff you need to figure out, but I saw this red and black and white painting, like a bull fight, very carnal, animalistic . . . and I couldn't get it out of my head. I took an Uber home and started painting."

"If a bar fight inspired art then it was worth it. You should go home and work. Don't let me keep you here with talk of divorce settlements and writer's block."

"Life inspires art, that's the only reason anything is worth it. That and the whiskey. But right now, all I want to do is sit in this diner with you talking divorce settlements and writer's block." He smiles sweetly and I grasp his hand. "And you know, I've been thinking about looking into getting an apartment in Boston. There are plenty of colleges there where I could grab a teaching gig, maybe tend at one of the Irish bars. I haven't lived in a city in a while."

"I know," I reply, not committing to anything. As I turn I see a hefty woman in a large salmon colored beach dress that I recognize. She's with a taller and slimmer woman, who's wearing nicely tailored white pants and a sailor blouse. Her hair is short and much more styled and I can see that if she were not at a Wellfleet diner on a Saturday morning, she might be wearing a business suit.

"Joanne," I call and the long haired woman looks over, smiles, nods, and bypasses the hostess to come and say hi. "This is the woman I met at the party the other night. My aunt's friend."

"Oh, right, Sarah's friend," Eamon muses, taking a small bite of his runny eggs. I don't know why he ordered them runny, he seems not to be able to stomach them.

Our red backed booth sits near the front and so it's not a major feat to come talk to us, though Joanne acts as if it is, the way she scoots past a woman with her chair jutting out just a bit too far. "It's so nice to see you again," I tell her and she opens her arms wide for a hug when I stand to greet her.

"Yes, Lorelei. I was hoping to hear from you. Have you heard from Sarah?"

"I talked to her the other day. We're having dinner tonight. But we should all meet for lunch soon." When she answered my call I wanted to ask my aunt about my mother's diary but she talked so fast, like she knew if she stopped another shoe would drop, and I couldn't get the words out fast enough. And so it looks like I'll wait until dinner tonight to broach the subject.

"So great about Sarah," Joanne says. "I was hoping to see her again. Maybe we'll go further down the Cape. I'll show you P-Town. They make the most delicious lobster rolls down there."

"I haven't had one of those since I came here. Lobster is definitely in order."

"Or you could just come to the house," Joanne goes on. She places her knuckles on the wood of the back of our booth and knocks twice on it. A simple gesture, but so like my mother it's hard not to notice. She used to have quirks like this, knocking on wood or reciting all the state-of-being-verbs off the top of her head while in line at the grocery store. "I can show you the bees."

"The bees?" I ask, looking to the woman standing beside Joanne who has just come up to meet us.

"We keep bees," she elaborates. "It was Joanne's idea. Something about the declining bee population and we have to do our part. We got a couple honeycombs, a queen, and a few workers, and started a hive a few years back. I was terrified they would all die our first winter, but they seem to be thriving."

"This is my partner, Tammy." Joanne knocks again on the back of the booth and this time Tammy notices. "She's obsessed with the bees now."

I nod to Tammy who says, "Not quite obsessed, but I do like them."

"She works at Saber and Thomas, but she's down for the weekend," Joanne elaborates.

"Nice to meet you," I say and this more professional woman smiles with tight, thin lips painted just a tad peach.

"Yes, likewise. Joanne said she met you at the *Maude* party. You know Sarah Moretti? That's wonderful. We haven't seen her in ages. How was the party?"

"Great," I tell her, aware of just how generic I sound. "We spent a lot of time talking about Sylvia Plath."

"Didn't she kill herself?" Eamon asks and we all stop for a second. .

"She did," Joanne says as a couple shifts around the tight space between tables. Joanne does not move to help the couple get around us but once they've passed she takes a seat at our booth, causing both of us to slide further in. Tammy points toward the hostess before walking over to see about a table. "I'll just be a second," she says by way of salutation. Then Joanne knocks twice more on the back of the booth before Tammy goes.

"She gassed herself, Sylvia Plath," Joanne elaborates once Tammy is gone. This seems a bit callous but I let it go. "Stuck her head in an oven."

"Wouldn't that hurt?" Eamon asks respectfully. "Wouldn't you burn to death first? Or wouldn't it just hurt so damn much, burning to death, that you'd stop."

"Ovens weren't like that back in the sixties," Joanne explains. "She didn't turn the oven on to heat it. She turned the gas on. Actually, what she did, was, she left milk and a snack for her children, then she sealed them in their own room, locking the kitchen door and putting tape and towels around the door so the gas would not get to them, she then went downstairs, and sealed herself in, then she turned on the gas, placed her head in the oven, which remained cool the entire time, and gassed herself to death."

"That's so meticulous. So thought out," Eamon comments before taking another bite of toast.

"It was. That's what's so terrifying about her suicide. It wasn't merely a childish impulse. She thought of so much, right down to how to protect her children, the ones her good for nothing husband left her with when he went off with his mistress."

"Wow," is all Eamon can say.

"Funny thing is the mistress, about ten years later, she took her and Ted's two-year-old daughter into the kitchen with her and gassed herself to death the same way. Didn't even think to protect the child there."

"Wow," Eamon breathes in astonishment. "I can't even imagine. Two wives and a child. What a terrible pattern."

"I know, poor guy. Wasn't the best husband but he didn't deserve that," Joanne responds before looking over at me like she's distracted. "Lorelei, I want to show you that manuscript. I think I have it in my car. I'll just tell Tammy I'll be a second and I'll get it for you." She turns around, knocking twice on the booth before moving to go.

"Really, you have it in your car?" I ask, surprised. This doesn't seem like the best place to keep a one of a kind manuscript.

"I carry it around with me sometimes. Do you want to read it? I can get it."

"Joanne, you have no idea what that would mean to me. If I could read it . . . maybe it would actually inspire me to write this damn novel I'm supposed to finish."

Joanne looks sideways at Tammy, who is now discussing seating options with the fifteen-year-old hostess, who does not appear to understand from Tammy's gestures that she'd like a table and not a booth even though from ten feet away I can clearly see that's what she's after. Joanne wrings her hands together and looks back at me. "Sure, yes. I'd love to show it to you. Just don't tell anyone, okay? Let it be our secret. I'll be right back with it. Tammy won't even notice."

Her voice is a little odd but hiding a lost manuscript by a famous author must bring out the paranoia in a person. True to her word Joanne slips out the front door of the diner and walks straight toward a navy blue Prius. Tammy sees her, I observe her watching Joanne with suspicious eyes, and hope I haven't started something.

I had not noticed anyone watching our table or approaching, but as if she has materialized out of thin air, a very thin girl with shoulder-length brown hair stands before our table, her arms folded across her chest, where she carries a green notebook like a shield. I can make out a pen in her fist, she grasps it as if she's holding onto it for dear life. She is like a miniature version of a journalist on a hard-hitting story, but she stares at the floor and her hands shake a little as she stands there.

"Excuse me . . . miss . . . hello," she finally says. Her voice is small and fragile like the shells on the beach tourists snatch up, the ones that break almost as soon as you touch them because the sea has already been so rough with them.

"Hello," I quietly greet her. Someone so timid must be handled with care. "Can I help you?"

"Yes, Miss . . . it's just . . . my name is Ashley and I was just . . . for school I was asked to speak to an author and I saw you here. The other day, I saw you in the store and I thought, oh, this was the woman whose book I read. It wasn't in school, your book's not for high schoolers, but I found it at the library and thought it was so good, the way you talked about marriage and family and children and I loved it. Could I speak with you maybe?"

"Hello, Ashley. Thank you so much for your kind words." I have published a book. I have been reviewed in *The Washington Post* and *The Village Voice*, Amelia was able to get a press release put through in *Maude Magazine*. I have done readings of my book where no one came up to me afterwards because they really didn't care, but this is new, someone out of nowhere, someone who is not the friend of a friend or someone my aunt knew, asking about my book. "Do you want to take a seat?" I move over and Eamon gives her a friendly nod.

"Oh, no, I couldn't. My family'll be back soon. We're on vacation here and this is just so lucky. I was just . . . what are you working on now, can I ask?"

"Are you sure you don't want to sit down?" It's funny, this young girl, she's so small, so thin, and I just want to take care of her. But those eyes, something about her blue eyes remind me of something . . . of someone. "Have I seen you before? Do you know where I live by any chance? Ever been by the house or lose something near a house in North Truro?"

Her eyes grow big and she steps back. "Oh no, I've never done that."

"It's okay," Eamon says. "Take a seat."

"I'm fine. Really. I can't stay long. But your next book, have you written it?"

"Kind of." I laugh at myself and look out the window. The road through Wellfleet is crowded, but something about the starkness of the Cape, the sand on the gravel, the little beach shops, makes it look primitive and lonely even in tourist traffic. Joanne, having come out of her blue car, marches back toward the diner with a brown rectangular manuscript box in her hands. I have seen these before. I interned at a publishing house in college and I know just what it is. "I wrote a large chunk of my second novel. Then after a few things happened I stopped. I tore a lot of it up. I thought about building a bonfire and burning it the way Sylvia Plath destroyed her second novel."

"Wow, that's crazy. But you did get rid of it?"

"Not so dramatically. I used the delete function on my laptop. But yes, I did. It wasn't working and after what had happened, it just wasn't in me anymore to write that novel in that way."

"It was more like your old novel and now you're a new woman?" the girl clumsily asks and for the first time it's like she knows me.

"Something like that," I reply.

Eamon laughs. "Something like that . . . it's exactly like that. Lorelei here needs to stop living in the past."

"I don't live in the past, thank you, Eamon, my dear. I must tell you, never hang out with artists, they're a bad influence."

"Yes," Eamon concurs good-naturedly. "We're a terrible lot."

"Oh I won't, I see," the girl goes on. "But can you tell me anything about your new novel? I want to read it as soon as it comes out."

"I don't have very much anymore. It's about a woman who's going through a divorce. Her husband cheats on her and leaves her with the children. The most notable thing about it right now is that the protagonist's three children are named London, Paris, and Sydney."

"Ah . . . all cities, that's cute." The girl genuinely laughs but there's something about the look on her face that also says she's being nice. The city names thing, it's a silly quirk, and really has to go.

"But to tell you the truth I don't know when the book is going to come out. I'm supposed to have a draft to my editor by the end of August, but I think it might be more like December."

"It's okay. I know. I've read about authors, second books are very difficult, especially if something has happened in their personal life. Excuse me if this is rude, I love books, but I really want to be a journalist and so I must ask, what happened in your personal life? What problems are you facing that make it hard for you to write?" The girl lifts her head and looks me in the eye for a single second before glancing away. Then she hugs herself tighter and I know she has steeled herself to be so bold and can only sustain this courage for a second. It's impressive in a girl her age.

"I'm sorry, I can't talk about that. But I like that you asked me the question. You know, my friend, who's staying with me, her name is Amelia and she works for *Maude Magazine*. She's the Celebrity Editor, it's not exactly hard-hitting journalism, but it's journalism. If you'd like to stop by my place . . . with your parents of course, you'd need their permission, but I'm sure she'd be happy to talk to you."

"Oh thank you. That would be nice," the girl says, wide eyed. "But I'd rather do an interview with you if that's okay. I work for my school paper. They'd love this story."

"That's perfectly all right, but ask your parents, okay?"

I can tell she has not thought about what this means, getting permission from her parents. Still, this Ashley seems like a nice girl and I want to help her.

"Here," I tell her, fishing into my purse and pulling out my card. It has my address in Boston on it. "Eamon, can you find a pen?"

He instantly starts patting his pockets. "Pen found," he announces after reaching into his back pocket.

"Thank you. My cell is on the card, but here's the address of the house in North Truro. Please, call first, but feel free to come by if you have permission."

"Yes, of course. The girl looks at the door longingly, an action I attribute only to her shyness. "Thank you, Miss." She hugs herself tighter as she walks toward the door. There's something about the way she carries her books over her chest that reminds me of a 1950s schoolgirl.

"That was odd," Eamon says.

"You think I don't have fans?"

"I think no one has ever approached you about your book outside of a pre-planned reading. And that's okay, no one has ever approached me about my art outside a gallery showing. Sometimes they don't even approach me then."

"This is so strange."

"What? That you all of a sudden have a fan club that consist of one teenage girl? Aren't your novels supposed to be for married women?"

"Who knows? They're not that racy but my first novel was about a thirty-year-old woman losing her job after having a baby and having to start over, not exactly an exciting read for a teenager."

"You can make anything exciting my dear, anything." He smiles at me before we both look up to find our new friend.

"Joanne."

She looks down at me. She hands the box over as if she's now in a major rush. Her semi-annoyance makes it seem like she's a different person from the woman who went out to her car five minutes ago.

"Here it is. I was just waiting for that girl to leave, I didn't want her to see it," she says awkwardly.

"It's okay," I reply, smiling kindly to calm her down. She'd seemed so proud of the manuscript the other night and I don't know why she's ashamed of it now.

"I have to go. When we talk next, maybe at lunch, we should talk about this. It's just . . . please, take care of it. It's a masterpiece and I wouldn't want it in the wrong hands." She then knocks once again on the back of the booth. "Knock wood." Is she wishing for luck? My mother used to do that sometimes when she was nervous about something. It used to drive my aunt Sarah crazy. And just then, the faux casual way she says it, reminds me of my mother.

"I'm so excited, thank you," I reply, waving as Joanne forces a smile, looking backward before approaching Tammy. "Well this is exciting," I tell Eamon, who has finally started on his eggs. "Aren't those eggs cold?"

"Eggs, yes, icebergs, but I'm hungry," he replies, smiling. "And, exciting, a new manuscript. Now you can read more and avoid writing. Let's open it up right now so we can start avoiding writing right away."

"I'm not opening it here. Joanne would kill me. You saw how protective she was of it. And I think right now I need to get you home, Mr. Snarky. A night of bar fighting and painting has done a number on you."

"Let bar fighting and painting do their worst," Eamon comments as I look up at the diner, which is still crowded with people in khaki shorts and polo shirts, women in nice Gap or Banana Republic dresses, and signal to the waitress that we want our check. "But, my dear, just let me make it up to you tonight, may I buy you dinner?"

"You may," I respond.

"Good," Eamon says.

Sylvia
1962

LONDON HAS SUCH large parks; Hyde Park, Kensington, Kew, and Convent Gardens, Sylvia thought. The city was chock full of these parks; sprawling and hill covered like you've just stepped into a Bronte novel. They reminded her of The Public Garden in Boston or New York's Central Park. Some of these parks were built up. There's the statue of the man on the horse here and there (what was it with Europe and statues of men on horses?) or the Royal Albert Hall just outside Kensington. Sylvia had just been to see the JM Barrie statue, the one of Peter Pan, the little boy who never grew up.

What people didn't realize was that the original story, *Peter Pan in Kensington Gardens,* the one Barrie was inspired to write while sitting alone in the park, was not about Neverland and second stars and Wendy and the Lost Boys. Lost . . . but it was about being lost. It was about a very curious and headstrong boy, an infant, who wandered into Kensington Gardens after dark and got stuck there. He was kept alive first by the birds and then he made friends with the fairies. The fairies in this story were very spiteful creatures who did not take kindly to outsiders and the infant Peter really had to work to get into their good graces. But he was destined never to grow up. And it was tragic, it was not a happy choice, but a curse, Peter's never growing up. Once he fell in love with a little girl who got lost there. He really fell in love with her and when she asked him for a thimble he gave her a kiss, a real kiss, and there were many thimble kisses after that. But the prospect of never growing up scared the girl and she ran away from him and Peter was cursed. Not like in the play, the play ruined everything, it made joyful and petty what had been tragic and sweeping and bittersweet. But the boy Peter stayed forever in Kensington Gardens protecting the children who got lost in it. And, when a child was harmed in the garden, he buried them.

But they really were magical places these London parks. Sylvia could see how these misty English landscapes, looking, especially in the London fogs, like they were out on the moors, could inspire such stories. It was the mystery of London, of these parks with their wild terrains that grab the imagination and hold on tight. Not just flower gardens but bramble where the weeds might take over, that's where Peter Pan came from. And really, these parks were not like Central Park where Sylvia used to go with Richard. But he'd left her and then there had been Ted and wandering around Yorkshire and now Ted was gone as well. Ted at the very least had taken the children for the day, once again to the zoo as if it were the only place he could think to take them. For such a celebrated poet sometimes Ted had no imagination.

Sylvia was just coming from an appointment. That was really why Ted had taken the children and if he hadn't she would have had to have hired a sitter as Doctor Horder did not like to allow her children to sit in the waiting room while she met with him.

And she'd thought of it then, the great mystical woman who could get men to bend to her every will and why couldn't she have done that? Lorelei, the Lorelei. *With richness, hair heavier/Than sculpted marble. They sing/Of a world more full and clear.*

Doctor Horder had said today that he didn't want to raise the dose of her medication. "Not just yet. You know, these things take time."

"Time? The reason you wanted me on these meds was because they took less time to start working."

"Do you feel better? Even a little bit?" Doctor Horder had inquired. "I remember the last time we spoke you said you were sleeping better. Are you having any more of those dark, dark thoughts?"

Really, what was she to say to that? These past few days it had been so much of those dark, dark thoughts. She had been a mass of them most of her life. They'd started when she was a child. When she was ten years old her father had died tragically. He'd been ill and then he'd had a fall down the stairs and did not recover. And it was as if God had purposely tried to hurt her, He really had. Sylvia, even at ten years old, when her mother took her to church and she saw the coffin and her mother had explained about Heaven and illness and that Daddy wasn't suffering anymore, still she could not forgive God. That had been the start of it, those dark thoughts, and they had never really gone away.

And Daddy had been German at a time when it was not a good thing, being German in America. Later Sylvia couldn't place it but she always felt this guilt. She'd loved the Jews and the summer they executed the Rosenberg's, well, she'd written about it in her novel *The Bell Jar*, which would be coming out in England soon. It had hurt her so much and she knew that if the Rosenbergs had not been Jewish they would not have been electrocuted. And she'd dated Richard, who'd been Jewish, and she'd loved him. But she would always look at him, into those great Semitic eyes, and wonder if he saw her pale coloring and light hair and remember the German in her. "My father wasn't a Nazi," she'd told him once and he'd only laughed at her. Richard had such a way of taking her in his arms and even though he was slighter than Ted she always felt safe. "I never said he was," he'd quipped back, but she knew in the back of her mind that Richard never forgave her for being German and it made her feel the darkness all over again.

She'd been able to stave the darkness off for so long. There had been so much joy after the first time she'd tried to die, to get back, back, back to Daddy. That had been ten years after her father's death. There had been Richard and going to Cambridge on the Fulbright, there was meeting Ted and falling in love—all of that had happened after the first time with the pills. She and Ted had gotten married so quickly, they just ran off while her mother was in town, booked a church, found Ted's family parish. But Ted didn't tell his family, not even his brother Gerald, who he was supposed to be so close to.

Then it was off to Paris and Spain to see the world. She and Ted had learned languages and wrote before Sylvia cooked dinner. Every night she made sure to make Ted a good English supper even in Spain where they didn't even have an icebox and all the meat had to be bought and used the same day. They had gone back to Boston for a year and Sylvia had taught at Smith, her alma mater. Then there had been the flat in London where Frieda was born and the house in Devon and . . . gone all gone.

But after the first time she'd tried to kill herself Sylvia had made herself well. Yes, there had been doctors and medicine and electroshock therapy, but in the end she had pulled herself up on her own. She'd crawled back out of the gloom her brother Warren had found her in after she'd taken the pills. They'd sent her to a home, first a very bad home with dirty floors and "crazy" people muttering to themselves all over the place and then to a nicer facility with people just as crazy though the curtains were white and the floors were clean so that the muttering was kept to a minimum. They had given her electroshock both places and eventually she'd come out of it.

Sylvia had made a life for herself after so much suffering. And now that life was gone and it was the darkness all over again. At least this doctor did not tell her to get a hold of herself. It wasn't like the first doctor, who'd told her to just try to remember all the good in her life. As if that was all it took. As if she could wave a magic wand and get better. Perhaps that little boy with a statue in the garden could help her . . . it was worth a shot if you're going to employ such witch doctor methods. But Doctor Horder, like Doctor Ruth Beuscher, who had helped her through this before, did not think she would just snap out of it. "It's not your fault, Sylvia," Dr. Beuscher had said while she'd been in the institution ten years ago. "It's a problem with brain chemistry. Of course you can't help yourself."

And of course she couldn't help herself. If only she could. Did they think that it's just a matter of getting out of bed? Did they think if she just thought happy thoughts she'd get picked up on fairy dust and flown away to a happy, happy place? But she had gotten out of bed this time. She hadn't sat in her room refusing to shower, getting smelly and not sleeping and then knocking herself out with those pills and sleeping too much. She was writing poetry. Every morning she was up at four a.m., it was four a.m. now, she couldn't help herself, the sleeping pills wore off and that was it. She couldn't take another dose of her medicine, not until at least five in the morning. But she could handle, at least for now, an hour of the pain, of the despair, the way she kept spiraling as if into a dark, dark hole. The Rabbit Hole. Oh Alice! And Sylvia remembered another English story that had been inspired one day when it's author had gone into an English park with a little girl and started telling stories.

Sylvia walked through Kensington Gardens. "I wonder where Alice in Wonderland comes from?" she pondered out loud. It was an innocent thing to say and no one looked over and thought her crazy. It was only that they couldn't see what was going on in her mind, the disorder, the constant confusion. The fact that it was dark, so very dark in her head, if they could see inside her mind they would call her mad. And society did not like a woman with depression. She's not happy, she's not conciliatory. Men don't like that. Other women don't like that either. And if she's a mother and she gets a little sad—well we can't have that! They all looked at her funny and then rejected her poetry when she sent it to them.

Sylvia could see the horizon, the end in sight, the threshold where the park ceased to be a park and became the city once again. There was a large concrete gate (it had probably been stone before The Blitz but they had replaced so much of the great stone or iron structures with concrete since the war). Sylvia wanted to pull the already opened gate as she walked out of the park and into the city.

It was the cars she saw first and then the people moving about. A mother pushed a pram, a little girl trailing behind her. Sylvia wondered if she was as overworked as her, if this mother worried about what she could and could not get done all day every day because there were children constantly trailing her. Then again the chances that this mother also wrote poetry . . . and even a job, a career, any other obligations a woman might be saddled with, are not the same as writing poetry. Poetry gets under your skin. You cannot *not* write it. There were days Sylvia sat at her desk and the words would come, flowing from her like a great fount. Other times she had to push them as she did her children from her body, the labor pains were that intense. Still other times she'd go back over what she'd written working and reworking a line until her fingers ached. Then the phone would ring. The children would awaken. She would realize the coffee needed to be put on or a friend was coming to tea and it was as if she were a great glass mural, shining and bright and then someone had thrown a rock at her, shattering her into a thousand dull pieces.

Sylvia watched the whiteness of the sidewalks and the black cabs that whooshed by. The red busses had been such a treat when she'd first visited London. The red double-decker busses fascinated the American tourists. But now London was home and to hop on a bus was no great feat, in fact she tried to avoid the rough, the jostling, the crowded experience if she could.

Sylvia walked on, down and then around Hyde Park Gate, which looped around itself. She'd visited this place before. At Cambridge there had been the young men of *St. Boloph's Review* and they had been such up and comers in poetry. That had been how she'd met Ted. She'd recited his lines of poetry at a party and he'd come up to her, they'd ended up in a bedroom together, he'd kissed her so raw, so passionately. He'd then grabbed her headband from her hair saying "Spoils." She'd bitten him on the cheek and left a mark that lasted for days.

But that was over and now she was here at 22 Hyde Park Gate, Virginia Woolf's girlhood home. Woolf had not been a poet but she had been a writer. And she'd been a woman and she'd done it on her own. Virginia had been just as unstable, if not more unstable, than she was. She'd heard voices and taken pills once, she'd jumped out of a window when she was a girl and then there had been the river. But before the river she'd had a great writing career. Yes she and her husband, Leonard, had had The Hogarth Press and he worked very hard on it, but mostly they got along with her writing. It gave Sylvia hope, even if she did not have a Leonard to support her, that she could do this, she could write poetry and raise children without Ted. Then again the Woolf's had not had any children.

Sylvia stopped at the house and looked up. Three artists had lived at this house. There was Leslie Stephen, Virginia's father, the biographer. There was Vanessa Bell, the painter, and then there was Virginia. *Virginia Stephen Woolf, writer, essayist.* And hadn't she said a woman needed a room of her own and her own income to write? Wasn't that all anyone needed in order to do anything? Space. And money. It wasn't quite so ingenuous, not like her novel *The Waves,* which seemed to understand all of humanity in one fell swoop. Still, Virginia Woolf had understood writing and art and women.

And she had gone mad. That was always it with women, great women. Why was it that they always went mad? Was it just that the only way to be great is to be mad and men are just better at hiding their madness? Or is it that society accepts mad men much more easily than it will ever tolerate a mad woman? Is it that a woman, when she's just a little bit off, when she will not get out of bed (or play excessively with her children or make her husband dinner) that she must be shot through the brain with electricity until she complies? And really, isn't that what happened to me? Sylvia thought as she looked up at that white house. Wasn't it just that I was sad and then . . . and then . . . they sent her away, they gave her pills and injections and then shot electricity right into her brain until she blacked out and everything was fuzzy and she could not remember, she simply could not remember? Did it really help all they'd done to her? Was it helping now?

She'd gotten another rejection today. She'd gotten three or four. Two of her poems had been rejected from *The Observer*. *The New Yorker* did not want her "Daddy" poem and *The Atlantic* was not interested in the story she'd written about her childhood on Cape Cod, "The Mintons" or some other such title, the one about the brother and sister who went into the sea. Too dark is what they said, too depressing, no one wants to read about that. But those little rejections she could handle. It was her novel, *The Bell Jar*, the one that would be published in England under an assumed name, though no American publisher wanted it. Her home country, where the novel takes place, did not want to publish her work. Too depressing, they said. Writing about madness, what's wrong with that? Why not be honest about what happens to the mind when a person, when a woman, starts to lose it? Men had been writing, had been publishing, about madness for so long. *Catcher and the Rye, One Flew Over the Cuckoo's Nest*, those books had been heralded as great works of modern literature and yet no publisher wanted *The Bell Jar*. They did not want to hear about a woman going mad. Men at least had the luxury of going insane and then being heralded for bravely telling about it.

Sylvia turned down the dead end road where Virginia and Vanessa Stephen had once lived with their family. Vanessa had died old at Charleston with Duncan and Clive and Virginia had walked into a river with rocks in her pockets and drown herself. And why, because her work had been rejected, her stories were not being published as they once had been. And that, more than losing a husband or having screaming children at home or having to worry about the chill that was now coming into the air, having no money and no family in England, that was nothing compared to the rejection. It was the rejection that was the mark of madness. To put your heart and soul into poetry and have no one care. To scream so loud and they just silence you, put a muzzle over your mouth like it's nothing.

No wonder artists went mad.

Lorelei

RESTAURANTS ON THE Cape run the gauntlet from tiny hole-in-the-wall diners with silver walls that serve fried eggs over easy and strong, black coffee, pizza joints inland with vinyl tablecloths and little glass containers of red pepper flakes, to the dainty places by the sea, the crown jewels where five-star chefs routinely take up residence in the summer. It is at such a place that I meet my aunt Sarah for dinner. A wall of windows looks out to the ocean, waves breaking fast over a near deserted beach. It's late in the day, almost seven o'clock. Even in the summer I watch the sun going down orangey and pinkish as it dangles like a mythic orb dying out at sea. I wait for my aunt at one of the back tables. Restaurants like this usually don't take reservations and I wonder how my aunt procured a table in the back by the windows without showing up first.

This is the kind of restaurant, on the third floor of one of the very nice hotels, where Sylvia Plath worked for a summer before her internship at *Mademoiselle*. This is the kind of place where Joanne met her. I can just picture her, very tall and thin with blond hair pulled back in a high ponytail, bright red lipstick, and a little blue eye shadow. She didn't like working at the restaurant, that's what her biographers, what Joanne, had said. Plath wasn't one for taking drink orders or pretending to smile when she didn't want to. It ended up making her sick, literally, and after a bout in the hospital she took a babysitting job. Joanne knew her then. Sylvia had hung out on the beach with that hippie of a woman beating bongos, writing poetry, and talking about life like young people do until they're blue in the face and they think they have it all figured out. And maybe they do have it all figured out, until the world changes and bills and love affairs and other complications muck it all up. Nothing stays the same, nothing stays sane forever.

"Sorry I'm late," my aunt Sarah says, hurrying to take a seat she pulls the white cloth napkin off the bread plate and puts it straight into her lap. "Martini, dry," she says to the waiter, who hovers over us. I realize I've been sitting with nothing, not even a glass of water, for the past few minutes.

"I'll have a French 75," I tell him and he nods to us, smiling graciously.

"I got caught up on a conference call. I tell you, when I started working in journalism dead time was torture. We always wanted to be working, but back in the seventies, the eighties, people got to have time off. We thought it was torture but now that I see this brave new world, being on call 24/7 no matter what, I don't envy the young."

"People do have to work harder these days."

"Work culture got messed up somewhere. So tell me, niece dear, how are you?" She fiddles with her napkin and then places it in her lap.

I watch her shifting the fork and knife at her place setting. My aunt looks young for her age. She's nearly seventy-two and though her hands are wrinkled, blue veins bulging in places, bearing the soft delicacy of the near-elderly, her face does not show the same age. It's not as if she's had work done, there's nothing unnatural or too overly made up about it, but her face has obviously been better taken care of, a nightly cold cream and mud mask ritual that her hands were never given. Her hair is frosted blond, very tasteful, and she dresses as if she's just walked out of a Manhattan Macy's. She was always this way. My aunt Sarah was older than my mother, much more mature, grown up and beautiful in a way that was professional. I remember wanting to be her, wanting to do what she did before I knew what it was. I just knew it was professional and powerful and very chic. She was a woman who was always in a hurry, who rushed through life in a business suit. Now I'm happy in leggings and a long shirt, something comfortable. But back then I wanted the power she exuded when she wore a blazer and high heels and walked around her office like she had thirty important places to be.

"So, I'm only here for a few days, maybe a week. I'm doing a story on Alex Baker, who runs this hotel. I guess he's doing a lot of tech investing and *The Times* is interested."

"Sounds great," I tell her, looking down at the white tablecloth. "Is that how you got us such a great table?"

"It is." She smirks. "They don't take reservations, but yes, I made sure he got us a good table. He thinks these interviews are just puff pieces, they're going to be a breeze, and great publicity for the hotel. I'll let him think that." I don't know what she means or if she's planning to attack this hotel owner who's been doing some investing but it's not my place. There is a reason I decided to write novels. It turns out the zoom-zoom life of the journalist elite was not for me. "So what are you up to? How's the Cape treating you?" Such casual, polite conversation and I want to dive in but I wait.

"I met your friend Joanne at the *Maude* party. She gave me something to read, a manuscript Sylvia Plath never published."

Aunt Sarah doesn't blink or say "wow." She also doesn't express complete disbelief. I know she's a journalist but my aunt has always had a literary bent and I thought she'd get a kick out of this. "Joanne Heinmann, I'm so glad you two met up. I was worried you'd miss each other. But she gave you a manuscript?" Her eyes roam back and forth, taking in the room as she shifts uncomfortably in her chair. "I should tell Tammy she gave you the manuscript. Wow. How is Joanne? How did she look? Did she say anything strange?"

"She's fine. She wanted to meet up, perhaps you could come to the house and see her bees. Apparently they keep bees."

"Yes, they keep bees how very, very Sylvia Plath." My aunt looks as if she might roll her eyes but she is much too classy, especially at a place like this, to do such a thing.

"Why tell Tammy? Is she not supposed to give it out? Is it a secret? I've read a few pages and it's really very good. Very much like *The Bell Jar* except it seems the writer has matured a bit since then."

"Plath was a child when she wrote *The Bell Jar*," my aunt replies. "She was a child when she killed herself in the grand scheme of things. But the pressures of those times, the sixties, into the seventies, especially on women, were tough. And let me tell you Ted didn't make it any easier. Not just the cheating, but leaving her with the kids all the time when he knew she was mentally ill, and there was violence in that marriage, you read between the lines and you'll see."

"I know they were supposed to be very passionate and destructive, but I don't know if there was violence."

"I have a reporter's eye for such things."

"A reporter's eye that sees the worst," I reply and she smiles sheepishly.

"Perhaps. But Joanne gave you a manuscript. I should really give Tammy a call."

"Is everything okay?" I ask.

She waves it away, smiles like it's nothing. But Sarah, being my mother's sister, is good at smiling like it's nothing when something is very wrong. She did that a lot on my mother's bad days. "Just watch out is all."

Our drinks arrive. The waiter sets them down carefully, one at a time, and I look up at him. It's the first time I've seen his face. He's young, at least to me, nineteen, maybe twenty, I bet he can't drink yet. His father must be a lawyer, I decide, his mother stays at home and works for the college football team in some motherly fashion, baking cookies, helping with the equipment. Am I projecting another era onto this make believe woman? He lives in a nice suburb near Boston, goes to a good school where he plays sports and studies prelaw or accounting. This job on the Cape is just for spending money and experience, a way to get away from mom and dad and live at the beach for the summer.

He looks down at us and rattles off a list of specials as Aunt Sarah sips her drink. Something about lamb, something about duck, a few freshly caught fish.

"I'll have the salmon," she orders when he finishes.

"I'll have the trout," I add and he smiles and grabs our menus.

"So, how're you doing, niece?" Aunt Sarah asks, the first look of sympathy on her face. "You know with everything, I never know how much of it to bring up. I don't want to talk about it all the time but I don't want to just ignore it either."

"He's out, Barry, her father. I haven't talked to Theo about it, but I got a call from Heather's father's phone the other day."

"I'm sorry, do you want to talk to them?"

"No. I should. But I can't talk to them. If I hadn't been her professor, if I hadn't introduced her to Theo none of this would have happened. If I hadn't talked to her mother—"

"You're allowed to introduce your students to your husband at school functions. You're allowed to be angry and try to find out what your husband's doing with your nineteen-year-old students when you find naked pictures of her on his phone."

"I didn't have to call like that."

"Did you tell the cousin? Did you even know she had a cousin capable of that kind of violence?"

"No but I—"

"Thoughts like that are dangerous," Aunt Sarah says. "We don't have to talk about this. How's your father? Is Florida treating him well?"

"He started talking about a woman, a widow down near Miami. Apparently they just play a little tennis together, but I think maybe . . ."

"Good for him. Joey deserves that. How's he liking Florida?" my aunt asks, then sips her martini.

"He's fine, it's just . . ." I look around the restaurant. Mostly it's families, that's who frequents the Cape. There are a few business people, but the summer at the beach is not a time for business unless it's business parties, there are a few couples, mostly younger ones, just married, or just dating. A pair of teenagers drink sodas at a back table and I remember those first dates, back before I could even drink, and how sweet they were. "So the journal," I finally start. "From the sixties. Do you know anything about this?"

I look my aunt in the eye and catch a glimmer of fear. It would be easy to miss, the way she glances so to the side, as if she's just thinking. "1968, that was the year her friend died. That was a hard time for her. Her mental health was not at its best. She had one of her break downs. It really scared my mom and sisters. I would venture to say it was one of her worst times."

"I know. I read the journal."

"You read the journal?" my aunt responds with resigned acceptance in her voice.

"She's been gone for a year, I didn't think she'd mind. I just . . . what I read, you're in it. What happened to her, is it true?" In that moment I don't want to say it. I just don't want to have to say it.

My aunt looks out at the ocean. Maybe she wants to fall inside the waves like I do, like my mother used to. "What did she say?" she finally asks. She's my aunt. She saved my thirteenth birthday by taking me to New York when my mother wouldn't get out of bed, she took me to dinner when my mother was in the hospital, she talked to me on the phone hour after hour when I was growing up and needed a woman, a woman who understood, to talk to. But just then, for making me say it, I hate her.

"She said she was pregnant," I let it out. "She said after her friend died she was really sad and she met a guy named Steve who raped her. He took her in a car, she was already so mentally unstable, and he raped her. Did she tell you that? Did she call you?"

"She did," my aunt admits. "And I wanted to go to the police. I told her to call them but she got so freaked out, she said she'd slit her throat if I told anyone and I believed her. Then to find out she got pregnant . . ."

"So you knew? I was hoping she was making that part up."

"Yes, I knew. She didn't want the baby. And carrying a child, going through the humiliation. She didn't have it in her, she really didn't, not after what happened to her friend. She heard voices that summer. She almost had a full break down."

"She said you helped her get an abortion. You found her a doctor and got her one illegally."

Her face falls. She looks out once again and it's the night sky, the moon inside it, it's so beautiful, so infinitely beautiful. How can time and space, how can the moon over the ocean, how can that be when there are mad women and secret abortions and ex-husbands and a student murdered by her unstable, obsessed cousin? How did mankind create such destruction in such a beautiful world?

"He wasn't a hack." My aunt singlehandedly defends herself and her sister. "He was a very good doctor and I wanted to have it done at his practice but Maggie wouldn't go there. She said she had to do it somewhere private, that she didn't trust it if she had to go out. Someone would see her, it would be a set up and the police would come. We should have done it in his office but she wouldn't hear of it and so he came to a place I was able to get. But we sterilized everything. He did a good job. So many women, during that time, were dying left and right from basically having a coat hanger shoved up their insides, but not this guy. He was good to her, he gave her antibiotics and painkillers. That's why there wasn't an infection afterwards though later . . . it was hard getting pregnant again, there was scaring."

"She wrote that there was a lot of blood."

"Of course there was a lot of blood. It was an abortion in a bathtub, of course there was a lot of blood. There's blood when you lose a baby. There's blood when you have a baby. Women are awash in blood, month and month, even though some people call it unclean. A lot of blood, it's the price we pay, some would say it's God's curse on Eve or whatever. But yes, there was a lot of blood but he helped her through that. He cleaned it up for us. He told her to stay in bed, to take care of herself but of course once he was gone she was up and out of bed. She could barely walk, but she insisted on taking the remains and burying them."

"The remains?" I picture this child. When did I start thinking of it as a child?

"What else do you want to call it? She was less than two months along, there wasn't even much there but she screamed at the sight of it. It terrified her, she couldn't think straight and I had to keep her calm. I didn't want her to look at it, to have to deal with it, but you knew your mother. She wouldn't stop screaming, stop pacing around until she knew it was buried and so we took it to the ocean at night in a bag. I wanted to just throw it out to sea. If anyone had found it they would never know, there wasn't the same kind of DNA testing back then. No one would have checked even if they could. But we buried it, she insisted. Look, I knew my sister, having a baby at that time would have destroyed her. She had these horrible fits and it wasn't until the mid-seventies, when they really started medicating her right, that she was okay. She still had her episodes, but she was more okay than not. And I knew she'd carry this with her but it was the best thing for her, once she decided she wanted it done there was nothing I could do."

"Why did she want to get rid of it?" I ask. "She could have gone away, given the child up for adoption. After what happened to her friend . . ."

"I think it was her friend. Her death really freaked Maggie out. She was so worried about ending up like Allison that she just wanted to get it over with even though Allison died during an abortion. And she was seeing things. She was hearing things. She tried to take pills to kill herself. I knew it was either help her get this done or we would lose her. And no one understood that then. I couldn't tell our parents. It was illegal and that's all they cared about. And the rest of society, teachers, doctors? They didn't care about her at all. They would have been happy to let her die."

"Then why did she have me, why have a child so much later?"

"She was older, it was during a time when she thought she was better. She hadn't had an episode in a while, she and Joey were doing well, she was going back to school and she felt better about herself. When she got pregnant she thought, 'Why not? I can do this.' Through the whole pregnancy she was very optimistic and honestly, after you were born, she did well. She really did wake up in the middle of the night, she swaddled you, took care of you. It was only years later, and as you were growing up, that she got ill again. Your mother loved you. It broke her heart to see just what her illness did to you."

"Where is the child?" I ask her. "Where did you bury the child?"

"At Breakwater Beach, near Orleans. Which is a bit far from the house. We never thought your mother would end up with a house on the Cape. When she met Joey and he had a place here it freaked her out. She thought the ghost of this child might haunt her. But it's good luck we didn't bury it near the house. Breakwater was a desolate beach then, no one was there, now it's more built up. There's a large formation of rocks where it's buried."

"It?" I ask again and my aunt Sarah takes the last sip of her martini. She looks over, eyes the waiter, then points to her glass and he nods, turning around to get her another.

"Do you want to give it a name? Lorelei, I'm sorry, I'm so sorry you found out, or maybe I'm sorry I never told you. Your mother didn't want you to know and I thought that was a secret I'd let her take to her grave."

"I know, it's okay. I just wish you would have warned me. I told you what I found. I wanted you to warn me."

"I didn't even think. It's not that I forgot, but I didn't even think, didn't put that together."

I try to picture it . . . everything. I see my mother at her friend's funeral. I see her with Steve, what happened to her. I see her in a doctor's office being told the news and then being told there's nothing she can do about it—nothing legal anyway. Then there's my mother and the doctor, lying in that bathtub, my mother at the ocean with the plastic bag in her hands. She was only seventeen. Did she cry? Did she wonder "what if?" Did she want to take it back? Or did she know, did she just know? The secrets, the lives we hold in our hearts, our minds, our spirits. People are never just one thing, we are one façade and so much trouble, so much damage and danger lies deep beyond the surface of the skin. It rests in the marrow of our bones, the shadowy crevices of muscle tissue we hide from everyone.

"There're more, more journals," my aunt tells me. "I have them at my place in New York. I can have Constantina go into my desk and mail them to you if you'd like."

"There are more journals. You have them?"

"She gave them to me to hide a few years before she . . . before she . . ." After nearly a year my aunt still can't get the words out. "But yes, there are a couple, mostly from after you were born, when you were a child. I didn't know about the other journal. I didn't know she kept one from that time. Funny that she hid it in the house, almost like she wanted it to be found after she was gone."

"Maybe." I sigh and glance back at my aunt and then out at the water, the white crests of waves tumbling, tumbling, tumbling. "I'd like to see the other journals if you can get them to me. I still have that Plath manuscript to read but later maybe the journals."

"Right," my aunt says, looking back toward the waiter. "The Plath manuscript."

Esther Greenwood
Salisbury, England 1958

THE BEES WERE buzzing outside the bistro mostly around the fresh honeysuckle. It ran up the little water trellis in these beautiful pink blossoms and reminded me of the lights in New York when I stayed at the Amazon. It was florescent, like out of a movie. But the town in southwestern England was nothing like New York, not anywhere near it. It was old and quaint with churches dedicated to long dead saints and martyrs. It had shoppes (spelled with two p's and an e at the end just like merry olde England) and I could almost smell tea in the air as if it were rising from the river that wound through it.

"Bloody insects," Tom complained, swatting the bees, which only made them angrier. They came at him; buzzing right at his head and Tom had to duck as we walked into this little French bistro. Tom is very tall, he towers over me, which is hard to do since I'm something like five-nine and they said when I worked at *Ladies Day Magazine* that I could have been a model. But I always wanted to be a writer and so here I am in jolly olde (also with an e at the end) England, having just finished my Fulbright Fellowship. I was looking for a way to stay on in England and it looks like I might have found it though I'm not sure if I want to stay on these terms, the terms being not professional but entirely personal.

"Don't swat at them like that. You'll only make them angry," I instructed as we entered the bistro. The floors were a kind of tile, like a bathroom and a mosaic all at once. The walls were painted white and there was minimalist art on the walls, which was all the rage since the war. Everyone just wants to be modern even in small towns like Salisbury. A tall man with very black hair nodded to us, his nose in the air, just to remind us that this was a French establishment. He then motioned with his head for us to take a seat anywhere. The place was empty, or nearly so, even though it was two o'clock on a Saturday and I was sure there would be tourists from Stonehenge somewhere about.

"So you know, Esther, it's going to be cutting it close, getting to Cardiff," Tom started once we'd taken a seat. Then the waiter was upon us, pouring water as if he were intent on listening to our conversation. "Are you sure you need to see the rocks?"

"Rocks?" I asked, a little put out. "Rocks? They're not just rocks. They're thousands of years old. No one even knows who put them there. You're an Englishman, how can you call them rocks?"

Tom laughed, he looked as if he was going to reach over the table and stroke my cheek but instead he leaned back in his chair and looked toward the waiter, who handed us two paper menus. "I think I'll have the chicken. Esther, you'll have the chicken too I suppose."

"I'm going to need a minute, thank you," I said to the waiter, who nodded before walking away. "But really, rocks, why call them rocks?" I wasn't really mad, though my voice might betray otherwise, but Tom knew how I could get, that's what I liked about him. Whenever I got angry and my temper flared Tom only laughed and called me silly.

"I can call them rocks because that's what they are. Don't get testy, Esther," Tom argued. "The chicken looks good. I think we should both get the chicken." He motioned to the waiter to return. "Really, Esther, just make up your mind. Even with food you're impossible."

The waiter returned as if at Tom's beck and call, but at the end of the day, everyone who meets Tom after five whole minutes are at his beck and call like he could command entire armies if he really wanted to. Not that Tom would want to do anything like that. Tom, like me, writes poetry. Commanding armies is just not in his genes. "I'll have the chicken," Tom said. "And bring over a carafe or something of your wine, the house wine, the white."

The waiter looked over at me and honestly, I really did want the chicken, it sounded good, with French herbs, and I was so sick of the English and their meat pies. But Tom was always telling me what to eat and I had to nip that right in the bud especially if I said yes to that question he'd asked me the other day. "I'll have the salmon," I said and the waiter nodded. At the very least it went with the white wine Tom ordered.

"The salmon, the chicken, white wine. Lovely, thank you," the waiter said and I noted that he had an English and not a French accent.

"I always wondered, after the war, if the English and the French were on better terms," I said as Tom still held the paper menu long after our waiter had left us as if he wasn't sure about what he'd ordered and maybe he'd call the waiter back and say he'd changed his mind. He had chosen the first thing he saw and maybe that wasn't the best idea. Tom was like that. We'd been going together for a while and a girl can tell these things.

"The French laid down and died during the war. Let the Germans walk all over them. We English know that. And yes England and France are friends now, it took seven hundred years of war and in-fighting to get here, but England is no longer interested in conquering France and France is no longer obsessed with staving off the English if that's what you mean. But no, I don't think we English have a new respect for the French after the war."

"What about the Germans?" I asked. Tom knew I was German. Not German-German, I was born near Boston, Massachusetts, a red blooded New Englander if ever there was one but my father had been born in Bonn. He left for America before World War Two broke out and so he'd had to deal with being called a "kraut" and "why don't you eat some liberty cabbage" and all that. My mother had been German as well. Her parents had come over from Germany just before the First World War and raised their daughter in a home that spoke only German. It had not been until she started school that she'd realized she couldn't understand a word anyone was saying. What a lousy thing to do to a kid, lie to them about what language they were supposed to know? Tell them the world is one way when really it's another. She then spent all her time watching people speak English, she read English as much as possible, stayed after school to make sure she knew it all. That's how she became such a good student. And it was because my mother was a good student that she met my father, her English professor in college of all things, and married him.

"The Germans," Tom said. "I mean, it's 1958 now, the war has been over for a while. But no, it's still on our minds. We don't hate the Germans, not since we basically conquered them. At least not the West Germans, but, there is that sting and when I hear a German accent I must say I still bristle."

I wanted to remind Tom that I was German. No matter where I was born a part of me would always be that Aryan blond hair, blue eyed, Glockenspieling-on-the-side-of-a-mountain kind of German. But I didn't. Instead I just sat there looking at him. At the very least Tom was something to look at, tall with light brown hair kept just a tad too long. He was always wearing this shabby black overcoat and after a while the shabbiness sort of wears off and all you see is the way it hangs off him so regal and proud. Tom's a real bohemian in some sense, but in others, he's a good upstanding man from Yorkshire, England who likes to hunt rabbits and run around in the woods. Then he sits down by a stream and starts writing poetry and there are times it's so wonderful I just want to cry.

"So, Esther, tell me, have you thought anymore about what I asked you?" Tom looked at me, his eyes right on me like his gaze had taken human form, as it rested on my body. He raised an eyebrow as if he were perturbed and it was that face he made, always that face, that said he was confused but he could handle it.

"Your question?" I asked coyly. "The other night, your question."

"You know some men, if he asked a question like that and got an 'I really just have to think about it,' he'd give up completely. He'd realize it wasn't worth it to keep pushing, but I know you, Esther, you can be indecisive and sometimes you don't know what's good for you. It's my job to push you, make sure you're on the right track."

"I know what's good for me. But you're right. I understand if you want to take it back but I really wish you wouldn't. It's such an important question and I think I'm entitled to a little time. It's 1958 women don't just go jumping into these things anymore."

Tom's face softened and he grasped my hand from across the table. "I know, Esther, I really do. And I'm happy to give you all the time you need."

"That's why you're so wonderful," I replied, squeezing his hand a little tighter. Just then our food came. The waiter swooped in with two piping hot plates, setting them down just as we withdrew our entwined hands from the table.

"The wine will be right up," he said and we smiled at him.

Tom dug right into his food and I watched him start to gobble, just gobble it. With any other man the scene might have been ridiculous but with Tom, even with his mouth full of chicken, he was becoming. And it really had been a very nice proposal. The kind that only Tom would make. It wasn't a big deal. At the end of the day Tom was not the type for those kinds of over the top things. We were standing in London, just inside Kensington Gardens and Tom was talking about the author Virginia Woolf, whom he loved so much, and he'd said something like, "You know, her father used to take her on long walks through the Garden when she was a girl. She did her first suicide attempt when she was just thirteen, after the death of her mother, tried to jump out a window only it was something like the second floor. But she'd walk here all the time in these gardens and talk about how they made her feel like a new woman."

"She was such a tortured soul," I'd admitted as we walked in the gardens. We had just reached the statue of Peter Pan. The sky was the normal London grey and it started to mist right there, right on us, and I remember looking at the flowers as Tom spoke.

"And she was a hard woman to live with, Virginia Woolf, but her husband, Leonard, took such good care of her and so she survived much longer than she should have, being as sick as she was. He knew his wife was special and he knew he could offer her safety and stability and that would give her the courage to live on. I think you need a Leonard in your life, Esther, and I would like to be him." I remember as Tom was talking I wasn't really sure what he was getting at. Sometimes I believe he is a much better poet than I am. He knows so much more about these things and so the metaphors didn't add up in my head the way they must have in Tom's and I just watched him for a while wondering what he meant.

Then I thought I knew. He was talking about my time at the hospitals in Boston, before I came to London, before I met him. After I left New York and my internship at *Ladies Day* I had gotten very sick, refusing to get out of bed, being unhappy all the time. I did the silliest, the stupidest things, like rearranging flowers in vases that other women had bought. I had been so obsessed with things being even and not necessarily right. And it had gotten bad and I had taken some pills and tried to kill myself, like Virginia Woolf, only she had done it a different way. And after that they put me in a hospital and gave me medicine that made me fat and they did electroshock therapy which was really very unpleasant the way the electricity just shoots through your head and goes down your whole body and it hurts so much and you're just powerless to stop it and then afterward everything is all fuzzy and you can't remember who or what you are but that's the point and then if you don't get better after that they do it again. But I had gotten better. I got a Fulbright Fellowship and came to Cambridge and met Tom and life has really worked out and so I guess you could say I'm better. I hadn't told him about the hospital, not everything, but just then I was afraid he'd asked my mother or someone had told him and he knew, he just knew. All my secrets had come tumbling out and he was just staring at them.

And so that was what I thought Tom was talking about but I can really be very dense, and then he got down on one knee. That was the strange part I always thought that if Tom ever proposed to anyone he would not get down on one knee but there he was and I looked down at him and the rain picked up and he closed his eyes because the drops were in his face and I looked at him. I just looked at him. Did he know that I'd seen my old boyfriend Micah the other day? Why in that moment was Micah the thing I was thinking about?

"Esther Greenwood will you marry me?" he'd said. Then he'd pulled out a ring, a little gold band, nothing too fancy as he couldn't have afforded anything more and I didn't really want much more than that anyway. I had wanted to say yes, but something, maybe it was what had happened the night before with Micah, came back to me, and so I just stood there dumbly (and really I did feel very stupid then) while people just looked at us. When a man gets down on one knee in public and pulls out a ring people stop to watch and I looked down at him and smiled. I pulled him up and he stood. I threw my arms around him and kissed him because people were watching and I didn't want to embarrass him. The people clapped but Tom knew I hadn't given an answer. He knew it was just for show. And he was nice, he was calm as we walked a little while down the promenade and then he turned to me and said, "You know Esther, I really do need an answer. That show back there, was that your answer?"

"No," I'd told him and he still held my hand as we walked. "I mean, no, that wasn't my answer and it's just that I don't know, not right now. I love you and I want to be with you but we only just met three months ago and I barely know your friends or your family and it's 1958 and a girl has to be careful about who she marries." But I knew it wasn't that easy.

"I understand," is all he'd said then, letting go of my hand. "Think it out, Esther, really. I want to marry you but I want you to be sure that this is what you want. Let's go to Cardiff tomorrow as planned. We'll drive to Salisbury and then see Stonehenge. You've been bugging me to take you there and then I'll drive us to that convention in Wales and it would be nice if you could give me an answer before the convention ends. That way I can tell my fellow poets whether or not I'm about to be a married man."

It had seemed a little too formal, poets shouldn't go getting engaged because of favorable logistics, but we had planned this trip to Cardiff for many weeks for a Poetry Convention that Tom was speaking at. We added Salisbury, the town near Stonehenge, and Stonehenge itself to the trip and I was sure those stones, those ancient stones, would help me to see just what I needed to see.

I looked over at the table and Tom had nearly finished his lunch. "You know you should really drink more," Tom said, emptying his third glass of wine. I hadn't even realized that the waiter had brought the wine or that someone had poured it I was so preoccupied. "It's very tasteful for table wine. The French, they know wine. I'm glad France is back on our side if only for the wine."

I laughed at Tom. "I'm sorry, I've just been thinking."

"Well think away. But I'd love an answer by tonight."

"Tonight."

"And when is your friend leaving England again?" Tom inquired matter-of-factly.

"Micah?"

"Yeah, the Jewish one," Tom elaborated with chicken stuffed in his mouth.

"Micah, I think he's going to leave in a few days, back to Paris or something. He's visiting his aunt right now. But he says he wanted to join the Merchant Marines, it's all up in the air."

"Silly Americans. Why on earth would you join the Merchant Marines, there's not even a war going on?"

"True." I sighed. And it had been so nice, seeing Micah again. He'd called spur of the moment. It had really been a whim and I'd met him first for tea and then we, both being Americans, decided at the tea shop to order coffee instead and they had looked at us funny, but they have coffee in tea shops now in England since so many Americans live here, since the war. I looked into his eyes, so big and dark, and I remembered how he used to take me in his arms. And years ago he'd left me, he'd gone back to America and told me in a letter to forget about him. But when we were in Paris together years ago, we had been together so many times and it was only because I missed Micah so much that I'd even started seeing Tom.

But the night before the proposal I saw Micah again. He'd called and first it had been coffee but then we walked along the Thames together and he held my hand and it was like wandering along the Seine as we'd done years ago. "You know, Esther, it's really just that when I'm with you, it's like I can't control myself."

"I never asked you to control yourself," I said, cautiously, because he had hurt me so badly when he'd left before. "But I do think you need to learn how to treat people. You shouldn't just run away."

"I know. I just packed up . . . I don't know what I want."

"I think you know what you want," I said.

"And then there's the whole Jewish thing. I don't think it's that easy, you know. Most of the people in my parents' families, the ones from Europe, are Survivors, or they're not survivors at all and my father still doesn't know where his sister is and that stays with a person, you know?"

"I know," I'd replied because really what can a German girl growing up in America say to that? "But I don't see a Jew or a German when I'm with you, Micah."

"I don't see that either," he'd said and right there on the bridge, one of the new stone bridges they'd built in London since so many of them had been blitzed in the war, he leaned down and put his hand on my face and it felt like fresh water to a dying woman, the way he touched me. He leaned in and kissed me and I forgot the last year of my life without him and he held me so close. But then he left, he said he had some things to do in England and maybe we would talk again in a few days. Then I went back to Tom and he'd gotten down on one knee in Kensington Gardens and it was so much. Just all so much.

"So you know, just across the way," I said, pointing toward the door, "That's the Church of Thomas Becket."

"Becket, eh? Is that right," Tom said, still shoveling chicken in his mouth. It looked very good and I wish he'd offer me some but he was almost finished and it would be impolite to ask.

"We should," I replied and just then Tom reached over the table with his fork and grabbed a large slab of my salmon.

"You're not eating it," he said, sticking it in his mouth. He was right; I had barely touched my food. I dipped my fork in and started picking since we really should get going.

The waiter was gracious when we paid the check, mostly because no one tips like an American and I did say a few words so I'm sure he caught my accent. Tom paid, but he tips well, mostly because he's with an American and he likes to play into that kind of stereotype. Tom's friends, his family, all call me the "rich American" and they don't even know. I grew up in a house with my mother and brother and grandparents, my mother worked two jobs to put me through college. I don't know what they think rich is but it definitely isn't me.

"Shall we?" Tom asked once we paid our check. "There's a little church over there." It was only a short walk, a few steps across an asphalt street, to the Church of Sir Thomas Becket. "Who was he again?" Tom scratched his head as I stared at the plaque in front of the church. The bees came back and Tom continued to shoo them.

"Becket? You don't know Thomas Becket?"

"I'm sure I should. The name's familiar. Who was he again?"

"The Archbishop of Canterbury. Now stop swiping at those bees and leave them alone," I scolded him and Tom put his hands down and the bees buzzed around his head for one more second before going on their way as I knew they would. Bees really are very calm, very helpful, creatures if you aren't tossing giant hands at them. "You know the book *Canterbury Tales* by Geoffrey Chaucer?" Tom nodded and I went on. "They were going on a pilgrimage to see the shrine of Thomas Becket."

"Is that so? Well, being a literary man I really should have known that," Tom said, scratching his head nonchalantly.

"But he's not just that. He was one of the major figures that helped unite the Anglos and the Saxons. You know, like the term Anglo-Saxon? That's from Becket and people like him. Long ago in England," I started. And I felt so silly, starting a sentence "long ago in England," to a man who had grown up in the country. But Tom only nodded and so I went on. "When the English had conquered the French yet again, there were two types of people living in England, the Anglos and the Saxons. The Anglos were the head honchos, you know, the people in charge. King Henry the First, he was an Anglo, and Becket was a Saxon. But Becket was really good friends with King Henry the First, despite their differences, and first Thomas Becket was just a man in the clergy. But, Becket, because he was so close to Henry, and they were very close, blood brothers really, so Henry the First made Becket the Bishop of Canterbury, which was a very important post. But Becket, as Bishop, started to really love the people. He wanted to take care of them. And so whenever Henry would decide he needed or wanted to do something that would hurt the people, the peasants really, Becket, even though he was close to Henry, would turn him down. Finally, Becket stood in King Henry's way one too many times and Henry had him executed. But afterward Henry had himself, the king, flogged something like sixty times to prove how bad he felt, because the people, loved Becket. But I think Henry had himself flogged because he loved Thomas Becket too."

"So why do you love him so much, Esther?" Tom asked as if he hadn't understood a word of what I'd just said.

"Because he is responsible for uniting a people. But not only that, he really wanted to help, to take care of people, and he was willing to lose his life for that. Now the term Anglo-Saxon means just one thing, one united people, and Becket had a very big hand in that. If only the world had a Thomas Becket now to unite people maybe the Germans and the Jews and the French and the English and the Russians and the Americans, would all be okay. And Becket, he lay down on his sword, he really did, for the good of the people."

"Isn't that like suicide though?" Tom asked as we neared the church. There was a sign that read "Church of Sir Thomas Becket." The sign was humble, made of wood and it hung right on the grey stone church.

"No, I think he was brave, very, very brave. He didn't care what the nationalities meant, he didn't even care about friendship he was above all that. He was a good man. A saint. A martyr."

"I see," Tom said, looking up at the large stone church. "So can we go inside?"

"The sign says we can," I said, walking through the wood and glass doors that had been put in more recently than the stone structure.

There has always been something about medieval architecture that fascinates me. It's just so big and still there is something so sad about it. It's not like any other kind of architecture. The way the stain glass windows hold pictures in such bright colors, even though the pictures aren't happy at all. They're pictures of Christ on the Cross and men being boiled alive in the name of greater things. There has always been something so raw, so subdue about these pictures.

Tom and I walked through the church. There was a little service going on, right in front of the altar, but visitors were allowed to go in, though there were signs every few feet asking that no pictures be taken. I walked up the first little hallway, past a stained glass window of the nativity and then another picture of a man with a very long beard giving bread to a peasant. Sir Thomas Becket was up in those pictures feeding the poor. Henry the First, egotistical king that he was, of course he had Becket knighted even though Becket was much too humble a man and never would have wanted to be called Sir. Thomas Becket probably would not have wanted his likeness portrayed in such a big stained glass window. Future generations, I have learned, never respect the dead.

It was a short walk through the church. There wasn't very much to see, but I felt welcome there, as if the church itself, the stone and the wooden pews, had reached out to try and bring me into something greater than myself. "You okay?" Tom asked at one point. "Are we done?"

I looked at the little service up front near a white marble altar and before a large wooden Crucifix where Christ hung dying on the Cross, a metal statue a monument to pain and suffering but mostly quiet, humble sacrifice. Tom shuffled his feet, he paced back and forth and didn't seem to be looking at anything.

"We can go," I finally said to him. I could have stayed. I could have walked those sacred halls for hours but Tom seemed bored and I wanted to see the rest of the town before we had to head to Stonehenge.

Tom put his hand on my back and ushered me out. We walked swiftly with purpose and it reminded me that we're young and tall and Tom is on his way to a conference in Cardiff where he had been asked to read a paper he'd submitted about the future of poetry and English modernism (as opposed to post-modernism). I turned back to the church at the last second, just as Tom opened the door, and took a final look. It was as if I would never be back here, as if this place would disappear if I wasn't there to look at it. Then again that's why I write poetry so that I can take each moment of my life and hold it up and keep it forever, a written record that's not quite as factual as the journal entries I write. I looked up at the stained glass windows and the grey stone while the people prayed up front. There was just so much stone. And Micah, even though he was Jewish, would have appreciated such a place.

"Let's walk through town," I suggested after we'd left Sir Thomas Becket and his church. "It's so quaint, look at those buildings," I pointed to the little shoppes (still with two p's and an e at the end). They were made of white material, like stucco only a bit smoother, and they had brown trim and thatched roofs with straw, actual straw. "This place looks like it hasn't aged a day since the thirteen hundreds."

"Something like that," Tom said, scratching his head as he took my hand and followed me down the tiny cobblestone street. "But my father helped renovate some of these old English towns in Yorkshire and honestly, the materials look old, but they're newer than you'd think. Even the straw has been sprayed with something so it won't catch fire."

I had expected a butcher, a baker, maybe even a candlestick maker to occupy these little shoppes. I pictured a clothing store with dresses that had been hand sewn and a stationary store with high-end parchment. But the street had none of that. "What is all this stuff?" I asked as Tom led me along. There was a souvenir shop with scarves and metal figurines and a place that sold plastic toys like hula-hoops and a magazine stand with the latest editions of all the fashion and business periodicals.

"It's what's here now. What do you want? Salisbury is modernizing, just like everywhere else," Tom said as I turned to find a high-end clothing store, the type that sold ties that had probably been made in France or China. Up the block was a place that sold malted milkshakes and a little further was a bookstore, classy enough, but a new bookstore selling all the latest bestsellers in paperback.

"I just thought things would be more . . . quaint," I said, looking up at Tom as he gazed out at the street, still squinting so his face looked mad and ugly.

"Merry olde England isn't stuck in the past," Tom explained. "I mean, they kept the kitsch of the town, but it had to modernize. And really what tourist only wants handmade candles and old-fashioned parchment? They want plastic toys for their kids, they want to read a book they've actually heard of. Supply and demand even in merry olde England. They should put in one of those grocery stores, the ones that are popping up, you know, there's three or four in the area."

"A chain?" I asked, stopping to look at his face, to just look at it. Really, Tom had such a nice face sometimes I felt like I was the luckiest girl in the world to be with him. And yet . . . yet I still had not answered his question and no amount of face was going to sway me. "What's wrong with chain stores?"

"I thought a town like Salisbury would have more of a connection to its past."

"Why?" Tom asked and I stopped to think. It really was a good question. What was wrong with modernity? Why didn't Salisbury have a right to move forward if it wanted to?

"I guess you're right," I said and Tom nodded, looking down at me for a second before kissing the top of my forehead. I wanted to laugh or say thank you. There was something about Tom's bigness, something about the way he usually put his hand on my arm, the way he kissed the top of my forehead, that made me grateful for him, and I almost said yes. Right there I almost said yes to the question he'd asked in Kensington Gardens.

"So, shall we run to the other church and then back to those stones?"

"I wish you wouldn't call them stones," I said, looking up at Tom I laughed at him. "Stonehenge, be a good English patriot and call it Stonehenge."

"As you wish my dear," Tom said, nearly bowing before we walked up the street with its many more quaint shoppes, many of which I wanted to go into, though Tom had seemed so bored with this excursion that I didn't want to ask him to walk into a specialty store to look at shoes or books or even bow ties.

I grasped Tom's hand as we walked through the town, which was really only one street long, taking up two, maybe three American city blocks. This town and this street had a single destination, all points converging on a large green lawn that stood before the next church, which was a much larger structure. I didn't even know its name, but it was a stone building towering over the entire town and so it seemed worth looking into.

"Should we go in?" I asked and Tom nodded down at me, smiling as if he knew this wasn't really a question.

"After you, m'lady," he said, bowing, and I almost grasped my arms around him. He really did love me, despite everything, and Micah had already left once.

I looked up at Tom and he was already headed toward the church. This church was larger than the one for Thomas Becket, it towered over the town, and as we drew nearer I turned to Tom and asked, "Isn't that the church we saw heading into Salisbury?"

"I think it is," he replied. "It's enormous just look at that spire. I wonder what it's like climbing up."

"Do you think they'd let us?" I asked as we reached the large wooden doors leading inside. There were no signs telling us whether we could or could not just go in but I saw two couples, the men wearing khakis and polo shirts, the women in collared dresses, enter with cameras and so I decided it was okay for tourists to just walk in.

"This isn't Rome, Esther, we can't just walk up any old flight of stairs. In Southern Europe they still don't care how many people put their sticky fingers in everything but here in England we show a little more discretion."

"I don't really feel like climbing a bunch of stairs anyway."

Tom's hand rested on my shoulder as we walked through the large wooden doors. This church was bigger but I couldn't for the longest time figure out who the church belonged to.

The walls of this church towered over us and Tom led the way as the colors from the stained glass windows danced on the floor. There was a chill in there, it was dark and cavernous and all the wood and stone seemed to mingle together in one cold shiver.

"So, over there," Tom said, pointing to a sign nearby, "it says Magna Carta Room, you want to check it out?"

"Sure," I said, not expecting much. All the rooms had such silly names in England. There was a Rosewater Room and a Baysriver Vestibule, a coat closet called Magna Carta Room didn't seem that far off.

When we got to the room, however, there was a line to get in. I only had to think for a second, "I wonder what this line is for?" before I saw a sign that read, "Magna Carta. This is the spot where the Magna Carta was signed in 1215. We have here the original version of that document on display. Please refrain from getting too close to this very old document. No pictures allowed."

"Is it the real thing?" I turned to Tom as if he, being an Englishman, would naturally know.

"I don't know why they would lie about it." Tom shrugged and we got in line.

"It's real, miss," a man with a cockney accent said, turning to me as I stood behind him. "They put it up here because this is the site where they signed the paper."

"To think that seven hundred years ago they signed the Magna Carta here." I took a deep breath as the line shuffled slowly forward. "I wasn't expecting to see this today, what a nice surprise." A breath of fresh air fluttered in my stomach and I looked out the window at the sun on the grass. I really was very happy. The Magna Carta! Of all things to luck into the Magna Carta.

"Get out of line," I heard the cockney Englishman sneer at the couple in front of him. They were young, a few years older than Tom and I, maybe twenty-five, twenty-six, both of them had dark blond hair and big eyes, though I couldn't make out the exact color. They were dressed conservatively, the man in a suit and the woman in a dress that could have been worn in an office in America ten years ago. The man had a crew cut, very five years ago, and the woman's hair was cut in a short pageboy that reminded me of the girls who always showed up in Humphrey Bogart movies. The couple looked back at the cockney Englishman with large frightened eyes and when I heard them speak I saw why the cockney man was so upset.

"Wir wollen wirklich nur Ihr Land, sir," the man said in German and that was it. No one else in line said anything to shame or defend them but the cockney Englishman did not let up.

"This is the sight of something sacred, something English and foreigners shouldn't be allowed . . ." The man went on but I stopped listening. I knew he did not mean all foreigners, he'd heard my American accent and had been perfectly fine with me, a good citizen of Allied territory. "My father fought you lousy good for nothings in the first world war and I fought you again in the second and it has not been long enough and the war will never be over long enough for you to go seeing . . ." Still the man went on but the line began to move and the young Germans, who probably had been very little children when the war was in full swing, were smart enough to face forward and ignore the awful man.

My father had told me a story about a time he'd gone to a gas station and the attendant saw his German name, Greenwood, on his license. He'd flat out refused to serve him. Then, he'd taken my father's license and wouldn't give it back, saying it was state property and even though that was illegal, the police just told my father to go get another one. My father had to wait a full two weeks for a new license and he couldn't drive at all during that time. Another time my mother was in a store and she wanted to buy some apples and they told her instead to buy sauerkraut because she was a lousy German and I have always been raised to believe that whatever happens between countries is between countries and what happens between people is between people.

The line moved as people walked into the little booth where the Magna Carta was kept. I couldn't see it from our place in line but I could tell that it was under glass. There was a woman upfront manning the station to make sure no one got too close or Heaven forbid tried to touch it or take a picture. In fact a man took a camera out and I saw the woman lift up her hands and he put it away.

Micah had told me about the Germans as well only he was kind enough not to mention their nationality. He'd only said what "they" had done as if what they'd done had nothing to do with where they came from. But I remember when he told me what it had been like for one of his aunts in the concentration camp. "She was almost gassed to death," he'd told me one night years ago when we were in Paris, looking out at the Seine. The city had been so lovely and we'd just had some wine and I don't know how we got to talking about concentration camps of all things but I can only imagine that stories like that, they stick with you, they reach into your blood and traumatize your family generation to generation.

"They took her to this room and had her take off all her clothes. She was with fifty or sixty other women and they were all stripped naked. Then they were put into another room where they waited before going into the gas chambers, their final walk. They all knew at this point, they'd heard stories, they'd seen the bodies, they knew what it all meant. And so, my aunt is standing in a room naked, with so many other naked women, and she sees a tiny window way up near the ceiling and she tells her friend to lift her on her back and help her up. My aunt was tiny and she thought maybe she could fit through that window. Her friend, with some trouble, lifts her up on her back and then onto her shoulders and my aunt said she had to get up on tiptoes and her friend almost fell over. In fact her friend did fall over but by then my aunt had opened the window and she hung from it for a second, until she was able to claw her way out. After she was out she had to jump almost two stories on the other side. She ran back to her bunk completely naked. She found new clothes and the guards never even noticed, they didn't know who was supposed to be gassed that day. She just slipped right back in. She went about her daily, horrible life at the camp for another three months before the war ended and the camp was liberated."

"Wow," I'd said to Micah when he told me. "What about her friend? What happened to her friend? Did she help get her out?"

"Esther, you couldn't think like that, not there. You couldn't think like that, it would drive you mad."

The German couple had come and gone, having seen the Magna Carta for a few seconds, and the line began to move more swiftly. I watched the unkind cockney Englishman stare at the document, his hand to his lips like he was trying to keep all the air inside his body. Stonehenge I had been expecting, but this was a complete surprise and sometimes when you are given something out of nowhere it's just so much, it's like it's bursting inside your stomach and you can barely breathe. Other times you expect things, like for people to understand that when you go to a hospital because you can't get out of bed or take a shower that you're sick and not a bad person but they treat you like a criminal instead and pump electricity into your skull. That just breaks you.

Tom put his hand on my shoulder as we walked over to the document. It was very yellow and seemed to be printed on parchment, but it also looked stretched like leather. The writing was very small. I couldn't make out a word of it, like it wasn't written in English at all. Tom gazed down at it with his hand on my shoulder. "You know, the noblemen, they were just so fed up with King John. They had had enough of his antics and his spending and they wanted to be separate from the King, they wanted their own power and so they basically put a gun to his head . . . more like a sword, and said, 'sign this or you're done for.' And so he signed."

"King John, he was Henry's son," I said, looking over at Tom.

"They were all sons of a Henry at some point . . . so many bloody Henrys on the English throne, I remember having to memorize the lot of them in school, drove me mad. Henry the this and Henry the that."

"Henry the First," I elaborated. "Henry the First and then Richard the Lionheart was king, after Henry died, but then it was John after Richard died. He got the crown even after being such a horrible brother to Richard during the crusades."

"That's what you get, dying without an heir, your lousy brother takes your throne and almost mucks it all up." Then Tom lifted his hand from my back and moved to walk away. "Take your time, I'll just be outside."

The woman standing guard over the document smiled at me as I leaned down and continued to look. I got closer, just close enough but I could tell that the woman would have pounced if I'd've gotten any closer to the protective glass. The writing seemed smudged and the words were written so close together but to think that those words written on that document had changed the course of English history. Someone had sat at a desk and written that piece of paper. They'd taken ideas and made them flesh. Just like what Tom and I do when we write poetry.

I nodded to the woman manning the document and she smiled. She seemed like a spinster, the kind of woman who went home to her mother after a long day of standing in a frumpy suit and sensible shoes. "Thank you," I said and she nodded as I walked away.

It didn't take long to find Tom in the courtyard. It was a beautiful day and the large open lawn was buzzing with people. Children ran around with toy hula-hoops and large balls as couples spread out with picnics on the grass. A few older people were standing around talking as well and that's where I saw Tom, standing with a group of guys tossing what looked like a tennis ball back and forth. The men were really chucking it at each other, getting in the way of the children trying to play.

A couple of girls stood near Tom. He looked over at them a few times as I approached. He wasn't talking to them, he was too busy concentrating on that ball, but I watched as they kept pointing at him and giggling. All of a sudden I felt very big and clumsy. When did college girls start to make me feel this way? They were so small and slim and young and I was a big old elephant now, nearly twenty-five. It was only a couple of years ago that I was a college girl myself giggling at boys like Tom as they tossed a ball in the park near campus.

"Tom," I called and the girls watching him looked disappointed when he glanced up at me. I must admit I got some satisfaction out of that. "Tom," I called again and he raised his hand to his forehead to shield his eyes from the sun and smiled.

"Esther, hello, have we finished our little English history lesson?"

"We have," I replied when I reached him. The men tossing the ball did not stop, they merely cut Tom out of their game when they saw that he was otherwise engaged. The girls quit staring at Tom and turned around to pretend they'd never noticed him. "We should head to Stonehenge if we're going to see it before Cardiff."

"Yes, Stonehenge and Cardiff, Stonehenge and Cardiff . . . seems as if we should come up with a nursery rhyme for that," Tom said, draping his arm around me as we moved to go. We walked off, off to Stonehenge and Cardiff, with thoughts of The Magna Carta and merry old England in our heads.

I put the manuscript down as I lay in bed, Eamon sleeping beside me. He is a mass of force, a mountain on my mattress. I reach out and touch the soft skin of his muscles and it's like I've found Esther's Tom, only I don't think Eamon would ever be so condescending. Sylvia Plath's words run through me. They're just like *The Bell Jar* only this books comes from a slightly older and more mature woman. I can tell the young poet has grown up as she writes this next chapter of her character's life.

Lorelei

THEO HAS BEEN in this kitchen before. When I first brought him home to meet my father he'd been a nice college boy. Theo grew up in New York City in a two-floor apartment on the Upper East Side. In college he studied finance at Columbia before Harvard Law School. He was a catch, especially for a bohemian artist, who spent more time in coffee shops wishing it were still the 1990s than worrying about tax law. We were going to move back to New York after Theo graduated. His father could line him up with a job there. Then Theo got a job at a big firm and we decided to stay in Boston. I did my thing. Theo did his. But we got married. We stayed married.

I don't know why I stuck around. Some people, my mother included, thought it was Theo's good job or the apartment in Beacon Hill and the house in the Berkshires. But it wasn't any of that. There had been something passionate about him and he liked the bohemian in me, he liked going for coffee instead of having drinks with the lawyers—at least at the start. Yes, he was a rich kid from New York, but you never would have known it when he visited my friend's apartments. He was fun. He liked art. He even painted. Then he stopped being fun. He stayed at work more and more often. He quit painting. In the end the inertia of a relationship in our twenties took hold and we couldn't stop it. I remember Newton's Law, "An object in motion will remain in motion unless acted upon by an outside force." It just took years for the outside force to act on our marriage. And she was one of my students.

"You know, when you inherit this place," Theo says, sitting at my distressed wood counter, on one of the white stools, "I'm entitled to half."

"I don't think that's right." We've discussed this before. The divorce decree has been handed down. There's been a settlement. I have not inherited my father's house and so Theo has no claim to it. "My father doesn't even have a Will drawn up, therefore it's not communal property. I might not even inherit it."

"But it was always implied," Theo starts. He's calm. He is always calm during these negotiations, it's what makes him such a success in finance. He smiles and nods and you like him, you really, really like him as he's screwing you over. "I mean, we bought that place in West Stockbridge because there was no need for a sea view."

"When on earth were you ever entitled to a sea view in this marriage? When did I ever say I'd bring that to the table?"

"It was implied, Lorelei, and when something is implied it's very close to a promise. I can fight you on this. Some things still aren't decided with the settlement, you know that, right?" The divorce decree has been submitted but there are still some details to iron out before it formally goes through. Meanwhile Theo keeps asking to amend it, to take more of my book deal, to get his hands on my father's house.

"And I was promised a faithful husband," I counter. "Remember our vows."

"That is not under scrutiny right now," he replies. There should be some sort of vitriol in his voice but he's still calm. "Love is different."

"You never defined what love would be for you. Apparently it was a nineteen-year-old who liked to send nude selfies."

"Stop it," Theo hisses, his voice shooting up. I see the crack in his face. I promised I would never mention it and I know this is going too far.

"I got a call from their phone, I think it was the mother," I offer. I need someone to share this with and he's the only one who really understands any of this. I picture a boxing ring, we're on opposite sides of it, Theo and I, and yet he's the only other person in the ring with me and that's something. No one else knows what it's like inside that ring. "He's out, the father."

"I know, probation. Should have served the full year and a half. That is nothing, nothing after what he did."

"He didn't know the cousin would go so far. He was her father, I'm sure the jury took pity on him."

"You're defending him? She was your student, you were so close to her. How can you defend him?"

"I'm not defending him, he's a grieving parent, I guess I just . . ." I don't finish, I can't. Theo just shakes his head. "It's that cousin, that entitled little shit, you know she told me how he tried to molest her when she was a kid and the parents didn't do anything. They knew about it. They talked to his mother but they let it go. They didn't press charges or call the police because he was a kid and 'boys will be boys.'"

"Lorelei just stop," Theo says, putting a hand up. "Look The contract you signed with your publisher, I want to go over that with my lawyers again."

"Why on earth do you care about my measly book contracts? They don't pay half my own bills and if it weren't for my teaching job . . . do you want half of that too, in addition to all the money you make?" I look him in the eye and he holds my gaze. He makes three times what I do if you combine everything, my books, the articles I write and my associate professor's salary.

"What if you have a bestseller?"

"You won't let me have a bestseller? Fine. I'll make sure to only write crap for the next three years, just to make sure I don't have a bestseller you're missing out on."

The back door opens and Eamon enters. He has taken to just coming in when I leave the door unlocked. He doesn't have a key, but when I'm home, he just comes in. I'm still not afraid of prowlers, not at night and certainly not during the day, not even after the little fiasco with the broken planter. When I lock the door, he knocks.

"No bestsellers for three years, I think if you try writing crap you'll have a real hit on your hands, Lorelei." Eamon nods at Theo. "Hello," he says half cheekily.

"Who is this?" Theo asks. They've met, but Eamon had been a little drunk then, his hair was longer and we were in the city. Somehow out here, the salty air just suits this Irish painter better.

"It's Eamon, Theo, don't be rude. Eamon and I have been seeing each other—"

"On and off, you know, just a wee bit," Eamon adds jokingly for me. "But then again quite seriously." He looks me in the eye and I smile gratefully.

"For a little over a year now," I finish for him. "I don't know, is it serious?"

"Apparently I'm allowed to just walk in."

"What's he doing here?"

"I don't know why you care," I counter. "Eamon, Theo thinks I should sell the house when my father dies and give half of it to him because it was implied in our marriage contract that he would forever have access to ocean front property I don't even own. I haven't even inherited it, nor have I been named as an inheritor in the Will my father has yet to draw up. Is that about right?"

"Seems as if your father should really draw up a Will," Eamon observes. "How does a man his age, with a daughter, not have a Will?"

"I just think—" Theo starts. His charms aren't going to work on this man who works at a bar—he knows too much about human nature.

"I think you both should cut your losses. The one time I got divorced, back in County Kerry, you know, she and I, we just said, well we both have a lot of debt and we don't make any money. We'll just walk away with our own debt and call it a day."

"You make marriage sound like a dreamboat," Theo replies before he turns exclusively to me. "Can I use your washroom? Do I still have access to that or would you like to charge me?"

"You know where it is."

"Thanks a lot," Theo replies as he gets up and marches toward the stairs. The sound of his feet on them . . . it's like he never left. Like his time with Heather

. . . what happened afterwards, never occurred. And sure the marriage wasn't all that great, but at least we were together, at least we were working and now . . . now there's still so much left unsaid, so much we can't or won't say and probably never will. We were married and now it's over and though we've both moved on it's still sad.

"You know, seeing him, he doesn't seem like a cold hearted guy. I certainly wouldn't think . . . after what happened to his mistress," Eamon starts, opening up my refrigerator and taking a bottle of water.

"I wouldn't call a nineteen-year-old girl a mistress. She was a smart kid. I just . . . she was young."

"I'm sorry, I didn't mean to dredge that up." Eamon sets the water down, walks over, and puts his arm around me.

"I have to learn to be okay with talking about it. I think I might have to talk to the mother soon. She called again."

"You do what's best, Lorelei, you're good at doing what's best."

The bell rings just as I consider grabbing my own water. Even with the air conditioning I persuaded my father to install a few years ago, it still gets pretty stuffy in the house, especially with the oncoming heat wave that's been forecast. Amelia is not at the door and my aunt is working. Theo is upstairs so I wonder who could be here.

"Maybe it's that Joanne character looking for her manuscript," Eamon muses like he's just read my mind as he glances over at the pile of papers I've left on the counter.

"It's very interesting. I'm starting to really get into the book. The voice is very reminiscent of Plath's from *The Bell Jar*. The way she talks about Esther's relationship with this guy Tom, even though she's obviously in love with this guy Micah, and then the little English town. The way she and the fiancé interact, it's like everything is fine but the end is in sight anyway. There's an undercurrent of violence in this couple, I feel it." The bell rings again and part of me wonders if they'll just go away.

In all honesty I have not had many visitors, not many that knock on the door when it's unlocked, and other than Theo I can't really tell who it might be. When I open the door it's the girl from the diner. She looks up at me with big eyes and I notice that she's carrying a novel and a notebook against her pink shirt. Her arms are folded over her chest as if she's trying to invent a shield to save herself from this place. If only she knew what she was walking into, she might have made the shield out of stone.

"Hello, Miss," the girl says.

"Hello," I reply. "You're Ashley?" The girl nods. "Didn't I ask you to call before coming?"

"My mom was passing the house and she thought, since we were here. My mom's in the car. She's happy to wait, she's on the phone with my sister in Michigan."

"Okay," I tell the girl, opening the screen door wider to let her in. I check the driveway and there's a strange car parked in it, a light blue Mazda with a woman on her phone in the driver's seat. I wave to her but she does not respond. "Come in, please, it's okay. You just surprised me. I went to Michigan once, lovely state."

"We visited in the fall, the leaves have so many colors. Last summer though, when I came to visit, I was stung by a bee."

"Ah, bees." I sigh as if I'm a wise sage and not a woman who can barely keep her head above water. "They sting, but it's because they're trying to protect the queen."

"My uncle used to say when he was a boy that he wanted to go into the hive and catch the queen. One time he tried and got his hands and arms stung so badly he spent a week in the hospital."

"Wow, that's tough."

"Served him right."

"True," I reply. "Don't mess with the queen."

"I was wondering," the girl says, getting down to business as I lead her into the kitchen, where Eamon still stands, this time with his head in the refrigerator, rummaging for food like a child home from soccer practice. I almost laugh at how naturally he's become a part of the landscape of the house.

"Do you remember Eamon? He was at the diner with me."

"Yes, I do. With the accent."

"That's true," Eamon replies, highlighting his Irish accent a tad more.

"I grew up in Georgia," Ashley replies. "My family works in Wellesley now. My father is a professor at the college and my mother is a secretary there. Professors move wherever they can find a job, you know?"

"I had a student with family in the south," I say, catching myself. "So, Ashley, tell me, how are you? What did you want to discuss in this interview?" It's silly to start with Theo upstairs but then again I'd rather talk to this girl than my ex. I already know everything he has to say and maybe with her here he'll be more apt to leave in a civil manner.

"What is that, may I ask?" the girl asks, pointing to the pages of the Plath manuscript.

"A manuscript a woman lent me. She says it was something Sylvia Plath wrote. Apparently Plath sent it over to her before she died. She says it's a new novel or the start of one. I just started reading it."

"Sylvia Plath, a tragic figure of post war feminism," the girl offers, not as if she believes it, but as if she's memorized these lines for a school project.

"She changed after her husband left. All the *Ariel* poems came after she found out Ted was cheating. She compiled them into a book just before her suicide. But this manuscript, from what I've read, cast a different light on the husband all together. Makes it seem she had another great love that got away."

"Ah, the one that got away." Eamon sighs nostalgically. "You got any of those, Lorelei?"

"Plenty have gotten away," I reply. "I just don't know if they were loves, more like, lost moments, lost friends, lost novels I should have written and never did."

"Do you think pain helps a writer?" the girl asks as if she's reading my mind.

"It can. It depends. Sometimes you just have to wallow in the pain for a while, let it really sink in, then you can harness it."

"If you don't mind," the girl starts again, still eyeing the manuscript. "If it's not too personal, I was wondering, do you have kids?"

"No," I quickly reply and Eamon looks over at me, noticing the bitter bite in my voice. "I was pregnant a while back, but I miscarried. Not really miscarried, I was very far along, almost five and a half months, the child is considered stillborn then."

"You did? I'm so sorry. If you don't mind my asking, was it your health?"

"No, not really." I could go on. I could say it was the divorce, the stress, the fact that after I found out about my husband's affair, and then what happened to Heather, it was all too much. I considered downing a bottle or two of wine but thought better of it because of the baby. Instead I just lay in bed until the labor pains started. I was only five and a half months along. Enough time to see an ultrasound, enough time to know the sex—a boy, we would have named him Nicholas, but apparently not enough time to gestate a child to a healthy full term. They thought they could stop the labor, the contractions, but it only got worse. I thought about calling Theo, but he'd just had some terrible news of his own and I didn't want to add to his stress. And I was still mad at him. He had talked about signing the child over to me, paying support but having nothing more to do with the life we'd created just months before our marriage ended. "I'm still dealing with the loss, but thank you," is all I tell her.

"And do you want more kids?" the girl asks and I remember Theo upstairs. I have not heard the whir of a toilet flushing or the water in the faucet in a thin spray. Theo is the kind of man who meticulously washes his hands.

"My husband and I are filing for divorce."

"I'm sorry," the girl goes on. She looks more comfortable now and places her book on the counter and opens the notebook as if she's about to get down to the real questions. "May I ask why you're getting a divorce?"

"I'm sorry," I tell her. "You may not."

The girl nods, expecting this. "So, why did you decide to write about motherhood if you're not a mother?" Her voice is calm and kind, much like Theo when he's about to strike. There's a bite to the words and for the first time I feel like one of those politicians who has been lulled into a very dangerous interview.

Then I wonder if she knows. Not just what I tell people, but the other things that happened with Heather.

"Motherhood has always interested me," I calmly answer. "I've always wanted to be a mother since I was a young child. My husband and I wanted to wait for a while, until our careers were in order, but at the end of it all, we realized we needed to start trying. It was hard. I saw a fertility doctor for about a year before I got pregnant. That's when some things happened in our lives and I lost the baby. To answer your question about when motherhood might happen for me, I don't know anymore."

"She's still young," Eamon says. "Thirty-two is nowhere near too old."

"Thank you," I say, my eyes telling him to stop.

"I see," the girl replies. She writes something down and I wonder what it is.

"But you had so much. A rich husband, why did you need a career? Why could you not be content?" It's the last sentence, the way she says it, that disarms me.

"Not everyone is content with a rich husband," Eamon butts in, a carrot, not a carrot stick but a whole peeled carrot, in his hand. He takes a bite of it and it's like he's Bugs Bunny. If I weren't so nervous I'd laugh at him. "Especially when that husband turns out to be a cheating bastard. Lorelei, are you sure she should be asking these kinds of questions? Is this what you signed up for?" I look over at him grateful that he's willing to jump in and help, the knight in shining armor once again.

"Do you think maybe your mother could come in? It might be nice if I met her."

"No," Ashley tells me, still looking in her notebook. "She does not want to meet you. She thinks a woman who would write about children without having them is odd. Who could imagine caring for a child without raising one? *I* wanted to know."

"What's going on?" I ask and just then I hear the flush of the toilet upstairs. What was Theo doing up there? Rummaging through my drawers? Trying to see if I'm hiding anything of value he might declare that he deserves half of? I hear the water in the faucet and know he'll be down any second, after he's dried his hands on the lily-white guest towels I keep out in case Amelia brings her publishing friends over.

"I just believe . . . You don't know me? You don't recognize me, not at all? Are you sure?"

"No," I reply and I hear a noise, like a wounded animal, behind me.

"Lorelei, what is this?" Theo demands, holding the red and black scarf. He waves it around and I step back.

"I don't know, I found it outside. I heard a noise and found it."

"You found it outside, what the hell? You don't know whose it is? Really?" Theo holds the scarf and I'm not sure what he's going to do with it. It's clear by the confused look in his eyes that he's not sure what he's going to do either. I was his wife for four years; I've seen him vulnerable, but rarely. He looks as if he might take a scissors to the scarf or hold it next to his face and start to cry. "It's hers, you didn't know it was hers? Heather, it was hers." I hear the tears in his voice though his eyes do not betray him.

"Whose?" I ask and that's when Theo turns and finds Ashley.

"I left it," she says. "I was holding it when I came to your house. I only came to look, I wasn't going to go inside or talk to you. I just wanted to see your house. I dropped my lipstick and when I bent to pick it up I knocked over your planter and then I dropped my scarf while I was running away. It was her favorite scarf and I loved it. I used to want one just like it and then one day Heather found almost the exact same scarf and got it for me. Not the same, it didn't have flowers but I loved it. We both loved it. I was going to go back for it but then your friend came over and you picked it up and so I left it." She reaches out, an action so brave considering how timid she's been, and snatches the scarf. "I want it back." Theo simply stares at her in disbelief, letting the billowing scarf fall from his fingers as if she's taking something precious from him. It's unnatural seeing a man like Theo this exposed.

"What the . . . ?" Theo asks as he stands in the kitchen looking stark and alone. "Lorelei, why on earth is she . . . ?"

"Heather? You know *Heather*?" I want to spit my words at her, I don't care if she's a child I want to shake her and tell her to get out.

"Lorelei, why is she here?" Theo asks again and this time his voice drips with vitriol. He stares me down like he's never done. After the divorce, I was the jilted woman, but he was hurt as well. I did not tell him when I went into labor, I gave birth to a stillborn son without him and still he seemed okay, sad sometimes, hiding anger other times, but just now it's as if I have unleashed hellhounds on him and he needs, he desperately needs, to fight back.

"I'm her cousin," the girl announces. "On the other side. Not related to that pig who killed her."

"Her cousin, you're her *cousin*," I say more to the girl, half laughing nervously at how ridiculous this is. Of course she's her cousin, I don't have teenage fans, she must have been looking for me for some other reason.

"You didn't know who this was? Were you paying attention at all to the last year?" Theo asks and his voice says that even if this is ignorance, it cannot be excused.

"I had a lot on my plate these last two years. A lot I didn't ask for," I sneer back at him. "She said her name was Ashley. She wanted to talk about my book. Really, until now that's all I thought it was. At least I didn't want to believe . . . She said she wanted to interview me." It was vanity plain and simple, a young girl admired me, a young girl was interested in my book, of course she was able to pull the wool so far over my eyes.

"You let Heather's cousin come in here? What is she doing?" Theo demands. Ice runs through my veins, a chill coagulating at the mention of that nineteen-year-old girl. "What are you doing here? Are you following me? Are you trying to get something out of me by going through my wife?" He breathes the word "wife" like it still means something, like those vows he took so many years ago matter now that our property has been divided and we no longer speak about anything but finances and fairness.

"No. I wanted to talk to *her*. I have nothing to say to *you*," the girl says. "She's a woman and she should have known better, she should have protected her student better. She didn't have to tell her mother like that."

"I'm sorry, I . . . I called Heather, I saw the pictures and I called Heather. Her mother answered her phone and it just came out." I feel so compelled to explain this to her. Just now I have to explain it to someone.

"It just came out?" Ashley nearly spits at me. "Telling her mother? That just came out?"

"There were naked pictures of her on my husband's phone. Texts that were so much more than friendly. I was really upset and I called her, I called Heather, and her mother answered the phone."

I look over at Eamon, who stands between the girl and me, a dumbfounded knight. "I think you need to leave, young lady." Eamon looks over at me. "Do you want me to go out and get the mother, ask her to come in and take her?"

"No, it's okay, she's leaving," I tell him.

"You should have thought before letting your filthy husband near my cousin," Ashley fires back. "Why did you not tell your husband to stop? Quietly make him walk away from our family."

"It's not my fault her cousin had a thing for her. That he felt the need to punish her for something that was none of his business. That he thought he had a right to lay his hands on a young girl. She had a heart condition!" I cite every excuse I've given myself, every line of reasoning that still makes no sense. Still I need to say it. I need to hear it myself but more than that I need this girl to understand. Instead she just stares at me.

"He didn't know about her heart. No one knew about her heart. But he—he knew that what he was doing was wrong and still he did it with my cousin, she was a girl, a *girl*," Ashley cries at us.

"I know calm down. I'm sorry this happened, I truly, truly am, I loved your cousin. She was my best student, she had so much promise, so much potential. But you can't come in here . . . you can't just go accusing people." I want to chastise her, I want to comfort her, but just now I look at the girl. Her wrists are small, her eyes big and heavy, but she is young, no more than seventeen, there is no way I should be arguing with her like this.

"She has to go," Theo barges in. "Ashley, I'm sorry about Heather, I really am. In my own way I loved her, I truly loved her. But you have to go. Do you need a ride?" He loved her? I want to be hurt but part of me always knew it was true.

"I do not need a ride, my mom's outside. Lorelei, thank you for answering my questions." The girl looks me in the eye. She grabs her notebook and her novel and carries them out, this time not across her chest like a shield, but at her side, as if she doesn't care. I watch her go, closing the door softly behind her, as if to cover her tracks.

"Theo, you need to go," I announce.

"What was that?" he demands, planting himself in front of me.

"I don't know. If I had known she knew Heather . . . I really thought this was over. I mean, what happened, it can never be over and I still feel . . ." Tears well in my eyes. We do so much, make so many mistakes. At the time, sometimes, we think they're right, these mistakes, at the very least we can justify them. We can push and pull at the ebb and flow of morality until it starts to make sense in our own warped worlds but then there is a comeuppance, always there is a comeuppance.

"I have a meeting tonight, then a stupid party. I wonder if I can just skip it," Theo says as if he's thinking out loud. "I don't think I can go now."

"You can't skip it," I reply. I don't know how I know the answer to this, but I do. I was his wife for four years and I know which parties he can and can't skip. "You should go. If there's more money issues, I think they should be decided through our lawyers."

"Sure, yeah, right," Theo says. He looks at the counter as if there's something there but it's just smooth sanded wood, grey and nearly naked. In the middle stands a blue bowl that should be used for fruit though I've never been the kind of woman to keep fresh fruit on the table. Maybe if I had put fresh fruit on the table, maybe if I had paid more attention to what was going on, my life would be different. But even these are poor excuses to justify the end of a marriage. "You know I loved her, right?"

I nod. It stings, after all this time, it still stings, but I just shake my head at him.

"Good bye, Eamon," Theo finally says, turning to go. I don't listen as he walks out, the door closing with more force behind him.

"So that was the cousin," Eamon comments after everyone has gone. "Not that I knew the girl had a cousin, but I guess families like that, they all have cousins. I remember stories of my Irish ancestors, the ones who were smart enough to move to America with the first wave of immigrants, they all had these families, so many damn cousins and over in Ireland—"

"I don't care about your family over in Ireland," I yell at him. His eyes bulge for a moment before he slackens. "I wonder if she tracked me down here or if her family really was on vacation and she saw me and decided to act."

"Both scenarios are pretty crafty," Eamon hesitantly replies. "You know it wasn't your fault." He places a hand on my shoulder and I see the knight in his face. "I mean, the cousin, that brute, who does that to a girl? To a kid? I mean, who thinks that's okay? I don't care if the cousin didn't know about her heart condition, that's no excuse."

"I know. And yet it's not enough. Having a single villain is not enough."

"True," Eamon says, looking out at the ocean. My eyes join his and it is only then that I hear the rocking of the waves.

I stop talking. I can't go on, not to him, not now. Eamon knows enough already. I hear my mother's voice through her journal. There's just so much we keep inside that never comes out. Should I have told him everything about my mother? Does Eamon need to know her pain to understand me? Is this my secret, my story to tell? My mother was able to keep so many of her secrets her entire life. She wrote them in a journal and it was only later, when a girl tried to break into our house not even to steal, just to see, that her story came spilling out like a thousand tiny beads toppled over after spending years safely compacted in a glass jar. She kept her secret and so did her sister and here I am now, telling Theo's secret as if it's mine to share. As if what happened to that girl has anything to do with me when we know that families hold mysteries so deep. How dare I go shouting them from the rooftops to anyone?

Sylvia
1962

SYLVIA HAD NOT been invited to many parties, not since the move to Devon, not since Frieda was born and then there was her separation from Ted. There had been near radio silence from the literary world when she was not banging on the door to be let in. She'd gotten a few invitations to dinner. She'd met Al Alverez near the square by her old place, the one she and Ted had shared. Jillian had been very kind always including her when she threw a dinner party but that was basically it. There were more parties, so many more parties, back when she was younger. When she and Ted had been together, especially before the children . . . But then again Ted had just published a book and there had been an award for something or other a few months back and so all the invitations were naturally coming his way. It always seemed as if Ted were in the midst of just publishing this or being honored for that. There was a book of poetry here (and then it would win an award) or a play there. His book of children's stories, the ones that had needed to be reworked because they'd been rejected for being too violent, had gotten so much acclaim once Sylvia had helped fix them. She'd typed them up so neatly so he could send them back out. Ted the literary genius, they all said, and no one bothered to thank Sylvia for helping rework the stories or for going so far as to type them up like his own personal secretary.

Sylvia could remember these kinds of triumphs from when she was a girl; she used to be the success, the one who could not go a week without an award or straight A's or something. Back in Wellesley she would sit and study at night, hour upon hour, until she couldn't see straight. It wasn't enough, just the act of studying, you had to accomplish something because of it. She had to make sure she got the A as well or what was all the studying but a waste of time? Then there was her book that they would not publish in America . . . and she was writing such good poetry these days and no one cared. A tree falling in the forest . . . why couldn't she get a single break?

But they had invited her tonight. She'd received an invitation in the mail three weeks ago. Susan, the girl she'd hired to take care of the children while she wrote, had brought the mail in, laying it on the table as she always did. Susan was a good girl, not a snoop at all, and Sylvia had found the very nice white envelope, it nearly looked engraved, with her name on it. The Blake Society of Saint James requested the honor of her presence at The Distinguished Poetry Award party in London. A new poet was being honored and they would so like it if she would attend.

The party was near Hyde Park. Sylvia had not been that far into the city, the part of the city that was really the city, the one tourists think of when they think of London. But it was always that one could only afford to live in places that are not the city, but only city-adjacent, even if the tube does go out that far and the taxes are the same. But in that part of the city, where she could afford to live (even in Yeats' House) the streets were just streets and any old shop was just any old shop and yes you have the expense and the hassles of living in London but at the end of it all was it really, truly living in London?

The party was held at a large white house, one of the regal row structures near Hyde Park, much like Virginia Woolf's old home. Only the society had not been lucky enough to have rented that for the occasion.

Sylvia looked up at the house, pulling the collar of her coat up over her neck at the cold. It was only early December but the chill in the air had grown worse and worse and the weathermen had said that this would be a one of the coldest, snowiest winters in London in years. A couple passed her on the steps, the man wore a suit and had sheet metal grey hair but a young face. The woman was plump but in a sexy way and her dress came to just below her knees and spread out like dresses had done in the fifties. They nodded to Sylvia, though she didn't recognize them, but Sylvia smiled, her lips tight as if she were holding a toothpick between them as she ascended the stairs after the couple. The door remained open for her though no one was there to greet her and it took a second for a man in a grey suit to come down the stairs and hold out his arms for her coat.

"Thank you, ma'am," he said just like an old English butler. Giles, Sylvia thought though he hadn't mentioned his name, I will call him Giles. There were times when Sylvia wondered how it was that the English could be so English. There were men standing up so straight it was as if tight strings were holding them in place and women with those careful smiles, as if someone had paused their faces. And here she was coming face to face with a real English butler. She could just see him asking if she'd like a spot of tea.

"Sylvia, you made it," someone came up to her. It was Al, the poetry editor at *The Observer*. He had been a friend of the family back when the Hughes had been a family, but Sylvia had seen him around London a few times and he'd been very kind to her. "It's ghastly out there and it's just early December, not anywhere near Christmas. I can't wait to see what this winter brings."

"They say it could be the worst winter in decades," Sylvia commented. Then she worried she'd over exaggerated. She had a tenancy to hyperbole, especially at parties, when she felt all eyes on her and the unease of having to talk to so many people.

"I know, I know. How are things over in Bethnel Green?" Sylvia asked.

"It's very nice really. Very nice being back in England. I did a guest-lectureship at a university in America last year."

"Oh my that's lovely," Sylvia said, remembering that Ted had said something about that. "I taught at Smith for a year when Ted and I were first married. I liked the teaching and the girls. It was so nice being at my Alma Mater, but it took away from my poetry. At the end of the day one has to decide teaching or poetry and poetry won."

"Yes, but as a critic, being taken away from your writing, sometimes it's more a blessing than a curse. Some people would be very happy if I stopped writing altogether. Then maybe there wouldn't be so many bad reviews in the world."

"I see," Sylvia said, laughing as she looked around. Everyone seemed to have a beverage in hand and she was sure most of them were alcoholic. Now where can I get one of those? she pondered as she looked Al in the eye. "So tell me, what was it like, living in America?"

"Oh, America, that's right, sometimes I forget, even when hearing your accent, that you're American," Al said, laughing at himself. "America was nice, although we were rather stuck out in the middle of nowhere. They had us in a house in the suburbs, and we didn't have a car so it was like being stranded. My wife hated it, just hated it, took our daughter and went right back to England after only a few months. But I stuck it out for the whole term."

"It can feel desolate," Sylvia replied. "Especially without a car. I remember in college I always had a boy to drive me around but when I didn't it was difficult just to get into town to see a movie."

"Everything is a lot closer here in England," Al said and his voice indicated that he was trying to move the conversation along. "But Sylvia, when you have something new you must send it over to *The Observer*. The boys in editorial haven't sent anything good to me in a while. I haven't read an ounce of decent poetry in so long I don't know if I'd even be able to recognize it."

You wouldn't, Sylvia wanted to say, but held her tongue. He, or *The Observer,* had rejected two of her best pieces recently. "Thank you, of course." Sylvia nodded politely instead, smiling and feeling silly. Does Al even read his own mail? she thought as Al moved to grab another drink at a table set up near the side of the entranceway as a bar. Sylvia might have followed him, she could use a drink herself, but she didn't want to feel as if she were hounding the man.

So many people, Sylvia thought as she wandered through this literary party. The rooms she walked through were richly decorated and there was something of the Victorian in them. Dark paneling went up the walls and the curtains in the front room were a very deep red while the curtains in the living room were hunter green. A large intricately carved and highly polished table sat in the middle of the room and on top of it was a lovely marble chess set they hadn't even bothered to move for the party. They must have a great deal of faith in the poise of these guests, Sylvia thought as she passed the set, her fingers gracing one of the smooth marble pieces. The children would have been all over this, she could just picture Frieda flinging the pieces around the room as Nicholas stuck one in his slobbery baby mouth.

Sylvia walked toward the food, which had been laid out on a poshly decorated table covered by a perfectly starched white cloth. Literary people always did go all out for these parties. When she had been with Ted they'd been too busy making conversation to really eat any of the food but food had always been important to Sylvia. She could eat very much without gaining weight. Her doctor swore she'd lost twenty pounds since this summer. "Eat, Sylvia," Doctor Horder had said. "Eat a whole cow if you can, spend the night at a sugar factory. We need to get some weight on you."

Sylvia inched her way toward the table. The room was not over crowded though it wasn't anywhere near empty. Still no one stopped her to chat as she walked a straight shot to the food. She took a white china plate and began to fill it with tiny crackers, little cakes and just a bit of caviar.

She had made that mistake, overindulging in the caviar, once during her time working for *Mademoiselle*. She'd taken too much of it, in fact she'd spooned the entire bowl of it right onto her plate and eaten it all in one gulp (perhaps it had been two or three gulps but it was very quick). The girls had all looked at her like she'd done something funny. One of them had even said, "Didn't you think someone else might want to eat some of that?" There had been snickers but Sylvia had kept composed. "I wasn't sure," was all she'd said. Then she'd allowed the conversation to move on as if nothing had happened. She'd then written out a scene like that in *The Bell Jar*, where her main character, Esther, sees a bowl of caviar and wants it all for herself.

With her plate full of food Sylvia realized that she was not going to be able to grab a drink. Still she'd prefer to eat. She really hadn't been eating much lately, not since the move. It was partly that there wasn't much money, not for anything worth eating and then there were the children and they had to eat and she had to cook for them and by the time she had them in bed she was too exhausted to think about food. But as she stood looking out at the party she became ravishingly hungry and placed a slice of some kind of bread cake into her mouth, immediately followed by another. She dipped her tiny spoon in the caviar and started to eat it. She considered sitting down, she really was very tired, but just then she saw a woman she recognized more from her book jacket photo than from real life and so she swallowed her caviar hard, wishing she could take just one more bite, before walking over.

"Doris," Sylvia said with a huge smile as she approached the authoress of *The Golden Notebook*, a book Sylvia had read a few months ago and loved. "Hello, my name is Sylvia, Sylvia Plath Hughes." She felt silly still holding her plate. She could not extend her hand out to Doris Lessing and she felt so clumsy just then, too big, too tall, too fat even, as she wondered if she had any food in her teeth. "I loved your book."

"My book, oh thank you. And tell me, who are you? Sylvia Plath Hughes?" Doris looked at her as if she didn't recognize her. Perhaps a fiction writer did not read poetry. "Are you married to Ted Hughes?"

"Ted, yes, we were married," Sylvia replied, thinking that the word "were" would create some female solidarity.

"I loved his collection *Lupercal*. It was really marvelous. The way that man can talk about nature . . . and still he's so modern. I met him once at a party a few months ago. Were you there?"

"No," Sylvia said, shaking her head. "We're separated, you see."

"Oh," Doris Lessing said, looking over Sylvia's shoulder as if this made her uncomfortable. "Well I'm very sorry. The condition of the modern world I fear."

"I fear it too," Sylvia agreed. "But I'm a poet in my own right. I published a book last year *The Colossus* and I'm going to have a novel out soon under a pseudonym."

"Really a pseudonym, why a pseudonym?"

"The novel is based on my personal life, it's based on a time when I was institutionalized and I talk about people I knew. It would hit very close to home for some people and I just thought it would be best not to use my real name. My mother was really worried about offending people, especially in America, if the book ever gets published in America, though that's been very slow going."

"I see. Well, I know that a novel, anything an artist makes, at the end of the day it is about their life, plain and simple, but I don't know about hiding it. If people are going to be offended, people from your life, your past, let them be offended. If you've written the truth then there's nothing they need to hide from. And if it's so close to your life, well that's something to think about as well. You're not writing autobiography are you, even if all art is essentially that."

"Yes, yes, you're right about the pseudonym," Sylvia said. She felt tears in her eyes and she wasn't sure why. Ms. Lessing was quite short, Sylvia could see her as a squat old woman in thirty or so years time, sitting in a large armchair beside a fire knitting. Still there was something strong about her. Sylvia had always felt the opposite, like a lanky giraffe with an inability to look people in the eye. They all said she was so lucky, being so tall, but it only made her feel unfeminine and out of place. She was tall and thin and she had delicate features and barely ever gained weight, even after two children, and yet she felt so awkward all the time, big and clumsy. With a certain kind of man, like Richard, she could not even wear heels because she would tower over him.

"I see you've met Sylvia," Sylvia's friend, Jillian said, coming up behind them. She had a drink in hand and suddenly Sylvia desperately wanted one.

"Yes, we were just talking about how all art comes from the artist's life, it's always their autobiography that we're experiencing."

"True," Jillian replied. "I wholeheartedly agree. And then it's the job of us critics to tell the artists why their lives are so boring or irrelevant or just plain bad art." She laughed at herself, throwing back her head as Doris chuckled along with her.

"Yes, there is something to concealing our lives, to taking our lives and making them seem so much better, yes. I know," Doris went on.

"You did that so well in *The Golden Notebook*. The theme of the artist's life and how they manage to make art out of it." Sylvia tried to break back into the conversation, though Doris Lessing didn't seem to hear her.

"But the only way to deal with the trauma of our pasts, and all people deal with deep trauma, whether it's personal or political, religious or cultural, the only way is to make something out of it. To mold it, using some kind of clay, or maybe we need to make the clay first, dredge it up from the mud in the ground, but we need to take life and make it something else, something other generations can take and do with it what they must, perhaps make their own art out of it. Tell me, Sylvia, do you agree?"

Doris Lessing looked at her with such big eyes but just then Sylvia only felt a lump in her throat. She looked down at her plate and shoveled a bite of caviar into her mouth so that it was completely full. It tasted salty and not at all refined and she imagined the salt of her tears as Doris and Jillian watched her. They were expecting her to say something, she had just proclaimed herself a poet, it was her job to say something. There was so much kindness on their faces, but in that kindness there was also pity. Sylvia swallowed hard and the tears squeezed tight at the edge of her eyes, constrained so hard in her throat.

"I'm sorry, yes. That makes perfect sense, it does, it really does," Sylvia fumbled, placing her plate on the nicely polished table near the chess set. She was sure she wasn't supposed to place plates like that. She had made some kind of silly gaffe. The British and their politeness and she could see them all staring at her, the tall woman, her hair entirely too long so that she must wear it in braids like a Swedish peasant, the clumsy American who had once been married to a great English poet. Now she was just a tall woman at a party who had eaten too much caviar and placed her plate in the wrong place.

"I should mingle," Sylvia said, swallowing hard so that the stoicism of politeness could take over. "Thank you, Doris . . . er Miss Lessing. I really did love your book. When my novel is out, I'll send it around."

"Yes, please, send it round," Doris Lessing said and Sylvia could see that this woman was seething with pity and politeness. Am I that obvious? she thought as she walked away. Can they see the tears at the edge of my eyes? Am I that sad and pathetic and hopeless?

Sylvia walked, though she felt more like she dragged, through the party. She did not want to leave, not really. She'd been invited and she had not been out in so long and if *The Observer* was going to reject her work the least she could do was meet the poetry editor at a party. Besides it was very cold outside and if she left she would not meet anyone else. She would not be able to talk about poetry or art. She would have been happy to talk about painting or movies, she'd even talk about the weather, she was so starved for adult conversation. So few people in her life came to see her now that she was hidden away in that cramped apartment and so she could not talk about poetry or books with anyone.

And the poetry, it flowed out of her every day. Every morning at four a.m. she would rise from bed, sometimes shaking, sometimes just about in tears and the darkness would take over. She could feel the darkness, always the dark, and still it was where the poetry came from, as if it were climbing out of the cave of her mind to the light. And why was she at this party now? Why was she not writing poetry? This party wasn't so great and if she went home maybe the darkness wouldn't follow her and she'd be able to write.

Is the light and happy phase of my life over? Sylvia wondered, immediately terrified by the thought. Am I now a creature of the dark? She had had light for a little while, with Richard, with Paris and the Fulbright, even with Ted, but that had been when she was young, a vacation really from Daddy's death, the breakdown, the electroshock. She was a creature of the dark, she always had been, and it was time to return to it.

Sylvia shuffled into a back room. There were a few people there, all with cocktails in hand. She moved toward the bar and a man in a grey suit, looking more like a waiter than a butler, looked at her and she said, "White wine, please." He gave it to her without making eye contact.

"The English and their politeness," Sylvia spoke aloud to herself as she walked into the back room.

She recognized a few people. The Frankfurts had come and Richard Murphy was in from Ireland, but she had been to so few parties this year, and Ted had been to so many, it was hard to remember who to smile at, who to speak to. Ted was off now traveling with That Woman. But he'd gone to all the parties this year and Sylvia, when she got an invitation she'd then learn that Ted was going to be there or she couldn't go because of the children or it was just (and this was more often the case) it was just that she had not been invited.

"Ted's not here," Sylvia heard a man say. She couldn't recognize him but she was sure she was supposed to know him. She would have known him if she'd been invited to more parties. "I heard he took Assia with him to Yorkshire. He's not even going home to see the family but he wanted her to see the woods where he grew up."

"Ted Hughes the gamesman," another man said. "It's too bad he's not here. Always the life of the party."

"Life of the party, that dark horse."

"I heard his wife is here," another man said and Sylvia wished she could disappear, as she stood in the back listening, just listening like some kind of sneak. Why am I being such a sneak? she thought. Why not just make my presence known? Would they even recognize me? But she was standing right there, right out in the open, and they didn't even see her.

"His wife, yes, isn't she a poet?"

"A poet, I think she is. Sally I think her name was? I'm not sure. But she's friends with Al, he published some of her work in *The Observer* and Jillian, Jillian insisted, she really wanted her here and Ted, we all knew Ted wasn't coming to this little get together. He hates parties. Doesn't like to go to them even when he's the one up for the award. I don't know how a man who hates parties always manages to be the life of them."

"Right, mark of a true poet that they hate a good party, even when it's all for them," said one of the men (they were all blending together, these men in suits, drinking brandy).

Sylvia turned away from them. She shuffled through the crowd gathered near the door. So many more people were coming and the Butler, Giles, his name must be Giles, was taking two and three coats at a time. It was very cold outside but it didn't matter. She would leave her coat. She didn't need it. She could walk the streets of London without one even if she caught a chill as long as it didn't interrupt her poetry.

And really, who did not like a party? What was wrong with liking parties? Why was Ted so much better because he hated parties? When she'd been in college she'd gone to all of them and they'd not been silly, they'd not been frivolous, they'd just been parties and she'd met interesting people and they'd had interesting, thoughtful conversations and it was really very nice, all of it, very, very nice.

Shaking, Sylvia glanced at the door as a breeze blew in a chill like the permafrost of Boston out on the Charles River when she would go there with Dick or Richard in college. She wanted to leave, to just walk out, but it was so cold now and she knew she couldn't leave without her coat. That had been a silly thought, leaving without her coat, what was wrong with her? "Could you go up and get mine?" Sylvia asked the butler as he carried a bundle of coats upstairs. "It's the grey one with the fur collar."

"Of course." The butler nodded a reply and she had the utmost confidence that he would get the correct coat. A seasoned butler like this Giles would never make a mistake.

"Sylvia," Jillian called, coming up to her she placed her hand on her arm and looked her in the eye with such concern. "Are you leaving so soon? Peter Redgrave is going to give a speech in five minutes and there's going to be the award presentation."

"I know, but I'm worried about the children. I should go," Sylvia said, plastering a phony smile so that her cheeks jutted out. And when did these things make her feel like such a phony? Her poetry, it was better than that, whatever they were giving an award to, her work was more these days and maybe it was that she simply did not have time for parties, for things like this anymore. Could that be it? And if so, was it really a mark of a great poet, hating parties?

"Are you sure? It wasn't Doris, was it? She can come on a bit strong. She's a great writer, but there are times when I wonder how much tact the woman uses."

"She's a strong woman and I love her work," Sylvia replied. "I admire her. And thank you, thank you for inviting me. But I'm inspired to write and there are the children at home, the girl didn't want to stay late, and I simply must go."

Just then the butler, this Giles, came downstairs with her grey coat. "Thank you," Sylvia said as he wordlessly handed it to her. "It's exactly the right coat, thank you so much." This Giles nodded and she smiled even more widely at him as if that would get him to react. And really why did she want him to react so badly? Instead, he turned from the door and marched toward the kitchen.

"The mark of a good British Butler, he never displays an ounce of emotion," Jillian said, rolling her eyes though Sylvia could see that she was only being nice.

"It's okay. I'll see you soon," Sylvia said, slipping her coat on and then reaching to give Jillian a kiss on the cheek.

"Of course, I'll stop by. Gerry and I really want to see you and the children."

"Wonderful," Sylvia replied, walking out the door.

She held her collar up around her neck as the wind blew. London was darker now. Even with the bright streetlights there was a certain darkness to the city when everyone is inside and you're the only one out. But here the city was, still hopping, with black taxicabs in the streets and bright red busses. Sylvia looked out, she wondered what it was like by the river, was someone standing near it now thinking of jumping? Could she stand by the river? Could she think about jumping? Just fall right into the water the cold would be such a shock but she wouldn't splash, she wouldn't call out, she'd just let herself fall down, down, down into the depths of the Thames and then everything would be all right. She'd fall right in the water, maybe with rocks in her pockets like Virginia Woolf. She held her coat closer to her body as the cold rolled over her and it was like she couldn't move for a second, as if the cold had gotten into her bones. She'd just had a drink, she'd just left such a glorious party no wonder she felt the cold so acutely. But maybe, just maybe she was becoming the kind of person, the kind of poet, who hated parties.

Sylvia held her hand out, calling a taxi. She wasn't at a stand but it was late enough and a car rolled over the cobblestone street to pick her up. She could barely afford this indulgence but she'd earned it tonight and it was really very cold and she needed to get home to her children and her poetry.

Lorelei

THE MADNESS OF drowning women, that's always what I thought when I thought about my mother. There was something off about her before I knew there was something wrong. We'd be at the dinner table having a nice talk and all of a sudden she'd start screaming at me. One time she threw her plate across the room and it shattered against the wall. My father used to come to my room at night and tell me that my mother didn't mean to act this way, she was just sick. Later, when I was thirteen, my mother took me to see one of her psychiatrists during one of her more lucid periods and he explained all about brain chemistry and how the pills my mother took helped keep her stable. And they worked, they mostly worked.

Except when she wouldn't get out of bed for a week straight.

Except when she took my friend, Tina, and I, in the car one day and drove around and around and around the block, she wouldn't stop, she wouldn't let my friend get out. We went around and around and around the block for hours until the car literally ran out of gas. She stopped the car and Tina threw open the door and ran away.

She used to cry in front of me. When you're young, around five or six years old, you're the one who does the crying, any child knows that. You're not supposed to see your mother cry. I remember the first time (or the first time I can remember), she was putting up a little fake Christmas tree in the study. It wasn't the big tree, the real tree, that tree my father would pick up at a tree farm two weeks before Christmas. But this little tree she put up right after Thanksgiving and the stand must have been wobbly because it fell over. A couple of the ornaments broke and she just crumpled to the ground. I remember thinking she'd broken like when my toys stopped working as she buried her head in her hands and sobbed. I ran over and hugged her. I didn't know what to do. I just hugged her and hugged her but it didn't work.

She was never happy. That's all I can say. Even when she was okay, when the pills were working, when she was mindful to do everything right. It wasn't my father. He wasn't a perfect man but he was never mean to her. When she screamed at him he just took it, usually he went into another room and let her cool off. When she wouldn't get out of bed he cleaned the house, made us dinner, the man worked nine hours a day as a plumber but he never stopped working, he never complained. I'm sure he wasn't perfect, he'd get fed up, he'd get annoyed when she'd break the TV remote for the third time, he'd yell back sometimes, but he was mindful, he tried. I tried as well. I tried to play with my mother as a child. I'd give her my dolls and she'd just stare at them like she didn't know what they were. I tried to talk to her as a teenager. I let her watch what she wanted on TV. Nothing worked. Some people are just not happy. But she's always with me, even now. She's been gone for a year but there are times I just feel her.

The ocean breathes, I see it, a very big thing out there just watching. I hold the letter in my hand, the one I got today. I thought this was over. Once the girl came by and left in a huff I thought maybe they'd gotten it out of their system and would leave me alone. The phone calls have stopped, but here it is, a letter from Connie Larsen, Heather's mother. It's been two years. Her husband has been in jail for a year and change. I don't need to talk to her but she sent me a letter and like my mother's journal, like her past that won't leave me, this woman has written me and I must read her words.

"Dear Lorelei," it reads. At least she's kind enough to use my first name.

"Let me start by saying I am sorry to hear about how my niece, Ashley, ambushed you. Her mother, my sister, did not know about it. She thought she was taking her daughter to see a friend. We are on the Cape for vacation, we didn't know you'd be here. We didn't know your house was around here. No one looked you up. We're not following you, cyber-stalking you, real stalking you, whatever. It was only that after my husband got out of prison we thought we'd take a vacation, not that a vacation will make up for it all, we know. We didn't know you were here but I'm very sorry to have bothered you, please forgive us and forgive my niece.

"I understand why you haven't taken my phone calls. If the situation were reversed I don't think I would have taken a call from you either. I thought about hiding the number when I called but no one answers from an unidentified number these days. Don't ask me why I'm writing, why I wanted to talk to you. I needed to get this out and I need an audience. I guess you're that audience. Thank you for humoring me. Now that my husband is home, now that life has come back . . . not all the way, it never will, but now that he's home, I feel like I must close this door. I must . . . at least say something to you. I couldn't look at you during the trial. You sat in the back, you didn't want to be there. They wanted you as a witness and you said what you knew, I understand.

"The people I know, when they find out about the affair, always say, 'You're such good Christians. You raised her well, why would she do something like that?' And I wonder the same thing some days. I remember taking her to church and Sunday school. I remember telling her about Jesus and forgiveness. 'Do not covet your neighbor's wife.' Is it that there's no commandment for coveting a husband? But it was wrong, what she did. I raised her better than that. But I would have forgiven her. We were angry. I said some things to her, I called her some names, but my husband and I would have forgiven her.

"She should not have let herself fall for a married man and yet I know she had an independent spirit. She did not want to play with the other girls in nursery school. She insisted on playing with boys. Barry thought it was odd that she was such a tomboy but I thought it was cute. When she was in high school my husband found some letters to a boy she'd met on the Internet on her computer. She said some very grown up things in those letters. She sent some racy pictures. Not quite like the ones she sent your husband but for a sixteen-year-old girl it scared us. We didn't even think that the Internet could be dangerous, not like that, not to our daughter. We kept her off her computer except for schoolwork for six months. But when she went to college . . . coming from a Christian family I did not want my daughter to be out in the world but I knew we had to let her go. I wanted her to get an education. We put her in a dorm with high supervision but college students get around rules. They all party from time to time.

"Her cousin Philip is another story. He was a strange boy. He was the kid who hit other kids on the playground, the bully people were afraid of. The bully other kids didn't like. Not the popular bully who only picks on nerds. He picked on everyone. His father left when he was seven and didn't keep in contact. His mother put him in therapy but it didn't work. He developed an unhealthy fascination with Heather. When they were little and she was swimming at the beach he used to hug her in the water. He used to try to touch her. I always tried to keep him away. My husband told me I was paranoid but I thought it was funny. One time, Julie, his mother, asked if Heather wanted to sleep over and I said, 'no.' I never let him around her unsupervised. But I never told anyone except Barry, my husband. He said Philip was confused. He had a tough life and we shouldn't blow things out of proportion, that's what he said. Even in high school, and starting college, Philip used to call and text Heather all the time. She'd ignore him but he didn't let up. And he was her cousin. She didn't cut him off completely. She was a nice girl. She gave people a shot. But what he did to her. Six years. That's all he got. I can't forgive him and I can't forgive the court for refusing to administer justice.

"I know you were upset when you told me about Heather. Sometimes we can't control our anger. If Heather had come to me I might have talked to her calmly. Instead I was embarrassed that her teacher had yelled at me when I answered her phone (I answered Heather's phone all the time, I was her mother). I was upset that her teacher had to inform me that my daughter was having an affair with a married man. We wouldn't have been okay with her having sex at all, but sex like that? Never. When you said you had pictures, you had texts and emails, I knew it was true. I didn't think you would lie but hearing all that embarrassed me and I screamed at my daughter when I might have talked to her. For that I was upset with you for months. I still am. But we all have gut reactions. We all make mistakes. I am trying to forgive.

"I do not believe my husband understood what was going to happen. When Philip told him he wanted to talk to Heather about what happened I don't think Barry knew there would be violence. I have asked my husband over and over again just what he thought was going to happen when he gave his nephew the keys to the factory warehouse where he worked. Why did Philip need to talk to her there? It makes no sense but then again none of this does. What was Barry, my husband, Heather's father, thinking when he let Philip of all people take Heather there? He will not tell me. But Philip beat her so badly her arm was broken. The doctors said it was her heart, her heart went out that's how she died. It was a congenital heart condition, no one knew she had it. It was only the stress of the beating that brought it out. She might have, she would have, survived the beating otherwise, that was my nephews' defense. He only meant to talk to her but then he got angry, and how was he to know she had an undiagnosed heart condition? That is why he only got six years instead of life. He got angry? It makes me sense. So what if he was angry it doesn't mean you can beat a person.

"But if she had been jogging and passed out, been taken to the hospital and diagnosed with this condition, she would probably have lived. They would have put her on the meds, she would have known to be more careful, people would have known to be more careful with her.

"But we have to move on. We have to heal. Barry is home now. He has not gone back to work. He just sits in his office and reads or watches the news. I have tried to talk to him about what happened. I have tried to listen but nothing comes out of his mouth. I live with a silent man these days. He is twenty pounds lighter, his hair is greyer, there is less of it. I live with a ghost of the man who left to go to prison. The ghost of him and the ghost of my daughter.

"Why am I writing you? First of all to thank you for not coming to the parole hearing. I knew that you were asked, that it was your right to attend. I also know you probably didn't care, didn't want to go. But thank you for not coming. I don't know if he would have been given parole if someone from the other side had contested it. I used to hate you. After that phone call. After I yelled at my daughter. After my husband threatened to pull her out of school. After everything. I hated Philip more. I hated Theo more. After all he had the affair. I know that. But I hated you too and now I don't. I can't. I don't know if you care but I wanted you to know that."

I didn't know that. It's good to hear. This all happened nearly two years ago but it comes back over and over. Just like my mother's past will not leave me, just like reading this Plath manuscript is a look back at another person's life, another person's pain. Like my mother's journal this letter is a beacon.

Heather was one of my Creative Writing students. The class was part of a mandatory English credit and so I didn't get a lot of gung-ho writers but I remember that the poetry Heather wrote was so beautiful. After she gave me a packet of poems to read before class, not an assignment, something she'd done on her own, I sat down in my office and read them three times. Heather was one of those students who always had her hand in the air. She asked so many questions, she offered so many valuable insights. I remember one time we were reading Sylvia Plath's poem "Mirror," and a boy had just said, "It's about a woman getting old, right?" and Heather had raised her hand and said, "It's about understanding your new reality." She was the student who came to office hours almost every week to talk. She listened to me talk about poetry and novel writing. Anne Sexton was her favorite poet and she went on and on about her. I told her she should submit her work to the school's literary magazine and she did. So few people follow through. Sure they want to talk about their interests but when you ask them to take the steps to pursue them . . . they'd rather binge watch TV. Not Heather.

She met Theo through the Lit. Magazine. He came to the launch party of the magazine and Heather had three poems in it. There was alcohol at the party but Heather didn't drink any of it. Theo might have had a little wine. I remember introducing them and not thinking anything of it. I walked away to talk to another student and she and Theo started talking. When I came back everything seemed fine. What I couldn't know is that they'd exchanged numbers that night.

And after it all, the emails, the pictures, texts, and phone calls, rendezvous in hotel rooms paid for with a secret credit card, I found out. I knew something was up, I could sense it. Theo was never home and when he was home he was distant. He was always checking his phone and smiling like a stupid teenager. I'd ask him what was up and he'd get defensive. And so I checked his phone. That's where I found pictures and texts, emails, and with some digging, hotel bills. I called Heather's phone, thinking I would confront her about it but her mother picked up and I couldn't hold back. "Who is this?" I asked when someone who sounded older picked up.

"This is Mrs. Larsen," a slow, friendly voice said. "Can I help you? I'm Heather's mother. She's just in the shower."

"Well maybe you should ask your daughter where she goes every night. Maybe you should ask her how long she's been screwing my husband. He's a grown man. He's married. I'm pregnant," I threw at Heather's mother. The woman was speechless. She said something about not believing me. I said something about texting her pictures. She said that wasn't necessary and that was the end of it. But I told on her. I was so angry, so hurt, so confused, and her mother answered Heather's phone and so I told on her. Then I didn't hear from her for days. I confronted Theo and he left. He stayed at a hotel. Heather didn't come back to school and then it was on the news. *Girl Found Beaten to Death in Warehouse—Family Member Suspected.* And how could I be mad at her? I could only hate myself.

I told Theo not to come home that first night and he never came home, not really. Those few days turned into a week and by the end of the week Heather was dead. After that Theo didn't want to come home and I didn't want him there. I stayed in bed barely finishing out the semester and then, being five and a half months pregnant, I started having contractions. I went to the doctor. I didn't even tell Theo I was going. I never told him there might be a problem. They tried to save our son but he was born too early, too sickly, and we lost him.

A little under a year after my son's death my mother committed suicide. As if I didn't have enough on my plate she added one more thing. The madness of drowning women . . . I still wonder what she would have said to me if she'd been more in her right mind during all this. But it's the baby, my son, who I'll never have, that I can't forget. He was our great loss and there are days I feel him so clearly. All the love I have for him, the love I can't give anyone now, rises in my chest like a frenetic wind. Sometimes it breaks me, it paralyzes me stiff, and I miss him. I never met that little boy and I miss him.

Sylvia
1962

IT WAS VERY cold in mid-December; the whole month was one giant ice storm. Virginia Woolf had written about this unseasonable English cold in *Orlando*. In the novel the Thames had frozen over and a great carnival sprung up right on the ice. They said it was based on a real life unseasonably cold winter and Sylvia could just see it now, this was worse than Boston in January, worse than New York. She was sure she'd entered the Arctic Circle . . . or one of the inner circles of Hell. The suicide rate, she'd read, had gone up considerably. They'd already predicted record cold but Sylvia and everyone she knew, the woman at the laundry, the man at the butcher shop, her literary friends and acquaintances, were all trying to push the thought from their minds as the month wore on and the freezing cold did not let up. There had already been power cuts. The other day Sylvia had snapped on the buttons of her heater. Two bars came up for a second before zzzp—nothing. There was no power. She'd lugged her eclectic heater, the only relief against this cold these days, from room to room, trying circuit after circuit (in case she'd blown a fuse). Finally she went downstairs and asked her neighbor, who said the workmen were on strike. There were power cuts all over London. Yes it was freezing but she'd have to live with it. Live with it! She had two babies how could she live with it?

At least the power was on today and Sylvia had remembered to bundle Nicholas in three layers. Frieda could barely walk wearing the two sets of leggings and the multiple sweaters her mother had put her in. "You don't have to swaddle the girl," Ted had said as Sylvia got both her children ready to go on this outing with their father.

They were going together, as a family, to the London Zoo. It had been Ted's idea. He wanted to take the children somewhere special and this was the only place he could think to take them. The London Zoo was a place the children had been numerous times with both parents. The parks were already frozen over and though the zoo was outside, it was still open and there were leaves on some of the trees and at the very least, Sylvia noticed when they reached the zoo, they were not the only people there.

It felt odd waiting in line to enter the park on such a cold day. The metal turnstiles felt like an entrance to the tube. There were signs for the penguins (it was certainly a day for them) with the grand white walkways they'd built in the penguin pen, the ones that looked postmodern like you were at a new age airport. There was another sign for the big cats (though the London Zoo did not have anything as grand as a lion), which were only in metal cages. Most of the zoo was metal and concrete. As a newly erected structure the zoo had come about in its present incarnation after the war and Sylvia could feel the hand of modernity all over the place. So many ultra white structures, so much metal and concrete it was as if these animals were to forget their natural environments and be happy to live in outer space.

Still, they felt like a family, mother and father and two children, a boy and a girl, waiting in line to enter the zoo on a quiet Saturday. Daddy was not off with That Woman and Mummy wasn't locked away in her room writing poetry. She wasn't standing at the window wringing her hands as the children ran around her ankles. Not that this was all domestic life was. Just the other day Frieda had helped her make dinner. Even though the girl was two years old they had had such fun together measuring flour and salt and stirring it all around with a great big wooden spoon.

"I don't know if many of the animals will be out," Ted said, grasping Frieda's hand as they walked toward the Big Cats exhibit just up a short hill. "It's very cold for them today."

"It's very cold for us today," Sylvia said, holding the baby tightly to her chest as he rested in his sling. She wanted to lean down and smell his soft, dark hair, but he was wearing a muffler over his ears and a hat over that.

When they reached the open space where the big cats, leopards and jaguars, ocelots and mountain lions, were supposed to be kept, there were none. "Mummy, where are the kitties?" Frieda asked, pulling on Sylvia's sleeve. Sylvia wanted nothing more, as Mummy, than to produce a big kitty for her daughter but it was cold and could the big cats, could any of these caged animals, really be blamed for not wanting to be outside? Better yet, why on earth were she and Ted outside, wandering around the London Zoo in the cold pretending to be a family? It was such a farce the two of them acting as if it were not cold, as if he did not live in a flat across town with That Woman, as if everything were normal when everyone who knew them knew very well that they were the farthest thing from normal.

"It's okay, honey," Ted told Frieda, bending to one knee to look her straight in the eye. It was like he was proposing, the gallant gentleman. He had not proposed to Sylvia that way. In fact she'd been the one to ask him to marry her and he'd only really said, "Why not?" Ted brushed a piece of the child's hair away from her eyes so gently and Sylvia could remember when Ted had done that with her on their honeymoon. They had been in Spain sitting out on their balcony. She'd turned to look at him and he'd said, "Here," and reached for her face to brush her hair out of it. She remembered thinking it was such a careful, such a sweet gesture.

Ted stood up, brushing his hands on his pants. He was only wearing the one layer and Sylvia was sure he was very cold. Still, he stood stoic in front of his daughter. "You know my collection *Wodwo* is being considered," he said off handedly to Sylvia. "I just got word from my publisher, it's going to be a beautiful book." It's going to be a . . . , Sylvia thought. It hasn't even been accepted yet and already it's going to be a beautiful book. She couldn't count any chickens until they hatched because most of her chickens didn't these days, but Ted could count on every success. Every chicken Ted ever counted, and some he hadn't even considered, hatched so perfectly for him.

"Congratulations," Sylvia said coldly. She had not meant to have such a chill in her voice but she couldn't help it. *The Bell Jar* was still not being published in America. Her last publisher had been shocked to learn that her pseudonym, Victoria Lucas, was really Sylvia Plath and her English publishers were sure this would help her case but it had not. They'd only been more kind in their rejection. It burned inside her body every little black and white letter that came stating "we're sorry to say" or "we have decided to go another way" or "does not fit our needs at this time." And don't they know what it feels like to write and write, to love something so much, to care for it as if it were a child, and to have it simply tossed aside as if no one wanted it? Like a child handing a prized picture she'd painted to Mummy and having Mummy toss it away right in front of her.

"Sylvia, I also wanted to bring up." Ted stopped and looked down at Frieda, who was now standing at the metal gates to the area where the big cats were supposed to play. "You know, we need to talk about selling the house."

"What about the house?" she asked, surprised. She'd had no idea this topic would come up. No wonder Ted had wanted her to come when he took the children out. This was not a family outing, he only wanted to be in public when he brought up selling their home and dividing the property.

"You're not living in it and we're not renting it out. I'm sure we could sell it for a good price right now. With the London housing market booming and people wanting to get out of the city, at least for a country estate, and the house is very big, Sylvia, I see no reason why we shouldn't get a good price for it."

"We? We? It was mostly my money that bought that house. You wanted to take a big loan out on it and I told you that would be wasteful, paying back all that interest. I took so much money from my mother and money from my family and from the sale of my book, so much of me is tied up in that house."

"I took an equal loan from my parents," Ted countered. "And my book sales were paying a lot more of our bills back then. My book sales pay a lot more of our bills now."

"Pay our bills?" Sylvia shot at him. If someone had been walking by they might take notice of the shrill in her voice. "You don't pay nearly enough of our bills. Sure you send some money for the children, but it doesn't cover the cost of food, Ted, and I had to rent out two floors of the flat because I live with our children. Tell me, how many nights have you spent with them? How many times have you put them to bed? Really put them to bed and dealt with them getting up in the middle of the night or Nicholas crying at two in the morning? When have you done that since you moved out of our house? And my expenses have more than doubled since you left, what with having to set up a new home on my own in London and I do my best, Ted, I do my best. Now you want to talk about selling our house? Why is that? So you can spend more money on That Woman?"

"Assia has nothing to do with this. She never even mentioned it. I just think it's practical. It's just sitting there and someone should be living in it. I can't afford to keep paying for the upkeep on that house."

"Then move in, Ted. Give me half the money and move into it."

"I don't want to move in," Ted argued and he looked like he might just start pulling his hair out. It was always like this with him. He would express some sort of opinion and she would start to argue and then he would get so angry and that would only make her angrier and this arguing had been going on for so long, well before the children . . .

"Is the house not good enough for her highness?" Sylvia asked, her voice turning eerily childish and singsong. "Does she want to live in the great big city, in the lap of luxury?" She spun around like a little girl playing ballerina while Ted just stared at her. "Tell me, has she left her husband yet? I heard he tried to kill himself when he learned about you two."

"Leave that out of it. It's not her fault she married an unstable man who cannot handle being left. And this has nothing to do with Assia, this is about the house and our finances." He came closer to Sylvia, grabbing her arm as she held the baby. He pulled her hard and she looked around, embarrassed that someone might see, that they might guess at what had gone on. Everything had been so neat and clean. They had been acting civil and then Ted grabbed her like that and she could feel everyone watching. He did not let go of her arm and half dragged her closer to a tree. "You know, Sylvia, why don't you make this easier for everyone and just kill yourself?"

"You'd love that," Sylvia countered. She tried to pull her arm away but Ted wouldn't let her, he held her closer and tighter. She felt his fingers digging into her skin even through the layers of clothing and wondered if he'd leave a bruise. Nicholas started to fuss in her arms and she finally yanked herself away from Ted, who let go, a sneer on his face. The poor baby was going to be hungry soon and she needed to find someplace indoors to feed him once she got away from her husband. "When you start taking care of your family's finances, Ted, you can start talking about selling the house." Sylvia walked away from him.

There were restrooms a few feet down the path. Nicholas was going to get hungry soon and he needed his bottle. Finally he wasn't breastfeeding. He was not latched to her body constantly, herself at the so primal beck and call of a squirming, living creature, but she still had to stop everything, take the already warmed bottle out and feed him. It was really not that much, not that hard, she was happy to do it. It was only that Ted drove her so mad and Ted never did things like help feed the baby anymore. She turned back to Ted, who was with Frieda, on his knees again talking with their little girl. Why did he never do this with Nicholas? Yes, he was a baby but he could show the child more love.

"Mummy," Frieda said, watching her mother with big, big eyes. "Can Daddy stay for dinner tonight? We're having Sheppard's Pie, can Daddy stay for it? He loves Sheppard's Pie, it's English like he is and we are."

Sylvia looked at Ted, who did not seem at all interested in her Sheppard's Pie. In fact he hadn't ever liked it very much when Sylvia made it for him while they were married. She plastered that smile on her face, the one she now showed to her family and friends, the one she gave herself in the mirror every day to tell everyone, to tell herself, it was okay. Everything was going to be okay. She was not going mad. She was not losing it.

"That depends on Daddy," Sylvia said, looking over at Ted she wondered if he could feel her seething. "He can only stay for dinner if he really wants to stay for dinner. But I believe Daddy is busy tonight, correct?" She looked over at Ted and he said nothing.

Esther Greenwood
Stonehenge 1958

WE COULD SEE it from the road as we were driving up. Right there as we turned a corner, in the middle of a long field of grass, like it had sprung out of the earth fully formed. It didn't seem at all as if ancient, human hands had dredged these stones from the sea and hauled it for miles. The field looked empty before we could see it but the road was crowded and we'd been in stopped dead traffic for fifteen minutes when we came over the crest of a hill and saw what all the fuss was about. It was far off and I wish I had brought binoculars. I could see it in my head, I'd seen plenty of pictures at this point, but there was something about seeing it in person, even through the glass of the windshield, even from so far away, that made me want to stop in my tracks and no wonder the traffic moved so slowly.

Stonehenge. Kinda made you want to get out and walk.

It wasn't that hard parking or getting to the site. "It's just up the path," a man in the lot informed us. "You'll see it. Don't even need to follow the path, just walk in the field. But watch out for sheep."

"As if the sheep would bother me," Tom muttered under his breath as we marched down the concrete walk that led toward the path to Stonehenge.

"You never know with sheep," I said, hurrying to keep up as Tom sauntered along as if we were late for something. "I heard somewhere that sheep can be incredibly intimidating when they want to, especially if you get too close to their young."

"Then I'll be sure not to mention that I want lamb for dinner tonight," Tom remarked as we walked toward the dirt path in the middle of a farmer's field. "I don't know why the government couldn't just buy up this field. Why do they let a guy farm here near such an important ancient monument?"

"Well, it's his land and they can't just take it," I said, defending a hypothetical farmer I'd never met.

"You're right." Tom sighed. "That would be bloody Communism."

We were in the middle of a field, wide and full of grass, some of it brown but most of it green. There was a little wooden fence that came up to about my hip and it was all very quaint and country as if we'd stepped back in time. Not to the time that those stones had been laid, there had been no sheep in England then, not sheep as we have now, and there were certainly no wooden fences no matter how tall. But I did feel as if we had gone back in time a hundred years as Tom opened the latch on the wooden fence that was marked "Path to Stonehenge." There was another little plaque on the fence and I stopped briefly to read it as Tom marched ahead on the dirt walkway. "Do not get between the animals and their young. This can cause them to act irrationally. Not responsible for attack by animals."

"I wonder what that means," I said to Tom, pointing backward toward the sign as he kept marching forward. "It says that they are not responsible for animal attacks."

"I don't think it's anything. Everyone is extra cautious these days. The sheep look perfectly harmless," Tom stated as he lifted his hands in the air as if he were going crazy or doing one of those very silly go-go dances that were so popular in London nightclubs. "Bloody bees, what is wrong with them?" He swatted at the insects as they buzzed around his head.

"You know, if you left them alone they'd go away," I said causally. I watched a family, a mother and father, run after two small children. At first it seemed like they were playing, something like tag, but after a while I could see that the mother was crying out in desperation as the father ran a bit too hard to grasp one child while the mother went after the other.

"Get over here, you!" the mother cried and I could almost hear the tears in her voice as she called to him. I almost wanted to laugh though I really did feel sorry for the poor mother. What was her life like running after children all day? Her face just seemed to crack as the children ran amok.

"You know," Tom started and I could hear it in his voice that I was in for a lecture. He had that kind of tone, one that said he was about to go on and on and on about something. "So you know," he went on. "They believe Stonehenge was built around 3000 BC. They think the stones might have been dredged up from the sea, that's something like hundreds of miles from here. But this kind of stone doesn't come from around here that much they know for sure. They're not sure just how the early people who built this thing might have gotten the rocks that far but anthropologists have decided that there are no rocks like this nearby. They believe this might have been an ancient burial site or, because of the way the sun hits the stones during the Summer and Winter Solstices, it had some sort of festival purpose."

"I see," I said, though I knew very well everything Tom had just gone on about and I said the next thing only to annoy him. "You know, some people think it was made by aliens."

"You can be so stupid, Esther," Tom scoffed and shook his head. We watched a small, rather stout and fat, man come close to a sheep.

"I wonder if it's a baby sheep," I said to Tom, pointing at the man as he stuck his hand out for the little sheep to sniff. The sheep did not appear to want to sniff his hand and only stepped back. The man then came closer to the animal and I could see more than hear the little sheep make some kind of noise.

"Get over here, you little—" I heard the mother from earlier, who was only a few paces ahead of Tom and I. She cried at her children, who only ran more quickly, though at least it was in the direction of the stones.

"I want to take one home, Mummy," the little girl cried, running away. "I want to take a big rock home and put it in the garden."

"Wouldn't that be nice," Tom stated, having apparently overheard the child as well. "A stone like that in the garden. Would make your property worth a fortune." The child ran right in front of Tom then, nearly tripping him up. "You might watch her better," he yelled at the mother, who looked down, embarrassed, as she tried to control her child.

Just then I watched the little man, who was still sticking his hand out to the small sheep as another larger sheep came at him. Tom and I stopped and I grasped his arm, it was big and muscular and I remembered why I was with him. At any rate at a time like this Tom could keep me safe. As the larger sheep approached I saw that it wasn't a sheep but a ram with horns and it reared its horns right at the stout little man and knocked him over. It didn't stop there and the man's arms flew in front of his face as the ram started to buck at him. I felt my stomach then, clutching it I worried that the ram might come at me.

"Stop it!" someone cried from behind us and Tom ran at the animal.

He was a hero sometimes, a real hero. He didn't even think about himself, not as he went at the animal, grasping its horns and tossing it a few feet to the side so it stumbled back, tripping on its own legs. The ram went at him and Tom jumped away and it missed, it tried to go at him again and he grasped his horns once more, this time holding

Jessica Stilling

the animal back. Tom's feet dug into the dirt as he held the animal at arm's length. The man who'd been attacked took a couple seconds to get up and I wanted to scream at him. "Move it, man, just move it, can't you see he's helping!" Here Tom was, risking his life, and the man just sat there as if he were playing dead. Finally the little man got up and scrambled, looking so unbecoming, so silly, as he tripped on himself and nearly fell over twice. Still there Tom was, holding himself together. Finally the ram gave up. The small animal, it must have been a lamb, had already lazily walked away and with it safe, the ram ceased its bucking and moved away from Tom, who let it go, cautiously stepping back as the animal walked in the opposite direction.

A few people who'd stopped to watch clapped as Tom returned. When he got close I grasped his hand and started fiddling with his coat. "Oh look, your black duster," I said. "It's torn and it was so nice."

Tom only smiled down at me grateful about the applause. "That's all right," he said, looking down and kissing me hard on the mouth before he finished speaking. He just grabbed me, he didn't even care if I wanted to be kissed. And I could tell by the way he kissed me, the way he held on too tight, that he was only doing it for the crowd he didn't give a damn about me. "You'll have to sew it up for me like a good little wife."

It had been so thrilling watching Tom save that man. Watching how he selflessly went into the lion's den . . . more like the ram's den, without thinking about his own safety. But why did he have to kiss me so hard that it hurt? Why did he need to mention that I could sew his coat for him? Was I being silly thinking that a man could sew his own coat? And to bring up my being his wife, I don't know why that bothered me, I did not want to be bothered by it and perhaps that upset me more and so I smiled politely (my mother had taught me to be polite). I kissed Tom once on the cheek (so as not to embarrass him around the people watching) and then I let go of him and marched toward those very big stones. If I had wanted to marry Tom . . . if I really wanted to marry him everything would have been all right but I couldn't shake the annoyance I felt at what he'd just said.

As we got closer to the stones it was as if they grew. They came out of the earth until they were on top of me. At first they were just rocks in the distance and I had to remember the black and white pictures I'd seen in the brochure Tom had given me last week, when he'd learned that he'd be speaking in Cardiff and we might as well try to come here on a little road trip. "I haven't been to Stonehenge since I was a boy," Tom had said. "And you know, you've been in England almost a year and you haven't seen it. What if you go back to America without ever having seen Stonehenge?"

"You make a very good point," I'd told him. But this was all before Micah had come to London and kissed me, before Tom had gotten down on one knee in Kensington Gardens.

I had never thought, not really, about seeing those stones but now that they were upon me it was their bigness that got me. It was not as if I were approaching them, walking a dirt path in the middle of a field of sheep with ten or so other tourists, it was as if the stones were moving, their ancientness producing a kind of magic. I walked up to them with so much ceremony as if this were a wedding.

"That was a good show back there, a good show," I heard a man say to Tom. "You saved that man's life."

"And really what was he thinking, there's a sign only a few feet away saying not to try and touch the sheep," a woman commented.

"Bloody idiot, should have obeyed the sign," Tom said as if he were the most sage mind in the vicinity. I hung back and waited for him. Who was I to throw a fit, to walk away from my boyfriend, after he'd acted so bravely? "It was instinct. I grew up in the wilds, I used to hunt and fish and my brother Marcus taught me how to act around wild animals. My brother, he's in Australia now, but he could wrestle a bull."

"Wow," a man said and I grasped Tom's hand as we continued our walk toward the stones. It was a decision really, a very conscious one, choosing between hanging back with Tom or running straight into the arms of those stones. The closer I got the more I could feel them and part of me just wanted to run to them and sit in their glory. But Tom was there. He didn't seem to particularly care about the stones and I had to think about him and what he wanted. Tom could get upset when I forgot about his needs.

Tom continued to talk about his time in Yorkshire and I'd heard it before. He used to spend all day fishing with Marcus. He would go into the woods for a week with his brother and never come out. He was going to move to Australia, where his brother lived, but at the last second he'd been hit by a bug that told him to stay in England and write poetry. I listened to Tom until we reached the stones and then I could hear no more and so I let go of his hand as Stonehenge opened before us.

They were a very big thing—those stones. I tried to take one of those gigantic breaths, the ones they are always talking about in movies where the air just moves through your body, but it was as if the air got caught somewhere, stuck in the ancient mist of an England that was not England, of a time before Arthur or Elizabeth, before all the King Henrys and their squabbling heirs. There were no Anglos or Saxons, it was a time when land was just land and the grass so green it ran for miles like the ocean. We reached the stones and everyone stopped. It wasn't just me, I wasn't special, appreciating such a sight, such a presence. We all saw, we all felt how powerful those stones were, but I couldn't be near people just then. I needed privacy to appreciate this. So I walked on and Tom did not follow me.

Who were these people who could make such a thing? It was the question on everyone's mind. Anthropologists had been studying this very thing for decades and while some stone utensils and clay pots had been found in the area no one could say just who, just what, these people were. Did they travel? They must have gone to the sea to get these stones but other than that did they go anywhere? Did the men hunt like Tom hunted? They must have used spears but had they invented something like the bow and arrow as the American Indians had? Did the women cook in pots, did they know how to wield fire . . . they must have but how well? Did they sit around at night looking up at the stars telling stories? These people, who had made such an enormous configuration, why did they do it if not in homage to a story, if not because they had looked up at the stars and seen and felt such wonder that they needed to tell stories and make art?

Then I thought, what if a stone fell off and crushed me? Wouldn't that just be a great way to die?

Had I felt that way ten years ago when I took the pills? Had it been a glorious death? Then again isn't every suicide glorious? To take a life, your own life, to keep it in the palm of your hand and just hold it there, wasn't that enough? I remember everything had felt so hopeless. I had been so hung up on purity then. This was before Micah. It had been Dick Norton and I'd thought we were staying pure together and when it turned out only I had been silly enough to buy into that sham it nearly broke me—all the lies the world was telling. I wondered which other things about the world, which other constants my mother and my teachers and society in general had told me, were false?

I didn't sleep at first and then I just slept and slept and slept and I didn't bathe and I started to smell but I just didn't care and after a while life got to be too much. The weight of my own body, which had gotten so thin because I wasn't eating, felt like too much and then it just seemed like what was the point? I took those pills and I lay down and went to sleep. It was glorious, just going to sleep, and I knew when I awoke it would all be okay even if it was all black. Even if it was all just over it would be okay. And then I'd woken up, the pills had not worked, and they found me.

It was the electroshock that was the worst. They placed me on a bed and tied me down and I thought, "This is only supposed to happen in the movies, they only torture people like this when it's not real." But the way those leather straps felt on my wrists, I wasn't sure how badly they were going to hurt me. Then they placed something on my head, they tied it right on and it was so very big and I closed my eyes before it even started. They put something in my mouth so I didn't bite my tongue, they said I might bite it right off if I didn't have it but I almost choked on it anyway. I felt like an animal bound and gagged and it was awful but what was worse was that I didn't know what was happening. No one told me. I just waited and waited and then it came like a great wave, as if the entire ocean had pummeled over me and it was like I was one of those great big rocks and the water just kept washing over me again and again, beating me, beating me down and I closed my eyes and wished it was over.

I remember it made me feel so incredibly tiny like I could hide in the fibers of the floor.

And when it was over my mind got all fuzzy, like I was looking at everything, at my whole entire life, from under water and I couldn't see. I couldn't really see except I was too screwed up to even wonder if I had gone blind. And I didn't really know who I was and the nurse, who I was supposed to know from before, I couldn't remember her at all and it was as if she were a stranger. It was as if my entire life were a stranger and that lasted a couple of days before I really woke up and realized what they'd done to me.

But I did remember and got better. They had to do it to me a couple of times, the electroshock, but I got better and they let me out and I finished college and got a Fulbright Fellowship and met Tom, a poet who is about to speak at a conference in Cardiff. Now he wants to marry me and why on earth do I need to think about it? Why on earth had I not just said yes right away?

But they all thought it had been school or the Fulbright or Tom that had made me better. But it had been Micah, Micah who fixed me. Micah took me to the opera and the theater. We saw all these plays from a school called "The Absurd" and Micah talked about how there was this new kind of way of making art that didn't care at all about realism but it wasn't fantasy either, it was just really strange, and how all the French directors were making such weird, wonderful movies called New Wave and he wanted to move to Paris just to see them.

We were sitting near the worksite of Lincoln Center, having just seen the Ballet do a new production of *Swan Lake* at Carnegie Hall one night and I had a kind of epiphany. We were looking at the beginnings of the white buildings and the yellow streetlights glowed right through the glass of the structure as if we were right next to the stars, like in a Van Gogh painting. "It's Modernism," Micah had said, draping an arm around me as we looked up. I had heard about Modernism in college. I had studied it extensively and yet I'd never seen it like this. There it was in that great big building made not of stone but of more modern materials like concrete and glass. "Or it will be when it's finished. You know, modernism, it's not about ornament, it's about the essence of the structure itself. Like Cubism, how an animal, a person, a building, a plant, a star, it's all just a series of lines and angles seem from all different sides. We can pretend there's something more, some essence, but the lines and angles, that's really their essence, that's really all we see. And the Cubists, like Picasso, they knew that. But the Modernists, they knew that as well. It's the essence, art in general is just trying to get to the very essence."

"No ornament," I had said. "But this place is beautiful."

"Something doesn't have to be overly done, overly made up, to be beautiful," Micah had said. Then lifting my face he looked right at me with his great big eyes and a tiny strand of his pitch black hair fell into his face and I almost moved it for him but he looked so innocent just a little bit ruffled like that. "Sometimes the essence itself that's the beauty of it. Sometimes, in great, rare cares, that's all the beauty we need." He kissed me then, lifting my lips to his and I melted into him. There had been no one else just a pure, near blinding essence.

I looked up at the stones. It wasn't a grey day. What they say about London and its fog is so unassailably true. But it was not grey or cloudy as I looked up at those stones and the sun shone through them and I saw it, I felt it. The very power of this place came over me and it was like the great electric shocks they'd given me and I was almost pummeled over.

I touched the white-grey stone once more, feeling its power as if a great force flowed through this monument, as if those ancient people, who'd created such a place, just as our modern people were making Lincoln Center, were running through me a great surge as if a fuse had backfired inside me.

I looked up and there was Tom talking with more people. He was standing there with three girls. They were tall, one of them blond, the other two had darker hair but their hair was long and flowing and they were thin. They wore skirts above their knees and tight little blouses and one of them kept getting closer to Tom, touching his arm every few seconds. He looked right down at her, smiling, and I could just picture the little twinkle in his eye as she touched him.

It brought me back to the time when I had been fat because of the medication I was on. I felt my stomach bulge and my thighs rub together. My shirts didn't fit, my arms were too fat and I felt big and sloppy. And why, why did I let those girls, who were really only talking to Tom, do that to me? I could no longer feel the stones, their bigness, their power. Maybe it's not even Micah, Micah was only a placeholder for something else, something more, and it's this feeling, this responsibility to Tom, that causes my gut to collapse every time I think about marrying him.

Tom walked away from the girls but I still felt big and clumsy, old and ugly and fat, the damage had been done even as he approached, even as he smiled and waved as if I were the only girl in the world. "So, what do you think, pretty big, eh?" He touched my shoulder and something shattered. It had shattered before but it shattered more now.

"They're just so big," I whispered and in their place, in a flash of an instant as if time and space could collapse, could fold and I could be in two places, two times, at once, I saw Lincoln Center and Micah. I wanted that moment back, not just home but that entire life and if only I could go back to that moment at Lincoln Center and live in it forever. I could just stand there in stasis, one single essence.

"So you know, I was talking to some girls and they said that there are some pretty happening parties out by the stones. They bring liquor and just set a fire off in the distance and dance around and I bet it's pretty cool, you know? Maybe on our way back from Cardiff we could check it out."

"I thought we had to get back to London."

"I don't know," Tom said. "But it might be interesting. They were talking about how the Conservation Society wants to outlaw the parties, but it's a public space, you know, it's for all the English people, and their guests of course, this is a monument to our past and the government shouldn't just tell people what they can and can't do unless they're really hurting someone."

I could have made an argument. I could have said something like, yes but what about keeping the stones as they are for future generations? What about protecting them? When did people have a God-given right to set bonfires and throw parties, that does seem a little excessive, doesn't it? But I said none of that. It would only make Tom angry and I did not like Tom when he was upset. I just looked out at the stones. Sometimes Tom has this look about him that takes my voice away.

If I looked out far enough . . . then I could feel the stones again. Tom wasn't there, I could make him disappear and there was no one else in the world. Maybe that's what I needed, not Micah, not Tom, only to be alone, for there to be no one else in the world.

Tom kept talking, he put his hand on my shoulder and finally I looked back at him. "Could you just . . . could we be quiet for a second? Could you just let me look?" I said it quietly. I wasn't angry, not on the outside, and Tom only nodded. He stepped back and let me look.

I could see it again, the yellow lights shining through Lincoln Center like a bonfire, the way the people had moved about the bones of those Modernist buildings. And these stones, what would Micah have said about them? I could just picture him talking about poetry and art and symmetry and those stones. I felt it again, those ancient people, as if the hands of the women who had beaten leather clothing with rocks to make a shirt, as if the religious figures that sat all day staring up to chart the stars, passed through me as Micah passed through me and it was all so still, so calm, so real, as if all of humanity breathed inside my body.

"And you know, I think we should take the back roads so we don't intersect with the London traffic," Tom said, placing his hand back on my shoulder. "The major roads are a mess now."

I turned around then and pushed his hand off. I didn't look back at him, I don't know what face he made but I just started walking. It was shattered, all of it shattered, and you can only hold all of space and time, such an ancient prophecy, for so long before the rest of the world comes in and shatters it. I know what people would say, if my mother knew I was having such strange thoughts she'd call me crazy.

She'd wonder if I needed the electroshock again. But every time I feel too insightful it seems someone wants to lock me up in the loony bin. That's why I try to keep my insights to myself.

I kept walking but I could hear Tom behind me, his shoes, the way his pant legs rustled as he marched. "Hey, wait up, where are you going?" he asked and I turned around and smiled. If I started a fight here Tom could get mean. If I didn't act annoyed, Tom wouldn't fight with me, that was his way. He could ignore things most of the time. It was only when he was really mad, only then should I watch out. He could just let things go when I'm quiet and at the end of the day isn't that what a girl wants from her husband?

"Hey where're you going?" Tom called after me.

"Back to the car," I said, taking a deep breath to calm myself. "It's getting late. Don't we have to get to Cardiff?"

"Ah, right, of course," Tom said, catching up he walked quietly alongside me.

I stopped and turned around and there they were once more. The stones. No one even knew what it was for, why an ancient people had made it, but there it was, such a very big thing. I didn't want a camera. I didn't want to take a picture so I could look back at it always. Besides, there are plenty of pictures of Stonehenge and it isn't as if it's ever going to change. That was the thing, it wasn't as if it's ever going anywhere. It was as if I wanted to create something, a time machine maybe, but not something so scientific, so silly, something more, something that came from the mind and the body and the sprit and I wanted to place a marker here, on this moment, like a bookmark or dog-earing a page to go back to always.

I stopped. I looked back. I wanted to close my eyes, to commemorate how sacred this place was but I couldn't. I couldn't stop looking. I knew Tom would call me, he would say something innocuous, like, "Shouldn't we be getting to the car?" or "Aren't we supposed to be on our way?" He would touch my shoulder again and it would be too much. It would all be too much. And so I did not close my eyes I just kept looking. I kept looking and looking until I knew the world had to take me away. I turned from the stones and the moment I could not see them I missed them. And I knew, I just knew I always would.

I close the manuscript and feel it then, the immensity of what Esther was feeling, the decision she was making, the one she'd already made. Life is sometimes just too inevitable. Theo called tonight, that's why I'm reading the manuscript. I needed something to get the bitter taste of his words about Heather, about the girl who visited the other day, out of my mind. Staring out at the sea I wonder if like Stonehenge this is all such a very, very big thing.

Lorelei

PROVINCETOWN SITS AT the edge of the world, the kind of place that speaks of sea monsters too far out. It was the first stop the pilgrims made before landing at Plymouth Rock. It's so desolate, so out of the way, even when it's built up, that the pilgrims who'd spent months at sea wouldn't even consider staying here. They didn't bother to drop anchor but barreled straight ahead to a place that looked more hospitable.

Years later braver interlopers settled here—the artists. The church and big business couldn't tame this place but the artists did. They came in a trickle and then in droves and it was the artists who made Provincetown what it is now. Eugene O'Neil used to live here at the turn of the twentieth century. He stayed in a white clapboard house and spent all his time wandering the beaches and writing and performing plays with his friends, Max Eastman and Jack Reed. Later Philip Roth vacationed here and Norman Mailer called this place home for a while. Poets and painters, actors and musicians, have built this place. Provincetown has had a rich history with its tiny winding streets full of clapboard buildings, little signs advertizing book stores, art galleries and candy shoppes (the kind with two p's and an e on the end) as the many colored flags fly every few feet. It's like the entire town, at least in the summer when tourist season is upon it, looks like a ticker tape parade.

"I really do love P-Town," Joanne says as we watch three all-male couples walk hand-in-hand down the tiny sidewalk. "A mini San Francisco, you know?"

"I wonder when it got this way," I consider.

"The seventies really, in the eighties it was full swing. Now it's just a part of the culture. You know *Long Day's Journey Into Night* was written a few miles away."

"I love that play," I say as we walk out of the hot and humid street and into an air-conditioned bookstore. It's small and cramped and musty, like any good bookstore. The walls are dark red and the shelves and floor are made of nicked wood. The contrast of heat and air conditioning sends a shiver under my skin as I walk toward the back, near a display of "local" poetry.

"I wonder if Sylvia used to shop at a place like this," Joanne ponders. I have never heard her referred to as just Sylvia. Her name has become such a bone of contention. Some saying her name is and will always be Sylvia Plath, while others call her Sylvia Plath Hughes even though she was about to divorce her husband when she died. The name Hughes has been scraped from her grave by vandals or concerned literary protectors, it depends on how you look at it, so many times that it might just sit empty now. "I remember when we were on the Cape together, she used to love coming to Provincetown just to see what kind of college boys were there."

"When she was in college, I think I read, she was boy crazy."

"Everyone was back then," Joanne replies. "I mean, I wasn't but even I pretended to be. I had to, it wasn't like today, if you weren't dating boys there was something really funny about you and I didn't want that. I wasn't strong enough to stand up for who I was until I got older. Girls dated until they were pinned, until they started going steady. It was a way to prime them for motherhood and those great domestic lives they were supposed to live. It really was sinister, if you think about it, the way it worked. But girls like Sylvia were encouraged to find a man, the 'right' man, to a certain extent, and then to keep him all her life. She had to hold onto her man for dear life because if she didn't her life was over. That's at least what the myth was in the fifties. No wonder Sylvia got so depressed after Ted cheated on her."

"Sounds stressful."

I walk back toward the display of poetry books and in addition to many authors I've never heard of, poetry being a medium that lends itself to obscure authors unless they are either very famous or very tragic, sits *The Colossus* and *Ariel*, Plath's two collections. I pick up *Ariel*. It's an older edition, maybe a first edition, though it's not marked as such. There's no jacket only a blue hardback covered with dust and gold letters. "*Ariel*" it reads, "Poems by Sylvia Plath." I touch the cover, then open the book and run my hand gently down its pages.

"It's about a horse," a voice behind me booms and I jump before I recognize Joanne. "The poem "Ariel," it's about a horse. I mean, that's the imagery she's using."

"But she was really writing about Prospero's Ariel, you know, from *The Tempest*," I feel the need to over explain. It's the English professor in me. "The spirit of the island that Prospero basically holds prisoner just like Caliban. Only Ariel is more ethereal, Ariel is content to just be until Prospero leaves the island and lets her go. She doesn't spend her time being angry, like Caliban."

"Were you a literary critic in a former life?" Joanne half laughs.

"I think I might be one now. My agent has asked me to write a review for a literary journal on a book she's representing. I think I should. It's the least I can do since I'm never going to be able to finish this novel."

"Too much going on?" Joanne asks as if she's about to play psychotherapist.

"Remember I told you about my former student who died? I got a letter from her mother. It wasn't bad but it's just putting it all front and center again."

Still holding *Ariel* I raise it up to show Joanne. "You know, I can see where the woman who wrote these poems wrote the manuscript you gave me. I just finished the Stonehenge section and I feel so much for Esther. I see so much of Plath in the way she pines after Micah because Tom just doesn't get her."

Joanne looks around, eyeing the clerk at the front of the store, a heavy man with greasy hair and large 1970s glasses.

"You know, I remember when she gave that to me. She said, 'Joanne, you keep this safe. Don't you let anyone touch it.' She said she'd stopped trusting Ted. She wasn't confident that he'd do what was right with her work. She didn't want her mother or her brother or any of her London literary friends to have it. She sent it to me because she trusted me so much. I was the only one who could have it because we were close, but not very close. It's funny because no one knows about me but I swear, Sylvia, the way she sent me that manuscript, it was like she couldn't trust anyone but me." Me, me, me, I had heard this kind of talk before from my mother but I don't want to see it now. Joanne is not my mother. She is a perfectly capable, perfectly fine New England woman. "And when she sent it to me she said that I was to keep it forever and never let it out of my sight. And I think I've done a pretty good job of it, right?"

"I'm really grateful you lent it to me," I tell her, looking away. I don't want to see what I think I see, the tremor in her voice, the way she won't look me in the eye. It's not that she's lying, it's more than that but I don't want to see it. "My friend Amelia has a friend who works in book publishing. I think he's an editor for Faber and Faber. Maybe he could take a look at it. And my agent, I'm sure my agent would love to get her hands on it. It's the least I can do after not handing in my own manuscript." I look her in the eye and I know. I have pushed the envelope. I should not have done that. I used to do that with my mother after a while. I don't even know why, it never felt good or right or helpful, but as a child I still pushed her a little too far. I didn't even know I was doing it with Joanne but I see it in her eyes now.

"No, no, no," Joanne whispers quietly. She places her hands on her head as if she's just heard a very loud and high-pitched screech. "No," she nearly shouts as if I have just given her the most terrible news. "I didn't give that to you to do whatever you wanted with. I didn't think you'd carry it all over town telling people about it."

"We talked about it at a party," I reply, unsure of her rising voice. "I thought that meant it was common knowledge. I don't have to give it to my agent, you don't have to give anyone permission to publish, I just thought maybe I could tell them about it."

"It's common knowledge that it exists, yes, I tell lots of people many things, but I don't go around trying to publish them. She never wanted that manuscript to see the light of day. It's her own private thoughts on her private life, a life that was violated when Ted cheated on her. A life that ended. It was a very bad time for her and she wrote that manuscript to deal with it, to come to some sort of catharsis and to think positively about how her life might have been. That's why she wrote it, she was in mourning for so much. That's what art does, it teaches us how to live in the world, how to be more ourselves, how to mourn, how to just mourn. But it is not your place to go showing people."

"I haven't shown anyone. I've barely talked about it. I just think it should be shared. The artist is gone, she killed herself, the least we can do is make sure her words get out there, that people read her and hear her. Ted has been dead for years, what could he do? You showed it to me, if it was such a violation why show it to me?"

"I thought it would be good for you. You looked like you needed it."

"Others might need it too. It could get others reading her poetry."

"People will always read her," Joanne cries out and the three or four customers browsing the bookshop stop and stare at this large long haired hippie of a woman as she places her hands on her head, pulling her own hair as if she might rip it out of her skull. "People will read her before they read . . . what is this?" she cries picking up a small book from the poetry table. "Kiefer Mayflower? Who the hell is going to read him?" She takes the book and throws it on the floor. "Or this lady Brooke Greenwald? What kind of names are these?" She throws this one on the ground as well. She picks up a bigger volume. It is pink with a picture of a cherry blossom on it. "Yokko Mitsusaka? Who the hell is this?" She opens the book and starts reading to herself, whispering words I can't make out. She tears one page after another. Page after page falls to the floor in a shower like cherry blossoms and finally I lunge for her, ripping the book from her hands. It pains me to see a book, even one I don't know, treated this way.

"I'm sorry," I tell the man in the 1970s glasses. He's done nothing, just sat and stared, while Joanne throws this fit. "I'll pay for that."

"I think it's time you head out," the 70s glasses guy says, leaning back.

"Head out, you want me to head out? I knew the greatest living poet and you want me to get out?" Joanne stares the man down. "You think I'm crazy?"

"Yep," he says matter of factly. "Don't make me call the police." This is a bookstore in Provincetown, a pretty nice tourist area, I can't imagine women come in and tear up books that often but he acts like this is par for the course.

"I'll pay for it," I reiterate and Joanne puts her hands on her head, she gives one terrifying scream turns around, and stomps out the door. I see a different woman, my mother, a woman with short black hair and tiny dark eyes. She wore stonewashed jeans and T-shirts everywhere. And usually she was okay, usually she was, but there were days my mother reminded me of this.

I feel the weight of the Plath book still in my hands. Turning it over I read the price tag. It's $1500. It must be a first, if not a very early, edition. At least Joanne had not ripped anything as expensive as that. I consider asking the seventies glasses man at the cash register why he would let such an expensive book sit out like this but it's not my business. I'm beginning to see that a great many things are not my business.

I put the book down carefully, like it's made of gold or diamonds, and crouch to the floor, picking up first the two poetry collections that survived Joanne's outburst and then the pages of the Mitsusaka. I might as well take the book if I'm going to pay for it. Fifteen dollars not exactly a bank breaker but more than I'd planned to spend here.

The way she left, the look in her eyes just before she turned away from me, I've seen it before. There is something, like a cornered animal that cannot focus, that reminds me of my mother. Most of the time she was okay. Most of the time I could go into the kitchen where she might be making dinner or sitting at the table with a calculator paying the bills and I would sit down with her and it wasn't ever very deep, neither of my parents were very deep people, but I'd tell her about one of my friends at school or how I really hated math or something on TV. She'd laugh, she'd smile, she'd nod and go on about her business. Life is full of nothing moments but it's the bad ones, the ones that sting, that follow us around. And as a young girl my mother had already gone through so much. How come it was only a few days ago that I learned this about her? She lived her whole life with those memories and I only know about them now.

I take the remains of the poetry collection and hand the man a twenty and wait as he fumbles for my change.

"You should get her help, you know," he tells me and I nod. It's not worth explaining to him.

By the time I'm outside, Joanne is nowhere to be found. Tourists crowd around fudge shops and little toy stores selling flimsy plastic snow globes and figurines. A large group of what must be high school students all wearing the same neon yellow shirt march down the street, taking up all four corners of it as they are led by a small, older woman carrying a sign that reads "Travel Club." Once they've passed I cross the street and march toward the ocean side of town. I can see it, the wide wisps of sand so very big, long tall dune grass coming up as if out of the sea and I wonder why anyone would build a town so close to such natural wonders. Mother Nature must be annoyed at the ruckus we've made so near her boarders. I find a short concrete path down closer to the water and it's there, at an open, ocean facing white painted art gallery that I see another familiar face, more like the back of a head.

"Theo?" I ask and he turns around.

"Lorelei, how are you?" Theo asks. "Fancy seeing you here." It's funny how much he is my ex, how much we have been through together, what he did to me, what we did to each other, and still when I run into him out on the street it's like any chance encounter . . . "fancy seeing you here."

"I'm with a friend. I got tired of sitting by the ocean staring out to sea like some sort of worried widow in a Victorian novel. I thought I'd see what big city life was like."

"How's it treating you so far?" Theo asks.

"I can't complain. Amelia wants me to go to New York with her next month, before the fall semester. She has to do an interview and it might be nice, maybe I'll get some writing done. New York hotels always did stimulate my creative juices."

"We should have settled there," Theo says with such nostalgia. Settled there, as if it is a place to mark your territory, an unexplored terrain in need of its own pioneers. "I'm about to do the Cape Cod Rail Trail. A few of the guys from work who are out here wanted to try it. Remember when we did that?"

"I do. We were out in the woods for hours. Afterwards you found a tick on my leg and two weeks later I had Lyme's Disease."

"Ah, yes. The great big woods never were very good for you."

"But I like them. There's something about being lost in them. You look up and there's this great green ceiling."

Theo laughs at that and turns back to the art he was eyeing. It's then that I see what it is, a fine, cubist-like painting of a girl with long blond hair wearing a University sweater. It's her eyes, that's the focus of the picture, they are so sad and helpless but there is something innocent and full of faith and love in them. "Is that yours? Are you selling it?" I ask and Theo nods. Theo only dabbled in painting in college and graduate school but after we separated he took a studio and had his own artistic explosion. Art and pain, at least for one of us it's been creatively fulfilling.

"It's silly, one of my partners owns a stake in the gallery, it's not like it's up on my artistic merits or reputation. But they're trying to sell a few of my paintings. I know it's a favor but it's still nice."

"Good for you." Looking over, I see another picture of a woman lying in a bed staring up at the ceiling only the ceiling isn't plaster, it's the moon. There's another landscape of New York City and one that's just splashes of color angrily crossing every which way. "Her mother wrote me. Probably because Barry is out . . . also because of the girl, her niece, but I think she just wanted to get a lot off her chest. Did she contact you?"

"No, and she won't. I just . . . I'm sorry, Lorelei, I can't do this, I can't talk about her now. I know I'm looking at her picture but I just can't."

"I understand. And I'm sorry about the other day, I really didn't know who the girl was."

"It's okay." Theo shakes his head as he steps away. His voice cracks and I know to move back, to leave him be. "Do you remember when we went to Cardiff?" he asks as if he can sense my desire to leave and so he must pull me back. "When we looked out at the bay? I remember thinking that it would have been nice to just walk into the water, just walk into it and never come out."

"You didn't seem to be thinking that at the time." I want to ask if he's okay but he'll only brush direct concern off.

"It just seemed so peaceful, you know? And in so many years, Lorelei, how much peace have we known?"

"I don't know," I reply softly, my words falling flimsy from my lips.

"I don't know either, I guess it's not my place to find out." He looks back at the painting. I move closer to him and he steps away and so I back away once again. We're in such an awkward dance. It reminds me of junior high parties.

"I have to go find a friend of mine. But your work is lovely."

"Thanks, get back safe," he says offhandedly and our pleasantries are over.

Provincetown is packed with tourists in shorts, many of them wearing hats and fanny packs, and I have to push through them, sticky arms and legs gracing my exposed skin, as I walk back out on the main street. Where could Joanne be? I wonder, about to pull out my phone. I know she likes books and Plath but beyond that I don't know where she would go after storming off the way she did.

As a wave of tourists part I find her standing at the glass counter of one of the many old-timey fudge shops on this street. They are all about the same, all purporting to serve only "homemade" products, all stating that they are the oldest, the most original of the original fudge shoppes (again with two p's and an e at the end) in Provincetown, as if fudge were the national commodity, something that grows naturally out of this salty ocean soil. This shop, reminiscent of something popular around the year 1904, has bright pink walls and a cotton candy machine near the back. A little kid runs in and his mother grasps his arm and pulls him out, but he reaches, as if he has an absolute need to get to the candy. I feel my stomach then and wonder how old my own son would be. A year or thereabout, I can't even keep track anymore. If I kept track, if I let myself think about it, it would break my heart. Even if Theo left me, I'd have had him, a little boy to cart around and pull out of candy stores. Sure it would have been difficult but he would have been mine and I would have something real to show for my life, something besides an unfinished novel.

"I'd like to try the cherry," Joanne says. She peers behind the counter to tell the teenage-looking boy complete with greasy red hair and acne not to mention that "I'm terrified of real adults" stare they sometimes get. "And the vanilla. I wonder how well they'd go together." The boy just looks at her as if he doesn't know what to do with such a large, self-possessed woman. He reaches under the counter and pulls out a tiny wooden spoon of red fudge. Joanne takes it, puts it in her mouth and says, "Mmmm, I like that, I really do."

"Hello," I say and Joanne half jumps like she's been caught before turning around.

"Lorelei, hello. I was wondering where you went off to." She smiles as she welcomes me. Her eyes are big and happy and it's as if she never ran off, as if she never yelled at me in the bookstore. My mother used to do such things. After a crying fit at a pizza place during my tenth birthday party, just as my father was cleaning up the mess from the fork she'd chucked across the room, my mother wiped her eyes, stood up, and said, "All right, girls, how about a trip to the mall? I'll give us all makeovers."

"I was just wandering," I tell her timidly, as if I deserved the scolding she gave me earlier. "I saw Theo, he's here."

Joanne grimaces as if she can't help herself. "Well then we best be leaving this town. I don't want to be in the same place as your good for nothing ex."

"He's okay. He's riding on the Rail Trail later."

"I love the Rail Trail," Joanne cries excitedly, grasping my arm for a second and I can see she's getting hyper. "We should do that sometime. It's supposed to be cool in a couple of days, too cool for the beach and who wants to come to the silly old city when they can be out in the woods?"

"Okay," is all I can say.

"Thewoodsyouknowwhatthatmeansthewaythewoodsarethesedaysandyouneverknowwhomightbethere," Joanne says. Her words blending together and she's talking a mile a minute. This is familiar. I've seen this before. "Iusedtotakemysistertothewoodsandthenmymwouldyellatmeanditwasreallyverywillall."

"I think I need to get you home. Are you sure you're going to be okay?"

"Of course, silly," Joanne replies, laughing extra loud now as if for the boy behind the counter's benefit. "Just let me buy this fudge. It's really important, I need to get this fudge for Tammy. If I don't come back from Provincetown with fudge it'll break her heart." There are almost tears in her eyes now and I wonder why this fudge is so important. Then again I don't wonder, I don't wonder at all, I've seen this with my mother and I know.

"Of course. Let's get your fudge and then I think I should drive us home." I know there's a way to handle this, a better way than I am. Yes, my mother could get this way but that doesn't make me an expert in these types of mood swings. People always think that, because of my mother, I'm an expert in mental illness. I wish this were the case. I wish I could have picked something up with osmosis but it doesn't work that way and when I see this, I'm just as frightened, just as clueless, as most people. My father tried to shield me from my mother, he always took care of her, but even him . . . it's not like either of us were medically certified to understand this and I can only be patient. "Joanne, are you okay? Do you need help? Should I call Tammy?

"I'm okay, totally fine. And besides, it's my car, I can drive us, honey," Joanne tells me, pointing behind the glass counter. "I need two pounds of cherry and seven and a half of vanilla, can you do that?"

"That's a lot of fudge," I pipe in, looking the boy behind the counter in the eye like I am the adult and he should listen to me. "It's just you and Tammy, I think half a pound each should be fine."

I wait for Joanne to counter, to insist, to start crying and accusing me of not understanding but she looks over at me, then at the boy, and nods. "You heard the lady, half a pound each and step on it." She laughs as I fumble with my bag. It's a big bag and the Plath manuscript is inside. I'm almost finished and I had wanted to use this time with Joanne to talk about it, but that ship has sailed, I know it. That ship has sailed way off down the coast and I will not be able to catch it today.

Sylvia
1962

THE SIDEWALKS WERE made of slush that gathered all around Sylvia's feet as the icy muck seeped through her wool-lined boots. She pulled her grey wool coat collar up over her neck and felt the chill of her leather gloves on her skin. She and the children had just gotten over a bout of the flu, there had been sniffling and sneezing, vomiting and just so much that it had sent them all to their beds for days. Sylvia was just getting her strength back when this new cold spell hit. And now it was the mucky brown water filling the tub and the heat going off. The gutters were bursting with snow and wet rot was seeping through the ceiling. Water might just burst over her while she was in bed. To wake to that! Or to not wake at all. But when Sylvia asked the estate agent about it he just looked at her with beady little eyes and said since the pipes were inside, even if they had frozen outside, they were not responsible. And besides all the workmen were on strike so there was no one to help with the leak anyway.

The weather had taken over even though there were nearly three more months of winter, Christmas wasn't even upon them and already the pipes were frozen. The landlord had sent Sylvia a letter telling her to be careful of the pipes, to always keep the heat going and so she'd been depositing coins into the heater so it might run. And to think, putting coins into a heater to make it run, Europe was so primitive. It was when the pipes were not used, the letter had instructed, when they were kept cold, that they froze and so one had to be forever vigilant during cold spells like this. She must always put coins in the heater as if it was her job to protect a home that she did not own. When she was away she told the girl to make sure even the rooms they weren't using were heated, though it was costing her a fortune in coins and she was constantly having to run to the market for change. If the pipes froze, the landlord had warned, it might be days without hot water and here she was with frozen pipes and no water for cooking or cleaning, for bathing or even drinking. And the baby's formula used water as well and it was such a pain having to run out for water all the time in this cold.

Sylvia walked the sidewalk, stepping over puddles as she made her way to Al's flat. She'd called him earlier that evening. It had been a whim . . . not a whim really, that implies a flight of fancy, a bit of whimsy. Women who live in the darkness she lived in did not just go with things, they did not have whims and flights of fancy. It had been an act of desperation, to reach out to someone, anyone, who understood poetry.

The voice of poetry had been echoing in her head. She felt it writhing inside her every morning at four a.m. She couldn't get out of bed somedays. It wasn't only the cold it was the darkness. The worst of the depression came just after she woke up. It was the paralysis of it. Like a hand holding her down so she couldn't move. And she wanted to move so badly. The poetry was still in her and some mornings it was strong enough, the poetry extended a hand and lifted her out of bed and she could write. But there were other times when its hand was not strong enough and she fell weakly back onto her mattress and felt nothing, absolutely nothing, all day. Even when she got up to care for the children or when the girl came and helped her fix breakfast or when Jillian came over to check on her still she felt nothing. It was really very kind of everyone to care about her state of mind but then she'd get a rejection letter and she would spiral, falling all the way down. It was as if her mental health were a staircase she was always climbing and when she reached the top something would slip, a heel would break, a puddle of ice appeared, and she'd go tumbling back to the bottom stair by stair. A modern day Sisyphus but all of life was like the myth of Sisyphus nowadays.

But Al had said that he'd be in at least in the early evening. "I have dinner plans tonight, Sylvia, but you can come for a drink beforehand." And so she'd come at a quarter to six to visit Al Alverez, poetry editor for *The Observer*. He had been a friend of the family years ago. He'd spent some time over at the house in Devon, he and Ted used to go for a drink at the pub when they'd first moved to London. It was all very friendly and while he probably still spoke to Ted, he had been so kind to her at the party last week and so what if *The Observer* had rejected some of her poetry, he was a nice man and he and his wife had separated and so perhaps he would understand her loneliness.

Al lived in a flat nearby on the second floor of a row house much like Yeats' house only the front was a little more run down and the rubbish bins had not been brought in from the street. Sylvia stepped over a discarded tin can, smiling at it. The image of it, as the streetlight shined down on the snow laden ground like it was the surface of the moon, felt like something out of a movie, one of those slow moving New Wave films they were making in France. Sylvia rang the bell and Al buzzed her in. She opened the door cautiously, taking the tight staircase to the floor where Al lived.

"Sylvia," Al greeted as he opened the door. "I was so happy you called. I'm sorry, I already had plans for dinner, but I'd been meaning to ring you to see if you'd like to come round and talk poetry."

"Thank you," Sylvia replied, as if he'd paid her some kind of compliment. "It was just that I had time tonight and I've been writing so much. I thought I might share it with you if that's okay. Remember years ago, you used to come by our flat and Ted and I would read you our poetry and then we'd all go have a drink?"

"I do," Al replied. "I was laid up at that time, broke my bloody leg. I remember hobbling round and you and Ted were always so kind to me. Tell me, have you heard from Ted, how is he?"

Sylvia's eyes went downcast. "He's fine." She wanted to put him more at ease after asking about Ted, to draw up the lines of her smile so he might see the happy Sylvia he'd known years ago.

"Well, I'm sure everyone is fine. Tell me, are you keeping warm? How're the children?"

"We've been holed up in the apartment much more than we'd like. The pipes froze so we're dealing with that. We all had the flu last week, a nurse had to come and sit with us because I could not get out of bed."

"I know, this chill," Al said, sighing. They were talking about the weather. Two people of poetry with university degrees, two people who had studied at Cambridge and traveled Europe and here they were standing in a chilly living room in London talking about the weather. "So, a drink, can I get you a drink? I'm having brandy, it's not the best brandy in the world, but it'll do on a cold night like this."

"Brandy sounds lovely, thank you. And you're right, brandy keeps you warm," Sylvia replied as Al went into the kitchen to pour her a drink. Here she was again, talking about the weather.

Al handed her the glass of brandy and Sylvia sipped it carefully, prim and proper as her mother had done after dinner with her father when she was a little girl. She hadn't drank, really drank, in quite some time, not since the party and that had only been a glass of wine. She couldn't really afford spirits, not with the children and it felt so wrong, drinking alone. When the darkness was upon her she didn't need a glass of sherry or brandy to make it darker and that was really all drinking did these days, it turned up the darkness until she felt like she was falling through a black, black hole. Still, she sipped her brandy, enjoying the warmth and the way it went straight to her head. She could forget herself, she could forget the rejections and Ted and That Woman, the children and the fight she'd had with the girl today about keeping the house clean. She really needed to get a new au pair.

"So tell me, what've you been working on? How's your poetry going?"

"Oh, it's going," Sylvia replied. Then she remembered how they had only talked about the weather and she couldn't have that. No more simple statements. She remembered her Creative Writing teacher at Smith who had said that writers should not make simple statements. "But really, I've been getting up early, before the children, and writing so much. It's like the poetry is just coming out of me. It's always been there but it's like these poems are pouring out like they have existed since the dawn of the universe and it was always my job to find them. I was chosen to find them."

"That's wonderful, just wonderful. I just got one of your poems, "Lady Lazarus" I believe, it just came across my desk. I was going to read it on Monday, I figured it would be a treat to start my week."

"Thank you," Sylvia replied. "Ever since Ted left something's been awakened in me. I feel it starting to pulsate and I must write. Maybe it's that Ted and I, I thought we were so happy, and that happiness made me complacent and it made my poetry complacent."

"It is the curse of the poet to feel so sad," Al said, taking a sip of brandy as he looked Sylvia in the eye and she remembered the way Ted used to gaze across a room at her always with a hint of malevolence in his eyes. She should have seen it coming, it was always there and she should have seen it coming. "Happiness never made good art."

"No one else thought we were happy though. My mother said the last time she came to London, before that horrid call from That Woman, that she'd sensed something was wrong and all my friends, especially my female friends, said they never trusted Ted, but no one ever said that to me while we were together. It was only after the fact that people started to talk about Ted's wandering eye."

"People never want to warn you about the lion's den when you're in it. And so many people are terrible about taking advice, even if they say they want it. Would you have listened to your mother about Ted before you had proof?"

Sylvia looked at the scratches on Al's hardwood floor, she held her bandy glass before her like a shield. "No, I probably wouldn't have. Then again I wasn't always good at listening to my mother."

"Ah, well, none of us are good at that. But I never thought Ted was a bad guy, I can't say I saw this coming, but now that it has, I mean, Ted always did have a bit of a thing for the ladies. And the poet and vagabond, the gamesman who just wanted to be outdoors, I guess if you want to say the signs were there you could, but then again . . . maybe you couldn't."

"Life is strange like that." Sylvia sighed, wishing she'd not said something so cliché. "But my poetry just keeps getting rejected. Even your *Observer* hasn't taken anything in a while. Not that I'm complaining—"

Al looked the other way; if he had been wearing a tie he might have awkwardly loosened it. Sylvia wanted to put him at ease but instead she just watched him. "My editors sometimes reject things without sending them by my desk. I don't know why they would reject you, except we did publish three female poets last month and sometimes they feel that's enough."

"Is there a cap on the male poets you publish?" Sylvia asked, heat building in her blood. She hadn't realized it had been a matter of female poets. How silly of her not to realize that there were quotas on how many female poets were allowed to succeed.

"But tell me more about your writing, your poetry, where is it coming from, this new burst of creative energy?"

"The darkness," Sylvia admitted. "It happened before, when the darkness came. It seems it comes every ten years and once tragedy strikes I feel as if the words start pouring out of me. Like someone has stabbed me in the side like Christ on the Cross, and I know that's a terribly bad metaphor, but I just . . . as the words start pouring out I feel so inspired. But then the darkness comes. I felt it once before; did I ever tell you about it? When I was in college I tried to kill myself."

"I know a little. You've written about it, haven't you? That "Johnny Panic" story Ted gave me, that came from your experiences, correct?"

"Yes, it's about losing your mind. Really and truly losing it. And after I left Smith, when I stopped teaching there, I took a job back at the same mental institution where I had had electroshock and I remember seeing the patients, how crazy they seemed. Some of them would just sit there staring, others talked so much to themselves or told such wild stories about their lives. Once I watched a girl lash out at her nurses, she thought she had a knife, though she didn't, and she just kept trying to stab them with air. I don't know why the nurses didn't start laughing, I honestly thought it was pretty funny, but then again, it really is very, very serious. Another girl tried to explain very rationally to me how she was the best friend of Jackie Kennedy and it was very obvious she'd never even met her. But it wasn't a conscious lie. She really believed she and Jackie Kennedy were best friends. To do something like that you must be sick, very sick. And I remember thinking, 'I was that sick once but I got better. Isn't it nice, I got better.' But now I'm not so sure that I got all the way better. Maybe the darkness is a sickness you don't get all the way better from. But that's something people, normal people, don't see, you're not being mean, or silly, you're not 'acting out' when you're having a breakdown, it's just . . . like having the flu or food poisoning and throwing up all over the bathroom, you can't help it."

"Our mental health is a very serious issue indeed. And people, 'normal' people as you say, don't always understand it. You know I tried to kill myself once."

Al? Al Alverez, poetry editor for *The Observer*. Sure he was divorced and he drank a bit much but he always seemed so . . . if not happy then at least content. When on earth did this happen? She looked at Al and could see it in the crevices of his face, the darkness. Why had she not seen it before? "Really? How?"

"Pills. The coward's way out when you think about it. And honestly, I don't remember a thing about it. I wish it were more engrained in my mind. I wish I knew what I'd done, really done. It was only after the fact that I learned. I had been drunk, really, really drunk. It was Christmas and I was sick and laid up in bed and people had come to visit me in my room all day like a little invalid. This was during my time home visiting England, during my year abroad in America. I was home visiting my family and my marriage wasn't working, we both knew it. I loved my daughter, I wanted to make it work with my wife but things were spiraling and it was my fault. I was drinking too much, all the time I was drinking too much, and after the party was over I guess I came downstairs and I drank some more and then I took some pills, a great many pills, and when I woke up I was in hospital and my stomach had been pumped but they were not sure I would survive. I had vomited into my lungs, you see, that's what would have done me in, and they had to get that out. It was all a mess, a big, bloody mess and I don't even remember doing it, taking the pills, but I had."

"How did you get the pills?" Sylvia asked. It had been pills with her too. She knew one didn't just come into them. It wasn't as if you could simply go to the pharmacy and ask for pills strong enough to kill yourself. Doctors must be consulted and then tricked into prescribing enough to kill you, usually over a period of time. It's a waiting game, getting those pills.

"Sleeping pills mostly, medications from my psychotherapist. I had to save them. We suicides, even when we're not consciously planning we're planning. But I guess you reach a point where the pain of living is more than the fear of death, only a suicide knows this. But I saved up the pills and I guess during that Christmas night, Boxing Day perhaps, I took too many pills and then my wife found me on the bathroom floor and called the medics and they rushed me to hospital. It was touch and go, they almost lost me. It could have gone either way."

"And what made you want to live?"

"I guess it was that I had failed. I know I should say something glorious, like I realized that I loved my family and myself and my life. I should say I saw a great white light and chose life but it was nothing like that. Each person who is mentally ill, suffering from one kind of depression or another, has their own unique story of how they survived, of how they got back and why they have not pushed themselves off the brink again."

"I took pills as well," Sylvia admitted. "Sleeping pills mostly, tons of them. I wrote a note saying I was going for a walk in the woods and then I buried myself in the crawlspace of our house, boxed myself right into this little section. I was right under everyone's nose for so long. My mother went out looking for me in the woods when I did not come home that night. There was a big search for days. I was lying in a little space, like a coffin, buried under the house and no one found me. But then I woke up. My body shot up and I hit my head on a pipe or a post and I murmured something. My brother Warren heard a noise and came running and found me and then they sent me to a hospital. My face was all puffy and bruised; it looked frightful, like a monster's face for days because of how I'd hit my head. The nurses wouldn't even let me look at it. They did electroshock on me, that was the worst, being hooked up to all those wires, the way the electricity flowed right in. I felt so helpless."

"Helpless, yes, helpless, we are all so helpless when we have lost our minds, when they start to believe that we can no longer be trusted. We're like little children being punished and we don't even know what for."

"Yes, exactly. I would have done anything to get them to stop the electroshock but there were so many times, even after the suicide, when I didn't even know what I'd done wrong."

"I know." Al sighed grasped Sylvia's hand. "Why did you do it?" But he must have known that there was really no good answer.

"I didn't feel like living anymore." It wasn't a very helpful response. She didn't have a good answer. "I don't even know why . . . life felt so silly just then and everything I was doing, the awards, the straight As, the stories I was writing and publishing, the poetry . . . none of it mattered anymore. But the novel I wrote, it's coming out soon in England, *The Bell Jar*, is about that time in my life."

"I've heard of your book. But yes, suicide, even to another suicide is hard to explain." There was a moment of silence and Sylvia sipped her brandy, once again allowing it to warm her body. Al slapped his knee changing the subject. "So poetry, you're writing poetry, I'd love to see some."

"I wrote a poem a little while back about my father. He died when I was ten years old and in a way that was my first suicide, my father's death. I didn't try anything, but I died that day, I died because I was so sad. I died because I chose to. I was so angry with my father the other day, for living, for dying, for being German, for leaving. I don't know and so I wrote this poem. The poem came from that anger, anger at everything, but also at Ted and my past and . . . I shouldn't really explain should I?"

"It's best not to explain poetry, Sylvia, I think you know that."

"You're right. May I read it to you? This poem is meant to be heard, not read silently in a sitting room with the heater chirping and cars going by."

"Yes, please," Al said.

Sylvia rustled in her purse and pulled her "Daddy" poem out.

"*You do not do, you do not do/Any more, black shoe/In which I have lived like a foot/For thirty years, poor and white,/Barely daring to breathe or Achoo,*" Sylvia started and Al looked at her, she felt his eyes on her as she read. "*Daddy, I have tried to kill you./You died before I had time . . .*"

They sat there is silence after she finished. The earth-toned furniture, the wooden table, blurred into the dim light and it was as if the flat had ceased to exist, as if the cold and all of London had floated away, and it was only her words that made the world, her words that created all of time and space. Al looked at her for a long, long moment, then he smiled and started to clap. It was not to please her that he clapped it was to recognize what he'd just heard, to fill up the silence with something glorious.

"Lovely, absolutely lovely, Sylvia. Now please, I want to keep this for always. The way you spoke just now, it was mesmerizing. Maybe I can get it on the radio. Those lines, the fact that it sounds childish, like a nursery rhyme, but it's not. And I can sense, no I feel, what you feel for your father but so much more. I sense what I feel for my father as well. Can I get the recorder? May I record you now? Are you ready?"

Sylvia smiled. She had always been a sucker for anyone willing to fawn over her work. And she had worked so hard on it and gotten so many rejections and really this was why she wrote poetry. This was why she wrote, to hear people like Al appreciate it. "Of course, please. I'd love to be recorded. I rarely hear my own voice come back to me."

Al got up and walked out of the room. She could hear him fumbling in the back and when he returned he carried a cumbersome black metal recorder connected to a small microphone. "Just speak into the mic, I'm sure you know how, haven't you done this for the BBC? Don't hold it too close or too far, just like that," he instructed as Sylvia moved the mic closer and then further from her mouth. "I'll handle the recorder. Nod to me when you're ready to speak and I'll tell you when."

Sylvia watched Al as he fiddled a little more with the recorder. He then looked up at her, their eyes met and a flash of something, it was poetry, all poetry, passed through them and she nodded that she was ready to speak. He then pressed a button, waited a beat and mouthed the word "when."

Sylvia started the poem again. Line after line. "*I thought every German was you./ And the Language obscene/An engine, an engine/Chuffing me off like a Jew./A*

Jew to Dachau, Auschwitz, Belsen./I began to talk like a Jew./I think I may well be a Jew." She was calm throughout the reading, though she could feel a lump in her throat, it came up her chest and everything, her childhood on Cape Cod, visiting her grandparents, going to school, her mother's constant worrying but also her constant, unwavering love, getting all those straight A's and how she had missed Daddy, who kept bees in the garden, flowed to the surface of all she was. She missed her father and she did just want to get back, back, back to him. Daddy . . . *Brute heart of a brute like you.*

"A brute like you," but who had she meant, who really? Who was the brute now? Sylvia felt Ted's hands on her the day before she miscarried, she felt him pushing her, slapping her face and then he'd come back and act so loving when it was all over. It was all there, bottled together with her poetry, Ted, herself, the darkness, this godforsaken London winter.

When she finished she paused, relishing the silence as Al carefully pressed the "stop" button and fiddled just a bit with the tape. "I'm going to play it back later, I'll make you a copy. Would you like a copy? This is lovely, Sylvia, your passion, your work, you're really coming into your own as a poet."

"Thank you, Al," Sylvia said. She could have sat in that room all night as if all of time and space were at their disposal. The words still whirled inside them both as they sat together. And there was nothing like sitting with a person once poetry was brought into the room. It added another element like introducing air or water to a world without it. It was the kind of alive that cannot cause death though the fall from it can be so great.

"Well," Al said, standing up after fiddling just a little more with his recording equipment. "I should be off. I really do hate these engagements but I've learned that if you want to keep your livelihood you have to learn to keep appointments."

"Of course, of course, thank you for listening."

"Yes. Any time. I'm so happy you thought to share your work with me. It really is something else. Next thing you have, send it over to *The Observer* and I'll make sure those crackpots don't reject it in hand."

"Thank you," Sylvia replied and she felt so close to him just then. She looked at Al. He wasn't so tall but taller than her. He was not as handsome as Ted but he had a certain kind of face, around the eyes really, the sadness. He was another suicide, he knew what it was to be afflicted with the same ailment. "You've been so kind. Would you mind if I came by again?" She placed her hand on Al's arm as he moved to show her out.

Al looked down at her hand but did not acknowledge it. "Yes, please do. I would love to record more of your poetry. You really are a talent, Sylvia. I hope you know that, sometimes the world doesn't recognize great poetry until it's too late."

"I do hope that's not the case with me," Sylvia said, moving closer to Al as he pushed the door open to draw her out. "I don't want the world to only see who I am, who I really and truly am, after I'm dead. What a horrible, horrible tragedy that would be."

"I know, but the poets who get the fame in their lifetime, more often they're forgotten by history. But the ones who have lived tragic lives, the ones who suffer in this life, it's those poets who live into eternity. Would you rather have fame now or for eternity?"

"When you put it that way, I'd rather live forever," Sylvia replied, smiling as she drew herself closer to Al. It had been so long, so very long, since a man even looked at her. She moved in then, brushing her hand on Al's chest. He looked at her for a moment, their eyes met and then he glanced down at her hand and gently took it off him.

"Sylvia, I'm flattered you see, but right now . . . this is not the right time in my life. I'm still getting better, you see, and it's just that . . ." He looked awkwardly at her and Sylvia smiled that broad, false smile.

"Yes, of course, silly. I'm sorry," she said. "I'll see myself out. Thank you so much for your help. For everything."

"Yes. And I want you to take care of yourself. Are you seeing a doctor for your . . . mental health?"

"Yes. I'll keep on top of everything."

"Good. Thank you."

Sylvia could feel her cheeks redden as she walked down the steps of Al's flat and back into the street. The cold came like a great slap in her face, another one after Al's rejection and five, seven years ago, before Ted, a man like Al would have been lucky if she'd looked twice at him and now he was rejecting her. Was she really so sad, so pathetic, so damaged? The wind came at her, a great gust of piercing winter, and Sylvia nearly fell over. In fact, she half slipped on the concrete stoop and almost lost her balance. She was about to fall right to the ground but she grabbed a pole at the last second just barely holding herself up.

Lorelei

PROPERTY OF MAGDALENA Bauer—My aunt hands me the journals she's kept for many years. My mother gave them to her well before her suicide. "She said she couldn't have them anymore. She was too tempted to read them but she didn't want to destroy them." My aunt Sarah has come by, a quick stopover with her Uber waiting, on her way to see Joanne. "We're just having coffee, you're welcome to come," Aunt Sarah says but I'm still reeling from Heather's mother's letter and Joanne's outburst.

"I think I should just stay in, maybe get some writing done," I reply, holding the journal. I know I won't write a word today but it's a good excuse for playing the introvert. "But thank you for this."

The Uber driver honks and my aunt glances over at him. "Do you want me to stay? Tell him to go? I can cancel on Joanne."

"No. Eamon's at his studio, he'll be back soon. I could use a little time to myself. It's just, Joanne was acting a little funny in Provincetown. Is she okay? Do you know?"

"Funny how? What did she do?" my aunt asks not as if this is strange but as if this is a concern.

"I don't know. She got really upset when I mentioned the manuscript. I guess she's a little protective of it. She was very hyper-active and not herself."

"I'll talk to Joanne. Lorelei, you have enough on your plate. Don't worry about Joanne. I'll call Tammy too."

"But is there anything I can do?"

"No, it's okay, you go back to work. Take care of yourself."

"I'm just going to read these. I think if I spend some time with them it'll open up my mother a little more, you know. Then maybe I'll be able to write."

"Okay, just don't let that time to yourself be full of regret and wallowing. Remember your mother loved you." She grasps my hand again and then turns to the Uber. "I'll see you soon."

"Wonderful, thank you."

After she goes I hold the journal in my hands. It's a different type of journal, black, like a moleskin, it's not decorative like the first journal I found but more like something I might have carried in college back when I thought documenting every stray thought I had made me very, very deep. *Property of Magdalena Bauer 1987-1992*. That's quite a long time. I was born in 1988, I was around four in 1992. The first journal covered 1968, what were her thoughts during the intervening years? Who was my mother then? Why was it not recorded?

I clutch the journal as the waves rock softly outside my bedroom window. The room, now it's my room, is white. Why haven't I noticed this before? Soft and downy with billowy white curtains and a pristine bedspread, it's as if a teenage girl or a young bride lives here. I sigh at all the white as I sink into the bed and start reading.

October 23rd 1987

It's been years, I know it's been years and I'm pregnant again. My mother just passed away six months ago. I miss her more than anything and now I'm going to have a baby and I have no one. Well, not no one. There's Joey, we've been married five years . . . there's Sarah, when she has time, but really, without my mother I'll be alone.

I thought I could prevent it. I don't even know how or why I thought that. Joey thinks we're unlucky, the fact that we haven't had a child yet but I always saw it as fortune. Since that time when I was a kid I really just haven't wanted to go through it again. Joey and I are okay. Our marriage is okay but I never wanted to do that again and I thought, since it never happened, that maybe I wasn't supposed to have a child. That's what those crazy voices told me when I was a teenager, I didn't deserve a child, but I'm better now. I've talked to my doctor about that, those voices are more or less under control. The strange feelings. The staying in bed and then the manic running around. I have bi-polar disorder—that's part of it. But there are other tests they're still giving me to make sure it's not more.

I still remember hearing Allison's voice at night. She told me I'd be such a terrible mother and I still can't shake that. I thought maybe something was preventing it but now I'm about to have a baby. It wasn't like I was taking the pill. I could have been but I talked to Joey once about it and he got so upset. He asked me why I didn't want to have his child? Why I didn't want a family with him? He was just so hurt, the way he looked me in the eye, like I was disappointing him. And a man like Joey, so male, so blue collar, why shouldn't he want a family?

But he knows now about how I get, how I am, he didn't know before we were married but he knows now. We all know a lot more about it now. He took me to the hospital two years ago because I cut my finger slicing a tomato and then, he saw it, he watched me do it, I just kept cutting. Those little thoughts just come and I think . . . why not?

It would have been an innocent little nick that first cut, but then I just kept cutting. I don't even know what made me do it. Maybe it was the sight of blood, or the way it felt. The pain, pain ran through me and I loved it. Made me feel alive and I just kept cutting. Sometimes my mind goes fuzzy, my meds don't always work or I need a new dose and I do things like that. Joey stopped me. He wrapped his arms around me as I kicked and screamed, he wrestled me to the floor and then he wrapped my finger in a towel and drove me to the hospital and told them it was an accident. Why the hell would he want to have a child with me after all that?

But here it is and after years of staving it off I don't even know how I'm pregnant again. But I have to have this one. I have to. I don't know why I feel this way but I think I'm ready. I have to be. I have to do this even if I hear Alley's voice I have to.

March 17ᵗʰ 1988

It's almost here. The baby. I could find out the gender, they're getting better at that these days. They don't always get it right but these ultrasounds or something, they can do it, my doctor told me. He told me so many things though, like what types of fruits and vegetables to eat as if I don't know how to take care of myself. I've lived off of rice and eggs for weeks at a time. Sometimes crackers are the only thing I can stomach, but I'm fine, eating like that. I'm fine and now I have this other person inside me and my doctor tells me how I should eat. I think maybe he's trying to over feed me. They talk about women getting fat after they have babies but I think it's the doctors, it's a conspiracy by them. They want women to get fat after they've had a child so that they have to stay with their husbands. Women have babies, they do this amazing thing, having a baby, and the men are so jealous of that that they make women fat, tell them they're lazy and that's why women don't rule the world. It's all because of the doctors and the way they make women fat when they're pregnant. But I showed him. I told him I was eating all those fruits, that meat he wanted me to make every night, but really I just throw it all up, stick my finger down my throat and heave it all into the toilet after Joey sees me eat it. I only need rice and crackers. This baby will be just fine.

May 3ʳᵈ 1988

I remember now more than ever, the first one. The way Sarah called that "doctor" and the blood that followed. I picture it too, bleeding out with this one. I haven't heard Alley's voice but I think about her sometimes. I remember her in junior high when we swam together or playing tennis in high school. She can't stop me now. I'm too far along and something like that would kill me. It's not illegal now but it's still dangerous. Alley knows that so she won't make me do it. Still, I hear its voice, the voice of the other child, it cries at night and wonders why I didn't want it. But I don't know if I want this one either, I just know I have to, I have to do this.

I feel it writhing around inside me. It kicks me now. I don't sleep anymore—two, maybe three hours a night and that's it. I'm up at all hours, till all hours, and then all of a sudden I'll sleep an entire day. Joey will come home and I'll be in bed, he'll come in, ask how I am, and then I'll just go back to sleep. Only to toss and turn the next night, the next night . . . I should be finished throwing up all the time but I'm still so sick and weak. This baby is sucking the life out of me. I swear to God I think it wants to kill me. I told Joey last night that we have to get rid of it. It's sucking me dry, taking all of me. All of me. I don't know what to do with myself. I was standing the other day just at the edge of the water at my in-law's little place at the Cape. They were all out front looking at the road, something about a new car they want to get, as if they can think of these things when I'm gestating a human being. But I thought, what if I walk into the water? What if I just throw myself in there? I really just wanted to toss myself into the water and die. I might have too, but Joey came out, he called me and I knew if I walked into the ocean just then he would have come in after me. It would have been a big To-Do. Maybe we'd've ended up at the hospital again and with a baby on the way I cannot be committed, they'd just have more control over me. Just like this thing growing inside me. Where is my sister? She's always gone, always away for work, for business, and I just can't handle it now. I wish my mother were here. She always knew what to do.

June 13th 1988

There was blood. So much blood. It started when I was in the shower. I couldn't get it to stop and the water ran red, so red. I thought maybe I had lost the baby. That Alley had killed it. It was just like before and I remembered everything that happened the first time, how much blood because we couldn't just do it in a hospital. Because they made me find my own way to get rid of a pregnancy I didn't want because of some law that didn't even keep. I called Joey, he was the only one in the house. I was crying when I was in the shower. I sat down right on the linoleum and that's where it happened. I could see it like it was happening all over again, the operation in the bathtub. The blood just kept coming and I started screaming and Joey ran up to me. He opened the shower curtains and there he was that brown hair shaggy and in his face, the slight hint of a beard. He looked at me and asked so calmly, "What's wrong?" As if there wasn't blood all over me, all over the place. I was going to bleed out. To just bleed out and he's looking at me like nothing is happening. "What's wrong?" What do you think is wrong, moron?

But there wasn't any blood, that's what he said. "Maggie, there's nothing, you're just sitting there, there's no blood. There's no blood."

He knows me. We've been married for years and he knows me. He knows I can do stuff like that. He knows that I freak out like this. And he's calm, he's just so calm and sometimes that's what breaks my heart. He should have married a normal woman. A woman that doesn't fly off the deep end but here I am and he doesn't know. I never told him about the time I took all those pills. My mother never told him, she said it would be our secret, he didn't know about the six weeks I spent in the hospital when I was nineteen. They gave me all these shots and then a couple of times they strapped me down and pumped me full of electricity just like Esther from The Bell Jar.

But this, I could see the blood, but Joey couldn't and Joey's brain isn't messed up like mine so I have to believe him. I finally got out of the bath. Joey gave me a towel. He dried me off. It's not his fault. He didn't know what he was getting into. I can be fun. So carefree. I'm pretty enough and he just didn't know. He didn't know what kind of cow he was buying and now I'm going to have his baby and he's stuck. But he tries his best, Joey, bless his heart. And he takes me to the Cape where his parents have a house and at least by the ocean there is some peace. Sarah and I went to the Cape before, when it happened, but this is different. I keep telling myself this is different.

He toweled me off and still I felt the blood. I saw it. But sometimes I can fake it. Sometimes I can just fake being normal. And so I pretended it wasn't there because no one else could see it.

July 27th 1988

The baby has been quiet inside my body and I've been quiet as well. Since I saw the blood, since Joey said it wasn't there, I've been better. I don't hate it anymore. Looking back I don't know why I ever did. I've slept a lot more recently, slept normally. Sarah thinks I'm going to survive this. I'm going to be okay. It makes me wonder what would have happened, really what would have happened, if I'd had the other one. I can't even think about that. I knew it was a boy. Obviously I wasn't far enough along, no one really knew, no one could tell, but I knew it was a boy. She would have had a brother. I haven't had the sonogram, I don't know the gender of this baby either but I know it's a girl. Lorelei. I am going to name her Lorelei, after the Sylvia Plath poem. Ever since last month when things finally started calming down, when I started calming down, I've been humming that poem to myself. She was a powerful woman, Plath. And the Lorelei, that story, the woman who could grab a man's attention and rule everything . . . I hope my daughter is that girl. I want her to be strong, unlike her mother. I want her to be powerful, unlike her mother. And no one hurts me. That's what my doctor says. When I act out. When I can't keep my mind straight, no one hurts me but myself. Joey is a saint and I only wonder what kind of mother will I be to this little girl? Will I harm her? Will she hate me? Then again what if she loves me so much and I let her down?

The ocean is calm tonight. The ocean is never really calm but tonight at least I don't feel the need to throw myself into it. I'd never say this to anyone else, even when I'm acting up I know to keep quiet about these wicked, wicked thoughts. But here I can write them down. I stared out at the ocean earlier and it was beautiful, just beautiful. I put my hand on my belly. I looked over at Joey and he seemed content. I think we'll be all right.

I put the journal down. There are more entries but I can't read them now. My mother wanted me and then she didn't. She thought of me so much like she thought of that first child and yet I survived and he (he?) didn't. My mother suffered. She was always suffering. She was on the verge of losing it so often. Even with the doctors, the therapy, her medication, she still lived on the edge of something I'll never really understand. I want to help her but she's gone, she took herself away before anyone could help her and I need to end on a high note, she seems happy there in that entry. I'm sure the other entries aren't so nice.

Esther Greenwood
Near Bath, England 1958

THERE'S SOMETHING ABOUT the land in England. When you get outside London, outside Cambridge and all those places where there are stone walls and cobblestone streets, iron posts and cities, there's land, rolling green hills and whatnot. But what's different about the land here from land in America is that the land always seemed to be working, doing something other than just sitting there, in the United States. In Massachusetts there were fields of corn or wheat or pastureland for cows or land for houses. I've seen a few cows in England but that's about it and all these rolling hills around Bath and Salisbury and Stonehenge seem as if they're just collecting dust. The grass sits in neat little rows, just like all those guards around Buckingham Palace, as if the place is about to be attacked by Nazis again. But no one does anything they just stand there looking neat.

"We shouldn't've stayed at the rocks so long," Tom said, annoyed. "I told you we should've left earlier."

"We have time," I said. "See it's only two . . . fourteen, is that how you say it here? Fourteen o'clock? You need to be in Cardiff at five to be early, you don't even have to rehearse for the reading until six."

"What if there's traffic?" Tom huffed and we both looked out at the empty road, just rolling hills and rolling asphalt. We hadn't seen a car in miles, just a little farm vehicle with the back end missing and that had turned off so quickly we didn't even bother passing it. "You never know, Cardiff could have traffic."

I only know a thing or two about Cardiff, mostly that it is still a fishing town, though it's the capital of Wales and they are starting to build it up more. After the war it appeared even the places that weren't all shot to bits wanted in on the great building boom. There'd be stores and restaurants, people bustling around, I was sure, but not traffic. "If there's traffic I can take the car and you can walk," I told Tom as he kept his eyes on the road.

"You don't even know how to drive on this side of the road. Silly Americans never learn anything about what happens overseas, you think people will just stop everything and let you do what you want."

"It's not like over there we think much about the other side of the road and if you want me to learn, I mean, this is as good a place as any. Look, it's an empty road, why don't you pull over and I'll drive?"

"Esther, you're not driving!" Tom cried, he yelled really, and I turned in my seat. I had been looking at him, the outline of his impeccable Roman nose sometimes fascinates me. The look in his eyes as he stared forward made me afraid of him.

Micah would have let me drive. I don't want to think this. I don't want to have Micah on my mind but I know as we're going, we're seeing cows now and longer stretches of rolling hills, but Micah, if I'd've asked he would have gotten out of the car and let me drive. He would have shown me where the stick was, how to turn the wheel. He might have given me a pointer or two on how to keep myself focused while driving on the wrong side of the road. I watched the road as Tom hummed. He seemed fine again; the little outburst was over—like a car backfiring. That's what Tom was like. That's what was so good about him. He wasn't like me, a little upset and I was down the rabbit hole, unable to get myself out of it for days or weeks. There was that one time it just wouldn't stop and I stayed inside the hole, caught up there for months until they sent me away, injecting electricity into my head and locking me up until I was better. But it had been Micah who left, Micah who never came back that time and then I'd met Tom and sure, Tom doesn't know yet, not really, not the depths of what happened when I had my breakdown. But who tells the man who is in love with them, the man who wants to marry them, so much of everything? Who does that? Really? But Micah, he may have left me, he may not have come back, but at least he would have taught me how to drive on the other side of the road.

Tom hummed in the silence and I just couldn't take it. Like there was this noise on a loop, this constant din and I wondered if that's what the people of London heard when the Germans were lopping bomb after bomb on them. Over and over again but Tom would not stop humming and I wanted to yell at him to stop, to cover my ears, but I knew he'd only start to fuss then and so I reached for the radio and turned it on. It didn't work right away. We were in the middle of the country, there were cows and sheep and a few fields but that was it, of course there wasn't much in the way of radio reception. Finally the little dial made a buzzing noise and I jumped I was so excited to hear something. I didn't even know who it was but when I heard that voice, it was Paul McCartney singing, "Lost My Little Girl." It wasn't always McCartney, he wasn't the only singer for The Beatles, but I loved his voice and there he was singing on the radio in merry olde England as we drove down a country road.

"I hate the Beatles," Tom said, looking out. "You know, I don't see what's so interesting about them. A bunch of pop trash just like everything else."

"I like them. They sound a little like Elvis, you know?"

"Since when have you liked Elvis? I thought you were a cultured girl. I thought you went to the ballet and the symphony and all that?" Tom looked over at me and half smiled, half laughed. "I guess the pop revolution is getting everyone."

"I can like The Beatles and still have culture," I replied, pulling my hand through my hair. It was getting long again but Micah liked it that way. Micah liked The Beatles as well. He was also a cultured person but whenever there was a party in New York he used to ask the host if they had any Beatles, and before that, he'd asked for Elvis, which is how I know about all this stuff. I didn't want to tell Tom that, he seemed upset enough.

"You can like whatever you want, Esther," he said and he let the music go. The Beatles played for a little while longer, the song was only a minute long but then another Beatles song came on, "Calypso Rock," and Tom shook his head and turned the radio off.

"You know, I've been meaning to talk to you," he said, looking over at me. "I just, when we were leaving, I wish you hadn't have walked away from me like that."

"I just needed space."

"It seems you need a lot of space from me these days." He sighed and looked out at the road. I could see a man on the side of the gravel part near the concrete, he looked like a farmer in junky linen pants and a flannel shirt. He wore a floppy hat on his head but I could see that he had grey hair and he pulled a brown and white cow.

"I told you, Tom, it's just that I need some time to think."

"All you do is think, Esther, don't you get tired of thinking?"

"I don't, not at all. You knew I was a thinker, you knew I was a smart woman when we got together. You knew I wanted to write and work and that I'm not just some little housewife."

"Do you think that's what I want, Esther, some little housewife? There are plenty of those all over England. I could have my pick of little housewives, in fact I already have, you know that, Esther. I can't believe you talk to me this way."

"I know nothing of the sort, Tom," I replied, looking out at the empty road. "What little housewives?" I could jump out, if Tom got to be too much, I could jump out and roll down the hill, the grass would catch me and I'd be safe. Maybe I'd keep rolling forever and ever, I'd become a great ball of earth and the ground would cover me. I looked at the empty road in this country I did not belong to and told myself over and over, "You're not helpless, you can get out, you're not helpless, Esther, you're not helpless."

"You know nothing, that's for sure, Esther, you know nothing. And earlier, when I put my arm around you, after I saved that guy and everyone else was so happy for me and you just walked away."

"I wasn't walking away!" I cried. "I just wanted to think. Like when you want to write poetry and I don't question that, I leave you alone."

"Except I haven't wanted to be alone, to write poetry, since I asked you to marry me."

"You are perfectly welcome to write poetry," I told him, looking away I stared out at the road again.

The Beatles weren't on, there was no music but I could still hear the car, I could hear it until it stopped. Tom turned it slowly to the side of the road, I heard the crunch of gravel as he turned the wheel, lowered the gear, turned the wheel again and then switched the car off. He slowly took the key out of the ignition, he didn't even leave it there, he put it in his pocket and turned to look over at me.

"Tom, we need to get to Cardiff, what's going on?" I asked. I wasn't afraid. It had happened before. Not often but that time in his room, we had been kissing, making out pretty thick and all of a sudden he pushed me off the bed. I stood up and started hitting him, hitting and hitting and hitting him and he pushed me harder and I hit my head and then he ran over, said he was sorry, it was just a game, he'd thought I'd liked it. And I'd laughed, what else was I going to do? Tom was my boyfriend, my new boyfriend at that point, and I just thought he liked being rough. I thought maybe if I played along he'd like me better. But in college with Buddy, I'd played along with Buddy as well and what had I learned about him? It was nothing I'd liked that's for sure. But Tom was different and he wasn't going to send me to the place I was when I couldn't get out of bed. He wasn't going to send me anywhere where they shovel electricity into my skull. Not again. I wasn't going to let that happen again. Not for Micah, not for anyone.

"I just wish you wouldn't walk away from me!" Tom cried so loud I wanted to cover my ears with my hands and chant "I'm not listening! I'm not listening!" Like what I did when I was a little girl, like what I had wanted to do when they told me Daddy was dead and wouldn't be coming home.

"Tom, please," I said calmly. It was best to be calm when he got this way. "Start the car, we have to go."

"What's going on with you, Esther, what's wrong?" He looked at me so pleadingly and maybe it was my fault. It was my fault for falling for Micah not now but so many years ago, for not really being able to forget about it. It was my fault for the problems in my head, the way my brain works and there are times I'm so sad I don't know what to do with myself. There are times all I feel is this darkness and of course Tom yells at me, of course he hates me. I'm a mess everyone hates me.

I just stared at him. I couldn't move. I didn't see the countryside around us I just stared at him. "Esther, what is wrong with you!" he screamed and it should have woken me up but I didn't feel anything. I could barely see and I just stared and stared and stared straight ahead.

Smack! He reached out and slapped me. I felt it sting my cheek. Smack! He hit me again and I put my hand over my face to cover it. I shriveled up into a little ball at the side of the car and he started hitting me, at first with his hands, slapping my shoulders, my side, then he made a fist. I didn't see it, I was too busy covering my face, but I felt it, pounding at my side. I could sense the bruises, they weren't there yet, they always took a little while, but they'd show up, that's why he punched my side. On some level Tom must have known not to hit my face since it would leave a visible mark.

"Esther, look at me, why don't you look at me!" Tom yelled and I did. I turned right over and looked at him. His eyes weren't big anymore, they weren't mopey and artistic and angelic they were something else, squinting as if he couldn't see. He grabbed my wrist and held it in his big hands and I winced because I knew he could crush it. "Esther, what is wrong with you? Why don't you say anything?" he cried and I just looked at him. "Esther I swear sometimes you're a waste of space, just a waste of space, why don't you just kill yourself." Kill yourself . . . I roll the words around in my head but they don't sink in. I wanted to fight back. I knew I couldn't, I would lose to such a big brute of a man but I wanted to fight back or at least I wanted to want to but I couldn't get a sense of it, like his words weren't words. I wanted to curl up into a ball, I wanted to hide on the floor of the car but I could feel Tom's grip on my wrist. Finally his teeth seemed to part like he was about to bite me but instead he tossed my wrist away. It hit the side of the dashboard and ricocheted.

"Ouch!" I cried and Tom stared forward. I don't know what he was looking at and I didn't care. I opened the car door and got out.

I don't know where I was going. I just stood there on the side of the road, in the middle of nowhere in merry olde England. I could run into the field of grass just beyond the hill, it didn't look that deep but maybe Tom wouldn't find me in it. I saw the landscape, it was old and so beautiful with the stone walls every few feet, miles of land just waving in the hills like a scarf fluttering in the breeze, the trees overhead and their green leaves formed a canopy. I felt like it was 1934 again, before the war, or 1912, before the first war, everything was so calm and peaceful, like going back to such a simple time and I just wanted to live there, looking out I just wanted to live in that peace.

A car went by. It was going pretty fast but in the opposite direction. I looked up too late to flag it down for a ride. It wouldn't matter where it was going. If they could get me to a house with a phone or maybe even to a train station that would be alright. Tom got out of the car and just stood there. I wanted to run away from him but he was so big and I didn't know where I was and I knew I couldn't go, not anywhere, not without him. Alone in a foreign country with barely any money, really, how was I supposed to get home without Tom? I was stuck as I had been when they put me in the hospital and shot electricity through my brain.

"Esther, get in the car," Tom said so calm now it was like he was a different person. I felt a pain in my wrist but I could move it. I looked down and flexed a circle just to be sure. If I could do that I knew it wasn't broken. "Esther, I'm sorry, I got upset. I'm just worried about tonight, that's all, that's really all. Please get in the car, let's go."

I looked out at the road again. Another car was coming, I could hear its engine in the distance before I saw it. It made a kind of whoosh like when the planes landed at the airport and all the air they generate just sort of swirls around in one place. I heard the engine again, it grew louder and when I saw a small work truck coming over the turn I stepped away from the car, I waved my arms in the air, then stuck my thumb out to hitch.

"Esther, don't be silly, get back here," Tom said, calm now, too calm. The car whooshed past. I saw the driver, another old man, who just looked at me. He looked right at me but he didn't stop, he didn't even slow down. No one was going to stop. Even Micah wasn't going to stop—he couldn't. No one would stop—no one could help. I wasn't good enough to help. I was too far gone and all I had was to submit to the darkness; to lie down, to never get up, to let it take me.

"Esther, come on now, you're being silly. I'm sorry, I really am. I got carried away and you know me. I'm passionate, I get a little crazy. It's my tragic flaw."

If that was Tom's tragic flaw, what was mine?

I looked at the little car and in that instant it seemed silly that the thing was so very small and yet it could carry us across England, from London to Stonehenge to Cardiff. I walked toward it and as I did, before I opened the door, Tom got in and sat down. I settled in and looked over at him. He put the key in the car and started it.

"You ready?" he asked as if all that had happened was nothing. I nodded yes but did not speak. I wondered if he would notice, if he would say something or yell at me again but Tom just nodded back before he turned on his signal and started driving.

And it was really silly, when I looked at it, the way he drove on the wrong side of the road. I don't think it's something I could ever get used to and yet there I was in a car on the wrong side of the road as if I were *Alice Down the Rabbit Hole* or *Through the Looking Glass* and this upside down world, this alternate reality that was England, was all I had now.

"We'll be there soon, a couple hours tops," Tom said. I didn't say anything I just looked out the window at the long, winding landscape. It went on forever and I wondered if I really was Alice, that girl who fell down the rabbit hole to a world so unlike hers.

Tom reached for the radio dial. Initially it was static but he found the channel pretty quickly. I heard the music first, then John Lennon's voice. And really, I liked Lennon better. Micah had always liked Lennon better as well. That was something, Micah had kissed me in London. And he liked John Lennon better than McCartney that was something.

"There, see," Tom said as he drove on. "I'm even playing The Beatles for you."

Sylvia
1962

THE LITTLE LAMP in the darkness of the flat reminded Sylvia of a roaring fire in a slow movie, the ones where you look into a great big room and wonder how rich all the characters must be. Except this flat was small, the wood of the walls, the carpets on the floors, it was all very neat and tidy but still so small and one only had to look in a little to see it was shabby. She stood at the window staring outside. Car after car; they were red and blue, and some rust color she couldn't place. So many of the cars here were some rusty color. She had been watching the cars for a while now. She couldn't hold the time in her head but the children had been asleep for hours, it had to be hours at this point—what had happened to the time? The sun had not quite gone down when she started staring out the window. Seven people had walked by. It was a slow night, no one heading off to the bars, no one loitering in the street, just your average Joe coming home from work, maybe a couple of night strollers, though it was getting too cold for that. It was pitch black now, the streetlights were on and she could see a man walking to the box to post a letter.

It felt like her life was cast in black and white and her character, Esther Greenwood, was in color. Sylvia had just finished writing about Esther in *The Bell Jar*. She was working on another book using Esther as her main character. Esther was so like her, really the character was a continuation, another version, of her own self and while *The Bell Jar* wasn't doing very well, Esther was the only character she wanted to write about. Esther had come to her in a whirlwind of thought and trauma and memory and she had written frantically, written furiously, for weeks to finish *The Bell Jar*. It had come to her just after her time in the hospital. She'd been laid up for so long, first she'd had Frieda and she'd written nothing but poetry but then there had been that terrible fight with Ted and the miscarriage and she'd needed an appendectomy right afterward. She'd been laid up in the hospital and it had been too much like that time, that time when they'd tied her down and shot electricity through her skull because they said she was crazy. They all thought she was crazy and what was there to do with a crazy woman but shoot electricity through her until she shuts up?

She'd remembered so vividly how her life had been so different, so unreal after the miscarriage and so she'd started writing about that time and low and behold Esther and *The Bell Jar* were born. She'd gone back to Esther a few times, Sylvia knew *The Bell Jar* wasn't the end of her story and she wanted to say so much more about her. But no one wanted to publish her novel, not in America and barely in England. It didn't matter if she used a pseudonym or her real name, no one wanted her work in her own country and how could she keep Esther alive, how could she keep writing about her, if no one cared? She felt like she was screaming, crying out in the dark and it wasn't that no one could hear her, they could hear, it was just that they walked right by with their noses in the air. They simply would not pay attention no matter how hard she cried out that she was drowning. And now she stared out the window as she waited for Ted to come and scream at her. Ted was always screaming at her when the children weren't around these days.

She'd called That Woman, she'd raised a stink today insulting her, screaming into the receiver and Sylvia was sure she'd tell Ted. She was sure he'd come and throw a fit. But she was so sick of hearing rumors. So sick of Ted not helping with the children so he could take The Woman on trips and buy her nice dinners. She had never gotten nice dinners or real trips—not in years. He'd saved all the nice things for The Woman and left her with diapers and messy rooms, changing tables, and having to pay all these bills.

Sylvia looked out the window, her eyes searching and it could have been hours, for all she knew it could have been days, but then the children would have gotten her and at least the children kept her grounded, at least the children gave her a sense of time. And they were so lovely, the children. They could be a handful, yes, they made life hard, but they also made it so good. Just then Sylvia wanted to wake them up and play with them but she knew that was a very bad idea. Sleeping children need their rest. Then she looked out the window and there he was, marching toward the house, his thick light brown hair tangled in the wind. It was so windy, so drab, these English winters, even in a city like London, they couldn't keep the brutal cold off the streets. Ted held his suit jacket close to him, and that silly duster he wore as if he were still in college, it was crumpled and unkempt but she remembered when she'd met Ted, how sexy he'd seemed in it. Apparently women still found him attractive.

Sylvia jumped away from the windowsill. The heat had been on all day, she'd plopped more and more little coins into the heaters and they'd been hissing, making a ridiculous noise like a little man was in there stoking a fire between bits of sleep and bouts of drinking. She had to keep feeding the heater, keep paying it and paying it or the cold would get in and freeze them. Her door buzzed and she knew who was there. It buzzed again and she did not ask who it was as she let him up.

She didn't wait for him to knock but opened the front door wide. "Sylvia it's pitch dark in here," Ted nearly cried at her, though she could see he was trying to keep his voice down for the children. "Have you been sitting in the dark all evening?"

"What does it matter to you?" she replied, trying to sound coy. She walked further into the apartment. It was still dark and she wondered if Ted could see inside or if he would even follow.

"It matters that my children are living with a crazy woman who prowls around with all the lights off," Ted replied his voice seething.

"Maybe you should take your children. Keep them at your place a few days."

"Sylvia, you know I can't do that. Assia—" He stopped. He had said her name. Sylvia wasn't sure but she was almost positive that she had made it a rule—That Woman—he was not allowed to say her name. "She can't be with the children. It's not that she can't be, she likes them just fine, it's just too difficult—"

"Having the children around is too difficult for her delicate sensibilities? Tell me, does she write poetry? Does she do anything except sit on that fat butt of hers—"

"Sylvia stop it, just stop it. She said you called today. You were very rude to her. I told her I'd come by on my way home and talk some sense into you."

"Talk sense into me, Ted, is that what you're doing, talking sense into me? Do I need some sense talked into me?" Sylvia crossed the distance she'd just trekked across the living room, getting close to Ted, nearly right in his face. She saw it then, outlined by the light in the hall, the sneer, the hate in his eyes. He could go from so calm, so kind, to such an evil snake of a creature. It had been true, the moment she'd met him and he'd pulled her headband, she'd bit his cheek. He'd had a girlfriend then but he'd left her . . . maybe she should have seen it, the way Ted talked about women, always he'd had a woman, always he was cheating on one girl for another. Why had she thought he'd be any different with her?

"You're a crazy woman, you know that, just crazy. You lied to me about your health when we got married. If I'd known they'd locked you up for going insane I never would have married you. Your own mother, your mother who dotes on you, even she couldn't handle what you did, Sylvia. How crazy is that?"

"How crazy is that? I don't know. Maybe I needed someone to be there, someone to listen. Maybe if you had stuck around you'd've been able to help."

"It was not fair to your family, your antics, and it's not fair to me."

"And your children, Ted, what about your children?" Sylvia asked, getting closer she pushed him in his chest again. He didn't step back, he didn't move away, he was barely phased by her tiny hands on him.

"Your children deserve a mother who is not going to go crazy on them," Ted said, his voice so calm, so cold, it brought a chill through Sylvia and she wondered if the heat was still on.

"I'm not crazy, I'll show you crazy!" she cried, her voice rising and she was sure one of the children had heard her. Her fingers flew magnetically into her palms, she made two fists and started hitting Ted in the chest, beating on it until he finally stumbled back. He nearly fell over, she saw he had to grab the wall for support before he gathered his composure. She ran at him again, hitting his chest until he grabbed both her fists in his big bear paws. He held her wrists as if he could swing her entire body around like a doll. A doll, but that is what she had been the last time Ted had grabbed her like this. *Already your doll grip lets go.*

They had been in London, Frieda was still a baby and she'd just come out with her first collection. She could remember that night. She was going to have a baby, another baby but not Nicholas, and she and Ted had started fighting. It was the other girls in his life or the baby had been fussy and no one could concentrate and that first flat was so small, just so small, that's why they'd been fighting. The moment she'd married him Sylvia had known she wouldn't be the only one, she couldn't be, he had all those women and she had never felt safe, not with Ted, not in this relationship. But it had been that night, that night that she realized she really wasn't safe with Ted.

There had been moments before. It wasn't all Ted, she had gone at him, kicking and screaming sometimes, fists at his chest. But she never left a mark and she was a thin woman and he was a man it was different, it really was different. He was so much bigger than her, so much bigger. He used to say how he was a hunter, a fisherman, a man among men and then he'd push her to the floor and sneer that she was worthless. He'd trip her while they were walking outside and she'd fall on her hands and knees, getting all dusty, ripping her skin and he'd laugh and call her clumsy. But it had been that time in London, when they'd lived only a few blocks away from here. Frieda was a baby and she'd been pregnant. The fight had started as all their fights started, the baby was crying, Sylvia was seething, she felt like she was about to cry herself and he'd hit her and hit her, thrown her up against the wall, she had never felt such tension, such violence from him. Sometime during all of it, or right after, the time just contracted for Sylvia, but she started bleeding down there and she knew. She knew. She was going to have a baby but she knew.

By the next day she was in the hospital. The doctor came in and told her she had miscarried. Ted came to the hospital with little Frieda and he was kind, so kind. They talked it out, they had always talked it out then. She'd gone to the hospital a few weeks later for an operation but she'd still felt Ted's hands on her and the blood that came later.

"Stop it, Sylvia!" Ted cried, raising his voice for just a second and she knew if he wasn't careful, if they didn't stop, he'd wake the children. Ted did not want that, she didn't either. They'd be impossible to get back to bed and Ted would leave, he'd just leave her alone to deal with this. He could come in, yell, raise a fuss and come to the defense of That Woman and then he'd leave her alone with his children, even as he'd just said she wasn't fit to take care of them. But she didn't want them with Ted either and definitely not with That Woman. At least with her the children were safe.

"Stop it!" she cried, going at him again. He grabbed her hands once more and pulled her out into the hall. Sylvia felt her feet sliding on the wooden floor. Ted held her back, pushing her against the wall. "Leave me alone! Get out, get out, get out! And do not think that I won't call your little mistress whenever I want. She's made my life hell, you think I won't make hers hell back!"

"Sylvia, so help me god, if it weren't for the children," Ted said. He pushed her back harder and she felt her head crack against the plaster of the wall. Her mind went black, she saw nothing for a second and she almost lost her footing. She felt Ted's hand around her neck. She was so thin, her doctor had said so, so thin these days and Ted only needed one hand wrapped around her throat and she couldn't breathe. Sylvia gulped for air but it did not come. Air . . . it was only air then, she didn't care about Ted or poetry, food or That Woman, she didn't see the children or the cold it was air, only air. She needed to breathe and she couldn't. Funny, how survival, when it seems so tenuous, is all that matters.

"Why don't you just kill yourself, Sylvia? Just kill yourself," he seethed. She gulped again and nothing came. Ted looked at her, she saw the bigness of his nose, the hate in his eyes as he sneered at her. "So help me god." He let go of her throat. "Just kill yourself. I can't do it, why don't you put everyone out of their misery and kill yourself?"

Breathe. Just breathe, Sylvia thought. You're not dead, he hasn't killed you, just breathe. She had been without air for what? Maybe a minute, a little bit longer, it couldn't have been much since she hadn't blacked out. And there were times, times not unlike this, when she had blacked out, passed right out onto the floor and Ted had stepped over her. Breathe, just breathe, she could concentrate on nothing else. Then she looked at him, he was still standing there on the landing to the stairs.

"I have to go," he said at her. "Leave Assia alone."

Sylvia shuffled to push her way past him. She needed to get home, get to the door, to her children.

Ted shoved her then, as she tried to walk past him, he shoved her shoulder and she lost her footing. She nearly tumbled down the stairs, in fact she felt her arms flailing her entire body elongated like a silly clown. She felt so clumsy but again her body wanted to right itself, to survive. She felt herself lose her footing as he shoved her and then she felt his hands on her, he grasped her back, pulled her up so she was standing.

"You only saved me because you knew what would happen if I fell down the stairs. They'd know then, they'd know. Famous Poet Pushes Wife Down the Stairs—I can just read the headlines."

"Can't have that." Ted sneered, stepping down two steps. The light in the hall illuminated his face and it would have looked angelic if it hadn't been so sinister. "Saved your life, Sylvia, remember that. Leave Assia alone," he warned again before turning around and walking away. He slammed the front door shut and Sylvia watched it, she watched him. She grimaced as he went but she watched him.

Sylvia took a deep breath, she gathered herself and went inside. It was cold in the flat. She'd forgotten to put more coins in the heater. She had told herself she would, once Ted was over, but she'd gotten so distracted, so upset. The heater had only been off for a few minutes but she could feel the cold seeping in. It got in so quickly, whenever she thought she was making headway, whenever she felt like she was on top of the heat, the winter snuck back in and she couldn't stop it. She had never been able to stop it. There had been doctors and friends, she'd written poetry and had children, she'd been a good mother and still the cold seeped in, the darkness. She couldn't help it, she couldn't stop the darkness.

She swallowed hard, a lump forming in her throat and she felt Ted's hand around her throat again. She saw the look of hate in his eyes. He had been so big and he could have pushed her down the stairs and the only reason he hadn't . . . they would have known then, they all would have known if he'd let her fall. She shouldn't have tried to save herself. She should have let him shove her, shove harder. What was her life worth the way Ted treated her? And the children, they did not deserve a crazy mother. It would be so much better if they were sent to live with her own mother in Massachusetts once she was gone.

Lorelei

"YOU SHOULDN'T TRY so hard to save the queen," Eamon jokes as I sit across from him at a diner on the other side of town. "She's there to protect the king. It's okay to sacrifice her."

"I refuse to sacrifice the queen for that stuffy old man," I reply and Eamon smirks and stares at the chessboard. I called him from a party with Amelia, another publishing shindig at another house on the water, telling him I was finished with the party and would rather hang out with him.

I move my pawn, leaving my rook unguarded and I know Eamon, he'll take it. "I don't know why you care so much, collecting queens," Eamon observes, and true to form he snatches my rook with his knight. "It's not as if a second, even a third queen, will necessarily save the king."

"Maybe not. But I'd much rather save my queen. I'd rather have a whole army of queens than one silly old king."

"Without the silly old king you're dead," Eamon observes and I move my pawn.

"Queen me," I tell him and he does. He then moves his bishop to take my initial queen. But this opens up a direct line for my new queen who is protected by my knight.

"Check," I call and Eamon stares right at me. "And mate." He looks down at the board and shakes his head.

"Well look at that. The queen wins again."

"She does," I reply, and after savoring the sight of the board, Eamon's lowly king in check by my pawn queen, I start to pick up the pieces. I set the pieces in Eamon's collapsible board, which he immediately stores on the seat next to him.

"So the party was a bust? You and Amelia," Eamon asks, sipping ice water from a glass slippery with foggy condensation. "You'd rather be here with little ol' me."

"Amelia is fine on her own. I'm going with her to another party tomorrow. My aunt's going to be at that one. And these days I think I prefer little ol' you to just about anyone."

"Well I prefer you too. I just wish you didn't beat me so much at chess."

"I was on the chess team in junior high, you never stood a chance." I smirk. "You know, I'm still reading this Plath manuscript and I feel like I'd rather be doing that than sipping champagne with Amelia's people. The main character is talking about her time at an institution and it's so interesting."

"An institution? What kind of institution? A mental hospital?"

"Something like that. You know, I read my mother's journal. More of it. It's just . . . the stuff in there, it's hard to think of your mother, even a mother like mine, suffering."

"But you saw her suffering?" Eamon asks. He knows about my life, the bullet points on an outline belonging to the kind of extended essay a life forms. Blue-collar parents, mother mentally unstable despite her treatment, college in Boston, marriage, book published, cheating husband, Heather (a great all-stop in the middle of everything) miscarriage, divorce, writer's block. There's much more to fill in but he gets the idea.

"I did, but this was a little different."

"Having it in your face, in this intimate way, it must be a lot. I'm sorry, is there anything I can do? You could not read it."

"Ever think about moving to Boston?" I ask carefully and he gives a secret smile.

"Say the word."

"I might." It's a trigger I've considered for a while but now that I've said it, I don't know if I'm ready to pull it.

Eamon laughs. "Take your time though, I can wait." He shakes his head and looks down at his water as our waitress brings us our food. I ordered eggs. Whenever I'm feeling off, not sad, not hurt, just a little disconcerted, as if my skin doesn't quite fit at the moment, I order eggs. My father used to make them every Sunday. He'd take a dozen eggs and crack them into a bowl. Sometimes he'd let me help. When I was young I used to crack the shells right in there too and he'd laugh and explain how the shells weren't food. I always felt bad for the shells being left out and discarded because they were hard and brittle. Even hard and brittle things should have a place.

When our plates come I immediately stick my fork into my eggs. They're overcooked but it doesn't matter, it takes a lot to thoroughly ruin eggs. Eamon takes a bite of his pastrami sandwich, only a little let down that they didn't have corned beef.

"So work was okay?" I ask.

"It's a good place to spend a Thursday night. The tourists go there and ask for the Irish guy and if I'm not in they ask when I'm working and come back then."

"All it takes is a funny accent," I say, shaking my head as I return to my eggs.

"Yep," Eamon replies, concentrating more thoroughly on his pastrami. "It really is a poor substitute for corned beef. I don't understand how hard it is to stock corned beef, it stays good for days, weeks if you don't mind it a little tart."

"You are the only person I know who can taste the difference between pastrami and corned beef."

I laugh at him and we eat in silence. Eamon is the kind of man you can eat with in silence. It's not uncomfortable and I enjoy being in my own head. I'm sure Amelia would say it's the writer in me. There aren't many people here this late. It's after eleven and only an old man sits at the counter, sipping coffee and reading the paper. A couple has taken a booth in the back, they're sitting on the same side, arms around each other as if they're about to start making out. It's quiet, all is quiet, this place doesn't even have music and I can hear the waitress and the cooks in the back talking shop as they wait for their shifts to end.

The bell above the door chimes a few minutes later, after I've almost finished my eggs, and Eamon has made a great deal of headway on his pastrami, despite the fact that it is not corned beef. I look up out of instinct and it's like time stops. I hold my breath but for a moment I don't recognize them, not really. They are there and not there. The diner moves in slow motion as I slowly digest this before it comes into focus.

The woman is older than she was the last time I saw her—by a lot. It's more than her years but after what she's been through I understand. It's not that I remember her that well, only a few glances in the courtroom. It's like seeing a child after a year-long absence. You just can't believe how they've shot up and how much older they seem. Maybe it's her stooped posture or careful movements as she takes a seat at a booth. No one else notices. They're just a slightly older couple coming into a diner a little after the dinner rush. She's a little heavy, her hair obviously, but tastefully, dyed blond. But he's very thin and wears a baseball cap pulled down almost over his eyes so I wonder how he can see.

"Are you okay?" Eamon asks. "Can I say you look like you've seen a ghost? Is that too cliché a thing to say to a writer?"

"It is. Don't say it," I tell him, half laughing nervously.

"I didn't say it then. Never uttered the words. Now, you ready to go?"

"Just about." Eamon looks around for the waitress to ask for the check. She approaches her new customers first but nods that she'll get to us soon. "It's just, I think Heather's parents are here. No, they are here. I recognize them."

"Wow, here, that's big. Do you want to talk to her? Should I try harder to get the check?" Eamon looks around until he sees her. When their eyes seem to meet he looks away.

I hold my breath as the waitress speaks to the couple, she orders something and then looks down at the table, her eyes avoiding mine. He doesn't appear to speak. Eamon lifts his hand again and the waitress glances over, he gives the international symbol for "check please," and she nods. She does not return right away but instead the waitress, an older woman with thin dyed red hair and hands knotted with veins, takes her paper to the back. She goes back to the kitchen and says a few words to the cook. She then takes her pad and places it on the counter, and then pulling a calculator from her pocket she begins to add our check. I watch it all as if time cannot move fast enough. Do I want these people to see me? Should I walk away without saying anything?

"Why are they here?" I ask Eamon. "I didn't think the whole family would be constantly around. I know they're on vacation but it's just . . . Why are they here?"

"They don't look like they'll come over. It could just be a coincidence," he reassures me. "I don't think they want to talk but if you want to go over there, say something, I'll go with you, or I'll stay right here, whatever you want." He looks me in the eye and I grasp his hand. Heather's parents don't look like they want to make conversation. They're entitled to a vacation on Cape Cod just like any hardworking New England couple. It must be a coincidence, I tell myself.

"I just, I have to get some air. Can you wait a little while? I think I just need to clear my head outside."

"Of course," he says very seriously. "I'll be right here. Wave if you need me."

I nod to Eamon, grateful, then I turn to the couple. They're looking at me, they're talking, they might come over but I head out before they can. I smell the ocean outside. I can't hear it, just the back and forth, the ebb and flow of cars on the road. It's almost the same whoosh, the same rush, and I wonder what it would feel like to have those cars, car after car, trucks, SUVs, pound my body back and forth just as I have felt the waves on my skin. I close my eyes and feel the soft summer air. The humidity doesn't linger tonight but I feel something, heat that is not heat, a toned down simmer as I stand in the parking lot looking at a couple of parked cars and a few neon signs.

I take out my phone, go to my contacts, and press the name "Dad." It's after eleven in Florida, we're in the same time zone, right on the same coast if you follow the curve of the country far enough. My father is an old man and after eleven is late for him but I know he'll answer.

"What's up, Pumpkin?" he asks, his voice chipper as if I have not just woken him up. I can picture him in bed, fumbling with the phone on his nightstand and wondering if something is wrong. He did this when I was in college. It didn't matter where I was whenever I was driving home late at night and I felt myself about to fall asleep at the wheel I'd call him and ask him to talk to me until I got home. We'd talk about the Red Sox and the Patriots, we'd discuss my Chemistry class or the Modern English Classic I was reading. I'm sure he was only half interested in the topics I brought up but I'm also sure he waited on edge during those calls, gripping the side of the bed until his little girl told him she was safe in her apartment.

"I'm sorry, Daddy," I say. I don't usually call him Daddy and I'm not sure why I use the word now. I can tell by the way he draws a breath that this takes him by surprise.

"It's all right, Pumpkin, how's the house holding up? Do you think it'll outlive me?" He laughs at this. The house has outlived his parents and his grandparents but when he says this I see my father's funeral, watching his black casket being lowered into the ground next to my mother's too early grave.

"I'm sure you'll outlive it," I say.

"I don't know. The house was made very well. They used to do things right back in the day."

"Kids these days and all that." I laugh at myself. His voice, more than anything, is a comfort.

"Are you all right? Is Theo bothering you?"

"No, Daddy. How's Florida? Still thinking of staying down there all year?"

"Oh, I like it here, you know. The women are much friskier."

"Don't talk like that," I half warn. "You sound like an old man trying to sound like a young man and you're not an old man. Just be a young man."

"I'm over seventy," he replies. "And the weather is nice down here. I met a man who wants me to work part-time for his contracting company. I'll be putting in cabinets three half-days a week. Easy work, nothing too hard."

"You'll be working again? It's been decided, you have a job? Do you need money? I can send you money if you need it. You shouldn't have to work."

"I have plenty of money. A really great pension. But I'm bored and I don't play shuffleboard or golf or any of that. TV is only so good. I need to get out there. It's boring being retired. It's what your mother would have wanted."

"It is," I reply. It's what she would have wanted on the days she was herself. When she stayed home and watched television, when she baked tuna noodle casserole and read her magazines, that version of her would have wanted him to move on. And she was that version, content, normal, just my mom, many more days than she was the other woman. So why is it that the other woman, her bad days, haunt me? "Why did she have to die?" My voice cracks and I hear only silence on the line. "Why did she do it? All she had to do was not do it in the bath and we might have saved her."

"Let's not dwell on the other stuff, let's remember how she was. The good times. There were so many good times. And your mother loved you. She would have been so proud of you."

"Stop it, it's not fair. What she did to you, what she did to us. How long are you going to go on not blaming her?"

"It wasn't her fault she was sick. I couldn't help her. Her doctors, the hospitals, in the end we just couldn't help her. But your mother wanted you to have the very best. That's why she took that terrible job at the Currency Exchange to make sure we could help a little with your tuition. Let's think about that."

"I know, but still . . ." Did a job at a Currency Exchange for six months make up for the fact that she embarrassed me in front of my friends, not like a normal mother embarrasses her child, but so much that my friends were afraid of her? Does it make up for the fact that I had to take care of her more than she took care of me? Did it make up for the fact that my poor father had to call me in the middle of the night and tell me my mother had just killed herself in the bathtub months after my baby was stillborn?

"Your mother loved you," my father says. "It's all fine, Lorelei, really. Anything she said, anything she did, she wasn't in her right mind then and she loved you."

"Daddy, I just, before I was born, was Mom ever . . . off? Did you hear about anything happening to her when she was in high school?" I ask cautiously, unsure if I want the answer.

"High school?" he replies suspiciously. "I didn't talk to her about that time. I know she lost a friend, she had some traumatic experiences and then she had that break. Needed to go away for a while. But they took care of her. She read a lot of poetry then."

"Are you sure she loved me? Are you sure it wasn't just out of obligation that she had me?"

"Lorelei, how could you say such a thing?" he asks as if he's shocked and I feel bad for hurting him. "She had her good days and her bad days but it wasn't any better or worse overall," he says so matter-of-factly like he's being interviewed for a documentary.

"Did she ever talk about kids? About wanting them or not wanting them? Especially just after you guys got married?"

"No," he says a little too coldly. "No, she never did. We had a lot of trouble conceiving you. She was thirty-seven when you were born, women her age didn't usually have children back then. We went to the doctor a few times, it took a while and after you were born, well, babies are tough on their mothers. It's a lot of work and so we decided it was best not to try for another one. But the doctors, they said we were lucky to conceive you." There's a pause and I swear I can hear the ocean but I know it's just the cars whooshing by. "But you don't want to know about all that, do you?"

I look out and I know I've put him through enough. "No, it's okay, Daddy. Thank you for talking to me."

Tears gather at the cusps of my eyes and it's not for my mother, not really, almost not at all, that they come. I see Heather in my class raising her hand and saying something so clever. I remember Theo and I when we were happy, and for a time I loved him, for a time we were happy. I watch that happiness fade like I'm watching my life flash before my eyes. I remember the disintegration of our marriage night after night turning to day after day. Before he even met Heather we were just going through the motions. Then there was the phone call to Heather and her mother picked up and I yelled at her, I told her mother instead of letting Heather do it. And then another call a week later saying that she was dead. I feel my womb where my unborn child once lived. All of it comes to me as the cars whoosh past. I sniffle, I try to hold the tears in but they come, of course they come. I know then what it's like, wanting to just walk in front of a car, wanting it all just to end. I know what my mother felt, at least I think I do, as I watch the road. But I'm not my mother, I know I'll get better. I know I'll survive and keep going.

"Do you think you'll ever sell the house?" I ask, forcing the tears back. "The memories, there are so many memories. Wouldn't they be too much?"

"Nah," my father says. "Other way around. There are too many memories *to* sell the place. I remember being a little boy there, I can't give that up. And my grandparents owned that place. Who am I going to sell it to some Wall Street fat cat who'll probably tear it down and build some modern contraption?"

"You sound like an old man again," I say, laughing through the gathering tears.

"Besides, it'll go to you someday."

"What if I don't want it?" I look back at the diner. Eamon waves and I raise my hand to wave back.

"You'll want it. You're not allowed to not want it."

I laugh at this and shake my head. "I'm sorry, Daddy. I have to go. It was good to talk to you. So nice to hear your voice. I'm sorry if I woke you."

"Of course. Anytime, Pumpkin. I never cared if you woke me up. It was always better to talk to my little girl than to sleep. I can sleep when I'm dead."

I see him in a casket again and a shiver runs through me. "Don't say that."

"Okay, I won't say that. Can I say good night, is that all right to say or do you need to talk some more?"

"No, I'm fine, thank you. Good night, Daddy," I tell him and hang up.

Eamon motions from the window. It seems he's asking if he should head outside to meet me but I motion back at him to stay put. I enter the diner, the metal counter; the chrome poles near the red vinyl backed booths are another time warp. Heather's parents look up at me, her mother smiles, it's a friendly but obligatory smile, and I walk over with my hands in my pockets.

"Hello," I say and her mother looks up, nodding kindly.

"Hello. Thank you for coming over. We were considering whether to say hello. We didn't want to bother you."

"I just, thank you for your note. I really appreciate it."

"Thank you for taking it. My sister wants me to apologize for Ashley's surprise visit. She didn't know she was driving her daughter to your house. She thought it was a friend. Ashley has her own ideas. She's willful."

"Willful like her cousin," Heather's father says, looking up at me.

"I understand. It's fine. It was a little surprising. It threw Theo for a loop seeing her. I hope she's okay." I wonder if they'll comment or cringe at the mention of Theo but after all that's happened they seem too embarrassed to react even to him.

"She will be," Heather's mother replies. "She's upset now. You know how kids are. They bounce back."

"And I'm sorry, I mean, the phone call. I guess everything. I just . . . I'm sorry."

"Thank you," Heather's mother replies, smiling serenely, not happily, as she looks up at me. "You don't have to be sorry but I understand. We're all just reeling from this. It's been over a year and it's not over. But we're here. We're trying to move forward, not on, but forward. Thank you for that." She grasps my hand for a second and I hold it. I could say more. I could go on but if I talk anymore it will be for me and not for them.

"I'll let you get back to your dinner." I motion backward in that awkward fashion and they nod understandingly when I start to turn away.

"Enjoy your trip," her father goes on as I go.

I walk back to Eamon. He's standing near the booth with the chess set under one arm. "All set. Ready to go?" he asks, putting his arm around my back as I move to leave.

"Yes, ready. I'd like to read a little of the Plath novel tonight, but I can wait until you pass out."

"I will not pass out, I'm capable of staying up," Eamon starts.

"You tell yourself that, Mr. Sleepyhead. You'll be asleep by eleven."

"You're probably right," he admits. "I have a busy day ahead of me in the studio."

"Good. Amelia will probably be back by now but do you want to stay the night?" I ask as if it's even a question at this point.

"I do," Eamon replies as I open the door for us. "I most certainly do."

Sylvia
1962

THE CHILDREN WERE crying. It was like the third world or somehow they'd been transplanted to medieval London, a time before all these modern conveniences when a woman with two children really and truly had to fend for herself, fend them off with a stick, because if she didn't the wolves, literally wolves, would be at her door. The grocery stores, the at-home medical care, reliable heat, that had all vanished with this horrible, frostbitten winter. Frieda stood under Sylvia's feet, grasping at her dress, pulling it down as if to try to strip her mother naked while Sylvia held Nicholas to her chest and tried to calm him as he wailed in her ear. "Mummy, it's cold, it's cold, it's cold!" Frieda cried. "Mummy I want to go to Daddy. I want to go home, to the house with the yard and the cows and the bees."

"We can't go back there, honey," Sylvia said, looking down at the girl. She was wearing layers, two pairs of socks, leggings and a skirt, two sweaters. Her hair was a rat's nest all stuck to the back of her head and her face wasn't washed. Sylvia could see smudges on her little cheeks like she was an urchin from a Dickens's novel but there was no hot water and black grimy sludge liquid in the tub and Sylvia wouldn't dare put anything cold on her child's skin even if it was to clean her. Not that anything could get clean in the dirt water coming out of the tap. "Devon is not our home anymore, we live here now," Sylvia said very calmly. And really it was just as cold at the house in Devon except in the country they would really have to fend for themselves out there with the fields and the cows. At least in the city there was some semblance of civilization.

"I don't want to live here!" Frieda wailed and Sylvia couldn't blame her.

The pipes had frozen again. She'd tried everything, keeping the heat on, running the water, the hot water, even when she didn't need it. Paying for all this cost a fortune, but she had done what the estate agent's letter had instructed. She'd followed the directions to the letter no matter how vigilant she had to be, no matter what it cost her and it still didn't work. In school she had been that kind of girl, when an assignment was due, she did it. She dotted every I and crossed every T and never left a thing out. She had never done less than an A's work and even then she felt she wasn't doing enough. It was work, work, work to succeed, succeed, succeed. But here she was and she'd done what the estate agent had asked and still the pipes froze.

It was twenty degrees out. Twenty degrees American, which was something like negative six Celsius. Europe and their fuddled calculations, Sylvia was sick of them, always reminding her that she was not one of them, that she did not really belong in this country because she wanted to drive on the right instead of the left, because she counted in Fahrenheit and not Celsius. Sylvia the spoiled American, that's what they all saw, Ted's family, acquaintances in London, her literary friends. Didn't they know that her father had died when she was ten years old, leaving her mother a widow who worked constantly to make ends meet? Didn't they know she used to sleep in her grandparent's tiny house because her mother couldn't afford their own place? She wanted to go home to her mother in Boston, where no one thought she was a snob simply because of her New England accent. And yes, it got cold in Boston but the houses weren't so old, the pipes wouldn't freeze like this.

It was twenty degrees Fahrenheit and Sylvia had stayed home all day with the children. There was no way to go out and so she had not sent Frieda to nursery school. She'd waited for Agnes, the new girl, to come to really get any work done. She'd gone out to see Doctor Horder yesterday. She'd braved the piles of snow, arriving there with her skirt soaked, her feet frozen in her wet, wet boots that threatened to turn to ice right there with her feet in them. It had been a good appointment, as far as these appointments went, but she had been so cold throughout it.

It's just that she could not get warm in this country.

"I can feel it," Sylvia had said to her doctor. "It's like I can't control it anymore. I wake up at three now and the darkness overtakes me. Some mornings I can still write, those mornings are hard but not as horrible, but it's the mornings when I can't even do that, and I just lie in bed. The other day the children were crying and I let the girl get them. Usually she doesn't come so early but I heard her come in and I just let her fix Nicholas his bottle, I let her tend to Frieda. I told her later that I was sick. It must be the flu. But really, I can feel it coming like it did before and I don't want to get out of bed. First it starts with this feeling that I simply can't go on. It's not for any specific reason. It's not because of Ted or the poetry no one will publish. I know that. These things hurt, but it's the darkness, it creeps in and takes over."

"I understand," Doctor Horder had said, nodding to Sylvia. With these doctors there was always so much nodding. So much scribbling on notepads, so much "ah-huhing" and "yes I see-ing." "Do you think you can control it?"

She wanted to spit at him. Control it? Would she be here if she could control it? "No," Sylvia had said politely. "Like I said, when this happened before, the first thing was that I felt this hopelessness, like no matter what I did life was never going to get any better. Then I stopped eating and I didn't even drink often. I don't know how my body survived at all with so little nourishment. I didn't shower, I just lay in bed staring into space and I can feel myself getting there, to that dark, dark place again. And now I can't even shower because they've asked us to conserve water because of this awful, awful frost and I have had the flu once already this awful, awful winter and the children have been sick."

"It's been a very difficult winter for a great many people. The worst on record in decades," the doctor had said, writing something on his little yellow notepad. "The suicide rate is up. And that's why it's very important, during this dark, cold, rather morose time, to keep your spirits up. Enjoy the children, Sylvia, enjoy yourself. Play with them. Write as much as you can. When it's dangerous to go out because of the cold and snow, well, try to make the best of staying in and whenever you can go out, make sure to do so and to enjoy it. It's important to stay out of bed as much as possible."

"But what if it's too late?" Sylvia had asked her doctor. She had not meant to sound so desperate. She could handle herself. She could write. She could take care of this little blip coming on her mental health radar. She'd done it before and she could survive again. She would not fail. Still, she felt it coming and she wondered if in the end she would be powerless to stop it. "What if the darkness . . . ?"

"Sylvia, how have you been doing on your medication? I think we should up your dosage, just a little bit. And I think, would it be a good idea if I tried to find you a place in a hospital? Just for a little while, a place to rest and relax. Could your husband take the children for a few days?"

A wave of relief washed over her. She hadn't thought of it until now, but yes, she could go somewhere. Maybe she would not have to be held so completely responsible anymore. She could go to a hospital. She could rest. Someone else would take care of her and everything else. They could watch her, keep her away from the things she needed to be kept away from. She knew how this went now, this getting sent to a mental health facility. Maybe they wouldn't even do electroshock on her. She'd read that these kinds of institutions were much more humane in England. She wouldn't see those great robed doctors, standing over her like priests. She wouldn't see the lightning and feel it surge through her like Johnny Panic was at her side. And maybe this would not be all on her shoulders and she could have a break and maybe even still write poetry but mostly it would not all be on her, whether the darkness came, whether she was kept alive. She wouldn't be solely responsible for the children, someone could help, her poverty wouldn't be so hard, and worrying about all these rejections. Someone else would watch her and that would mean she could rest.

"Could you do that? I'm sure Jillian and her husband could help. Or Ted, maybe Ted, but I'm never sure with Ted taking the children. That Woman, I don't think she likes to be around them, and I don't want them around her either, she poisons them against me when she's not outright mistreating them . . . but I think that if you could get me into a facility, it would be very helpful. At least for a little while, until I'm back on my feet. Jillian, my friend Jillian, would be happy to take the children." "Back on my feet," Sylvia felt herself saying the words, "back on my feet," as if she'd just had a bout of tuberculosis and her lungs had been deflated. Deflated but really wasn't that what this was? Didn't she feel as if all her organs were sinking, as if there was nothing, absolutely nothing, inside her? Not even numbness, she couldn't even feel the numbness.

"The hospitals are crowded right now. And as I said, the suicide rate has more than doubled since this weather took such an awful turn, but I'll start calling round today to see if I can find you a bed somewhere. It might be a little while, but I'll put your name in," Doctor Horder said.

"Thank you," Sylvia had replied. "If you could try it would be marvelous." Marvelous. She had not used a word like marvelous in so, so long.

But it had been straight back to the flat in the blinding snow. She had not been able to find a cab and the first bus she'd tried to get on was chalk full and so Sylvia had waited and waited as the snow came down and her feet turned to sheets of ice. By the time she got into her own stairwell, the modicum of warmth it provided made her feel whole again, as if finally her icy self might melt. Then later that day they'd learned that the pipes had frozen. After everything she'd done to prevent it, still they had frozen and Sylvia wanted to fall to the floor she felt so helpless. It didn't matter what she did, how many rules she followed, the problems came, like the darkness, and she was powerless.

Earlier, she had put the children in layers as if they were going outside. She'd draped blankets over them and they'd all huddled together on the bed as they waited for the heat to come on. "The water, it won't even come, I don't know how I'll make them their supper," Agnes, the girl, had said as Sylvia sat in bed, huddled with the children. Agnes hugged herself standing in the doorway and Sylvia didn't know what to do. They were all looking at her, she was the mother, she was in charge, she paid the bills and cleaned the house and they looked to her to know what to do. And why, why was that? Why did she have to take control over everything? Didn't they know she could hardly handle herself, let alone the lives of two small children? Where was Ted? Why couldn't he help? She couldn't do everything, not on her own, not like this.

"You know," Agnes said now, entering the kitchen from the other room. "I'm not sure, but I think the gas in the oven works. I wonder if we just turned the oven on and let it bake us. Maybe the heat would travel through the flat. If we just stayed in the kitchen we could all keep warm?" It was a time for desperate measures, Sylvia could see it on the girl's face as she stood in the kitchen with her crying children, bundled in layers.

"We can't turn the oven on, Agnes," Sylvia told the girl. "The gas might poison us all. You have to be careful with these modern ovens, sure they're useful, but they can also be very, very dangerous. Starting an oven is not like lighting a match and having a campfire. I've read about the carbon monoxide poisoning that can happen when you leave an oven on."

"I didn't think of that, Ma'am, I'm sorry," the girl said, hanging her head as she swiftly picked up Frieda, who'd been just under her mother's feet all day.

"Mummy! Mummy! Mummy!" the little girl cried, reaching for her.

It had been Frieda's prying hands on her, the desperate look in her eyes, that made her walk away. Sylvia loved the children, she wanted to protect them so much for so long, and then something like this happened, just two little hands a little too desperate for a little too long, and the tension broke like a great damn and she couldn't take it. Sylvia swiftly marched with Nicholas out of the kitchen and into her study. It was dark in there. The electricity had not failed yet but Sylvia was trying to conserve it. There had been a letter about that from the estate agent yesterday; apparently there was a chance the power might fail as well with this weather.

Sylvia felt a chill come through her study like the ghost of something and she looked out for more candles. She had some in her desk but she wanted to keep them handy in the kitchen. Just then Nicholas started to cry harder, his little hands clung to her chest and Sylvia kissed the top of his head as she rifled through her desk one handed.

What she saw were papers. So many papers. The drawer was full of rejection letters for her poetry. And then there were her poems; some of them neatly compiled, others scattered around. And even Al had said that she was writing such great poetry these days and still no one wanted it. She bared her soul. She gave of herself. All her life she laid out on a platter and no one would even taste it. There was her poetry, piles of it, and so much unpublished. It felt like a dead baby, all that unpublished poetry, stillborn and empty as if it did not exist. There was no feeling like it, none on the planet and she could have handled anything, this cold, losing Ted, if only there was not so much unpublished and therefore unappreciated, and therefore unread and unloved, poetry.

Sylvia wanted to grab it all, the letters, her new poems, the drafts of the novel she was working on, and throw it all away. There was more to Esther's story and she just wanted to write it, to tell her own story through Esther Greenwood. But in that moment all she wanted was to grab it all and bring it to the stove and light it up as she had her last novel just after she'd learned about Ted and That Woman. She'd start a great big bonfire right there on the kitchen floor. At least it would keep them warm. It would be good for something. She could just picture it, smoldering at first and then, poof, a great big fire, warmth, it would be red and yellow and orange, maybe even a little blue, jumping about. Her poetry, at least it could keep them warm.

Nicholas wailed in her ear and Sylvia could hear Frieda crying as Agnes tried to tell her to calm down in her kindest, calmest voice. Sylvia marched out of her study and into the kitchen leaving the rejection letters and the poetry. "Here," she said, handing the baby over to Agnes, who took him awkwardly in her arms as if he were a cumbersome piece of furniture she couldn't figure out how to upright. "I'm going downstairs." The girl just looked at Sylvia her eyes so wide and helpless. There was really something so innocent, too innocent, about that girl and Sylvia wanted to wake her up to the world.

She walked calmly at first but then ran down the stairs, the coldest part of the flat. She heard her shoes banging, slapping really, on the wooden steps and wondered if this had ever happened to Yeats. Had he dealt with such cold? Had he written poetry by candlelight or had he sat huddled in his blankets, praying to keep warm?

Sylvia knocked steadily on the door to the downstairs flat. She and her neighbor, Trevor, had had their differences. Apparently he'd wanted the rooms upstairs, just the second and not the third floor. He'd inquired about them after Sylvia had put down her deposit, but Trevor had said to her once, "You know I needed those rooms for my family. My children stay with me sometimes and there's hardly any space for them. By rights, as the tenant downstairs, I was entitled to those rooms first but then you swooped in before there was any time . . ." It had not been a pleasant conversation but since then she and her neighbor had mostly kept to themselves. But in times like these really all of London was in crisis and neighbors should help one another.

Sylvia knocked politely on the dark wooden door to the flat downstairs. She used the knocker and not the bell but found when she finally rang the bell that she couldn't hear anything, not even inside. Perhaps the cold had done something to the bell? Sylvia knocked politely once more and then started banging. She banged so hard she wondered if she might cause a picture to fall off the wall and still she banged. She could feel it, the darkness, it wanted in, and if only she banged on this door as hard as she could she could help herself and the children. Help. She needed to find help. It was her job, she was a mother, she needed to bang down this door until someone helped her.

"Coming, I'm coming," she heard a voice call as the slight hint of movement came from behind the door. "Just a moment, please," the voice went on and

Sylvia heard a metal lock click and thought with such relief, We're saved, we're saved finally.

When the door opened and a little man with messy greying hair appeared Sylvia could only look down at him, gaping. Saved? By this man? And what exactly do I want? What exactly can he do? How on earth can he save us? And still she went on looking at him. There was nowhere to go, nothing else to do.

"Can I help you?" the little man asked and Sylvia looked down at him. Can he? She wondered. Can anyone help?

"Please," she finally said. "It's just that the pipes have frozen and I called the city and it looks like the men who do these things are on strike and they won't be in to fix the pipes, not for days. I told them I have two babies and they said it didn't matter, so many people are old or ill or have small children and they can't help. It's freezing in the flat and I was just wondering if you had anything, anything at all."

The little man looked at her. He had not always liked her but his face melted and Sylvia glanced in the mirror. She really did look a fright, like Medusa, *lens of mercies*, her brown hair was disheveled and flying every which way, her face was wan and ghostlike and she was thin, so thin. When was the last time she'd eaten, really eaten more than a nibble while standing above the sink scrubbing dishes? And I used to be beautiful, she thought to herself. Men used to love me and I gave myself to Ted, all of myself, and I fixed his home and helped him with his writing career, I had his children and got older and tired and then he up and left.

"We live in the same flat and therefore we're in the same boat. My pipes have frozen too," her neighbor told her. "I can't get water and the heat is on the fritz. It really is a bad, bad winter. A friend of mine slipped on the ice over in Hampstead a couple of days ago. He banged his head on a pole and it was bleeding and he went to hospital for stitches and waited there seven hours just to be seen. Everyone I fear is in the same predicament. It's best to stay inside."

Sylvia watched as the man marched through the entranceway, where he left her to come in on her own, as he made his way back to his kitchen. He came out a couple of seconds later with a metal torch and a brown paper bag. "Here," he said as she stood in his living room. "I have an extra torch, it has batteries in it but I don't know how long they'll last. And here's some bread, it's really all I can spare. But I've seen your children upstairs and I don't want to think of them starving."

"Oh, thank you," Sylvia said. "I fear we'll run out of milk, but I still have the stove to heat up the baby's formula. But thank you, I'll give the bread to the children at once, thank you so much for your kindness."

"I understand, I completely understand," her neighbor said, moving toward the front door as if to see her out. Instead Sylvia took a seat on a chair near the hall and the little man just looked at her, helpless as Sylvia collapsed in his living room. She couldn't leave. She couldn't go back to that. She barely knew her neighbor, he hardly liked her, she was not welcome here, she was imposing, she knew it and yet it was better to just stay here than to return to her life upstairs.

"It's just that it's so hard, you know, with the children," she nearly cried into her hands, though she kept her head up.

"I know. I have children. When their mother brings them round for a visit, when I'm alone with them, it's not always easy. You have to keep them clothed and fed, but you also have to entertain the little buggers." Her neighbor smiled at that but Sylvia couldn't bring herself to understand his joke.

"It's just been so much, since Ted, my husband, left. And I've been writing so much poetry and this darkness, I feel it coming. You know?" She looked at her neighbor and wondered if he had ever felt the darkness. He didn't look like the type and the expression on his face seemed to state that he didn't really understand. Not everyone was of the darkness. Not everyone understood what it meant to see it coming.

"When my wife and I split up it was the same way. But I can't imagine it's easy, getting the bad luck of a winter like this on top of everything else."

"It's all piling up, all stacked against me. And I cannot get my poetry published, that's the biggest thing. A friend of mine said maybe it means that my poetry is too good, too ahead of its time. That's a nice thought, wouldn't it be good to tell yourself that? You're too much of a genius to be recognized? Isn't that convenient? And if it is too good, if I'm to be one of those tragic poets who only gets recognized after her death, well then, I don't know if that's any consolation now. It certainly doesn't pay any bills. Doesn't help my life. Doesn't help me raise my children. Is that selfish? I guess that's completely selfish and I should want to help future generations of poets. I should stop caring about paying bills when there is eternity to think about. It's just that Ted has all the friends, Ted has all the influence and they don't like me the way they like him."

"Poetry?" her neighbor asked. "Poetry, you write poetry?"

"I do," she replied, wiping a couple of tears from her eyes with one hand as she held the torch and the bread in the other. "I used to publish pretty widely and I have a book coming out in England. But that's it for now."

"Sylvia Plath? You write poetry. Ah, I'm just putting it together and I read something of yours in *The Atlantic* not too long ago. Hughes, I always thought your name was Hughes, but here it is, you're Sylvia Plath. I read your poetry and I liked it, I really did. I didn't realize you were her, one and the same. How silly I didn't put it together. I didn't realize you were Sylvia Plath."

Esther Greenwood
Cardiff, Wales 1958

CARDIFF WAS A blue-collar town, like parts of Boston. When people think of Boston they picture the capital building with the shiny gold dome on top. They think of tiny cobblestone streets and people with money shopping at high-end stores like Filenes and Lechmere's because they got their college education at Harvard or Radcliff. And that's one part of Boston but the heart of the city has always been men working on cars in side alleys and guys in overalls at the docks shipping out crates of flour and lumber and other necessary supplies. Boston is waitresses with big hair and women who scrub toilets for a living more than it is anything so high end as Copley Square and this is the vibe I got once Tom and I drove our rented Morris into Cardiff.

We looped around the city, heading first toward the docks, which were not where we wanted to be but Tom had gotten lost and didn't follow the signs right. "Just pay attention, Esther," he screamed at me. "Learn how to follow directions!"

Then we went back inland where tiny row houses stood one next to the other their white paint chipping. There's a heart to the city that is not so neat and clean. But Cardiff had just been declared the capital of Wales and so it did have a few streets of stores and restaurants near the Empire Theater and the Jones Hotel, a brick and concrete structure with a large red and white sign where Tom and I were going to be staying. The hotel wouldn't let us stay in the same room, because we weren't married, and when we went to check in and leave our bags at the front desk Tom commented, "Maybe next year we won't have to worry about a silly rule like this." The concierge only raised an eyebrow as I signed the register.

"So, the theatre is just across the street," Tom observed after we'd checked in and left our bags at the pretty stark lobby sparsely furnished with cheap love seats and stools. "It won't open for another hour then I have to meet Preston and the guys before my reading. Where do you want to go until then?"

"Back to the water," I said. "The Warf is only a few blocks away."
I had been eyeing it as we drove past earlier. Cardiff lies on the sea,
unlike London, which is landlocked and can only be traversed via
water by a river. And the Thames really is a very grand river but it's
nothing like the sea. There's not even salt in the water. But Cardiff,
it looked out to a fjord-like inlet that led right into an estuary that
goes to the ocean. The water was so blue, a dark blue at this dusky
time of day, and it lapped gently at the surface of Wales as if that very
big ocean had been subdued by the whimsical charms of the ancient
Celts.

We walked a few blocks past parked cars and little shops selling
scarves and hats. We passed a butcher that reminded me of a man my
mother used to use in Wellesley. The shop had a big white sign out
front with a bloody meat clever on it, very unbecoming, some of the
parents of small children had complained, but there was something
charming about a sign that could be so honest about what was going
on inside. At least they didn't try to cover up what they did with a
picture of a smiling cow, as if cows liked being chopped to little bits
and fed to people in carefully portioned sizes.

I could smell the water, and the wharf, the moment we walked
near it. "They've just started to build up this part of Cardiff," Tom
explained. "This place used to only handle shipping. The city just
became the capital a few years back, you know. The navy has a port a
little ways away, used to all be commerce, the raw side of commerce,
the crates and boxes and men lifting things side of it, until a few years
ago when they put in a couple of restaurants."

"What's that?" I asked, pointing to a big red structure, something
very official with a three-storey clock on top. It looked like a toy,
something you'd put near the train set under a Christmas tree.

"The clock tower?" Tom asked. "I think that's where official business
happens. The mayor's office, stuff like that."

"I see," I said as we walked down a strip of newly paved sidewalk
and toward a couple of shops by the water. "I smell the sea."

Tom nodded as if this observation were more than a little keen.
I could feel it, that cool breath of salt water ran across my skin like
Celtic fairies skipping about on tiptoes and it was like I was back with
my family on Cape Cod.

"I'm famished. Stonehenge took a lot out of me. That was quite a
walk and quite a drive on all those little backcountry roads. You know,
the peasantry here really should learn how to step on the gas," Tom

said, patting his belly as if hunger were a physical thing he could grab and throttle if he wanted to. It seemed he'd completely forgotten our fight. Perhaps that was for the best though I could still feel a dull pain in my wrist when I twisted it. Still it was best not to remind him of it.

It had not been a terrible drive after Tom's outburst, he didn't hit me again or yell, he didn't even think to, didn't even try but still I felt such darkness as we drove. I'd put the radio on and tried to find station after station, switching the dial as we entered yet another small town with a new frequency but I couldn't find any more Beatles and that was a shame. Tom, however, did not like that he couldn't drive very fast not like on the highways they were starting to build around London. These highways, like all progress, another byproduct of the war.

"Do you want to grab a bite?" Tom asked, his hand still on his stomach as he pointed to a little café a couple feet away. It had iron tables out front and had been painted white at one time. But I could see the blackened grime on the upper walls near the roof and the large glass windows were streaked as if they had not been cleaned in a while. Still there was something very Cardiff, maybe it was that it seemed blue collar, about the place and so I nodded yes to Tom and we walked toward it.

"I'll have the fish and chips," Tom ordered the second we sat down at the little patio outside. The waitress, she was tall with short blond hair and tiny facial features, took out a little pad and quickly started writing as if brusqueness like this was a part of her job description. Her tiny features all seemed to fit on her face, but they looked scrunched up as if her face were falling in on itself. I wondered what this girl would look like as an old woman. This was not the kind of face that aged gracefully but got uglier year after year until it's that of a shriveled old hag.

"I'll have that as well. And some coffee, do you have coffee?"

"Sure thing," the waitress said and I could pick up her Welsh accent. It was slightly rougher like this coarser land.

"I'll have some tea," Tom added just before the waitress walked away.

"So, Esther." Tom got down to business just after she left. "You know, I've just been thinking about the hotel and that silly rule they had. If we're going to travel like this, especially in other parts of Europe . . . I mean, you said you wanted to go to Spain and Italy and France, and these are not places that take kindly to unmarried couples traveling together."

"It's 1958, Tom, I'm sure we'll find a place to settle for the night. Even this hotel, it's a very nice hotel, very old, but if we went somewhere a little less nice—"

"But why should we have to do that? I mean, I don't want to go on some kind of crusade and say that all people everywhere should now allow unmarried couples to stay in the same hotel room together. Hoteliers should do what they like. But if we're going to be doing this, traveling, reading papers and poetry at conventions, writing, working together, doesn't it just make sense to get married?"

As I looked out on the water I saw Lincoln Center as it would be when they finished it, mingling right there with the silver lights reflecting off the sea. A life in New York with Micah came into my mind full force as if it were a wall I'd walked smack into. Could I live here in England with Tom? Could I just say yes? Could I ever get used to the fact that they drive on the wrong side of the road or that they still drank more tea than coffee and in London I would be forced to eat so many meat pies? Should a decision such as choosing the man you are to marry be made, not because of love or logic, but because of the state of the meat pies in the city where you'll live? But with Micah in New York there would be culture and books and poetry, still poetry, and no meat pies. He was a man who could take me in his arms and if he had asked me to marry him I would have said yes.

"I'd like to just be here now, in Cardiff. I love the wharf, do you smell the sea, the salt, feel the air? I don't know, there's something about water, when I get near water my mind starts wandering and I want to write poetry." It pulled me out of the darkness, that's what it did. But I didn't tell Tom that because he'd only wonder what I meant.

"I know, Esther, me too. It's not very built up here but it really is a beautiful place." Tom looked out and I wanted to ask him what was in his head. What was he seeing? He was concocting some kind of poem in his mind and if only he'd share it with me, the words that were forming to create a whole, the words that would make a poem that would fit in a book of poems that would be published for the entire world to see. And Tom, he really was a great poet and if only he would share that poetry with me, share it while it was happening and not afterwards when everything had been formalized and crystal clear, if only he would let me see it as it was happening, I would love him more and I would have said yes to him. But Tom keeps everything to himself, he hordes like a common sneak, and then complains later that I'm not chipper enough.

"You know, that's one of the topics up for debate at one of the panels. The idea of the poet as the last great Bard, the poet as the traveler who goes round the world seeing life, feeling it, and bringing it back to the people."

"That's a very interesting topic," I said, looking out.

"And Wilson is going to be directing an open mic later, Esther, maybe you could read something."

"I'd like that very much."

"You know, it's just that, with the way poetry is going, and writing in general, the creative side of it, it's becoming very academic in its own right. I'm not sure what that means for people, but I think that at the very least, with Creative Writing as a topic discussed in Universities, it will give it some credit, you know? When I publish a book maybe someone outside of a select circle of people will read it. And you have to admit Esther, that circle has always been very small and very select when it comes to poetry. Maybe a professor will assign my work in school and college students twenty, thirty years from now will be able to read it and think about it."

"I was an English major," I told him. "You don't want English majors getting anywhere near your poetry. All they'll do is tear it apart. They'll think they're getting down to some kind of universal truth, some kind of essence, when really all they're doing is making themselves look smart in front of their professor."

Tom laughed at that, placing his hands on the table just as our food came. "Looks good," he said. "I always did love fish and chips in Wales. I don't know what it is, I think they fry it up better." The waitress smiled and nodded down at Tom and I gazed back out at the water as Tom dove right into his fish. A man walked into the café and marched directly to the back, ignoring the waitress who had just set down our check. He picked up the receiver at a payphone and I realized that the café had a whole row of them.

"That's what we're known for," the waitress explained. She must have seen me watching. "Ever since we put the payphones in the back we have people coming in all the time, during the work day, at lunch hour the guys from the docks come in and stay on the phone a whole hour, sometimes there's a line to use them. It's been great for business but it's really tough for a working girl like me."

"I bet," I said. "And let me guess, they order a cup of coffee and hardly tip."

"Hardly tip," the waitress reiterated as Tom wolfed down his fish and chips and I realized that I had barely touched mine. At the sight of my food I felt a pang of hunger and stuck my fork into a slice of fried fish and started to pick at it.

"Are you going to finish that?" Tom asked after a couple of seconds and before I could answer he reached down and grasped half a slab of fish and started chomping on it. "You like the chips better anyway. What do they call them in America, French Fries? Why exactly are they French?"

"I read about it somewhere," I replied as Tom dug into his wallet and pulled out some bills. He seemed to be in a bit of a rush now and so I quickly downed a couple of chips. "It has something to do with the way that the French cut their potatoes, julienned I think."

"So if you cut them in bigger wedges they'd be British Fries?"

"Maybe." I shrugged and Tom stood up.

"I have to run to the theater. I'm supposed to meet Preston and Wilson there in ten minutes. Do you want to stay here? Maybe finish your meal? Take your time and come back to the theater when you're done. Just make sure you don't take too long, Esther. Don't let your head get stuck in the clouds. I'll be very disappointed if I have to come looking for you." He gave me a dark, warning look and for a second he reminded me of my father. Except Daddy was never mean like that, never so controlling.

"All right, thank you. I'll be there soon. Good luck." I smiled up at Tom and the look he gave frightened me for a second.

"I don't need luck, I just need to do a good job."

"Of course," I replied as I watched Tom leave the restaurant his back so broad as his disheveled hair blew in the sea breeze.

I took a few more bites of the fish and chips, mostly chips, Tom was right, I didn't much care for the fish, it was just so fried and greasy. Grease always stayed in the pit of my stomach, I felt it sliding around and it made me sick.

"He's a catch," the waitress said, coming upon me and scooping the money off the table with a single hand.

"He's a great guy," I told her, looking up at her with big eyes. There was something about that moment, the weight of it, that made me feel so helpless.

"Really, handsome, strong, he seemed nice too."

"He can be. Thank you for dinner. It was lovely," I said to the waitress and she nodded as I stood up and walked out of the patio area.

I could see the water from where I'd been sitting but something about the air made me want to get closer to it. I closed my eyes and took a few steps and finally reached the end of the pier. Looking out at the sea, the water stretched for miles and I knew that if I kept going, if I jumped in and swam maybe I could make it back to my mother in America. And Micah, Micah would return to New York in a few weeks and maybe if I swam the entire sea, if I did not go under but used all my strength as the ocean pummeled me, I could meet him there. I could show him that I could do it and wouldn't he love me then?

It was such a very big thing, the sea at Cardiff, and even in this blue-collar city with only a few nice buildings, many of which were not the towering colossuses of London, the horizon seemed to last forever, sea touching sky and I wondered if there was a place they might meet. I saw them then, those rocks at Stonehenge, big and powerful they made me feel so small. And then it was Lincoln Center as it soon would be three buildings connected by an inner sanctum of concrete, another piece of art for another place and time just as big and I, Esther Greenwood, was so very, very small.

It was then that I wanted Micah. I had to tell him everything and hope he could understand me. I felt him, an ache in my chest it ran through my nerve endings, away from the chemicals in my brain and right to my soul.

I turned back, away from the water. Part of me would miss it when I wasn't looking at it, but I felt as if Micah was in my bones and I had to get to him. I didn't have any money but I knew I could call collect, Micah's family were the type of people who would accept a collect call without asking too many questions. I walked back through the patio, smiling tightlipped at the waitress, a smile that I hoped told her not to talk to me. She knew where I was going and left me alone as I picked up a payphone receiver and dialed the number Micah had given me the other day in London, "Just in case you need to get in touch." I had memorized it. I hadn't even had to bring it with me. I'd stared at that number for so long that night as I lay in bed thinking about him. I'd wanted to be with him so badly and his hands had touched that paper, he had written on it, and I wanted to keep it with me always.

"I would like to make a collect call to ----," I said after the operator asked me what I wanted.

"Just a moment, I'll connect you," she said and the phone went quiet for a second before ringing ensued and a woman answered.

"Hello?" she asked, very confused. But this woman had accepted the call and that was something. If I'd gotten a collect call from Wales from a strange woman I don't know if I would have accepted the charges, but Micah's family is apparently very progressive.

"Hello, Miss. Are you . . . ?" I searched my mind for her name. Micah had given me his aunt's name, I'm sure, but I couldn't remember it. "Are you the aunt of Micah, Micah Rosenberg?"

"I am. My name is Frieda Rosenberg," the woman replied very prim and polite.

"Thank you. I was just wondering if I could speak with him. I'm sorry for calling collect like this, it really is an emergency. I really need to speak to him. I promise I'll wire him the money so he can pay you back."

"Of course, dear," the aunt said, her voice very kind. "Don't worry about the money. I'll put him on."

It only took a second for Micah to get the phone. I heard rumbling as the two of them exchanged the receiver. "Hello?" Micah asked and I closed my eyes, his words, his voice, was like water and it was only then that I saw how thirsty I was. "Hello, Esther are you okay? Is something wrong? Do you need help?"

"It's just . . ." And the tears came. I thought I could hold them in but like the ocean they were so very big and they came from my eyes even though I didn't want them to. And why, why do tears come, shouldn't something so sacred, so vulnerable, be voluntary, why is it that anyone should be forced to cry when they don't want to? It's seems much too intimate a thing to be so involuntary. Like being forced to walk around naked. "It's just that I wanted to hear your voice."

"Oh, Esther." Micah sighed and I knew just then that it was not the same as before. He was not the same and he deeply regretted those last hours we'd spent together in London. I felt it all in his voice. "Esther, we do need to talk you know, but I thought maybe when I returned to London."

"Micah, you don't understand. It's as if I spend all my days, even when we were apart, even those many months when we didn't speak or see each other, I spent all that time thinking about you. You're in my blood and that's such a silly, cliché thing to say and I really don't want to have to say it, a poet should do better, but you reduce me to clichés, Micah. I see you, I feel you inside me and I just . . . I want to be with you so badly. And Tom, Tom took me to Kensington Gardens the other day and got down on one knee and proposed and I told him that I couldn't do it, I couldn't give him an answer, not yet and I wanted to say no, no right there but I didn't and now he thinks I'm thinking about it but I'm not thinking about it because there's nothing to think about because you're all I think about, you're all I need and when I see Tom again I'm going to tell him that because I really just want to be with you Micah, do you understand that? Tom is such a brute and he makes me feel bad all the time. I feel the darkness come in and I'm worried that if I stay with him I'll need electro-shock again and it will kill me this time. It will kill me. Tom can be so mean and he doesn't understand me, Micah, not like you do.

"And I don't care at all about the Jewish thing. I would convert for you if that's what you need. I would go through the process, talk to a rabbi, I would. I'd go to synagogue with you every Saturday and do the Friday night meal with the blessings and the candles and you could light the candles and see, I do know some things about the Jewish religion and I would be so happy just to be with you, Micah, and this time away from you has taught me that. It's just such a thing, such a very, very big thing, my feelings for you and so I had to call you, call right away so we could speak about it properly." I was trying to keep him, that was all, I felt it right away I was just trying to keep him, to hold back the halt in his voice, the silent suffering. I almost collapsed right there and if I had been alone I probably would have started wailing but I held my tears. But I had said it, I'd made my confession, and there was relief in that. This had been on my mind for so long, the pressure of those feeling like those stones pressing the earth, like the waves against the rocks, it had all been bursting inside me and I finally said it.

"Esther," Micah breathed calmly and I could picture him, tall and thin and very, very logical, standing by a phone and speaking evenly. Micah, for all his passion, knew how to speak to me when I got frantic. He would be so good for me when I got sad, he'd make it so I wouldn't need to go away—not ever again. I couldn't get him off my mind, I went round and round on him—obsessing. "Esther, we do need to talk. It's just that, being with my aunt, you know she survived Auschwitz and she told me such awful stories about what the Germans did to her."

"But I'm not German!" I said. "I'm not German at all, not like that. I was born in America, just like you. My parents both came over well before the camps . . ."

"I know Esther and it's not as if I blame you. It's not as if I or even my family would ever think to blame you or lump you or your family in with the swine who did such awful things to my family. Your family wasn't even in the same country, I . . . we, know that. But the stories my aunt told me, the things they did to them, it's all too much, Esther, it really is. And I think I need to pay homage to that. I need to sacrifice for my religion, my people, really and truly because the faith has been through so much in the last twenty years. And I was really very silly the other day in London. I'm over emotional and I do stupid things and people get hurt. I'm sorry. I got carried away and I shouldn't have. You know we're not meant to be. We fought a lot when we were together and yes, sometimes it was nice, and I really did like you. You're a great girl, Esther, but you know it would never work. We're not compatible. And I just got carried away, it didn't mean anything, the other night in London, you know that, right? Both of us are a little too sad . . . we're both just not together-in-the head enough. We both need someone more stable than we are to keep us grounded. You know that, right, Esther?"

"No," I cried into the phone. "No, Micah, I do not know at all." Anger built in my chest and I wanted to throw the payphone, the whole booth, across the room. Then I wanted to get down on my hands and knees and beg Micah to love me. "No, no, no!" I cried at him, tears falling down my face. The waitress turned and looked at me. It was a lucky thing there were no other customers because she probably would have told me to leave then. "What do you mean? You thought you'd have a little fun, a little fling, while you were in London? Is that what this was? Were you just playing around? Is that what I am to you, Micah? I love you."

"Esther, calm down. We're not in love. In the grand scheme of things we barely know each other." And how could he say such a thing when I was ready to throw everything away, Tom, my religion, my life, for him. "Esther it was one night, a nice romantic night but you can't base your whole life on that."

"I said I'd convert!" I cried. "I would convert, I'd make that sacrifice for you. Do you want me to convert?" I would do anything, anything for him. I felt the confusion in my mind, the sea, the smell of greasy fried fish, Tom and Stonehenge and Cardiff, it all swirled around me and I grasped the phone booth as I lost my balance and fell over.

"Are you okay, miss?" the waitress asked, coming to help me into a chair. I sat up and put the phone back to my ear without even acknowledging the woman.

"But it wouldn't be the same," Micah went on. "Your family wouldn't be Jewish, the faith, the customs, they would never really be a part of you. And even if you did that's not what this is about. We're not good together. I apologize if I gave the wrong impression the other day. I took things too far and I should have realized with someone like you . . . We just can't, I'm sorry."

"You're sorry?" I said quietly into the phone. "You're telling me you're sorry you just got carried away. It didn't mean that much to you."

"Yes," Micah said definitively. "Yes, but you know it's not that simple. It's not about any one thing, Esther. I'm sorry if last week meant more to you than it did to me."

"All you have to do is love me," I cried.

It washed over me then, a great numbness, a darkness, and I felt as if I wasn't there, as if the waves had already pummeled me and there was no more Esther Greenwood. I closed my eyes and pictured the sea, I saw Stonehenge and what there was of Lincoln Center and they were all so very big and I was so very small and I just wanted to cower at it all I felt so worthless. It was like the day my mother told me that Daddy had died. She was calm and slow and I was ten years old and he'd been very sick and I'd felt so helpless. "Daddy," I'd said, missing him so much. I knew then that I was powerless to get him back. I would never see him again and I wanted those moments back, that time with him, I wanted to snatch it up and carry it in my pocket forever. Micah, I had lost him just as I'd lost my father. He'd never really cared about me it was all just some silly story I'd blown out of proportion and still I felt like I'd lost him. I was prone to big stories, prone to telling myself things that weren't true and it was happening again. I knew it. It was happening again. Whatever was wrong with my brain was repeating like some sort of broken record. I looked out at the wharf, at the water, and finally, finally I felt nothing.

"I'm sorry, Esther, I really am," Micah said out of nowhere and I just stared out.

"Good bye," I said, hanging up. I let the great numbness wash over me and just then I wanted to go to bed.

I stared at the black receiver hanging on that silver metal contraption and it really did look so modern, especially inside this whitewashed shack of a restaurant and when did the two connect, this rustic blue-collar place and all the conveniences of modern life? The waitress came out and started to wipe off a couple of tables and I sat down at one that she hadn't gotten to yet. The need to write poetry was so very strong and I felt it in the core of my stomach. The words existed as if they always had. It was only that I, the poet, had to find the right configuration to bring them to life, like Michelangelo chipping at that raw, unnaturally beautiful marble. But the words came as if they were inevitable, as if this poem, these words in this exact order, had always existed and it had taken this pain to get it all out. This undeniably numbing pain had been the catalyst, the juice, that had brought the poem to the surface so that it might exist for the world to see.

And what was art, any art, but a byproduct of damage, of pain and loss so unimaginable? Very big things . . . grand, immense, eternal . . . one struggles to find the right word and what kind of pain had the creator of the ocean felt as He made the waves so violent they trekked across the sea pummeling rocks and sea creatures, entire mountain ranges in their wake? What kind of pain had the makers of Stonehenge felt? What were they looking for, what did they need to know so badly they had to pull stones from the sea and drag them hundreds of miles?

What were they trying to find out?

I took out my pen and notebook from my bag and wrote. I wrote furiously. It didn't stop the pain, it didn't help at all but the words were in me and like my tears, which I could not control, they had to come out.

For Micah
By Esther Greenwood

If I were a beekeeper's daughter I might have fallen from London Bridge
I, who love so much those rivers
I stared out at the Thames but never considered doing it
Tell me
Does that make me brave or a coward or just completely, utterly absentminded?
And I never knew how you could love me
And still
Wear that yellow star upon your chest
The one that binds you so tightly to a world, a life
The chosen people and you made your choice

One big family reunion into all eternity
The hat you used as an oven mitt
And it was all a game
Some sort of mad scientist experiment?
Fall so easily and walk away
And still you cannot answer a phone on Saturday
And you loved me and loved me and loved and yet
It was so, so easy to forget

When I was finished I looked out at the sea and it wasn't as beautiful anymore, without Micah it wasn't the same. I put my notebook back in my bag. I had laid it out, all we had done together, our entire relationship, our love boiled down to a single thing, its very essence contracted to the head of a pin. It would be the sole survivor of our love because Micah and I, we weren't . . . we just weren't and never would be. It was just a story in my head, a manifestation of my chaotic mind. I had been crazy. I was not worthy. I had blown it all out of proportion. Tom was right about me. I knew that then.

The waitress nodded as I left the café. It was time to meet Tom. In fact I was late and he would be wondering where I was but I couldn't face him just then and so I walked toward the water. It was very close, so close that very big thing and I could just reach out and touch it as I stood at the wharf in Cardiff Bay. Had I ever even wanted to go to Wales before this point? Did I ever care about the sea so much? But now I had lost something and this numbness . . . but at least the ocean, it's big, just so very big. There it was and I gave in to it. I walked away from the docks and toward the beach, my feet on the rocks. I took off my shoes one at a time, tossing them to the side. Then, I took off my stockings, gentling placing them on the ground before I turned and walked into the water.

I could sense the sea, its soft, cool breath and wanted it. I knew more than anything that I wanted it, that very big thing to swoop in and take me, to tie me up as I had been tied up when they ran electricity through my brain because I was a mad woman. I put my foot in the water and it was cold, a kind of baptism, the round rocks of the shoreline shifting under my feet. It almost felt jagged even in their smoothness. You'll get used to the cold, Esther, you will, you really will, I told myself. You'll go numb again, you always do. And had it been cold after I'd taken the pills? Had it been like this?

I walked out, one step, two, I wanted to feel the water at knee level but I never got that far. "Esther!" I heard a voice and turned around. "Esther!" the voice cried sharply one more time and I saw Tom running at me.

I stood there, I didn't move for the longest time and it wasn't until he reached the shore, until he stopped to see that I'd taken my shoes and socks off that I walked back to him. I saw him coming but what I saw was his light brown hair and the fact that he was very tall and there was poetry and hunting and Yorkshire, that's who he was, a good Englishman who would not punish me for being German because to him I was only an American, a girl from Massachusetts. That was enough for him and he wasn't perfect and maybe he wouldn't make me entirely happy but it was something. A girl should at least have something if she can't have everything.

"Esther, what on earth? Did you think you could go for a swim before my reading?" He didn't even think, didn't comprehend, the idea didn't even cross Tom's mind, what I was about to do. He didn't know. He didn't know about the pills and the hospital and electricity running through my brain. I was only a very silly girl who had decided to take her shoes and stockings off and wade in the water before her boyfriend's reading. "Esther, come on, don't be a dope."

Then I realized something. It was all planned out just like those leather straps on my wrists on the day electricity surged through my brain. I had not chosen. The choice had been made for me just as I had written those words and made poetry. And we would fight and Tom would hit me and sometimes I'd hit back but that's what I was for.

Life. Fate. Inevitable.

"Tom," I said then, my stomach dropping inside me. "Tom." I said his name again as if it were a brick in my mouth and the rest of the words, all the words I had in me, could not get past it.

"Esther, are you all right? You look cold, you're shaking," Tom said, draping his arms around me he held me close and I felt safe. At the very least with Tom I felt safe.

I pulled away, I looked up at him and tears fell from my eyes once more. Only they were small tears and in the right light I'm sure someone might call them happy tears. "Oh, Tom, I've been thinking," I said. "And yes, my answer is yes. I will marry you."

"Yes?" Tom said, his eyes going bright and then he stooped down and kissed me hard on the lips, holding me so close. This time I did not feel safe but only constrained and shaken and it was not at all the way Micah would have kissed me or held me but I couldn't think about that anymore. Micah was not mine and he never would be. "Of course, yes! Wonderful,. I'll call my parish when we get back to London. We'll get married there as soon as possible. We'll get you a dress, some flowers, a few friends can come but we should get married right away, Esther, right away."

"Of course," I said, forcing a smile as I held Tom close once more. "Of course, we'll get married right away and it'll be lovely."

"You know, I was a little upset that you took so long coming back, that I had to come and get you, then I saw you playing by the water and thought, 'What the devil is she doing?' But if it took that to get you to come to your decision, if you were just thinking and you needed the water's help, well that I understand, and I'm so happy you went out to the water."

"Thank you for understanding," I said softly, moving toward my stockings and shoes I put them on quickly. I stood the entire time and Tom grasped my arm, holding me in place as I hopped a bit to get my shoes on.

"All right, let's get you back to the hotel so you can freshen up before my reading. We don't want you looking like a little urchin if you're going to be my wife."

"Let's do that," I said, standing straight now.

Tom walked away. I saw his back, it was like a mountain and I wanted to climb on top of it as he marched back into the heart of Cardiff, away from the sea and the smell of salt and the great bursts of cool air. I saw the buildings descend before us and wondered what this city would look like in twenty, thirty, fifty years, when Tom and I had children and grandchildren. Would we visit this place? Would all of time converge on us or had I lost the ability to make a moment last forever as I had at Stonehenge when the world sprawled before me? I wasn't sure if I wanted this time back, if this moment, even this moment, was worthy of remembering.

Tom was still ahead as I turned back to the sea. There was just so much of it. Ocean after ocean after ocean, such a very big thing and part of me wanted to walk back into it.

"Come on," Tom called and I turned around to see him waiting. "Follow me."

I looked once more at the sea, my stomach, my limbs, my mind empty and sinking. I turned back to land and followed Tom.

Lorelei

I PUT THE manuscript down and it's the waves, coming out of the darkness as if from the great primordial soup, that I see. There was a scientific study done once that argued that time was the first thing ever to enter the universe, not matter, not light but time. It was when the clock started ticking that the universe began and the great cosmic soup spat out the universe just as Zeus fought Kronos to release his siblings. It's been sixty years since Esther's story, it's been nearly as long since Plath's suicide, and still I feel as if time has converged and I'm there with her. It feels so timely now, Esther's story, I sense it inside me as I look out at the waves. This is a woman felt so much, she basically walked right into an abusive relationship out of desperation, out of just wanting to find a place in the world. I want to call Joanne and thank her for giving me this. I want to ask her for more but I know there isn't more. The author is dead and all we have is one book and her poetry. I'm lucky to be allowed to read it.

I set an old seashell my father always kept on the small metal table on the porch on top so the pages won't fly away. I stare out and feel it; something I haven't felt in two years, something I've pushed myself to do, unhappily, unwelcomingly, unsuccessfully, for too long. I want to write. But this is not the novel I've been working on, that story isn't right, it isn't working. A flood of new words come and I have to get them out. I grab my laptop. I don't know why I thought to bring it when I took the manuscript out, but it seems so obvious here against the sea with Sylvia Plath ringing in my ears. I have been writing the wrong novel, London, Paris, and Sydney, that silly gimmick, and now I hear the words of a new piece.

I picture Theo and the girl . . . the girl she's not Heather anymore, she's only the girl. I see a man who is Theo and not quite Theo, a woman who is me but not really me and a girl who is Heather and still something else. This is what I have to write. This is what I must purge. I know there's more than what I saw or knew, what I felt and understood on my end. And in so many ways we're all at fault. My husband fell in love with a young girl and she died. It's this story I have to tell . . .

There was the moment he saw her, looking out across a crowded room as if looking out and crowded rooms were not the most cliché avenues for adventure. But there it was, her eyes, all eyes. The girl, he would think later, had the most beautiful eyes. There was a song when he was young "Betty Davis

Eyes," and he had looked up who Betty Davis was when he was younger and yes, like that, she had those eyes.

He did not approach her. Later he would think it was the wife's fault, it must have been the wife's fault, she put her arm around the girl and walked her over, delivered her right into his hands. "This is the girl I told you about," she'd said. "Some of her poetry is front and center in this semester's literary magazine." It was all so simple.

He would remember later, when his wife walked away, how this girl looked up at him and he felt a sense of adventure. He'd traveled to Europe once a year for a decade but he'd never been to Africa or China, never went off that beaten path. He never really saw the world. But this girl, he saw the world in those eyes.

And they got to talking, he looked deep into her and she laughed, looking down, covering her little mouth as she smiled but he could see her lips turned up and he just kept talking. "You know, if you want, here's my number," he said, knowing it would be the final words of an unwritten story. Knowing full well it was wrong he still handed her his card. "Just text me whenever you want." That had been it and a little bit of him died that day, before it even started he knew it was the end and yet he'd given her his number, he'd wanted her to text him.

He'd looked over at his wife and she'd smiled at him but he couldn't help but be annoyed at her, annoyed that she was there, that she was the wife, the woman he'd be going home with and not that girl. He knew while he was doing it, this nineteen-year-old girl, she was too young, and from their conversation he could tell that she came from a very Christian background. Despite her penchant for poetry and big cities her family was conservative. Still she had taken his number, slipped it quietly away as if she too knew it was wrong but she wanted it. As if she knew that she couldn't help but step further into danger.

She texted him the next night. At least she knew the rules of protocol, don't sound too desperate, don't text that night, wait at least a day. And she had and during that day he'd jumped every time his phone buzzed, even at work as he sat at his desk looking at the tax forms of wealthy businessmen, thinking about how he could help them pay less money to the government so that they might have more boats and nice vacations, perhaps they would go to Africa. He looked at the numbers, the cold hard numbers and thought long and hard about them. He made them work for his clients and in return his clients paid for his nice house, his great apartment in the city and a few vacations a year. But he never went to Africa, he never went anyplace interesting.

But the girl's text was a beacon of light and he had not followed protocol (which told him to wait at least an hour before replying). He'd texted her back right away. "You want to meet up in the city sometime?" Sometime, he said sometime, as if he didn't mean right then. But she'd said yes, right away, forgetting protocol as well, she'd just said, "Yes." And they'd made a date for coffee that afternoon, after his real work was finished. He called the wife, said he'd be home late. She barely noticed.

Since she'd gotten pregnant she didn't seem to care. It was all getting the baby's room ready, reading all the books, talking to her girlfriends about "the first year."

It was coffee once at a little place in Beacon Hill, a nice place with art deco on the walls and a barista who smiled and knew all the regulars names. But he wasn't a regular; he was just a man waiting for a woman . . . not a woman, a girl. He was in his late thirties, quickly falling toward forty, and she wasn't even twenty . . . my god was she even more than half his age?

She met him at a coffee shop and the girl didn't even drink coffee, didn't want caffeine, she said it was bad for her. She drank herbal tea and had a cookie, a little butter cookie like a child and an old woman all at the same time. But he talked to her, he told her about his job and she listened. She looked at him with wide eyes as he explained tax law and accounting to her and she said, "My mother wants me to be an accountant but I want to make art." Make art and he had wanted to make art too even though he wasn't good at it. Still, he'd been a rich kid growing up on the Upper East Side of Manhattan and so his mother had bought him art class after art class and they all praised him even though he went to MoMA on the weekends, he went to The Met, and he knew he wasn't any good.

But she wanted to see his art and so after the coffee he brought her back to his office, not his home, the wife was there by then. He kept the two decent paintings he'd done in his office anyway. He wasn't sure why but the wife never seemed to appreciate his art and while the big tax attorneys, the company men and women who came in to meet with him, didn't notice the art either at least he expected it from them.

He brought the girl in. It was around six-thirty, people were still at the office, a few young lawyers, just out of law school and striving to move up, a few secretaries. But they didn't notice when he walked in with a teenaged girl. Maybe they thought she was a client.

She walked right into his office and looked up at his wall and there was a painting of a man staring up at the sky. He'd been trying to replicate Van Gogh's style, he thought maybe he'd done a nice job and the girl, her eyes got so big and she looked up at it with such awe, like she was seeing real art for the first time. And the wife, he remembered the wife had said that this girl had a taste for art and so if she liked it . . . if she liked it, and for a second it wasn't as if she liked him but she liked his painting and that meant more. "You want to go to Africa?" he asked and the girl giggled.

He looked over at her, he came closer and kissed her, then he brought her closer. At first he wasn't sure that she would let him, he told himself if she pulled away at all, if she looked even the least uncomfortable he'd stop but she leaned in when he brushed her face with his hand, she closed her eyes and when he kissed her she kissed him back. He drew her closer and kissed her again and again. Right there in his office and it didn't feel wrong.

That was the thing, it didn't feel wrong. Not when he kissed her, not when he texted her that night and told her he wanted to see her again. "You make me feel like a different person. Like I'm me and not me, don't you understand that?" And she'd said, "Yes." She'd said that she understood. "And you make me feel more too." And so two days later he asked to see her in the city again.

One night he looked her in the eyes and he was so happy. But he knew something had broken. He loved her but he knew he'd broken it. "Your wife," she'd said. "I can't help thinking about your wife." She looked like she was about to cry and he'd said, "I love you. It'll be okay."

There were dinners and movies. It was like he was dating again. There were phone calls late at night like he was back in college. His wife would be asleep in bed, having conked out hours ago, and the girl would call and he'd sit on the couch in the living room just talking to her for hours. Hours! Like he was back a kid. There were dinners at restaurants he'd never take his wife. There were hotel rooms and racy texts, pictures and emails. Too much of a trail. They left too much of a trail.

And then one day his wife found out. He wasn't sure if she had a suspicion. Maybe he'd been away too often. Maybe he was just acting funny. But she found the texts and the pictures on his phone. She did some detective work and found receipts for hotel rooms in the city. And that was enough. She tried to call the girl but the girl's mother picked up and she told her. His wife told the girl's mother. Once again like he was back in college when mother's had a say in things that went on between consenting adults.

The day after his wife told the girl's mother he tried to text the girl and someone else came on. "Do not contact this number," the text read. He knew it wasn't her. "Stay away from our daughter." That was it. He tried to get in touch, he called her dorm, called the school. Then the wife called him and said, "We need to talk." And he went home and stood in the living room and let her scream at him. He watched her cry, her long, brown hair looked stringy and haggard like an old woman's and he knew he had to take it, he had to listen. All the while all he could think about was the girl and how to get back to her.

It wasn't so bad, what he'd done, he told himself. It wasn't so bad because he loved her.

He went to a hotel and tried to call from there but they wouldn't let her speak to him. He thought he'd be funny and pretend to be one of her professors. He remembered the name of one of her male professors and called the house and said, "This is Professor Jameson from your daughter's Art History class, I need to talk to her about her grade for a minute."

He wasn't even sure if it worked, if they believed him, because the man who picked up the phone only said, "Her cousin just took her out. She is not to take any phone calls. If you would like to talk about school, you may talk to me." He could only assume it was her father. But he had not called to talk about her studies and so he hung up, shaking. She was with her cousin . . . but he knew, he felt something sink inside his stomach.

He tried to call again and again, he texted her and texted her from different phones. He went to her parents' house but no one was home and he wasn't sure why. The entire place was dark like it was boarded up for a hurricane.

He saw it on the news. No one called to tell him. Didn't they know that he loved her? Didn't they know how much this was killing him? His wife wouldn't speak to him. One of her friends, the reporter, took his calls and basically told him to go to hell every time he tried to contact her. "But we're about to have a son," he'd cry at the friend and she would only hang up. Then one time he called and the friend picked up and she was more calm, more kind. "Do you know what happened?" she'd asked quietly and he'd said no. "Do you watch the news?" she'd asked and he'd said no. He used to watch the news, he used to care about his work and his family but that had all gone out the window when he'd met the girl. "Just watch the news, look it up online or something."

"Can't you tell me?" he'd said, tears in his voice because he knew . . . he didn't know what, but he knew. That sinking feeling once it's there you can't deny it. Heads in sand and all that—it just doesn't work.

"No, I can't . . . I just can't," the friend had said and she'd meant it, not meanly, she really couldn't. It was too much for her.

He tried the news but there was only something about the Federal budget, something about some war somewhere and maybe they were up in arms about protests across the country—all stuff he used to care about but now didn't. He went to his computer and typed "College girl," in the search engine. He wasn't sure why that word popped into his head. He knew her name but college girl, somehow that's the word he knew would work, and there it was; "College Girl Killed By Cousin." He read further, "A nineteen-year-old college girl died last night in the hospital after suffering a severe beating by her cousin. The girl had recently confessed to an indiscretion with a married man and the cousin had taken her to a warehouse to 'teach her a lesson,' in the girl's father's words, and there she had a minor heart attack as a result of the beating. She died at the hospital last night from heart complications. Police are still investigating."

The cousin beat her? He thought. Because of me he beat her? He'd taken her to a warehouse. Why the hell would anyone let that happen? Who does something like that? This wasn't the Middle Ages when women had their ears cut off for minor affairs. He pictured the warehouse dark and murky, dusty, machines everywhere and then that cousin started to beat her and he had not stopped until she was dead. He hadn't even been there; no one had allowed him to protect her. Later he'd learned that the girl's father had given her cousin the keys to the warehouse where he worked. Why would he do that? What did he think would happen there? What kinds of lesson can one learn from such violence? She was dead . . . dead and he had loved her and she was dead and all the life went out of him. He fell into his starched hotel bed, he felt the flimsiness of the sheets and cried. He cried and cried and cried because he had loved her and she was dead.

I set the computer to the side. Virginia Woolf once said, "Fiction has more truth than fact in it." It's not all fact here, but there's a lot of truth. It's the start of a novel I can feel it. I'll make it better later, flush the story out, add more fiction to the truth, the essence of the story. All our lives, they lie dormant unless we use them, unless they come out in the least destructive ways and that's what artists do, poets, painters, all of us, we take our lives and make art. Sylvia Plath was a confessional poet. All our art really, all our lives, are some kind of confession.

And that had been the thing, after Theo found out, after he called the house and Amelia answered and told him to check the news, everything broke. The truth . . . all of it was some sort of truth, but now I picture how he felt, I get inside his head, his heart. I know some of it because the night after he found out he came to the house. I was sitting on the couch, a box of tissues at my side, and Amelia had let him in because he'd looked so pathetic she couldn't help herself. He'd come in and just cried. I had just found out that he'd had an affair. I'd called the girl to confront her and gotten her mother. I'd told her mother and that's what started it all. I couldn't forget that. I couldn't get those moments out of my head. But I didn't think the rest would happen. I didn't think that the cousin would take her to a warehouse . . . But there Theo was the day after he found out and he just lay on my couch and cried. He cried and said he loved her. I couldn't even fault him for it, it cut me each time he looked up, still tearful, still pathetic, and said, "I loved her, you know, I loved her."

"I know," was all I'd said, feeling our child, nearly five months along at the time, in my womb. I wanted to hate Theo but I couldn't in those moments, he was too sad and I knew he'd loved her. It was only later, after we lost the baby, that the war was on.

The manuscript sits next to me as I push my laptop further away. I'm finished writing for tonight but I know now that I'll write more later. When a novel comes, when it really comes, it lives in your muscle tissue for years. Oh Sylvia! I can see it in this manuscript, Sylvia, not only Esther, but Sylvia Plath as well. She knew how it felt to have a husband whose love was suspect. Sylvia's husband had loved another woman as well. She knew what it felt like to be left so much with nothing and it's through her words, her pain, that I have found my own.

Sylvia
1962

SYLVIA HAD GOTTEN gifts for Christmas. A necklace from Olive Pouty, a fine, rich writer who had written many bestsellers and sponsored her education at Smith. She'd always been kind to Sylvia, inviting her to tea when she was in college so they could talk about writing and later, after her first breakdown, she'd paid for her to be transferred away from that horrible state hospital to a nicer facility in the country. This Christmas Sylvia's mother had sent her money and toys for the children, there had been a card from her brother Warren. Many friends had called to check on her and Ted had come to visit the children, bringing presents, toys, more toys that would make a mess in her living room, more toys for her to put away. Toys that would break and cause crying. Didn't Ted ever think?

And yet, despite all the gifts and well wishes, it had taken quite a lot of scrambling to find an invitation to Christmas dinner. Sylvia hadn't even thought of that, what to do for the holidays now that her family was decimated. She couldn't very well spend the holiday with Ted and his family in Yorkshire, not with Ted off with That Woman and rumor had it they were leaving the country for a while. She couldn't see her own family all the way in America, they were just too far and she didn't have the money for a trip across the ocean, especially not with children. Sylvia wished she'd gotten closer to her friends but she was just so busy with the children and the housekeeping and trying desperately to be, to stay, a writer. Jillian and Gerald had been especially kind to her and there were the Frankfurt's, they'd been very good as well, Katherine had even found a suitable nursery school for Frieda. But there were no friends who felt like family, no one she could just go to without reservation and ask to be taken in for Christmas dinner.

I have lived the wrong life, Sylvia thought to herself as she parked the car near the Macedo's London flat. It was snowing very hard, blasts of hard winter pummeled the car and Sylvia did not want to take the children out in it. Instead it would have been better to stay home, she could have cooked a roast and potatoes, maybe a pudding of some kind. The British loved their puddings. But no one would have come and it would have been so lonely, just her and the children on this cold, snowy Christmas. And so she'd had to scramble and piggy back on the plans of her friends last minute.

After they'd parked Sylvia waited in the car. She could feel the heat of it, it was barely a breath but it was something in this late December chill. "All right," she said, looking back at Frieda and then Nicholas in his car seat. "We're going to have to make a run for it. The flat is only a few feet away. Do you think you can do it, Frieda?"

"Yes, Mummy," the little girl cried excitedly. "I'll run and run and run."

"Good girl," Sylvia cheered. She then maneuvered her body so that she was half in the backseat, her knees only slightly strained in the front. Ah the contortions a mother must do! She then reached and pulled the straps from Nicholas' car seat and pulled him out awkwardly. He cried at being jostled like this, but it was the best she could do. "All right. I have the baby. When I open the door, you crawl out his door and we'll run."

"Run for it!" Frieda cried, up for the challenge.

The challenge, it would seem, was a bit more than Sylvia had bargained for and the moment she stepped out of the car she found her feet in five inches of sludge. "Oh my goodness," she cried, holding the baby close as she grabbed her bag and slammed the car door. Frieda came out and started to cry as well.

"It's cold, Mummy, it's cold. I'm wet, I'm wet," she said, dancing on the snow covered sidewalk.

"Take my hand, let's go," Sylvia said and she rushed with the baby, her bag dangling from her arm. She clasped Frieda's tiny fingers with her free hand and rushed toward the Macedo's front stoop. She couldn't even see the color or make out the number of the flat, she only had to go on memory.

Sylvia knocked softly at first, even in this snowstorm she wanted to be polite, but when no one answered she banged harder with the iron knocker until the door opened. She could not see a person before her, not with her worry over the children or the blinding snow. She could only see the flat and the large open room with wooden floors and a Turkish carpet. She saw chairs and tables and lamps and the seeing, more than the feeling of all this, made her sense the warmth inside.

"Of course, of course, come in," Suzette Macedo said, a lovely woman with dark hair and angular features.

They brought water in with them, or more appropriately, wet, sliding, dripping, clinging wet. Sylvia could feel ice in her shoes as she hurried to take them off on the little rug near the door. Snow dripped from her coat as she peeled it off and handed it to her hostess. Suzette then knelt and helped Frieda with her jacket as Sylvia stood, feeling a little better now that their wet things were off.

"I'm sorry about this weather. I really thought this winter would let up for Christmas," Suzette said, as if she had anything to apologize for. "Wishful thinking."

"I thought so as well," Sylvia replied. "I thought the gods of the weather or the gods of London or the gods of Christmas at the very least would take some pity on us."

Suzette laughed and walked further into the flat with her heels clicking on the hardwood floor. "Helder," she called for her husband. "Look, Sylvia and the children are here." She then walked back, leaving Sylvia with little Frieda and Nicholas.

She could hear others in the living room. She had not thought of this, that she must be imposing on them. Of course Suzette and Helder had invited friends, closer friends, or family, to Christmas. She'd called at the last minute. She'd grown frantic and called everyone and only two people had offered an olive branch, only two of her friends allowed themselves to be put out by Sylvia Plath, the abandoned wife of Ted Hughes, and his two children.

"Sylvia," a man said as she and the children entered the room, feeling like they had come in from a shipwreck they were so wet, ragged, and tired though it had only been a walk of a few feet from the car. "How lovely to see you."

"This is my nephew," Suzette said. "And this is Carl and Mirada, friends of ours," she went on with the introductions. Each person nodded and Sylvia stood there smiling, all she could do was smile and hold the baby close to her body like some kind of shield. She felt all their eyes on her and knew what they were thinking. There she was a young mother with two children, who did not even have her own invitations to Christmas dinner. She had to go calling around, she had to go begging and it really was only because of the kindness of near-strangers that they had anything at all. And really, how close were they, she and the Macedos? Didn't Suzette also see Ted? Hadn't she mentioned that she'd just seen Ted and That Woman the other day and wasn't it such a nice surprise, the way he was getting on?

"Hello," Sylvia said, placing a hand on top of Frieda's head. Her hair was soft and smooth. Sylvia could remember when her own hair was like that. "Thank you so much for the invitation. I won't be a bother, I promise. This is my daughter, Frieda, and my son, Nicholas," she said, nodding to the baby still swaddled to her chest. It was warm there and he didn't appear to want to move.

"Hello, Sylvia, how lovely to see you. It's terrible out there isn't it?"

"Oh, yes, the weather," Sylvia replied. "Of course, the weather. It really is awful. I wonder how we'll get our car out . . ."

"Don't worry," Suzette's husband Helder, a Portuguese critic and translator, said, coming in with a glass. It looked like he was polishing it with a white cloth napkin. "We'll dig you out if we have to, we have plenty of shovels."

"And plenty of good men to be put to work," the nephew said, making a false muscle with his bicep as the other two women in the room laughed.

"So tell me, how has your Christmas been so far?" Suzette asked still standing in the doorway between the living room and kitchen like the dutiful hostess.

"It's been very nice. I saw Al last night. We talked for a while. He's been recording my poetry. And I had tea at the Frankfurt's before coming here."

"Ah, tea at the Frankfurt's, tell me, how are they?"

"They're doing well," Sylvia replied. "Very nice people. Frieda enjoyed it there."

"They gave us cookies," the little girl chimed in and the whole party laughed.

"Well, I just have a few things in the kitchen to take care of, please, make yourself at home. Tell me, would you like a drink?"

"Brandy," Sylvia replied, nodding to Helder as he shuffled toward the wet bar, a few crystal bottles of brown or clear liquor on a silver dish, on the other side of the room.

The conversation that seemed to have been going on before went on as it had been. There was more about the weather (it really was unbearably cold), something about a mutual friend Sylvia did not know (a bad case of the flu, like in 1915, that kind of flu) and something about television (apparently the BBC would be airing a special about great English writers very soon). "So, Suzette tells me you write poetry," the nephew finally said turning to Sylvia.

"That must be fascinating," Miranda chimed in, leaning back in her chair.

"Yes, it is . . . it can be. Thank you once again for the invitation," Sylvia said as Helder handed her a brandy.

"Of course," he replied, smiling. "I heard the city is thinking of declaring some sort of emergency with all this snow. You know, it really is a crime, workmen going on strike at a time like this. I'm all for the working people, you know I am, but sometimes you just have to think of your fellow man."

"Your fellow man, yes," the nephew repeated and Sylvia took a seat at the edge of an empty couch, perching herself as if she might slip off. She got a glimpse of herself in the darkened glass of the back door and thought she looked something like Rodin's *The Thinker*, expect for the brandy in her hand.

The conversation rolled along. Some other acquaintances were mentioned and Sylvia remained quiet, keeping her eyes on the children, who were both now on the floor playing with the pieces of a chess set.

"Do you think they should be touching those?" Sylvia asked, though really she didn't want to stop them. It was only out of politeness that she inquired.

If the children were happy that was all she wanted. If they were quiet and not in constant need of her, if she could sit with grownups and have a brandy on Christmas Day, that was enough for her. Still, if the chess set was expensive or an heirloom or important . . .

"No, it's fine. It's fine," Helder said, getting up he moved toward a large cupboard. He reached the top of it and grabbed two wrapped presents. "For the little ones." He handed one to Frieda and the other to Sylvia to open for Nicholas.

"Oh, you really shouldn't have, you've already been so incredibly generous."

"Oh, but of course. That's what we want, to make sure the children have a happy Christmas," Helder replied.

All eyes were on the children as they sat with their presents. There is always something so jolly about children getting presents. Even people who aren't fond of children, Sylvia found, stopped and stared whenever there was a child with a wrapped gift to open. There was something about the eyes, the rapt look on their faces, and the innocence of it all. It reminded everyone of their own childhoods, of the good times, like sitting around a fire with their own families on Christmas day. This kind of joy could not be replicated in adults.

Sylvia opened the box for Nicholas; it was a little rubber rabbit, just big enough for him and perfectly safe for the baby to put in his mouth, which was important, as everything went directly there these days. She handed it to the baby, who grasped it for a moment before gumming it. Frieda tore into her paper, opening the box it came in and pulling out a black toy piano about the size of a loaf of bread. "A piano, Mummy, can I play it, can I play?" she asked, her eyes wide as everyone chuckled. Really it was a very nice present and it would be wonderful to hear her play it for a few minutes. But it would get very loud and Sylvia was sure it would wake her in the morning when Frieda played it at the crack of dawn as she surely would and her neighbor would complain about the constant noise of the thing.

"Thank you," was all she said to Helder as he proudly watched the children play with the gifts he'd given them.

With the children safely on the floor Sylvia stood up. "I'm just going to see if your wife needs any help with dinner. Will they be all right in here with you?"

"Of course, they're wonderful," Helder said, looking back up at his other guests before returning his eyes to Frieda. "Why don't you play me something, little woman, anything at all, whatever you want."

Frieda started banging and Sylvia winced. To the Macedo's this "performance" would last a few minutes and therefore they could enjoy it. Then she would be on her way home with these cumbersome packages and she'd hear the instrument for days. Sylvia walked slowly toward the back of the flat. She had only been here a few times before and then it had been for a more full party and she wasn't quite sure where the kitchen was. Before she could reach it, she saw that Suzette was standing off to the side of the stove, on the phone. Sylvia stopped, not wanting to disturb her.

"She's here with the children," she heard her friend say into the powder blue phone. "And I wonder if she's found out about the baby . . . oh, I know, I know. Assia would never in her life dream of keeping it . . . She'll take care of it, she has before . . . I know, I know . . . but after Christmas she'll go to France and take care of it."

Sylvia stopped. She'd already heard about this but she didn't see why her friend needed to be on the phone with . . . whoever she was on the phone with, talking about Ted and That Woman. Was it really that she was such a topic of gossip, a woman alone on Christmas, without any family on the continent? A woman in a foreign country trying to live on the meager salary poetry provided, with friends who could only be so kind for so long.

Christmas had not been like this in America. Her mother had never had much money but she scrimped and saved to make sure she and her brother always had plenty of presents. She bought Sylvia books, so many books, and fine paper and journals. Sylvia's mother bought her brother a fishing pole one year and both of them such nice outfits for the family dinner. They'd sit with her grandparents and eat a roast or a ham, whatever her mother felt like preparing. They would visit friends and neighbors and it had all been so lovely. In America there had been snow on Christmas but not like this, not this giant, wet typhoon. And yes, Boston could get very cold, but still she had always been warm, not like in London where the pipes froze and the heat went out. When she was older, no longer a little girl, she would visit Buddy Willard and there had been Richard and the time she went to New York with him just after the holidays. It had all been so nice, so lovely. She'd had a life, a real life, and it could have been wonderful if only she'd kept it. If only she and Richard had worked out. If only she had stayed in America and never met Ted—that brute.

Sylvia turned back toward the living room where polite conversation was still rumbling. "You know, I think that Macmillan is thinking," the nephew went on as Helder sipped his brandy.

"Oh, but who cares about the bloody prime minister," Miranda said, tossing her head back and Sylvia really wished she would not use that word in front of the children.

She watched Frieda and Nicholas, who were still playing on the carpet. Frieda had Nicholas' toy rabbit now and he was reaching for it as she laughed at him and called him a "silly baby." It was all so natural, so normal, the children playing with toys at Christmas and yet there was something forced, something unreal about it. The children were surrounded by strangers. They were taking it so well, and maybe they didn't notice (though Frieda had asked "where's Daddy?" a number of times today), but they were outsiders here, with people who did not entirely love them like Sylvia's own mother loved them. Her mother would have gladly welcomed them all home if only she could afford a cross Atlantic journey.

Sylvia turned around and went back to the kitchen without being spotted. "Sylvia," Suzette cried when she came into the kitchen. "I'm sorry, I didn't see you there, how are you?"

"I'm fine. I was just wondering if there wasn't anything I could do to help? I didn't even bring a hostess gift, how silly of me. I was in such a rush to figure out Christmas that I forgot to offer to bring anything. Can I help?"

Suzette looked at her long Formica counter, it was blue and white, something that had been all the rage in the 1950s. Sylvia remembered that her mother had had one like that at the house near Cape Cod. The food smelled delicious, like meat and gravy and butter and potatoes and at least she would be giving her children a good meal this year.

"Everything is fine, all in order. Please, Sylvia, it's Christmas, relax and enjoy yourself," she said, placing a hand on Sylvia's bony shoulder as if to push her away.

"Thank you, Suzette, I really do appreciate it. I mean, I know things with Ted and I are strange and you must feel in the middle of it and I want you to know I'm grateful for all you've done." And she meant it. Suzette was being kind. She had offered her a place to go on Christmas. What more could she ask for?

"Of course. And I never thought . . . and she was my friend too and I didn't think she was that kind of woman. And Ted . . . but I just . . ." Suzette said but Sylvia only smiled.

"It's okay, it's not your fault." She would forgive her; she would not make her explain her continued friendship with Ted and That Woman, that would be her gift to her hostess.

"Thank you," Suzette replied, turning back toward the oven. "Dinner will be ready in a few minutes, just a few minutes."

"I'll tell everyone," Sylvia said, turning out of the kitchen.

She meant to go back into the living room, to brave that party where she felt as if everyone was staring at her. She could feel their eyes burrowing into her pale skin. There was still the snow outside and after dinner she and the children would have to run out in that and she would see if she could even move her car and then she would have to drive back home and park and take the children back into that dark flat where the heat may have gone out or the pipes might have frozen again and maybe the workmen wouldn't come. She felt herself shaking as she walked, not back to the living room, but to the washroom. They called it such silly things here, the WC, Water Closet. But why would it be a closet? Sylvia thought to herself. Why not a room, a bathroom . . . why not call it like they did in America? England was starting to feel like such a silly, silly place and why was she here when she could be at home with her mother?

Sylvia shut the door to the bathroom. She pulled the toilet lid down and sat on it, at the very edge of it like she was about to fall off. Teetering, teetering, always she was teetering just above a precipice and when would the darkness come, really and truly come? When would she fall off?

But That Woman, That Woman was pregnant. She had gone and gotten herself pregnant and it was Ted's, it had to be. That Woman was still married, but everyone knew she wasn't with her husband, everyone knew the baby was Ted's. And what would people think of her, Sylvia Plath, the jilted woman whose husband had just gotten his mistress pregnant? Sylvia had heard stories about That Woman as well and she had ended many other pregnancies in an unnatural way, and everyone was sure this would happen again. She didn't even have the courage to have and raise a child. Ted didn't want any other children, she'd seen him after Nicholas was born, he'd barely wanted the baby. And if he could take only Frieda he would. She saw it when he came to pick the children up. It wasn't fair to her son and she had to keep her children together, she had to keep them always with her, their protector. If something happened to her, would Ted even take Nicholas or would he just run off with Frieda and leave him to an orphanage? At this point she could put nothing past that man.

Sylvia sat, still on the edge of the toilet seat, her head in her hands. She'd promised herself she wouldn't cry, she simply would not cry at Christmas. She'd tried to be happy. She'd tried to find a place, a good place for them to go, to be taken in and fed because she and the children were without family. But she felt the tears, they were a knot in her chest and she felt them come up and it was so good when they finally came. She'd been holding them in all day, for so long. She'd cried a trickle but never this torrent. And maybe what I need, Sylvia thought, is to flood this water closet with my tears. She cried, tears coming and coming. She closed her eyes and breathed and still the tears came with the darkness.

She could feel it. The darkness was almost here.

Sylvia heard the party going on. Dinner wasn't ready yet but Suzette had joined them in the living room. They were laughing, having fun. Even the children, she could hear Frieda's piano and Sylvia kept crying, crying and crying, and no one came to look for her.

Lorelei

"WE KEEP THE bees outside, obviously," Joanne says as I come around back to see the hive. It's a large rectangular box on faded sawhorses with a few drawers, almost like a rustic, wooden filing cabinet. It's blue collar, like my father's workbenches. The bees aren't flying around, there's not a giant plume of them, though a couple buzz about the structure as a few fly to the pink flowers along the chain link fence at the end of the yard. I picture plumes of smoke, the kind beekeepers use to calm the creatures, and wonder what's inside those dripping honeycombs. "They make really good honey," Joanne goes on, skirting the fence where the bees are kept. "I'll have to bring you some. We've considered selling the honey but Tammy and I are comfortable, we'd rather just give it away."

"When I was a little girl, my best friend's father used to talk about keeping bees. Every year he swore he was going to buy a honeycomb and start a hive, get a queen and the little workers, but it never panned out."

"It's hard work. Sometimes it's not just a matter of getting a queen but the *right* queen. She has to connect with the hive. Usually, if you don't separate them, the new queens will kill the old queen when they hatch. You have to be very careful about that. But the bees have to work with their queen. They have to want to serve her."

"I can imagine," I replied, fascinated by all this. Queens deposing queens just like a medieval fairytale.

"You know," Joanne goes on as she ushers me toward the screened in back door to her and Tammy's cottage. "Sylvia Plath's father, Otto, used to keep bees. Wrote a couple of books on the subject. He was interested in the power of the queen."

One woman served by so many men. Sylvia Plath's own "Lorelei."

"That's right, I think I read about that in a biography," I tell Joanne as she holds the screen door open and I walk inside, hit first with the smell of patchouli and then the stark chill of the air conditioning, so different from the warm, sea air outside.

It's like returning, or entering, the 1960s, inside Joanne's house. Not the sixties of sex, drugs, and rock and roll, but not the perfectly cleaned up version either, women in pillbox hats and sack dresses. This is bohemia and bongos sit in the corner as knick-knacks litter most surfaces. Yet there is a neatness, a calm to this house near the ocean. Joanne's house, what one might call a bungalow, is situated a few streets inland, near Fairview road and across the street from a causal looking Italian restaurant, the type that tries to be fancy, but really their vinyl, checkered tablecloths and parmesan shakers resemble a glorified pizza parlor.

Inside Joanne's place there's a beanbag chair in the corner and a couch upholstered to look like those thin and scratchy loveseats from the sixties. The smell of incense permeates and there are black and white framed photos of women with big hair, on most of the seashell pink walls. The color scheme is not exactly Joanne, who is more of a hippie than a housewife, but there's green shag carpet to counter that.

"I'm sorry it's such a mess," Joanne comments as she comes in, carrying a tray of coffee. She does not seem like the kind of woman who would carry a tray of coffee but it smells good, made strong and just a tad bitter. She serves it in dainty china cups as if she's a little girl playing tea party. The place is not a mess and there are only a few things out of place. After I learned about Heather, before the funeral, before my miscarriage, I couldn't bring myself to clean my house and it became such a mess so quickly. It's funny how you can lose control of a home so fast once you stop working on it.

Joanne is dressed in very baggy jeans and a large men's collared shirt. Paint stains litter her white dress shirt like a Pollack and she wears a long seashell necklace that looks as if it's been made by an artist who holes herself up in her studio nine months out of the year. I want to ask her if she's okay after her outburst in Provincetown but she seems fine now. "You know, Tammy is usually the one who takes care of the house on the Cape. We like to do it ourselves, you know?"

"I know something about that."

"And you, Lorelei, how's your book coming along?" Joanne falls into the beanbag chair across from me as if the orange filling will suck her in. Her large body, clad in such flowing clothes, looks like a child's for a second. I don't see her grey hair or the lines on her face as I picture her as Sylvia Plath must have seen her when she knew a younger Joanne in the fifties.

"Yesterday, when I finished the manuscript, I was so caught up in Esther's story that I started writing something. It's a rough sketch now, but something based on my own life, on Theo and myself, looking not just at my pain, but his pain as well."

"You want to write about your own life, turn it into art? That's just what Sylvia did. Confessional Poetry I think it was called. I approve."

"I was thinking about that as I was reading the manuscript and thank you so much for letting me read it. Her writing is so confident, so real. And that poem at the end, what she says about the words just existing, the art, it's already out there somewhere in the universe and it's her job, Esther's job, as the poet, to find it. I feel like I was telling the wrong story with this last novel and then I started to hear the voice of another story in my head. I was so inspired I just started writing right on my porch. Do you know the story of Michelangelo and the marble?"

"He was a sculptor, correct?"

"Yes, during the Renaissance. He did the sculpture of *David* and *The Sistine Chapel*. He used to say that the sculpture, the work of art, always existed, he just had to free it from the marble. I think that's the job all artists have. The book, the painting, the film, has always existed somewhere and it's the artist's job to find it, to go out and bring it into the world in its most perfect form. That's why some works of art . . . like Plath . . . those *Ariel* poems, the way she writes, it feels inevitable like something the universe was meant to have and it was her job to discover it. It was the same with my first novel, it wasn't all fact, writing about motherhood when I wasn't a mother, but there was a lot of truth, since I was mostly writing about my own mother. The book just existed, it was in me and it had to come out. Like freeing the statue in the marble."

"That's so beautiful," Joanne says. "I feel that same way about my own writing, magazine writing though it is, but I never would have articulated it that way. Tammy thinks I should write a memoir."

"How are things on the home front, how is Tammy?"

"Tammy's a saint. But you know, I always knew I was meant for her, even when I was with someone else, when she was not so happily married to a man, I always knew it, somewhere deep in my spine I always wondered, why am I so drawn to that woman? And then . . . it took a year or so, but it happened."

"Tammy was married to a man?"

"She was," Joanne replies as if this is a simple fact. "It's not a big deal anymore. But you read the Plath? You liked it?"

"You know, when she's talking about her lover, I know it takes place at a time in Esther's life when she's not a wife, but it's the inevitability, the fact that she's living a life she can't control and she must do what's acceptable in the end, which is why she decided on Tom. And Tom, isn't that the name of Esther's husband in the few stories Plath published about her? But, I really felt her pain. Who Sylvia Plath really was. I've studied her before, I've read everything she ever wrote, but it never hit me like it did this time. I'm so sorry the world will never see it. But thank you so much for letting me read it. I felt her so clearly, more so than when I read *The Bell Jar* for the first time." I reach into my bag and pull the manuscript out. I've been holding onto it. I've been keeping it, hoping, not realistically, but on some back burner in my mind, really hoping that I could hold onto it forever.

"She was so upset after she found out her husband was cheating on her," Joanne says. "I remember reading her stuff in high school. She used to publish in *Seventeen* and she did that *Mademoiselle* thing. She wasn't considered a genius when she started writing. She was good, everyone thought she was good, but she wasn't pushing herself. Then her husband got that mistress and he left her with two kids. She was alone in a flat in London during one of the coldest winters of the year. No one would publish *The Bell Jar* in America, her poetry wasn't doing well. And she wrote. All she could do was write. They said that winter she wrote like a woman possessed and that's where we get the *Ariel* poems, from a place in her deep and blackened and broken heart. That's what made her an artist. She could have lived her whole life with a successful poet husband and two children, publishing quaint little stories for *The Atlantic*, poetry that would have wound up in *The Saturday Evening Post*, but then she got her heart smashed wide open and she became the artist, the dark figure of poetry, to so many people."

"The heart, when it's broken, does the most powerful things."

Looking up at one of the black and white pictures on the wall, I recognize the women in the picture. One is Joanne, I can see the same square bone structure, her short brown hair that is now long and grey. Young women are supposed to have long hair and so Joanne kept hers short as a girl but society says that older women are supposed to grow up and cut their hair and so Joanne has done the opposite. The other woman is more enigmatic, but I know her as well. She is tall and blond with wide eyes with a smile that is so kind, so polite, but so deep. "That's me," Joanne explains. "With Sylvia Plath."

"I envy you so much, you actually, *actually* knew Sylvia Plath."

"I didn't know her that well but I knew her some. I met her on the beach when she was waitressing one summer at The Belmont. I was a little older than her and my friends and I were sharing a place. We used to smoke pot and beat the bongos all day long. It wasn't really her thing but she loved visiting. She really did like getting away from those silly, silly boys she dated then and that crystalline world. She was such a miss perfect in college, straight A's, the kind of girl who would have fainted at the sight of a B+ on her record. But there was something dark, a fighter, in her and it took being left by her husband, it took his horrible mistress and living alone with two children, to really bring it out. But it was there, even that summer so many years before her dark times, the bohemian was always there, encased in marble as you say, and heartache had to sculpt it out. You know, I ended up in a Psychiatric facility at one time as well. Pain drives people, without it we're just swimming with the current."

"Really, Joanne, I'm so sorry." I barely know this woman but just now it feels like we're old friends and she's revealing something so precious and deeply buried. I'm honored she told me. I remember her reaction the other day, the way she stormed away from me in Provincetown, and how much like my mother it was. This revelation is not a shock, not at all.

"I was twenty-three and honestly, I think it was all the lying that was getting to me. I'd moved back in with my mother in New Bedford for a while. She was ill and my father was away on business a lot. I had graduated from journalism school at that point but I wasn't really working. But my mother was an old-fashioned woman. My father had fought in World War Two and come home to marry a woman who popped out two kids and started to chair every committee she could get her hands on. She kept the house clean, all that jazz. But to know her daughter was a lesbian? My friends knew, some of my colleagues in college knew, but my mother, my family? I couldn't tell them. One time I was caught kissing a girl and my father beat the shit out of me. Not that he didn't beat the shit out of me for other things, but it was the forties, then the fifties, and daughters didn't talk about that stuff then.

"But I'd hide up in my room and stare at girlie magazines as a kid. I didn't even like them but they made me feel connected to who I was. I'd bring girls home when my mother was out and I'd feel so ashamed of it. And it wasn't what I was doing that made me feel bad. I was a stubborn woman, I wasn't ashamed of who I was, but I was ashamed of the lying.

"Finally, one day I got so sick of feeling so bad. That's how it starts, you know? You go down this road and the hurt just keeps going. You think it'll get better, that you can live with it, but you can't and something has to change but you don't know what that something is and so you think that if you just stopped . . . really just stopped. And one day I locked myself in the bathroom turned on the water, took some pills and cut my wrists." I watch Joanne closely. I do not gasp. I know what's coming. My mother did the same thing only we did not catch her in time.

I look at her wrists as she offers them to me like a Christ figure seeking redemption. Tiny white lines, slivers nearly the color of the moon, dangle down her arms. These scars have been thinned over, diluted, by time. She did it right, the scars go down, not across. She actually meant to do it. "My mother had a neighbor bang down the door. They found me, called an ambulance and sent me to a psych ward. I remember when I was there, and I was there for a good three months, I remember that it was a lot like *The Bell Jar*. Sylvia got it exactly right, especially the electro-shock and the way men look down on you when you're in there. The book hadn't come out yet when I had my suicide attempt, but it resonated when I finally read it. I remember thinking, that's exactly what it's like, mental illness, especially with women. It's like you're stuck and you can't get out. The entire world just feels off. You sleep too much or you don't sleep enough, or at all. You do the funniest things. I remember once I tore out all the pages of one of my mother's big coffee table books because the pictures weren't all symmetrically aligned. And what was more, I thought I was helping. I didn't even consider that my mother would be upset that I'd ripped up her book. You're like a child and the world just keeps scolding you, expecting you to get it right, but you don't get it right. You just keep making the same mistakes over and over and over again until you don't know what to do with yourself and they lock you away."

"How did you get out?" I ask as if she escaped some sort of foreign prison.

"I got better. I mean, honestly, they diagnosed me with depression and a personality disorder. But a woman, it's like when she's a little bit off, when she's feeling not right, the world knows it and they judge her so harshly. Especially in the fifties. And in the end I'm glad I got help. It did, it does, help, but the way it happened, the way I was treated then, could have been better."

"They said no one would publish *The Bell Jar* in America because America wasn't ready for a woman to talk about metal illness in that way even though Salinger and Keasey had been writing about it in regards to men for years."

"There's a double standard, women still bear the brunt of their mistakes. Women are watched like hawks."

"I sometimes wonder about my own mental health," I confess. I don't know why I'm telling Joanne this. She's a near-enough stranger but it feels right. Joanne looks at me with such sad eyes and nods as if she understands what I'm offering her. "Did I tell you what happened two years ago? The story I've finally decided to write." Joanne shakes her head and so I go on. "My husband Theo cheated on me."

"That I knew. Are you okay? Was it the kind of cheating that can be forgiven or was it directly-to-divorce cheating?"

"Maybe we could have worked things out. But things got bad afterward. He was cheating with this nineteen-year-old girl, she was one of my students and we were close. I found some pictures on his phone. Then I went through his texts and there were some really explicit ones from her. I was upset—"

"Of course you were," Joanne says.

"So I called her. I had her cell, maybe she'd texted me about the Literary Magazine before, but I called and her mother picked up. It was so innocent. Her mother was visiting her dorm and her daughter's phone rang and I guess she was used to answering her phone. But when I got her mother I just unloaded. I was so mad and I guess I blamed Heather, the girl, and her mother, for what was happening. I wanted to tell her mother on her. Like I was tattling on the playground. It was so silly."

"No it wasn't, you were angry, that was all."

"I keep telling myself that. I was upset. I had every right to confront her. But her mother was shocked. She was upset, but you would expect a mother to be. I was furious at Theo, he got a hotel room because I didn't want him in the house then, but honestly I think we could have worked things out. I was pregnant at the time and maybe that would have brought us back together.

"But then, it turned out the girl's mother had told her father and somehow the cousin, who was always odd, who had this strange, possessive crush on her, got word of it. He took her to a warehouse late at night and beat up her. He beat her so badly, the doctors said there were bruises all over her body, and her arm was broken. The cousin testified that it was not supposed to be so much but he so upset that Heather had been messing around with a married man. But he beat her up until her heart stopped. She had a heart attack right there. Apparently she had some kind of congenital heart defect no one knew about. The beating caused her to have a heart attack and they took her to the ER but by then it was too late. She died. She died because this possessive little shit beat her up and he beat her up because she had an affair with my husband. And the only reason anyone knew about it was because I had to open my big fat mouth to her mother."

"He beat her because the cousin was an animal who could not understand how women too deserve freedom, even the freedom to fuck up marriages. Is he in jail?"

"Yes. The cousin got six years for manslaughter, her father served a year for knowing about it, at least they think he knew about it, and giving him the keys to the warehouse where it happened. Apparently he didn't defend himself at all at trial."

"Wow. You've had a tough few years," Joanne replies. We both know it's an understatement.

I glance over at the manuscript and feel so close to the author. There are artists who speak to you, who reach between time and space and call to you. I sense Plath as I watch Joanne stroke the side of the pages. She must know this woman too, perhaps better than I.

After a moment a car rumbles outside and Joanne stands up. She smiles and it's somehow fake, like a girl in a movie version of a fifties housewife. I picture her ample body in a checkered dress, her hair is curled and she's wearing bright red lipstick like Sylvia Plath.

The door opens and Tammy, this time really wearing a business suit, walks in. Joanne's smile ramps up and she starts fussing with the knickknacks on the shelves. "You know, this place is still a mess, a mess. You should've warned me this place was such a mess, Lorelei. And I was going to put steaks on tonight," she says into the air.

"Hello, I'm home," a voice calls before Tammy appears in the living room. Joanne swoops up the manuscript as if it's a dirty secret. She rushes from the room with the pages over her chest like armor as she passes Tammy, softly rubbing shoulders for a second.

"Hello?" Tammy asks, looking at me. She doesn't appear to blame me for Joanne's odd behavior but she senses that something must be up.

"Hi, I'm Lorelei," I tell her as if she's Joanne's mother and I must mind her. "I was just returning the manuscript."

"Hello, of course, I remember you. How are you?" She stops to take stock of what's been said. "The manuscript?" I hadn't thought I'd have to clarify. If I had a secret manuscript left from a famous author the person I lived with would certainly know about it.

"Yes. The Sylvia Plath."

"The Plath?" she asks as if this is some kind of code. "Shit, the Sylvia Plath," Tammy says more to herself.

"Do you know about it? I just thought, I mean it's beautiful, I've read it, it's really beautiful."

Joanne appears, sticking her head in as if she's been listening. "The steaks are going on soon. I can make a salad, finish the steaks in ten minutes, Tammy. Lorelei," she looks over to me, "do you want to stay for dinner?"

"Sure, why not?" I shrug, looking over at Tammy, who nods as if to indicate that this is a good idea. I feel the need for Tammy's permission—like she's in charge more than I know.

"Great, dinner in twenty minutes tops."

"I should go change . . . but in a second," Tammy tells me. "Just wait here, we need to talk about the manuscript. I really didn't realize she'd actually let you read the thing."

"What's wrong?" I ask. "Is everything okay? Is Joanne okay?"

"Five minutes, I'm going to change and check on my wife, I'll be right back," she says and I wonder if I should worry.

Minutes pass and I hear movement upstairs. Tammy says something to Joanne, who murmurs back. I hear Tammy on the phone in some kind of one-sided conversation but I can't really make out the details as I sit in the living room looking at Joanne's pictures. There's another snapshot of Joanne, her hair cropped short, wearing Capri pants and a short sleeved blouse, standing next to a very lovely, smiling Sylvia Plath.

"I'm just going to get the salad ready," Joanne says, coming into the living room.

"Can I help?" I ask, half standing until Joanne motions for me to sit.

"Not, it's okay. You wait here. It won't take a minute." Joanne turns back. I hear her rustling around in the kitchen, chopping lettuce and carrots for a salad as I wait for Tammy, who appears shortly after.

"We should really talk about the manuscript, Lorelei," Tammy says first thing when she comes downstairs in a pair of white shorts and a short-sleeved sailor blouse. "I'm really sorry, I hadn't realized she'd given it to you. Did you tell your aunt about it? Does she know?"

"She does," I reply. "Why does that matter? Is this a legal thing?"

"She's used to keeping secrets. I don't know why she agreed to keep Joanne's."

"What are you talking about?"

"I'm really sorry to tell you this but the manuscript isn't real. Believe me, I looked it up. I've taken it to Sotheby's. I've run it by a few friends I have in publishing. It's not real," Tammy explains so quickly like ripping off a Band-Aid.

"No," I respond without thinking. "I've read it, it sounds just like Sylvia Plath." Tammy nods understandingly and I can tell she doesn't enjoy being the bearer of this particular bad news. My heart slides down my chest and it's like it was the first time I felt Theo was cheating on me, like the moment I lost the baby, or when I heard about my mother. They had been inside me, those words I read in that manuscript. They said everything I felt as I was hurting. Who could have written them? The words existed, I'd read them. How could they not be real?

"Look, Lorelei, I have to tell you something," Tammy goes on, taking a seat next to me on the couch. "Joanne has a personality disorder."

"I know, she told me, but she said she was all right. She seems okay. There was a little incident in Provincetown but she seems fine now."

"Yes, most of the time she is," Tammy explains calmly. "But sometimes she's a little delusional. Sometimes, really most of the time, she's perfectly fine. In fact most of the time everything is all right and then out of the blue she starts to talk shit. Once she told a friend of mine that she was the long lost relation of Mary Queen of Scots. She went so far as to get herself DNA tested. Another time she went through the whole process of trying to prove that she was one quarter Native American, tracked down a tribe and everything, when we knew damn well she wasn't. But the Plath manuscript, that one she's been using for years, well before she met me. She shows it to people every once and a while. And it's not a lie, not to her. I mean, she knows I don't believe in it. I just . . . she knows not to bring it out around me. I think she knows it's a lie and believes the manuscript is real at the same time. I don't know how else to explain it."

"Why on earth would she do that? Who wrote it?"

"Well, I mean, Joanne did meet her when she was in college. There are those pictures they probably got along. Everyone got along with Joanne. And *The Bell Jar*, I guess with the right mindset you could really channel Plath with that as a base. It's not Sylvia's work though, believe me. I think Joanne wrote it sometime when she was having a particularly bad breakdown, after she found out about Sylvia's suicide. Until we met she had been in and out of hospitals her whole adult life for this disorder. She still sometimes needs to go back in. I thought she was over the manuscript, it's been a while since she brought that out."

"You think Joanne wrote it?" I almost spit the words at her I can't believe them. "But they felt so real . . . so . . ."

"I've been trying to ask her for years," Tammy interjects. "They're pages of a novel, yes, they were a channeling of Esther Greenwood. That doesn't mean they're fake, it just means they're not Plath's words. But still, if they meant something to you . . ."

Tammy is now acting like my aunt when my mother would break down, as if she's trying to let a child down after they've found out there is no Santa Claus. "If they meant something to you," those words just then are such a cop out. "If you know all this about her, that she does this, her problems, why are you with her? How can you let her tell people this? How can you let her make people believe this bullshit?"

"I can't watch her all the time. I know it's hard to hear and I'm sorry—"

"You're sorry? Do you have any idea what I thought I was reading? How special it was?"

"I know," is all she says. There's silence for a second and then Joanne calls us.

"Steaks are out. I set the table outside." Her voice is so crisp and clean and I can't reconcile them with the woman who gave me the manuscript only a couple weeks ago.

"How can you stay with her?" I ask. "I know it's none of my business but I guess I just . . ."

"You take people as they are. Joanne saved my life as well once, when I fell in love with her. Even when she's acting up, I love her. She makes life interesting and she's never broken down, not completely, not on my watch. Maybe I have something to do with that."

Joanne begins fiddling in the next room. I hear metal objects clang and the refrigerator door opens and closes as Tammy sits before me. "Dinner is ready," Joanne calls once more and Tammy stands up.

"I understand if you don't want to stay."

"No," I say, shaking my head. "I'll come."

I follow Tammy outside. The bees are still out, hovering over their wooden hive. I can just picture all the intricate honeycombs inside. I look at the table, it's already set with a pitcher of water and a bottle of wine. The steaks sit blackened and glistening on a red plate, a salad bowl sits in the corner, near three smaller stacked plates. It all looks so neat and orderly, so not the Joanne I thought I'd met. I look at the table and remember the manuscript. Is anything real?

"Just take a seat. The steaks are all medium, I hope you don't mind."

I feel so fake just sitting down to dinner like I know nothing. But for a moment I'm frozen. Joanne serves the steaks, lifting each one with a fork as Tammy watches me. She gets up and pours the water but doesn't bother with the wine, it's like she knows even after this whole dinner charade that I won't be staying.

"You know, I got these at the grocery store the other day. I asked the butcher and he said they were the best he had," Joanne announces once everyone has settled.

"So what are you reading now, Lorelei?" Joanne asks as if she doesn't know. There's a phoniness to this question, like she's protecting herself. She looks over at Tammy and smiles and it's like I'm in another world, like everything we'd just talked about an hour before never happened. Tammy just looks at her plate, embarrassed. Just like my mother her mood, how she acts, can turn on a dime.

"Reading?" I ask. "What am I reading? Joanne, why don't you tell Tammy what I've just been reading? What I've just finished?" Joanne stares at me with a deer-in-headlights look and I can't tell if she's scared or confused. I can't read her, I just can't read her and she's so like my mother just now. "Go ahead, why don't you tell Tammy what I've just been reading."

"Lorelei, is everything okay?" Joanne asks.

"Who wrote it?" I put my fork down I can't even pretend to eat. "The Plath, who wrote it? I guess I shouldn't call it the Plath. I just . . . I don't understand why you would tell me that, why you would make me think that?" It comes out, this anger, and it's not all for Joanne but now this, on top of everything else. My husband lied to me about so much, my mother lied about her condition, my aunt lied about how bad everything was and now this, on top of everything else there's this. "I know about the Plath. I know it's not real. How could you? Just . . . how could you?" I know she's delicate, my mother was delicate as well but I can't calm down, I can't take her condition into consideration as it all tumbles on top of me. Here I am, Lorelei who knew nothing about her husband, nothing about her mother's pain in high school, nothing about her own life.

Joanne doesn't say a thing. She just looks at her food, scraping her fork along the plate every couple of seconds. "I don't think you have to raise your voice, Lorelei, I think that's very uncalled for," she finally tells me and I shake my head. I can't take it. I can't be here. I push my plate away and get up. I can't believe it's gone this far, this ridiculous dinner.

"I'm sorry, I have to go. Thank you for the steak, I'm sure it's delicious," I tell her and Tammy looks up at me, a mask of worry on her face.

I walk away from the backyard and into the driveway. I've lost it, Esther's story, my own understanding of it, as if a great something has been taken from me. The manuscript wasn't real? It never was. I make a fist and shake my head as I sit in my car, festering. How could I be so stupid? How did I not see this? No one comes to check on me, Tammy and Joanne stay in the backyard and I have no idea what's going on, what they're talking about, how they're handling this but I can't care. I just can't care. I take out my phone and call my aunt.

"The manuscript wasn't real, Tammy told me," I say into the phone when she picks up. I don't know why this is the last straw after everything else but something breaks and I can't put it back together. "The Plath. I told you about it, did you know?"

"I did. I'm sorry," she admits. "I should have told you the other night I just wasn't sure how you'd react, how Joanne would react. Tammy told you? I guess she thought it was best. I've read it, I've read it too and it's still such a beautiful story."

"A beautiful story that was a lie. Like when my mother said she was well. Like when Theo said our marriage was okay. And that journal, what happened to Mom, you knew about it. It seems all you do is cover up people's lies."

"I hope I do the opposite, considering what I do for a living," my aunt retorts and I want to hang up on her at such an ill-advised attempt at humor.

"Theo said he loved me and then he cheated. Heather was my student and she came to class and smiled and spoke up and all the while she was sexting my husband. And I can't even be angry with her, angry with either of them, because after everything how can I be? He fell in love with a girl and she died, how can I fight that? I have no right."

"You have every right to be angry, it's okay. You need to be angry. You need to heal. I'm sorry you found out this way."

"It's like I don't know anything, the world is going on around me and everyone I know is not who they say they are."

"It's hard to know everything that goes on in people's heads. Everyone has secrets, everyone is hiding something. I'm sorry I never told you about your mother. We can keep on talking about this, I deserve it. She didn't want her secret out and it was hers, I had to keep it. With all that went on with her, they'd send her to a hospital if they knew what she'd done when she was seventeen and then she'd have no agency at all. I needed to keep this one thing, this one secret just had to be hers."

"And what about when she died? Didn't I have a right to know?"

"To know what? That your mother had an illegal abortion in the sixties? That she sat in a bathtub and let a strange man poke and prod her and yes I'm being polite here, that's not what he did, but she let it happen because a doctor wouldn't let her get a sanitary operation on her own body when she was a seventeen-year-old rape victim. I'm sorry, but she'd been mistreated enough I didn't need to mistreat her by telling. I wanted something to be hers." Movement rustles on my aunt's end and wonder what she could be doing in her hotel room.

"To find out like this? Why did she write it down if she didn't want anyone to know?" Tears well in my eyes but I hold them in. I look back at Joanne and Tammy's bungalow and remember the bees. They had been so fat, so perfect, those bees.

"I guess the words were stuck in her, they ate away at her just like the memory and she needed to get those words out, to purge herself. Why does anyone write? Why do you? Why do I? Why does Joanne go around pretending that a long dead poet wrote that manuscript? To dictate a story she never got to tell. But to also tell her own story without telling it. There are a million reasons for anything and they all stand straight up when you think about them."

"I'm sorry, I just . . . it was a shock. After everything . . . And my father—"

"Don't you dare tell your dad," Aunt Sarah says, her voice rising. "It'll kill him and it'll kill his memory of her. She spared him having to wonder 'what if.' She spared him and it is not your job to take that away from him. And I'm sorry I didn't tell you about Joanne. This has happened before with the manuscript, but it'll be okay."

"It'll be okay?" I nearly spit the words. "It's that simple?" How can it be simple?

Lorelei

September 30th 1988

She screams constantly, this baby, Lorelei, that's all she does. I gave her a bath the other day and I swear to God I do not know what kept me from holding her under the water and just letting her go. I think I might have but then I remembered that the police would find out. Whenever anything happens to a baby they blame the mother. I try to get her to eat. She's over a month old and she still has trouble latching. All the mothers in my little group, they all think it's so much fun, breast-feeding. They think they're doing their motherly duty or something, and this baby won't even eat from me. She will only eat from the bottle and my doctor says I have to keep trying the breast milk. I have to work at it. I don't have anything else to do, I don't have a job, why can't I just feed my child? It's been over a month and she's just not taking and I swear the screaming, the crying, I do not get a moment to myself and I want to walk out of here, to leave her in her crib and just walk away. And what stops me is they'll find me. I'll walk into the street, I'll try to hide but I swear to God they are watching me and they'll find me.

January 27th 1989

Sarah came over today. She's been spending so much time away. When I couldn't figure out how to get the oven to work last month I called her up, the baby was screaming in the background and I was so far gone, I felt like I was drowning in her cries and Sarah came over. It took her hours but she took the train and then the bus and she stayed with me until Joey came back from work. He's got two jobs now, his regular union job and then he took a night shift at this plumbing supply place a few nights a week. It helps with the money but he's never home and I never get any peace, none at all. But there were times when Sarah was in Iowa to cover a convention or California to do a story on some tree in some forest and who the hell cares? But she's not around to help enough and I don't have any other family really. My other sisters barely talk to me and I never see them. Sarah's work sends her everywhere. Her life is amazing, she does what she wants.

I don't understand why I'm the one with the husband, the child, and my sister is the one with the life. Why is it that women can't have that? Can't have both? Then again I know it's my own damn fault, I made this decision. I was smart; I could have done something with my life. I could have finished college but it was all too much. I couldn't focus, not with my meds, and then I'd have a breakdown and not do my work and the school never cared. I tried to explain it to one of my professors once and he said, "And how is this my problem?" That's the year I dropped out of college. And today, this week, I just kept not getting out of bed. I just kept breaking.

But Sarah came over today and she held the baby. Lorelei cries and cries with me but when Sarah picked her up she felt safe, she was happy. The damn child stopped crying. I talked to Sarah about college, maybe taking a couple of classes. She told me not to hold myself back. That I can do anything. I know she believes her lies but they're lies all the same, we all know that. And Joey just last week said it was a silly idea, my wanting to go to school. Then Clara, from my Mother and Me class, is taking this pottery class or something at the community center one night a week and I wanted to do that maybe. Joey said that he gets home from work too late and we can't really afford a sitter so I can't even do that. I just feel trapped here, like the mess is piling up, my life is piling up and why, why on earth did I decide to do this?

March 21st 1989

It was the smell today, the smell that made me run outside. There's all this dirt on the floor and I don't know what to do with it all. There is garbage on the counter and I swear to God I throw it away and it's back again. Like it crawls back from some gutter just to haunt me. It's like my entire life, my home, is rising up against me. I cannot see straight with the smell, with all this garbage, that's a smell.

Just the other day I sat in the kitchen, on the yellow linoleum floor and cried. I just cried and cried. The baby was screaming, I'm sure the neighbors could hear her, could hear her for miles, but I just couldn't get up. I sat there and cried while the garbage piled up, while there was dust on the windows. I can't live here. I feel the walls closing in on me with every scream and I still have this kid.

November 26th 1989

Sarah came over for Thanksgiving. Last year she wasn't in town for any of the holidays but I'm happy she's here. She helped me clean the house. I've been better at it. Joey hired a cleaning woman to come in two days a week and that helps. I still have to try to keep the house clean, I still have to pull my weight but I've been seeing a new doctor, a new therapist, and he seems to think that if I just focus, if I try to control myself, my energies, it'll all be okay. I slept last night. I hadn't slept in days but I slept last night and having Sarah here helps, especially since Joey's family, his parents, his mother, they can be so unkind to me. I see the way they look at me, especially when they hold the baby. His mother just today said, "Here, let me take Lorelei." But it wasn't that she said it, it was the way she said it, like she knows, she knows I can't handle this. She knows I don't sleep at night, that I toss and turn, that I just want to go back, go back, I don't even know what to, I just want to go back to something better. I wonder what would have happened if I had had the other one when I was seventeen? Would I have gone crazy sooner, felt this trapped sooner? Would it have been better if I hadn't have had Lorelei at all? I feel like such a failure, such a horrible person, because I feel the walls closing in on me every time my baby cries. I feel myself shrinking into this other person and why, why am I so horrible? I hear the voices now. They were gone for so long but they've come back and they tell me, "Leave it alone, let it cry." I don't sleep and then I sleep too much and the baby wakes me and I just want to ignore her. I can't tell my therapist about the voices, I have to just let them pass. Joey will take care of it, that's what I keep thinking. Joey will take care of it.

February 15ᵗʰ 1989

I haven't written in a while because they took me away. I'm in a hospital now. Everyone says I need to be here. Just for a while until I'm better. It was for the best it really was. The voices were getting to be too much. Right before I went into the hospital, before they gave me this new medicine that they swear to God will work, I was giving Lorelei a bath and she wouldn't stop crying. I turned the water up, I made it hotter and hotter, so hot I don't even know why I was just sick of the screaming and I thought it would help. I put her into the water. It was so hot she turned bright red right away, the screaming got worse and then Angie, the cleaning lady, came in and pulled the baby out. I just sat there on the floor, my knees to my chest, staring into space. Angie called Joey, Joey came home from work, he called the doctor, brought me to the hospital. Sarah came from New York and they put me away, put me away at this hospital with shrinks and medicine and I honestly do not know what else . . . no . . . no I know.

February 27ᵗʰ 1989

They did it, they finally did it, hooked me up to the electricity, shot it through my brain. They call it ECT now, not Electro-shock, but it's the same thing, or close at least. I felt the power, the raw power of it. And I don't remember it hurting, I can't feel the pain but I know there was pain, somewhere my mind told me that logically there was pain and I felt it. Some things were fuzzier after that but then again some things were clearer. It was so strange but for the first time in so long I could hear myself think. I just kept going down, down, down and there was this darkness. This unbearable darkness. No one would help me. They strapped me down and let it happen.

March 1ˢᵗ 1989

In the hospital I've slept as I had not slept in ages. I rested. Joey waited a while after my ECT before he brought Lorelei. It's hard for a child to come to a place like this. But I get visitors now, the women from my Mother's Group, a few of them anyway, some of them still blame me for I don't know what, being a bad mother probably.

I'm okay now. I'm never going to be better, that's what the doctors told me. I need to go to therapy. I need to make sure that I monitor my behavior and keep up with my meds. This is all very important, I know that. But I think I'll be okay. I'm never going to be the perfect wife, the perfect mother. I don't even think I'm going to be a happy person but at least, at the very least, I can be okay. I can survive and that's something.

March 27ᵗʰ 1990

I can survive, that's what I said the last time I wrote but I wonder what it means, to survive. Today Lorelei wouldn't let go of my legs. She goes to nursery school two days a week and still she's so clingy. I was trying to make lunch, those silly cheese sandwich things she likes, the silly sandwiches that are all she eats and she wouldn't let go of my legs. It's all, "Mommy, Mommy, Mommy," and I swear I'm suffocating, I swear I can't move and I don't know what to do with myself. The doctor tells me to breathe, to just breathe, but then I can't hear myself think and my stability goes out the window. My willingness to even try, it's like I just give up.

I called Sarah today. She's staying at a hotel in Philadelphia for some story but I really needed her and so I called the paper and they gave me the number of the hotel and at least she was able to talk to me. She told me about our mother, how our mother used to understand me, how she used to try and help. I can make it through these days because there are days when Lorelei and I have so much fun together. We go to the park and she slides down the slides and I think if only this moment could be all moments, if only it could last forever. And I love her, I really do. I feel the strain of it all but I also feel the love and I wonder if this is what all women feel. Yes, I have this illness, the peaks of mania, the valleys of depression, and all the whatnot in-between but still, I wonder if all people go through some version of this. This love? This dread? Lorelei wouldn't let go of my legs but finally I pried her off of me and now I think we're okay. I'm learning tools for how to handle this, how to handle me, handle us. She laughed at me and called me, "Silly Mommy," and that made it better. We're going to be okay.

The journal ends there. I was around two years old. I do not remember holding tight to my mother until she was thoroughly annoyed. I do not remember being put in a scalding hot bath as a child (then again I never had any scars so it couldn't have been that hot). I only know that there was something wrong, something was off. My mother would act so strangely, talking a mile a minute about a TV show we'd just watched like it was the most important thing in the world one day only to completely shut down the next. And the sleeping, I knew there were nights she didn't sleep, I could hear her in the living room when I went to bed and then again when I woke up for school she'd still be awake. Then she'd sleep for days and my father would take over as if she didn't exist anymore, as if we were just going to leave her in bed and see what happened.

The sadness, the pain of other people, we never really know it, not until it stares us in the face, not until they tell us in no uncertain terms, this is how I feel, this is what I want, what I need. This is who I am.

Who else is suffering and what have I not seen?

Lorelei

AMELIA'S NEXT *MAUDE Magazine* party is on the beach. It's their third party this season but the first one to actually take place on the water. They've put a floor down, wooden planks covered by a swanky red carpet so the women can still wear high heels. Music flashes in waves like at a nightclub but the lighting is more subtle, only lanterns, the kind sailors might have used a hundred years ago, tastefully shine at the corners of the party while one large chandelier falls prominently from the middle of the oversized white tent that resembles a long, flowing, on-the-beach wedding dress. The ocean is out there. Poseidon is out there. I hear him. I feel his soft whispers on my skin. It's dark and the light, this party, blocks my view and I can't quite see just how big the ocean is.

It's the same people as last time. Except Joanne. I called today not just to see about the party but to see how she was. I shouldn't have overreacted so much, I shouldn't have yelled at her the other day and I wanted to apologize. "Joanne can't talk," Tammy told me. "She's away right now. I don't even think they invited her to this one, but it's okay," she brushed it off politely. "Maybe the next party."

There are men in suits, women in nice dresses. Many of them carry champagne flutes or mixed drinks and I picture Eamon still at work at Lairs peddling beer and shots of cheap liquor, the stuff the locals like. Then again I've met the locals, when I was a girl taking summer vacations here, my father a plumber, my mother a housewife, we were locals as well, no matter the luck we had inheriting the house. My father would have had a beer, my mother maybe an iced tea, she couldn't have anything else with her medication. We ate pasta more often than fresh seafood, even when it's local it's hard to afford.

"You really have to try the duck," Amelia nearly cries over the music, coming up to me in a red dress. She looks like someone else, like she should be parading around the streets of Paris, not on this beach. There is a playfulness in her small hazel eyes and I want to pull her aside and ask her if she'd like to be somewhere else. Though I know the answer. Of course not. Of course she does not want to be anywhere else. There are things about Amelia that are not like me and I've learned to embrace them. When a friend is there for you, when she stays with you while you cry your eyes out in bed, when she comes to the hospital and insists on seeing you after visiting hours are over because she knows you have just lost your child and your husband isn't there, you can begrudge her nothing, especially her need to invite you to swanky parties. "I just talked to Mindy Freidman, she wants to discuss doing an interview with Starla Harris next week. It means I have to get into New York soon. You still want to come?"

"To New York?" I ask as Amelia stands glassy eyed with her drink. "Yes. I should get back to New York. Theo is going to start complaining that I spend too much time at this house, not that it's any of his business. I still think he's going to try to get half of my next book contract."

"He has enough. He's really an ass. He doesn't need to take money from your writing."

"Thanks, Amelia." Looking into my friend's tan face, so much makeup so expertly applied, I'm grateful for her. "He might start keeping tabs on how much I write. Maybe I'm just being cynical, I'm sure a lot of Theo just wants this all to be over."

"I know," Amelia replies, draping her arm around me. Now she is not just a girl at a party, a girl who has to make contacts to keep her very cool magazine job, she's Amelia, the girl I meet for coffee once a week, my very good friend. "Are you okay?" she asks, looking me in the eye and I'm unsure what to say. I'm okay. Now. I'm okay at this party at this very second but who's to say what the next second will bring? Being okay like mental health is not a one shot deal, a straight line hurtling toward better or worse, it's the waves at sea, sometimes up, sometimes down.

I look out and there's a man in a suit I recognize. He has short black hair and stubble on his face. He's carrying a glass of whiskey and it looks like he's about to check the cell phone he keeps in his pocket. I know this guy. He works with Theo. "Thanks so much," I tell Amelia as I watch her eyes pan out. She also sees someone she knows.

"I should mingle. And so should you. Mingle, mingle, like you're single," she says to me, a plastic smile spreading on her face as she steps away.

I don't plan to approach this man I recognize, but we walk in the same direction and he half smiles and waves when he sees me. He does not go for the phone in his pocket or turn tactfully away. "Lorelei, right?" he asks, his index finger pointed in my direction like he's about to accuse me of something.

"Lorelei, yes. And you're Richard."

"Richard Willard, the one and only. What're you doing out on the Cape?"

"A friend of mine works for *Maude*. I'm here in the summer."

"Right, the family home, Theo told me about that. How's everything going?" he cocks his head, his voice like a frat boy's.

"Everything is great." When talking to a frat boy it is best to just say that everything is great since they do not comprehend any other response. I plaster that plastic smile and I know, just then I know, how Amelia fakes it so well.

"How about you?" I am myself and not myself. The words, "how about you?" in this context are not so strange and still they feel off, like I'm parroting something I heard on television.

"Can't complain. Rex and Buddy just made partner. We're working on a few cases right now. Theo's doing really well by the way. Am I allowed to tell you that? Did I just give away some sort of big divorce secret?"

"No," I reply, getting more serious. "Nothing like that. We've basically worked it all out financially."

"Theo's in town, right? Where's he staying? Do you know? Is he with you?"

"No, he's got his own place. He said something about Airbnbing a condo."

"I know, he likes his privacy. We offered to let him stay with us at the rooms the firm took at the Fisher's Head but he said he needed some time alone. Needed to sit and think. I'm not sure what that means." He doesn't seem like the sitting and thinking type. "He's been working really hard lately. Really throwing himself into it, you know?"

"I know, he always could be a work-a-holic," I reply, looking out at the party. "If you see Theo before I do, give him my regards, Richard." I touch his suited shoulder. It's made of fine material, soft and strong, I'm sure it breathes well on the beach.

"I will," Richard replies, looking away as if he too sees someone else.

There is quiet, actual quiet, except for the rocking of the waves, and then a voice comes up behind me, soft at first, but with a little force. "Hello stranger, everything okay?" a woman asks. I recognize her right away. The hello stranger, she used to say that to me when I was a child.

"Sarah, how are you? I didn't think you were coming."

"I really didn't want to. I still have a story to do for *The Atlantic* but I was invited and I've always found it's best to come when you're invited to these things. Small world, the Cape in the summer."

"I know, exactly. I've been pulled from party to party the last few weeks and so much stuff is going on." I laugh more to myself, looking around to see if there's anyone else here I recognize. My body slackens. At least now I'm with someone I know and the familiarity of my aunt is like putting on a warm fuzzy sweater.

"*Maude* does know how to throw a party. I remember in the seventies, *Cosmo* and *Mademoiselle*, all the ladies magazines, the high fashion, high profile ones, they were always throwing parties. After I graduated and moved to New York, I was a bright-eyed young thing. I remember those first few years, I wore entirely too much plaid. When I first came there I worked as a secretary for *Cosmo* but very soon it became my job to put on the parties."

"Sounds like a great gig," I say.

"I know, it does. But I was terrified. In the beginning, I didn't know what hall to hire, what vendors to choose. It was a job for a very cool person and when I first started doing it, I wasn't very cool, not at all. I had to work at it, becoming who I wanted to be. That's what we do, we're all artists, we all make ourselves, our lives. We have to work at becoming who we want to be, we can't simply be who we want by inertia. You know, they always say 'be yourself,' and there is something to that, there really is, there's always a kernel that is only the essential you. But also, you have to find the essential you. You don't always know her when you're ten, fifteen, twenty-three, forty. You also need to be who you *want* to be, who you aspire to be, that's the essential you as well, and that doesn't come out of the womb fully formed."

"That's really wonderful advice." I wish she'd given it to me ten years ago. "I read the journals," I tell her and her eyes look downcast for a second.

"Was it all they were cracked up to be?"

"I just . . . I guess maybe I shouldn't have insisted, I feel like the moment I found the first one it was Pandora's Box opening and on top of everything else."

"I know." My aunt grasps my arm for a moment before gently pulling back. "I'm sorry, but once the box was open I just thought you had a right to see."

"Thank you."

My aunt smiles kindly and grasps my shoulder for a long moment. "So how's Joanne doing?"

"We had a fight. I tried to call today but Tammy said she was away. I think she might be mad at me. I kind of blew up at her about the Plath manuscript. Why, how should she be?"

"You heard right? What happened?"

"No," I reply cautiously. "What happened?"

"It's just, I spoke with Tammy and Joanne is back at the Behavioral Health Center for a week or so. They talked about it and agreed she should take a break for a while."

"Behavioral Health Center? I didn't even know there was one on the Cape." This does not even ring familiar. When I was younger there wasn't a place like that for my mother to go when we were out here. Once my father drove her to the regular hospital after she'd tried to cut her finger off and they just stitched her back up as if it weren't the strangest thing, a grown woman admitting she'd sliced her finger open. "Remember Mom, there was nowhere for her to go out here, not really."

"I know." My aunt nods sadly. "I'm sorry. I shouldn't have said anything. Apparently she's been spiraling for a while. Her moods, her disorder, it comes and goes, but you know, sometimes she needs to go to The Center just to get herself and her meds under control. She's usually okay. Her life, the world she's built for herself, it's usually fine, but sometimes she just goes under. She started talking about that manuscript again, that was the first sign. Once that comes out it's the beginning of the end."

"The end?" I ask, a knot twisting in my gut.

"I'm sorry, Lorelei, that was melodramatic. And I wouldn't have said anything except when I spoke with Tammy the other day she said she'd explained Joanne's situation to you. And you seemed so close with her. I thought maybe you knew more than I did. It really is a predictable pattern. She'll go into the hospital for a while, get reset, she'll get better. She'll move on with her life. I swear, sometimes Tammy considers taking the manuscript and tossing it in a fire, just like the real Sylvia Plath did with the novel she wrote about Ted. But Tammy knows Joanne has to get rid of it herself. It's not her place to make that kind of move. Not only would it be too devastating but it wouldn't help."

"I didn't know it was that bad. Tammy made it seem like it had been under control for a while."

"I know. It was at one time but mental illness stays with you. You have to manage it. Take care of it. You have to deal with doctors and medications your whole life. It's like having cancer except there's little hope of remission. I'm not going to say it's just as bad as cancer, that's not my place. But what Joanne has, it's not a cold, it's not even pneumonia, it's a chronic illness that has to be treated, cared for, for the rest of her life." I want to tell my aunt that she seems to be speaking from experience, watching her own sister go through all she did.

"I'm sorry I didn't know Joanne was that ill. Maybe I should have. I was so harsh with her after I found out. I'm glad Tammy is there."

"A saint, Tammy is a saint. That's what fragile women need sometimes. Virginia Woolf had Leonard for the longest time and that man loved her. He kept her alive for so much longer than she would have been if he hadn't have been there. He kept her alive and he kept her out of institutions, away from prying doctors that in her day would have harmed her, not helped her, mental hospitals and medications for the mentally ill being what they were then. And Sylvia, she was in the opposite boat. Sylvia Plath had Ted, who cheated on her and left her, who some say abused her. I don't blame the man entirely for her suicide though. But someone should have helped . . . helped more than they did. Just like you wouldn't simply leave a woman with cancer to fend for herself . . . " My aunt stops. No, she does not stop, she halts, as if a sign has been raised, as if an authority has come up and told her she can go no further on this subject. She closes her eyes, shakes her head, and downs the rest of her champagne. "I'm sorry . . . I . . ." She looks toward the ocean. I wonder if she sees what I see. I wonder if she wants to walk into the water, to see how far out she can go. They say these things, mental illness, runs in families, like a great grey stain mother to daughter, sister to sister. Did she ever wonder about herself? Did she ever show signs? I wonder all the time. The possibility of contracting my mother's illness haunts me.

"It's okay," I tell her. "Can I see Joanne, is that possible, do you know?"

"Probably in a little while. She's been away a couple days. She'll be able to see people soon, with Joanne, it gets bad, but never that bad that she's locked away without a say in the matter. Joanne always signs herself in and signs herself out."

"That's good to know. Thank you." I grasp my aunt's arm this time as she plasters on that same plastic smile (it must be required at these parties), waves to someone over my shoulder and moves to walk away.

"It was nice speaking with you, Lorelei. Now I have to talk to these people. You know, if I don't, what was the point of coming? I'll check back in later."

"Of course." My cell phone buzzes in my small handbag and I move toward the back of the party, away from the cool people and the drinks (though also away from the ocean) to see who's called.

When I check my phone it's Eamon. "I'm off," the text reads. "Fancy a drink at a bar other than Liar's?"

I look out at the party. I know no one. Not really. Amelia will come home tonight, maybe soaking wet from having jumped into another pool. My aunt has given all the sage advice she's going to give for now. And there's nothing I can do for Joanne at this time of night. It was nice to see Richard but we won't talk again tonight. I hold my phone and press the Uber app. They say my ride will be here in five minutes.

Sylvia
1963

"I FIRED THE girl," Sylvia said into the payphone down the block. London was behind the times when it came to phones just like it was behind when it came to plumbing, and there was a waiting list months long to even get the phone company to put a line in. And so whenever she needed to speak to someone Sylvia had to walk down the street, even in this cold, to use the public pay phone near the grocery store.

"Sylvia? Is that you? Are you okay?" Jillian asked.

"I'm fine. I really am. But I fired the girl. Completely got rid of her."

"What happened? Are the children all right?"

"The children are fine, but they very nearly weren't. I came home from shopping and the doctor and when I walked in the children were in their room, the door was closed and I heard these noises coming from the spare room. I knocked and no one answered and so I opened the door, it is my house you know, and I opened the door and she's in bed with a man. She said it was her boyfriend but I don't even know who he was, he could have been any man off the street."

"I'm sure she at least knew him. I mean, Agnes is a nice girl and I don't think she would just let a stranger into the house," Jillian said. "But I understand, she needs to be minding the children, she shouldn't be doing those things in your home. She can get a hotel or go to his place. We don't have to be Puritans, but still."

"I am not a Puritan," Sylvia nearly cried into the receiver. She felt the blood drain from her hands, her knuckles going white in this cold as she clutched the phone. "But the children were awake, Nicholas was crying and what could I do? She left them alone to go to bed with a man in my home. I told her to leave. I took her clothes from her suitcase and tossed them on the floor, I told her to pick them up and leave. I threw the man right out."

"Well that was sensible, Sylvia. He shouldn't have been there, not at all."

"And then that little bitch had the nerve to ask for her money! I told her if she wasn't going to do her job then I wasn't going to pay her. I told her I'd toss her things out the window if she didn't go right now and she ran out."

"Well, that was good. Though I think you should still pay the girl, at least for the week she worked. It's not fair to leave her high and dry. What is she, Irish? She's in a foreign country and all."

"She isn't getting my money!" Sylvia screamed into the phone. Her breath created a giant cloud in this cold and two people turned to stare at her when she yelled. "She isn't getting anything. Ted has enough of my money. And to think that I spent so much time saving and trying to put this family in a good position, and he goes traveling around with That Woman, gallivanting off with models."

"It's okay, Sylvia, calm down," Jillian said. "Are you going to be all right? Do you have someone to look after the children while you look for someone new?"

"I don't know, Jillian, I just feel so lost and everything was starting to come together and there was the girl to help out and we were just getting over the flu and the cold, it felt like the chill was finally letting up and now this on top of everything else."

"I know," Jillian said calmly. "Sylvia I'm worried about you. I want you to come stay with us tonight. I can pick you up or you could drive here, just for the night, you and the children, need to get out of that flat. You three are too cramped in there and it's starting to drive you mad. And with this winter, you really need to be in a better area. It's all madness right now." She paused, Sylvia could hear the halt in her voice and she knew it so well. People were always tiptoeing around her, refusing to utter, to even think, that word. Mad. Crazy. Off her nut. She'd heard it all. And yet it was there. Between Sylvia and the world it was always there. She had not meant to say it, but she had said the word. "Mad Girl's Love Song," had she not written that poem years ago? Did she not know this was coming?

"I don't even know where to go or what to do," Sylvia cried and she felt the tears inside her body. They always started in her lungs. She wasn't sure why. Then again, where did tears come from? The head, they were all in the head. And wasn't everything, the darkness, the sadness, the anger, the tears too, wasn't it all in her head?

"Just take the children and come see us. Bring a few things, Gerry and I will take care of you."

She wanted to tell Jillian that she did not need taking care of, but she wasn't sure if that was true. "Okay," she finally whispered, sighing over the outstretched telephone line. "I'll be there in an hour, maybe a little longer."

"Wonderful, we'll get the guestroom ready. Please, we want to try to get you healthy again, Sylvia."

"I know," she replied, hanging up the phone before marching back to the house.

She had only left the children alone for a minute but when she came back they were crying and wailing and Frieda had made such a mess of their toys and her clothes on the floor. Sylvia wiped Frieda's tears. She told her it was okay and then got to work getting ready to go to Jillian's. She really should pack a few things for them. But then again she wanted to get out before the girl returned with that man and demanded her money. She did not need any screaming fits outside her flat. That would only upset the children.

"Come," she said to Frieda, grasping the girl's hand as she moved to pick up Nicholas. "We need to go see Auntie Jillian and Uncle Gerald, is that okay, honey?"

"It's time for dinner," Frieda said. "I'm hungry."

"It's okay, we'll have dinner, don't you worry," Sylvia replied, her voice sugary sweet again as it usually was with the children. She looked down at her daughter, grabbing her keys and her purse and nothing else she headed out of the house.

When they left Sylvia saw that the girl was standing outside and true to form the man was with her. Whenever there's a pretty girl there is some man following her around. When she was in college the men were always there, waiting in the wings, until one day they weren't. One day they went off with Some Other Woman and forgot completely about her. This man looked bigger now. Maybe it was the suede fringed jean jacket. His hair was long and slicked back and in the right light he resembled, at least a little bit, her old pen pal Eddie Cohen.

"I want my money!" the girl cried at Sylvia, who grasped Frieda's hand more tightly and walked quickly with her to the car. "You owe me a week's pay and I deserve it, the way I look after your kids."

"Then you shouldn't have been a slut," Sylvia shot at the girl. She opened the door of the old Morris and slammed it once Frieda was inside. The little girl looked shocked, but she did not start crying. She was used to such things from mummy. "When you act like a slut you get treated like one," she said, holding baby Nicholas close to her.

The girl came at her and tried to punch her in the face but as she took a step Sylvia pushed right back, knocking the girl to the ground. She lost her balance pretty easily and plop, she was right on the wet, London street. If she hadn't had the children with her, if this weren't so serious, Sylvia might have started laughing at her.

"You're lucky you have a baby," the boy behind her yelled, swooping to pick his girlfriend up off the ground. "You're just lucky your children are with you. You're some piece of work, lady. Agnes said you were crazy. You're some piece of work."

"You won't get a dime from me," Sylvia cried before placing Nicholas in his car seat and getting into the Morris. She looked back at them from the rearview mirror. The boy was still dusting the snow off Agnes' coat and they were both shaking their heads as Sylvia felt the adrenaline rush as she started the car and took off down the road. They were going in the wrong direction, but she didn't want to turn around in front of those two, better to make a grand exit. She could go around the block.

"Mummy, why did you push Agnes?" Frieda asked, wide eyed.

"Mummy's sorry," Sylvia said softly, looking at her daughter through the rearview mirror. "Mummy was angry at her for not taking care of you. Are you all right, Frieda? We're going to Aunt Jillian's tonight, is that okay?"

"That's okay," Frieda said, looking down at her hands in her lap, she fiddled with them as Sylvia continued driving.

And it had already been a day, such a day, she really did think things were going to get better and then she'd gotten home and found that girl in bed with a boy and what a boy he was, just a thug from the streets, not even that interesting looking.

She had seen Doctor Horder again, that's where she'd been. He'd talked once again about her medications. "I think they're working," he'd told her as she sat on a couch looking at him sitting there, just sitting there, in his shabby brown suit writing in a little yellow notebook. Did he even look at what he wrote afterward?

"But I still feel it, the sadness. It's so dark and so deep," she'd said to him. "There are times when I can beat it back and there are other times when it's just too much and I want to throw myself into a tub of freezing water and just stay there and turn to ice."

"Sylvia, you know you can fight it. And I really am trying to help you. I spoke with a facility in North London, they said they had a bed, but I asked round and it's really not the best place for you. I fear it might do more harm than good, going into a facility that isn't right for you."

"But I need help," Sylvia had cried to Doctor Horder, who now held so tight to his little yellow notepad as if he were using it as a shield against her pain, the pain he could fix if only he got his act together and got her into a facility. "Maybe if I go there and then another bed opens up—"

"That's not the way it works here and once you're in, that's where you're at, we can't have people switching willy-nilly." The way he said it, willy-nilly, as if he were talking about what kind of cake to buy for a child's birthday. "I'm sure a bed will open up soon. But the medication is working and I think if we continue to speak every day it should be all right. Will you be okay, going home? When you do go into a facility, will you have somewhere for the children to go?"

Sylvia had wanted to tell him that Ted could take his own children but she wasn't quite sure. He was off now with That Woman, who had had the operation and taken care of her pregnancy. She couldn't say for sure that he would even consent to watch his own children while their mother was in hospital. And she had never, not once, been able to count on Ted's family. They very rarely visited and never had Ted's mother come in to help during a crisis, not at all, not like her own mother, who would have moved in after the separation if she didn't live a whole ocean away. She was stuck in this country instead, with this cold winter and Ted and his distant family.

"Really, I just . . . there are times at night I don't know if I'll make it. I'm teetering so far over the edge it's like I'm about to . . ." She wanted to say jump but she didn't dare. Yes, she wanted to go to a facility but not the kind that would tie her to a bed and surge electricity into her brain. But what the hell, what did it matter anyway?

"There are times, I swear I get up in the middle of the night and I want to do it, I just want to do it. And I already tried to kill myself once and because of that the prospect seems more ordinary. It's as if I think some nights when I'm lying awake, I tried before, why can't I try again? And I'm so close, those nights I'm so, so close."

"Sylvia, I'll get you into a facility, I will. It just needs to be the right one."

"I know," Sylvia had said, giving up. And so Doctor Horder had taken more notes and talked about her medications and facilities where beds might open up. Then she had come home to that slut in bed with a man and it was too much, really it was all too much.

"Mummy!" Frieda cried as Sylvia reached the final leg of the drive. It started to snow, the cold, the wind was picking up, as she made her way to the Becker's flat. "Mummy, where are we going to sleep?"

"Just with Auntie Jillian and Uncle Gerald tonight. You'll have your own room, Nicholas will probably sleep in Mummy's bed."

"Can I sleep in Mummy's bed?" the little girl asked. Sylvia couldn't see her face in the dark and so she was only a disembodied voice from the backseat.

"I'm sorry, love, but I think it would be best if you had your own room tonight."

Frieda did not respond as they traveled down the cold crowded London streets toward the Beckers. Once they arrived Sylvia parked in front of their house. She turned the car off and then slid around to look at the children. Jillian was outside, she pounced upon the car just as soon as Sylvia grasped her bearings and moved to undo Nicholas' seat.

"Sylvia, are you okay?" Jillian asked as she helped Frieda out of the backseat. The girl swung her legs out expertly avoiding most of the snow as Sylvia grasped the baby to her and marched toward the flat. "Did you bring anything?"

"Just ourselves," Sylvia said, smiling widely. Now that she was out of the car, now that she could breathe, she needed to put her best face forward. She couldn't let Jillian see the darkness, not all of it. "I didn't think we needed anything. Is that all right?"

"I just thought you'd bring some clothes for the children and yourself. What are you going to sleep in?"

"We'll figure something out," Sylvia replied, still smiling as she followed her friend up the steps to the flat. "I used to sleep in my bra and panties all the time when I was in college."

"But this isn't college," Jillian said, opening the door for them. "But please, make yourself at home. Dinner is almost on the table. Would you like to freshen up?"

"Maybe a little bit," Sylvia replied. "You know you British, you are so unbelievably polite. There are times when it's unbearable." She smiled again to smooth things over as Jillian betrayed a disconcerted look. Her mother had always said, when you're a guest you want to make sure to be overly polite to your hostess, as long as she also thinks you're sincere. You never want your hostess to think you're a liar. "But never you, you're just the right amount of polite, Jillian."

"Thank you," she replied. "You know where the WC is, if you'd just like to take the children. Or would you rather go right to your rooms and worry about eating later?"

"Don't be silly, of course we'll eat, I'm famished. I haven't eaten in so long, not a nice home cooked meal. I don't know when the last time was that someone cooked for me."

"Of course," Jillian replied as Sylvia moved to take the children into the WC. She wanted to check Nicholas' diaper and see if Frieda, who was still training, needed to go, but other than that she was ready to face dinner. She was really very hungry and she'd been so silly, calling Jillian so frantically before, but now they were here and she needed to take care of herself. She knew it would get bad again, the darkness would come, it always did and really would it be so hard to just take a few more pills, to just jump? It always got worse, like a monster terrorizing her. At least she would be with friends tonight and maybe that would stop her.

Once the children were situated Sylvia ushered them into the dining room. The Becker's had such a nice dining room. It was very formal with a long polished table set with twelve places. They were not a good silver and china kind of couple at least not at first glance, Jillian was really down to earth, but they did have very lovely flatware. Jillian was the type who wore those long skirts and sweaters, the kind for cold weather climates and Gerald had always been overly friendly, never very stuffy, around Sylvia and Ted. And Gerry had always been so very good about playing with the children.

"Dinner is served," Jillian announced, a smile on her face as she pointed toward the plates she'd set out. There was a platter of chicken and some kind of potato dish, also a large salad and another piping hot platter of carrots. "It's nothing much but we knew you'd be hungry."

"Thank you so much," Sylvia said, taking a bite of the chicken before she even started seeing to the children. They watched as mummy shoveled forks full of food into her mouth. "You know, Doctor Horder has been worried about my weight lately."

"Sylvia, you do look thin," Jillian replied, glancing toward Frieda, who was having trouble with her chicken. The little girl fumbled, trying to cut it with her dull fork. Jillian got up when Sylvia did not move to help the little girl. Instead Sylvia shoveled more and more food into her mouth. Just like with the caviar, she thought. I had been so hungry in New York and I needed all the caviar just like Esther. She wasn't sure why Jillian was looking at her that way, so funny, but she really was very hungry and the food was right there. Jillian cut little Frieda's food for her and then set her white adult sized napkin in the girl's lap. Sylvia looked over and admired her daughter. She really was lovely at the dinner table looking all grown up. "How much weight have you lost?"

"Something like twenty pounds since the summer."

"I'm worried about you too, I must say, you really should eat more. You have to keep your strength up, you have to take care of yourself," Jillian offered as she sat back down to her own dinner.

"Can't have you wasting away," Gerry chimed in good-naturedly and Frieda laughed. At her laugh Gerry made a funny face and Sylvia almost laughed with them, but instead she dove back into her food. She finished a full piece of chicken, it was savory, cooked right on the bone, and then grabbed another with her own fork, ignoring the serving utensil. She had eaten this way the first time she'd stayed in New York, when she'd worked that summer for *Mademoiselle*. The girls had thought she was mad the way she grabbed at the caviar and crab salad, the steaks and whole slabs of chicken she'd eaten right in front of them as if she were a bottomless pit. But she'd never gained an ounce of weight not until the head doctors got a hold of her and started giving her those nasty insulin shots. Then she'd blown up like a balloon getting so fat that summer her body was disgusting, she didn't even want to look at it. But she'd gotten her figure back once the electro-shock was over.

"Sylvia, we can cook you up some more food," Gerry teased as Sylvia kept eating. She hadn't eaten like this in ages but when she was a girl she used to stuff her face all the time. Here she was, a grown woman and food had not been offered to her, not like this, in so, so long. It had been ages since someone had made her a meal she hadn't cooked. She could not stop eating it, mouthful after mouthful it was as if she had been starving, in a desert really, for so long and she was finally, finally coming out of it. She could feel it filling her, not just her stomach, it clamored around the bones in her face, her arms and legs that shook sometimes she got so nervous. If I could only eat, Sylvia thought, eat and eat and eat, I'll nourish myself better. I won't be mad anymore.

After dinner Gerry helped the children up to their rooms. He carried little Nicholas and helped dress him while Frieda remained in the jumper she'd been in all day. "We have a little crib for Nicholas, a friend of ours brought it when he and his children came to stay and left it here. It's just been sitting in the room, collecting dust. We thought it would be best if the children slept together so Sylvia could have her own room," Gerry explained as they began the good-night ritual.

"They're going to have to sleep in their clothes," Jillian instructed her husband, who smiled and nodded to his wife, casting no judgment. He was going to be taking orders on this one tonight, Sylvia could see that. Taking care of a friend this sick, she knew, was not something he was used to and Gerry deferred to his wife.

"You know, I can call on the neighbors tomorrow, I believe they have a young grandchild, maybe they'll have some clothes for the children," Jillian offered as she handed Sylvia one of her old flannel night dresses to change into. "It's very cold, even with the heat on, and we're so lucky the heat hasn't gone in this part of London. The pipes haven't frozen either, that's a blessing."

"It's just been so hard right now, being in London," Sylvia said to her friend, sitting on the edge of the bed she grasped her hand and Jillian held tight to it. She looked Sylvia deep in the eye as if she were trying to decipher the depth of her damage. "It's so cold and I've had the flu twice already and even the nurses they send, I mean, the British health services have been very good to us considering the circumstances but it's not enough, it's just not enough."

"I understand. On top of everything else, Ted, your health, your work, and now this weather."

"Why is everyone always talking about the damned weather!" Sylvia cried. She stopped herself, listening to see if she'd disturbed the children, but they seemed fine, Gerry was still getting them settled. "I wrote a book. I wrote a brilliant book. I put my heart on a platter, I cut it right out and I said to the world, 'Look, look at this, isn't it interesting? This is what I've heard and felt and dealt with every day and please, please listen. This is me, this is all of me.' And I did all that and the world turned away with deaf ears. And I can barely publish my poetry. Everyone thinks it's because of Ted, that's why I'm so upset, that's why I'm losing my mind, but a writer, an artist, a man doesn't make her lose her mind, only her work and its deepest rejection can do that. Do you know what it's like to create something from your mind, from your soul, and have so many people reject it? I feel it in my core and I hate myself. I hate myself because the world has said it hates me."

"Sylvia you must know it's not a rejection of you. It's not like Ted—" Jillian started, coming close to Sylvia. Just then she wanted to shoot to her feet and tell Jillian to stand back she felt so unsure of herself, so unstable, like a bomb about to go off and she didn't want her friend caught in the wreckage of her life.

"Shut up about Ted. This is not about Ted or my father's death. My doctor keeps saying I need to deal with my father's death, but he doesn't know. He doesn't understand. It's not that I feel a deep-seated abandonment. It's my work. And yes, other things in my life are hard but I can handle it all expect this, the constant no's. When I was a girl all I heard was yes. When I was a girl, before I came to this country, people accepted me."

"Sylvia, I understand. I really do. And Gerry and I, we've talked, we want you and the children to stay here with us until Doctor Horder can get you into a suitable facility. We don't want you going back to that cramped, cold flat. I know it meant so much, getting Yeats' house, but still, you need to be among friends right now. You need to be taken care of, dear. Okay? Will you stay with us, just for a little while? You can write and I'll cook and help you with the children."

"Thank you," Sylvia said, smiling calmly now. She could make that face. She could disguise the darkness. Put a cloak over it so no one saw. And really, even if they knew she had the darkness, they only wanted her to disguise it, they only wanted to turn away from it, as if the darkness were something you could toss out in the refuse bin. Only she was forced to feel it. She made the smile wider, brighter, she felt it in her eyes as she looked at her friend. "Thank you, you've been very kind. I need to take my medication. I always feel so much better. The darkness subsides so much after I take my medication."

"Of course," Jillian said, getting up as Sylvia garbed the cup of water she'd gotten from the kitchen. She then grabbed the pills, the ones Doctor Horder had prescribed for her depression, and took them. One, two, gulp, gulp. She then opened the bottle of prescription sleeping pills and took two of them. She used to be able to take only one but now she needed two to knock herself out. "I'll take these and be out like a light. Are you sure the children are all right? They're in bed?"

"They are, everything is fine. I want you to sleep, Sylvia. Rest, sleep, take care of yourself," Jillian said, pushing the hair back from her face as if she were a mother cleaning her child before bed. Sylvia climbed under her covers, she felt the warmth of them, the warmth of this house, as she watched Jillian go.

SYLVIA SLEPT. SHE always slept. It had been a cycle for some time, one she had been on before, when she'd had her first breakdown. First she could not sleep. That was always the first sign. She would toss and turn at night, she'd get up, she'd read, she'd write poetry or sometimes she'd just lie there looking up at the ceiling. Her mind would race and race with thoughts so silly, so scary, but they kept her up 'til all hours. It was funny because then, like now, all she could focus on was how hopeless everything was. And it was funny, there had always been so much to do, so much to study (she had been in college during the first breakdown), so many places to go (she could have gone out with friends or stayed out with Buddy or one of the other young men who'd courted her so much in school), she could have read or written or gone for a walk. But it was sleep she wanted. The human body craved sleep and she would stare at the walls and beg, just beg, her body for it.

Then there were the times she would sleep all the time. She couldn't get up she would just lie there, half awake, as if the world didn't matter, as if she were in a netherworld halfway between existence and nothing at all.

But it was the sleep she needed and a doctor would prescribe pills. First she went to the family doctor, who had given Sylvia a prescription and later Doctor Beuscher had gotten her better sleeping pills. And they worked. They knocked her right out and she was dead to the world. And something that had been so hard coming would just come. It was so easy, too easy—just pop a pill and that was it. She would sleep and it would be glorious.

But now as she kept taking them the pills wore off sooner and sooner and then she was awake in the dark at four in the morning and her life was her life and she always, always remembered that Ted was gone and she'd been abandoned with two little children and there was hardly any money and Ted was spending all of it on That Woman anyway. And the more she wrote, with more and more of a fury, about this illness, losing her mind, about Ted and the children and Daddy . . . even now they did not want it. They did not want to hear about a woman going crazy better to just pat her on the head and tell her to buck up, she'd be fine. And Sylvia woke up at night, always she woke up when the pills wore off. Her depression medication could take the sting away, even if it never cured her, but taking the sting away, even for a little while, was something, but it wore off at night and she couldn't just take more.

When she woke up at four in the morning it was to the darkness. She opened her eyes except it was like she hadn't it was still so dark and she remembered with a frenzy all the horrible things like a big fat bolder sitting on her chest weighing her down and she could not acknowledge, not at all, the good things in her life. It was like they weren't there, like there was no light, none at all it was just responsibilities and Ted and unpublished poetry and she couldn't go on, she knew she just couldn't. Sylvia sat up in bed, not bothering to even turn on the light. "Jillian!" she called her friend's name. "Jillian! Jillian!" she called more frantically, not thinking that she might disturb the children or Gerald or anyone else happening to pass by the flat so late at night.

The door swung open and Jillian appeared. Her hair was up in a bun and she was wearing flannel pajamas just like the one's she'd given Sylvia. She looked like a housewife, a school marm, with her glasses on and a little piece of hair falling into her face. She sat on the bed and pushed Sylvia's hair back and it was like she was at home in Wellesley with her mother. Her mother had come every time she'd called her, and yes, she could be overbearing, but Sylvia always felt loved in her mother's home.

"Sylvia, what's wrong, are you okay?" Jillian asked, turning on the light and brightening the room.

"I can't explain it."

"It's okay, you don't have to. I'm here. You'll be okay."

"It's just that at night like this I feel so bad. It's this time. I used to write poetry but now I can't even move. And Ted is gone and no one will publish my poetry and my friends don't even speak to me, not like they used to, I have two children and the heat goes out and there's barely any money and Ted has everything, he travels, he lives with That Woman or he's off with some model, and the pipes freeze and this winter . . . really it's just that I don't even know anymore. What am I supposed to do? Except I can't go any further, I can't move. I just sit here and stare at the darkness and it's like I'm empty. I can't feel anything. How can a woman who cannot feel anything write?"

"I know, dear, I know. You're going through a rough spot, but you'll be okay. I'm going to see if your doctor can't get you on better medication. You need to go to that facility. I know it's hard right now, this winter is sending everyone into a funk, but you need to get into a facility that will take care of you and give you a rest and let you reset."

"But they can't, they're all full and it won't matter this will only happen again. I'm just too broken, too defective. I can't be fixed, not for real, not forever. This happened once before and if I get well now it'll only happen again. It's hopeless and I'm worthless."

"Sylvia, don't say that. You know that's not true. Maybe you're too sick to see, but that's why we need to make you better so you'll be the wonderful girl I met again."

"It's just, it's before five, and they were very clear, I cannot take my medicine again until five and so I have to wait. It cuts the edge, the edge I'm teetering on, and I know I'll be better after five, when I can take my medicine. Can you sit with me? Help get me through this time? It's a terrible hour, the one between four and five."

"Of course," Jillian replied, grasping her hand. "I'm right here and I won't leave you. I'll get you through this hour and then you'll take your medicine and perhaps you can use the rest of your morning to write or read or take care of yourself or go back to sleep and I'll be here to help with the children when they get up."

"I think I scare them. I think I scare the children."

"You're their mother, you don't scare them."

"The darkness . . . I really hope it's not hereditary. I hope I didn't give it to them."

Lorelei

THE PSYCHIATRIC CENTER, the technical term Tammy used when I called earlier this week to see when I might visit Joanne, is in Hyannis. Hyannis is near the house of Joe Kennedy, the son of bootleggers who got both his sons, John and Bobby, into politics. I grew up on stories of the Kennedys. If you went to the beach where the Kennedy's lived at a certain time of day in the fifties and sixties you could see the family, John and Jackie on the porch, Bobby Kennedy off playing volleyball somewhere. My father used to say that one time, when he was a teenager, he saw John and Bobby at a restaurant eating fried fish in paper baskets. They were young men, tanned and handsome with their short cropped hair, square jaws and big, genuine smiles. My father had stared at them in awe, these senators and congressmen, men of politics. "Bobby came right up and said, 'You'll be a good citizen one day, right young man?'" my father had said to me once. "I just stared at him. The two men, they were really amazing to look at up close. Larger than life, no wonder people called them American royalty."

This is just the kind of place John and Bobby would have commissioned, a gift to the community. The hospital is very new. It looks like it belongs in the suburbs not out by the water. It's one of those concrete monstrosities stone and brick on the sides but mostly concrete and metal in the bones of the place. A sea of a parking lot stretches around it like an expanding puddle or high tide and I park near the Wellington Entrance, where Tammy told me to meet her. I march toward the entrance in my tennis shoes, my oversized purse dangling at my side.

"Good afternoon." A woman smiles and nods as I enter. It's chilly, the air conditioning is on overdrive even though it's a very nice day. "Can I help you?"

"Yes. I called earlier this week. Tammy Greenbrier sponsored me, they told me to come and visit Joanne today."

"Joanne, yes," the girl, who has short blond hair and sharp, fringe-y bangs, greets me. "Yes, Joanne was just saying that someone was going to come today. Someone besides Tammy. Tammy's always here." I wonder if this girl should be telling me all this. She must be new. "You can just have a seat, we'll call you back in a moment."

I look toward the green upholstered chairs. They're nice, made of wood and cloth. The floors are thinly carpeted grey and light green. Everything is new. Everything is nice. Large picture windows stand against the massive walls and there are four or five skylights letting in natural sun. A few people are already seated in this large, well-lit place. There's a man in a suit and a woman in nice casual wear probably bought at Anne Taylor. There's also a younger girl, seventeen, eighteen, who's also well dressed. I gaze out and see a woman wearing a white sweat suit following what looks like a nurse in light pink scrubs and realize that they let the patients come right out. Had I expected them all to be locked away? Had I expected straight jackets and dull, doped up faces? Why is this the image I get when I think of the mentally ill, especially after what I've experienced with my mother? There were days she was unkempt, didn't take a shower, wouldn't brush her hair, but it was nothing like those black and white movies with shrieking, disheveled women. This girl being led away looks tired, like she's spent some time at a hospital, but her hair is neat and combed, her expression is calm but not lifeless. Real people come here, real people live here and get better, they live productive lives but my mother lived until 58 and then the illness took her.

We'd sent my mother to junkier places. We didn't want to, but we had to. It was all we had. My father couldn't afford to send her to one of these nicer places, the insurance wouldn't cover it and she ended up somewhere in the city. I remember when he took me to visit her, the one time he brought me, it was the dirt on the floors, a film of filth that permeated the surroundings. The windows were foggy and I wasn't sure if it was on purpose. The people working there were scary, not like you picture people in those movie versions of metal hospitals, people with missing teeth and scraggily hair that jump out at you. They weren't like that, they just weren't well kempt. There were people with poorly applied makeup, one man behind the counter actually took out a cigarette and started smoking. But it was the 90s and things like that were still done back then.

When she was in there, when I saw her, my mother just stared off into space, looking like she was going to cry but then again also like she didn't care. "Mom?" I remember asking. My father stood behind me, his hand on my back, ready to pull me away from this brink. She just looked at me. First she was confused, I saw her eyes change, a constant sorrow, then anger flashed in them, mixed with a tinge of annoyance and she said, "I'm sorry, who are you?" That was it. "Who are you?" I pulled away from her and stood up. I understood then that she, in those moments, was not my mother.

It was then that I started worrying that I might catch it. I went to the library. I looked up mental illness in books, severe depression, bipolar disorder. The worry was that I'd get it. "Mental illness runs in families," I read in one book.

"The patient usually starts to exhibit signs in their teens but it can sometimes take until the patient is in their thirties to show signs of a breakdown." When I went to college without any signs of the illness I almost threw a party. I started seeing a therapist in my early twenties and though they wanted to treat me for minor depression, they couldn't see anything beyond that. "But you never know," my doctor had told me. "Mental illness is not a one shot deal and I'd still be careful." I have, since that time and before, always been careful, trying to keep away from stress and situations of heightened emotion (though I have been doing a poor job of that these last two years). It's as if avoidance will keep me healthy the way washing your hands and applying sanitizer might prevent a cold.

"You made it," Tammy says, taking a seat next to me. "Was it hard to find?"

"No. I know Hyannis. I just didn't think there was a Psychiatric Center here."

"They built it about ten years ago. They got a lot of money from the Kennedy Estate actually. Some of it is state funded but it's mostly private."

"So does that mean Joanne's insurance won't cover it?" I ask. Not that this is any of my business. Why is it, when things like this happen, even the most on-the-periphery busybody thinks they have the right to ask, 'how are they going to pay for it?'

"It covers part of it. We're lucky Joanne still has a little money left over from her parents' trust and I have a good job."

"You really are a saint," I tell Tammy. I wonder if she's knows people have been calling her that behind her back lately. Her smile is small and tight and I can tell that other people have told her this before and she does not entirely believe it.

"When you love someone, you do what needs to be done. She'll be out in a couple of days. She'll be the same Joanne I fell in love with. She's always at the end of the day the same Joanne I fell in love with."

"She has to stay in that long," I ponder.

"Sometimes she stays in longer, a few times they've let her out after a week. She really needs the rest and to get herself under control. Her meds were a little out of whack but we're adjusting them. She'll be okay, back to the old Joanne in no time, I promise. And the woman you met, the woman you know, that's mostly Joanne. Even now, she's mostly Joanne. She's not going to do a quick surprise change. I hope you know that."

"I do, but thanks. That's good to hear," I tell her and the conversation peters out, waning as we watch the teenage girl go back behind shut doors as the man in the suit swipes his phone.

It's a few minutes before another woman in scrubs, this one older, thicker, with short brown hair and very big brown eyes, comes out with a clipboard, looks up, looks down and then says, "Lorelei Bauer?"

I raise my hand as if I've just been called on by the teacher. We all feel like eager students when we're out of our element and our name is called. The woman nods, smiling, she must smile a lot like that, as she motions for me to come back. I follow her through a large wooden door marked In-Patient Care, it's all so cold and clinical, but this is still friendlier than the alterative I'd pictured. I believe the hospital my mother went into called her wing "Long Term Facility Treatment." The tiles are bright white with little specks of black in them, they look like they might be swirling trying to mesmerize the patients. The lights are also bright, as if the hospital is trying to show you something. The walls, the ceiling, everything white like a new age movie.

"Have you been here before?" the nurse asks as if this is some kind of attraction I'm visiting.

"No," I reply. "This is my first time."

"No problem. Joanne is in the common room, that's where most visits take place. You're cleared to stay with her in there. There might be a few other patients with visitors but don't worry staff will be watching as well."

"There'll be guards around?" I ask, unsure of how this works. I try to picture what it was like with my mother. Did men stand around like officers ready to pounce if a patient started kicking and screaming, if they grabbed a visitor's throat and started throttling? But I'm sure I'm making this up, it really wasn't that bad. Out of control was usually just standing up and yelling just a little too loudly.

"Just a few of our medical staff remain in the room," the nurse reassures me. "Everything will be fine. The doors to the waiting room will be locked, but just press the white button on the intercom on the side of the door and someone will buzz you out."

I want to ask her what happens if someone gets out of control but it's a very rude question. I'm sure they have a procedure in place.

"How's Joanne doing?" I ask, mostly to be polite. The woman looks back at me for a second and then continues marching down the hall.

"Oh, we can't talk about that. She'll be in the room though. You're cleared to speak to her."

"Of course, thank you," I reply, looking down at my feet as the nurse stops at a white door. There is a window above the doorknob made of frosted glass no one can see through. She presses a few buttons on a pad near the side and when a green light flashes she expertly pulls the silver metal knob and lets me in.

"This is the Visiting Room," she announces and I look in to see bright white lights and white tiles, white walls, just like the hall. Three large round tables make a pattern like a Mickey Mouse head with two big mouse ears. Red and orange plastic chairs stand around the tables like we are students at a progressive Middle School. A few nicer wooden chairs line the back and a bin rests on one table with what looks like art supplies. A man wearing a security uniform sits in a corner with a clipboard in his hands looking out while a woman in scrubs bustles around speaking with an Asian woman sitting with an older man. A young man in his mid-twenties speaks with an older woman who, judging by the look of concern on her face, is probably his mother. At least I'm not the only person visiting someone today.

"Take a seat, Joanne'll be right in," the nurse tells me and I pull one of the red chairs out and awkwardly settle. A few sheets of paper sit in the middle of the table and I grab one of them. It's blank but I pick it up anyway and fiddle with it. I can't hear what the other people are talking about but I can tell they feel my presence as they keep on with their conversations.

After a few moments a door from the back of the room opens and Joanne comes out. No one is with her, not even a nurse to guide her in. She's not infirm she just needs help. She looks older, under the weather and tired, a softer shade of herself but she smiles when she sees me.

"Lorelei, thank you so much for coming," she says, pulling out a seat, though she doesn't sit down. We just stare across the table and I can see by the two people stationed to watch the room that we're not really supposed to touch each other. "I was wondering when Tammy and I checked me in here if I would see you again."

"Oh, Joanne, of course you would. You don't have to worry about that. How are you? I'm just sorry I didn't know . . . I didn't see . . ." I stumble, sitting back down as Joanne follows my lead. "I'm sorry about the other day, I shouldn't have gone off on you like that."

"It's okay, I lied to you, you were upset. And you didn't set me off, not with that, you didn't set me off with the manuscript either, Lorelei, it was already there."

"I had a mother like this . . . I should have seen the signs," I counter. And I should have. I have experience, why did I look the other way? Why did I not see what was right in front of me? This is exactly what happened with Theo and Heather. Sometimes it's just easier to assume everything is okay than to face what is so obvious.

"The signs are hard to spot unless you're used to them. Tammy has been a saint, but she always is when this happens. Once the manuscript is on my mind, once I'm thinking about it . . . it's coming, that's all I can say, it's coming and something . . . I want to say manic but that's not the right word, but yeah, something manic happens."

"That must be so hard. To know it could come back."

"Yes, well, it's like Tuberculosis," she says and I wonder how on earth she could make such a comparison. "You know, TB, when it doesn't kill you, it comes back. I remember hearing stories from my grandmother, who had the disease, and every few months, sometimes she'd get lucky and go a whole year without a relapse, but every now and then, the TB would come back and she wouldn't be able to breathe. It was like a big fat dragon was sitting on her chest; she just couldn't get air in her lungs. They'd have to deflate her lung because that was the cure back in the twenties and thirties. So just picture it, having this thing inside you that is going to come back, it always comes back and when it does you're stuck in bed for two, three months while they deflate your lung, which is incredibly painful. That was TB. Well, this mental illness is kind of like that. You know it's there, it's in me, it's going to come back and it's going to hurt, it's going to disrupt my life, and it's never cured, never gone for good. Yes, I can manage it, but I have to be aware, I have to take care of myself. But even then it can come back and when it does I mustn't blame myself. Above all things, I cannot blame myself. I have to focus on getting better again, on prolonging the good times, the well times, and making sure I take care of myself."

Did my mother ever think about her illness like this? Did she live her life wondering when it was going to happen again? "Best to just ignore it," my mother told me once. "If I pretend I'm okay, I'll make myself okay." Sometimes it worked, other times that way of thinking only made things worse.

I look at Joanne, her eyes are so tired, her skin like paper as if she hasn't gotten enough sleep. I grasp her hand and look out at the room to see if anyone will tell me to pull away from her. They do not and so I grasp her more tightly. "I'm sorry," I tell her and I know it's not the best thing to say. What does an "I'm sorry" really mean to a sick person? "I'm sorry you felt like you had to hide it. I'm sorry I didn't see it. I didn't know."

"I'm good at hiding it. But that day at my place I was getting pretty manic. The way I just started hopping around when Tammy came home. I know you thought it was odd. You didn't call me on it, it would have been impolite, but that was a bad night. Not just because of the manuscript and I do understand, but with the manuscript—the way I lied."

"So whose is it, the Sylvia Plath manuscript?" Bringing up the manuscript, the thing that sets her off, is bold, but Tammy has already told me that Joanne has to face it.

"The manuscript," Joanne repeats. "I've had that thing a long time. And every time I end up coming back here I think to myself, it's about time I get rid of that manuscript. I'll just throw it in a fire the way Plath did her own manuscript. I tell myself I'm going to do it but by the end of my stay I know I can't. I want to, but I know I can't. And I don't think that means I'm any sicker than I already am, it's just something I can't let go of, not yet. But I do hope I can stop telling that lie and let it be what it is."

"What is it?" I ask. It has been there, this manuscript, this secret, lingering between us. "I mean, how did you get it. Who wrote it?"

Joanne looks down at her hands. She has to have known this was coming. "I wrote it. I really felt like I was channeling Plath, that she was inside me, when I wrote it. But it's mine. And it's not just about Sylvia Plath, it's about my life as well, how I felt as a lesbian in the fifties and sixties, loving someone I couldn't love, just like Esther loved Micah. And everyone who really studied Plath and reads the book, they think Micah is a stand-in for Richard Sassoon, her other great love, who was Jewish, though I don't think he would have left her for not being Jewish, there was more going on. But no, Micah is a stand-in for loving something so big, for needing something with all your might and never really being able to have it. That's how I felt living with my prejudiced mother, it was like being in a box I couldn't get out of. I had an abusive father, not just the normal discipline. Whenever I acted up, talked back, anything, he'd whip out a belt and it never ended well." She closes her eyes and I want to tell her not to go on but she does. "And I had a brother who abused me. He was six years older and he used to come into my bed at night and I didn't even know what he was doing. I was ten when it started and I just thought it was something brothers did for a while. But I knew I didn't like it and no matter what I said he wouldn't stop. He'd get mean and mad but he wouldn't stop."

"Did you tell someone? Did he ever get in trouble? Joanne that's horrible."

"I never told, not as a kid. My mother never knew. Because then, two years later, when I was twelve and he was eighteen, he died in a car accident. A friend was driving too fast and hit a tree. It drove my mother to bed for weeks. Then he was the golden child. And how do you hate, how do you compete with, the memory of a dead brother? What was I supposed to say to my mother about her darling dead boy?"

"That's really tough. And you used Esther's story to help combat it?"

"Look, Esther is headed for an abusive relationship. Tom is not a nice man. And so many men in my time were so mean to women. They thought so little of us. I know, there's a long haul for women, but it was worse, you should know it was worse. I didn't want to go overboard but that scene in the car, I didn't want to make the whole story about the abuse but that's going to be her life for a while. That scene in the car, Tom stopping, hitting her, yelling at her and making her feel like shit. That was life for so many women. Just like my father was abusive. Like the men I dated were either womanizers or bullies. And I know all men aren't like that, even in the fifties, I guess I was unlucky. Or I only dated a certain kind of man, the kind you date to cover the fact that you prefer women."

"I'm so sorry," I whisper.

"Don't be sorry. It's okay."

"But, that's beautiful . . . I mean, it's sad, but it's striking. I just wonder why hide all that now? If hiding hurt you so much, wouldn't hiding hurt now? And why tell people Sylvia Plath wrote it when your story, your parallel, is also so compelling? I mean, that scene where she calls Micah, it broke my heart but knowing it was about so much more . . . breaks it into more pieces."

"Because I wanted it to be hers. After she died I always felt as if she could have been the world's next great writer. She was such an amazing poet and her stories, and *The Bell Jar*, were amazing, but also the work of a young woman, unpolished, not quite in her prime because who is in their prime when they're just thirty? Her poetry was more mature, but her fiction . . . it was good but I know, I felt it in my bones the moment I learned of her suicide, that she could have written so many great things it just would have taken time and time was not something Sylvia Plath was allowed. When I heard later that she'd destroyed, actually destroyed, one of her novels because of Ted, that just broke me. I wanted to read it so badly, whatever she'd written I wanted to read it. And again, when I read that there might be more journals, that there might be a whole other novel that her husband and her family or someone from the estate, had lost or destroyed or just not let out into the open, I felt like she'd been silenced yet again. That great voice, that wonderful woman, they silenced her. First her mental illness silenced her, then her marriage held her back, then the fact that she stayed home with children in poverty while Ted ran around sleeping with models and finally her death, the ultimate silencer. And there might have been a whole other novel that we never got to read, it never got to have its say and so *she* never got to have her say. It creates quite a mystery, you know?" I shake my head yes. "And I just kept thinking, 'Why, why do they want to silence her?' And if she'd gotten help, if people had been more receptive to what was going on inside her instead of judging her all the time. Instead of calling her crazy and telling her to buck up and take her meds and just be happy. It's not that easy that's what some people don't see. It's just not that easy."

"But why write it? Why tell people the manuscript was Sylvia Plath's, especially if you're just going to keep it hidden from most people? It's yours?

Don't you want to take responsibly for your own work? I mean, I read the novel, it's really good. And the emotions hit me so hard there were nights I'd just be struck at how beautiful it was. It made me feel so close to Sylvia, but why couldn't I have felt close to you? Those feelings of alienation, of losing it, the abuse, they were yours."

This conversation is so heavy and I wonder if it's good for Joanne's health. But her eyes light up, her voice rises, in a good way, as she looks me directly in the eye. "When I met her I loved her. And I did meet her. We were barely acquaintances but you saw the pictures we hung out a few times. She was so happy, so carefree. The Sylvia Plath who was a college student at Smith, the Sylvia Plath who interned for *Mademoiselle* and published in all those journals and magazines, she was blond and happy, tall, and beautiful and carefree. And yes, there was always a sadness about her, something else was there, a burden she carried, and we who carry similar burdens, we see it, we understand. Only an artist, a poet, could hurt like that. But I loved her.

"I met her at a diner after one of her waitressing shifts. We talked about poetry, all she wanted to do was talk about poetry. We didn't spend much time together. We went to the beach a few days in a row. She had me over for dinner at the house of the family she was the live-in babysitter for. I remember she was so good with the little kids, she used to play hide and seek with them before bed. And the parents loved her. Everyone loved her. But at night she would start to read poetry. We'd sit on the beach, a fire burning between us, and she'd read me poetry. It was so beautiful. The way she read with this very grown up but sing-song voice like a mother. She'd tell me about the men she was dating. I always thought there were too many men, but it was the 50s and girls were like that. She'd talk about Joyce and Yeats and how much she loved their work. One time she even told me the story of her father. How she sat in her room cursing God after he died. She just felt so abandoned and all her life it looked like she was seeking someone who would not abandon her. Her entire life she just wanted to be able to trust someone.

"When I heard about her first suicide attempt when she was twenty, the one she wrote about in *The Bell Jar*, I felt so responsible, like I should have kept in better touch. I wrote her, but she was dealing with her own things and she never wrote back. After that I didn't want to bother her. I remember thinking, 'I just want to tell her it'll be okay. They put me in the hospital, they gave me electro-shock, and I came through it.'"

"And what was that like, what they did to you?"

"Electro-shock?" Joanne asks as if she has been pulled out of a trance.

"Yes, I mean, was it inhumane?"

"It was. They don't do it anymore, not like that. But it wasn't like you see in the movies, they didn't put me in a straight jacket, they didn't tie me down or electrocute me like a man on death row. But it did hurt. I remember when the electricity went through me and I felt that raw power, I felt so very, very small. I had no agency over my own life, my own body. The fact that this could happen to me, that they could just do it. They could take away my rights, my power and pump my brain full of electricity just because I wasn't like everyone else. But I came out the other side. Apparently they only do it to the most hopeless cases now. What I remember though, after it happened, was that everything felt fuzzy. I wasn't myself anymore. That's what it does. It takes the parts of you that are bad, that are sick, and it doesn't make them go away, it only made them fuzzy. But it makes everything else fuzzy too. All of who you are goes away."

"I'm sorry," I tell her. I can't imagine, I can't even imagine. But my mother, they did it to my mother as well when I was a baby. She called it ECT and it was probably different. It was thirty years later and the procedure had probably changed but they did it to my mother as well.

"It's okay. But I remember." Joanne returns to her story and I look out at the room. "When I heard about her death. It happened in England, but it was in the newspaper in Wellesley, where her mother still lived. And though she became much, much more famous after her death, it was really years before people thought of her as a tragically great feminist icon, cut down before her time. But her death announcement was in her hometown paper right after it happened. I remember reading it and thinking, 'If I had only kept in contact with her. This is my fault.' And of course it wasn't but when you are mentally ill sometimes you can take something and make it more than it is.

"I became obsessed with her once I knew she was gone. I went to her mother's house and tried to speak with her but she wasn't home. I remember I pounded on the door and I wonder what they would have thought, if it would have hurt them, my coming like that. But no one was ever home when I came. I read and reread everything she wrote. I tried to get my hands on her old letters from me, the ones her mother had, but again, her mother never answered my letters, I wonder if she ever got them. And I remember thinking . . . she could have said so much . . . so much, there were so many more words left in her and they're gone, silenced. Why did they silence her? And I was losing it, that's part of why I got so obsessed; I ended up back at a psychiatric facility soon after her suicide.

"That's when I started writing the book. I was in a frenzy, one of my manic phases. I just kept writing. At first I didn't know what it was this thing I was writing but I thought I was channeling her. Sylvia Plath, she was inside me and I felt her. Every word I wrote, they weren't mine, they were hers and I was giving voice to the voiceless, to the one who was gone.

"I don't know what I think it was, how it even happened. I didn't plan to write the manuscript but there it was and when I finished it, I signed her name, Sylvia Plath. I typed her name on the cover. And there were times when I really did think she'd written it. I'm sure there will be more times like that. Her experience was my experience. Her illness, her feelings of abandonment, they were mine as well. My brother died in a car accident when I was just a child and that broke my mother. My father was never home, always away on business and when he was home he was so abusive to myself and my mother it was like being abandoned by him. I felt like I was silenced by society and it wasn't until feminism really took off in the 1970s that I ever felt I could be who I was in public. The fact that my mother wouldn't speak to me after I came out, that it took me years, decades, to find someone to love me the way Tammy does. I know how Plath felt. My husband didn't abandon me with two children, but there are other ways to get to the same place, that's why art is so powerful, the experiences of so many people from so many walks of life are essentially the same even when our lives are so vastly different."

I try to picture Joanne as a younger adult sitting alone at a desk writing the words I read. Of course they are hers. Looking back, I feel her, the way she speaks about losing herself, about loving someone and what that means, how it can harm you, really and truly harm you. Being with the wrong person, *being* the wrong person, it's so similar. "If you took Sylvia Plath's name off it, if you said it was an homage, a derivative I think is the technical term, I bet you might get it out there for the world to see."

"I don't want that," Joanne tells me, sadly shaking her head. At least she's not angry this time. "I like sharing it, but I don't want strangers to read it, to know . . . to think . . . and what I did . . ."

"If you published it and told the story, you wouldn't be able to say it was Sylvia Plath's anymore. But don't you think people should read that story? Don't you think it would be good for people to know that it is definitely not Sylvia Plath's, that it's yours and your story is just as big, just as real?"

"The lie would be over," Joanne tells me. "And I'm not ready to give it up. I guess I'm not that okay yet."

She's not that okay . . . still I know in a few days they'll let Joanne out. She'll take meds, more meds, different meds, maybe they'll just put her back on the same meds. She'll see a therapist more often and she'll be fine. She'll go out to dinner, have conversations, walk by the ocean. Tammy will take care of her, but this thing, this very big thing will always be with her, always almost, maybe, about to strike. And yet she'll get out. She'll be okay until she isn't again and all she can do is try to make herself better as soon as possible. "You know, the fact that Sylvia Plath inspires you to write, the fact that you got a whole other story or set of stories from the stories she told, from the art she made, that's the mark of a great artist."

"Great art inspires others," Joanne goes on for me. "It's the raw human emotion, the fact that we see ourselves, our lives, in great art. That's what matters, that's what divides art from entertainment. We see our lives reflected back at us, the truth in those stories, not the facts but the truth, those made up characters, those words that could have been written a hundred different ways but they are written this one way, that's what connects us to our humanity."

"Someone told me that art is a symptom of damage. That a culture only has great art when it has been damaged, like after World War II or during The Great Depression. And people, they only create, truly create, when they're hurt. And yet the most awe inspiring thing we can do is create, to make something from nothing."

"It's a way to make sense of ourselves, a way to deal with the damage. And people, all people, no matter what they say, are all damaged. Even the happiest of us."

"There's always something."

"True," Joanne replies. "Cue that REM song, right 'Everybody Hurts'? I can just hear it now."

"Ha." I actually say the word "ha" before laughing at her joke. She has told a joke. She has confessed to me. We have discussed not only our own damage, but damage in the world and with that, it feels like things will be okay between us. "I should really head out. Tammy wants to speak with you and I don't want to take away from her time."

"Thank you. She sees me every day, but I agree, don't take away her time, she's a saint, the way she treats me. Not that she doesn't know it, but she doesn't think it. The woman I love is much too humble for that."

"It must be part of the reason you love her."

"I'm sure it is. But thank you. How long will you be on the Cape?" Joanne asks as she stands up. She holds her hand out and I shake it like we're parting at a bar or restaurant, only to see each other again after a few emails.

"About a month. But I'm heading to New York next week for a short visit. Then I have to get ready to start teaching. Next semester I have four classes."

"Don't you have a novel to finish?"

"I know . . . I should have thought of that. My publisher is going to be pissed but maybe this is what I need. I need to just hunker down and write. I see another novel, no London, Paris, and Sydney, it's a different story, the right story—inspired by the manuscript. I need to write that. But this thing you wrote . . . whoever wrote it, it's inspiring. It makes me want to write."

"Thank you," Joanne replies, smiling as I take a couple of steps toward the intercom and the door. "Call me next week when they spring me from here."

Sylvia
1963

THE CHILDREN WERE settled in bed but Frieda had gotten up asking for milk twice. She'd taken to wanting a cup of warm milk just before bed. Sylvia had done the same thing to her mother until she was seven years old. It was a way to keep the lights on, to look downstairs and see what the adults were doing. And really, what kind of mother could begrudge her child milk? Sylvia's father used to say, "Aurelia, you spoil the child." But her mother always gave her warm milk. And Daddy never really minded if little Sylvia had been spoiled. Daddy loved his little Sylvia and little Sylvia missed him every day.

"Frieda, remember, Mummy is just going to heat this up on the stove and then you're off to bed," Sylvia said, patting her own hair, which she had cut recently. It had been so long for so many years. Since Ted really Sylvia had stopped cutting it. In college she used to wear it in an elegant pageboy, her hair had been so blond, almost white in the summer when she got so much sun, and she had been tall and thin and tanned and stylish. And then she'd met Ted and it really wasn't his fault, but first her hair had turned brown, a mousy kind of light brown like those girls who are destined to be old maids. It was as if the stuffy church-mouse world of old Yorkshire with Ted's stick-in-the-mud mother and his snotty sister who'd never, ever liked Sylvia and had told her so one Christmas in the midst of a blow up fight, had rubbed off on her. Since Ted it was as if the light had gone right out of her skin, sucking up its radiance and then turning her hair such a mousy brown.

She'd stopped cutting her hair. She wore it in a braid down her back or on top of her head like a Swedish peasant. For so long she'd looked like a rustic bumpkin who did not dress well or care about her hair or wear makeup. But that part of her life was over and Sylvia knew that she must come back to herself. And so she'd cut her hair and she'd put some makeup on and she had not bought a new dress, she didn't have the money for that, but she was wearing her old red one, the one she wore with Ted to a party at the Alverez's before their divorce.

Jillian had asked her not to leave their house. Sylvia had stayed at their flat for a couple of days. She'd eaten heartily. She'd sat and played with the children, she'd once even gone for a walk even though it was so cold outside. They'd gone shopping, she and Jillian, just for groceries and provisions, but it was enough of an outing that it helped her spirits. And every morning, early, at four a.m. when her sleeping pills wore off and it was *that* time, the middle of the night darkness, she would call out for Jillian and Jillian would come and hold her hand and tell her it would be all right, she'd get her through it until it was time for her next dose of medication. The darkness came and there was a whole in her heart and sometimes she missed Ted and sometimes it was only the life they might have had and it had been so close, she'd almost had everything but now he was gone, *it* was gone, that entire life and she was only living this one, a life where she saw fewer of her friends and she was away from her family. There was the pull, the constant pull of the children on one side and poetry on the other and it was just so much. Who could write under these conditions?

And so after a few days of Gerald and Jillian's help, after Doctor Horder had told her that he was still working to find her a spot in a suitable facility, she decided to go back home. She did not want to overstay and no matter what they said to the contrary, she knew it was very possible, especially with so many needs, with two children, to overstay one's welcome. And so she'd gone. She had packed herself and the children and the few articles of clothing that Gerry had picked up at the house the day before and she'd gotten into the Morris and driven the children home.

"Are you sure you'll be okay?" Jillian had asked, such worry on her face. "What can I do to get you to stay? Can I make you stay? What if I called the police and told them you needed to stay with me would they believe me?"

Her friend's face showed so much desperation but Sylvia knew, she really knew, that Jillian would be happy to get rid of her. Happy to have her house once again to herself without a helpless poet who could not sell her work and her two screaming children.

"Mummy, why are you in your red dress?" the little girl asked just as the kettle boiled and Sylvia moved to give her daughter her warm milk.

"Oh, it's nothing really. Mummy just felt like wearing it."

"You look pretty," Frieda said, still looking up at her mother, all wide eyes, as she took the cup.

"Now sip it carefully, it's still hot."

"Okay." The child carefully took a small sip and stopped. Sylvia knew she'd save the rest for when she was safely in her room. It really was too hot right now to just gulp down, Sylvia could remember this from her own cups of warm milk as a child.

"Now run along to bed, Mummy needs to clean up in here."

"Okay," her little girl said again and Sylvia turned to putter in the kitchen. She opened the refrigerator door and there was the champagne. She didn't dare tell little Frieda this, then she would insist on staying up, but Ted was coming over. He wanted to talk. He had been so nice on the phone and really, she would be happy to be nice to him if he could only be kind to her.

Sylvia ran a damp rag over the counter. So much gunk had accumulated near the oven! She really needed to learn to clean up better. Ted would be over soon. Sylvia pulled the rag over the oven, taking one of the burners out to make sure she got all the gunk around the edges. It was a grey surface, not as bad as her mother's 1950s white oven, but still it showed so much grease. Sylvia had just read about a man the other day who'd stuck his head in an oven and left the gas on. His wife had just left him and taken the children and so he'd decided to stick his head in the oven, turn on the gas and wait, just wait, to die. It seemed so curious, so ceremonial, waiting to die.

Pills, Sylvia had thought as she read the story, one must take pills to knock oneself out first then it would all be so much easier.

After the oven had been cleaned Sylvia heard a knock at the door. "Oh no, oh no, oh no," she said to herself, rushing to wash her hands. Now she smelled like wet rag, why on earth had she done that? It was only that there was always something to clean, always something weighing on her. She scrubbed and scrubbed her hands as the knock still sounded. She ran into her room, her hands shaking how, she could feel a tingling in her legs as she grabbed her perfume and sprayed it all over herself. She took a big whiff . . . it was too much, she'd put on too much, but there was still the knocking and her neighbor would complain soon or the children would hear and what else could she do?

Sylvia closed the door to her room, perhaps the stench wouldn't follow her, she took one look in the mirror, at the eyeliner around her eyes (she had never been one to do that, but women wore so much eyeliner all the time now, it was worth a shot and she had only worn a little). Her cheeks were red with a touch of rouge and she'd put on the light red lipstick, the one she'd been wearing, or very nearly the shade, on the night she'd met Ted at a party in Cambridge so many years ago.

And really those years, they'd melted by and she could see them, could feel them on her body and in her poetry and all the things she'd done with her life and . . . but the knocking continued and Sylvia pulled the handle, answering the door.

"I was afraid I was going to have to break in," Ted said, laughing. It was like old times. Such a simple, a silly joke and just like him in that booming Yorkshire voice. His light brown hair fell into his face, it was a commanding face and Ted was so tall, the way he stood over her. Sylvia, being five-nine, had to make sure at all times that she was with a man who towered over her.

"I'm sorry, I was doing some dishes and then I had to run to my room for something," Sylvia said, wringing her hands in front of herself as she walked into the living room. She took a seat on the couch, the long brown one upholstered poorly so the stitching came apart in places.

"It's fine, Sylvia, it's fine. And how is Jillian? How's old Gerry?" Ted asked. He took a seat, not on the couch next to her, not as he would have done when they'd first met, when they couldn't keep their hands off each other. Even later with the children he sat next to her but now he took the chair, the big armchair like the man of the house, Sylvia could just see it. But if That Woman were here, would he have sat with her? Would she have taken the armchair and made him stand? Maybe that's the kind of woman Ted wanted. Lorelei, the Lorelei, a woman who could command him. Ted lifted his nose in the air and sniffed. He smelled the perfume . . . it was too much, but Sylvia had been such a lady in college, she knew to just ignore a faux pas, even when she made them.

"The Beckers are fine. They've been very kind through everything."

"And you're okay?" Ted asked, his eyes big now, big like little Frieda's and Sylvia could see the resemblance between father and daughter. They were so very much alike and maybe it was her job to be like her son. It would be the only protection little Nicholas had, the fact that he was like his mother. "Jillian, I mean, she didn't go blabbering, she really was just worried about you, but she did ask me to look in. She said that after you left, you seemed better. But you're on your medication? You're okay?"

Ted watched her. The way he asked those questions, always he asked questions as if to give you the right answers. He only wanted to hear what he wanted to hear. He'd come to check up on her, that was all. He'd come to make sure he had not left his children with a raving mad woman, though even if she were raving mad she didn't think he would take them away from her, that would be too much work, too much dedication, more than Ted was willing to put into anything that wasn't himself. "Ted, I'm fine, perfectly fine, I don't know why you came over. Did Jillian put you up to this or That Woman? Are you here on a little errand just to make sure old Sylvia doesn't lose it on you? Then you'd have to pay my medical bills, with a sick wife and all, and I don't think it's fair, you asking for a divorce at a time like this. You just don't want to have to pay my medical bills."

"I just think, I mean" Ted closed his eyes, composed himself. "Sylvia, remember how we used to meditate together?"

"You mean do I remember how you used to hypnotize me? You used to try to get me to go to sleep when you wanted me to go to sleep or live in the country when I wanted to live in London. You even told me if I wanted to kill myself to just kill myself."

"It was never like that. Just a healthy interest in the occult, that was all. My mother always said we were guided by the moon and the stars and it was never anything more than making you your fullest self. I wasn't ever trying to manipulate you."

"But weren't you though, our whole marriage you were trying to mold me into your little wife and more and more it was a way to control me and after I had our children, then you met That Woman. And you didn't ask her to have your child, you were perfectly happy to let her throw one away."

Ted winced. He took another deep breath but remained sitting in that armchair. "Sylvia, if you're that jealous why don't you just kill yourself? Really, why don't you?" He sneered at her. "Don't say things like that. I'm only here because I want to come to some kind of equilibrium. If you want to continue with the legal separation, maybe divorce later, when you're ready, I'm fine with that. So is . . ." He stopped, Sylvia knew it, he was going to say her name but instead swallowed the word and went on, "everyone else. No one wants to push you. But yes, Doctor Horder is worried about you and I wish that quack, I mean, I know he's helping you and your medicine does seem to work, even I can see a difference in the way you're acting on it, no matter how slight, but he needs to get you into a facility."

"Oh stop it, Ted. I want my mother. Why can't my mother come from America, let her have the children for a while. Or they can go to her. They can see Boston and Wellesley where their mother grew up."

"The children are not going to America. I'll never get them back if they go there, Sylvia. Your home is here, in England, you'll get a handle on everything, you really will. You'll be okay."

Sylvia stopped. It was really something, the desperation on Ted's face. He looked so sad and maybe he was just trying to help her. "Okay," she finally said. "Okay. I'll call Doctor Horder again tomorrow. I'm writing more poetry, hopefully I'll sell some soon."

"That would be nice," Ted said. "And I always did love your poetry. You're going to have to read it to me sometime."

"I could get it, I could read you some now," Sylvia said, nearly dancing in her seat she smiled so wide but Ted shook his head, dashing her hopes.

"Not tonight, I'm afraid, I have to go soon. But please, take care of yourself and know that I'm here for you. I really am. I want to make a new start. I want everything to be okay between us, not only because of the children, though that's obviously on my mind, but because of you."

He smiled again and Sylvia shot up. She wanted to walk over and hug him but she was afraid he'd reject her, just as Al had rejected her. "I have some champagne," she said. "It's in the refrigerator. It was a splurge, but I figured I owed it to myself and let's have some. Let's toast to our new relationship, to getting along and taking care of the children." Giddy she nearly dashed up and started dancing. All at once everything seemed so clear, so right, she would get well. Everything would be okay she knew it.

Ted looked around the living room as if something was missing and he had to find it. He glanced at Sylvia for a second but then his face changed, as if he'd made a conscious decision. "Fine, all right. Get the champagne, we'll have a toast. I can stay for that. A toast to our new friendship."

"Yes," Sylvia said, bouncing back toward the kitchen to ready the celebration. "Yes, to our new friendship." She walked into the kitchen and opened the fridge. The bright, nearly florescent light of it beamed out at her as she looked at the shelves of bottles of milk and tins of tuna and beans. It was such a mother's refrigerator, just like so much else in her house, it reminded her of her childhood. Then, she grabbed the little greenish bottle of champagne and forgot all about that. She saw the bubbles and the cork and it all looked just like a very grand party. That's what they were having, a very grand party. And she would get better and Ted would like her and she'd write poetry and be happy, just so happy!

She grabbed two champagne flutes from the top of the cabinet; she only really had to go slightly on tiptoes to reach. Sylvia held them in the same hand she held the bottle like a perfectly trained waitress as she bounced back to the living room. "To us," she said, putting the champagne flutes down on an end table as she handed Ted the bottle. "To us and the fact that now everything will be okay."

"I'll drink to that," Ted said. Sylvia had not seen his face like this in so very long. So happy Ted was, like those days in Spain and Paris and Boston, seeing the world with him when they were both young poets about to conquer the literary landscape.

"Everything is going to be okay," Sylvia said, believing it.

Lorelei

THEO CALLS WHILE I'm on the beach. I can still hear my mother's words from the journal ringing in my ears. I read both again, the entire story. From the horrors of her teenage years to her struggles as a young mother and I think I can start to make sense. Reading her words has done more to help me understand her struggle than living my childhood with her. Here she is brutal. Here she is honest. Here she is free and I am starting to understand.

I called Eamon today and told him that he should look into finding an adjuncting gig (or two) at a Boston university this year and he'd said he was on it. Joanne is still at the hospital but apparently my aunt is going to visit her soon and I have been asked to tag along. I wrote three thousand words of this new novel today. Whole chapters are happening in my head. Things are moving along and after this trip with Amelia to New York I'll be ready to face Boston and another school year.

The phone rings. I check and it's Theo. The ocean pulses a few feet away and I wonder what would happen if I threw my phone in or if I walked into the ocean and ignored this call. I don't really want to talk to Theo right now but finally I answer.

"Hello?" I ask though I know who it is. Calls are no longer a surprise, names, numbers, pictures, and lists of what the caller had for dinner now pop up on our screens.

"Lorelei?" Theo says my name as if he's choking on it. "Lorelei, hi, is that you?"

"You called me," I reply. "Is anything up? Do you need something?" Theo has never needed a thing, not in our marriage or during the divorce.

"I know, it's just. Do you remember that vacation we took to England a few years ago?"

"I do." It was the last vacation. He hadn't met Heather yet. I don't think his eyes were quite wandering but we were still trying really hard to have a baby, he was working a lot and things were strained. "You kept talking about how you wanted to meet Princess Kate and everyone laughed at you."

"I know, the people we met at the pubs were hilarious. I wonder what they'd say now with everything that's happening with English and American politics."

The way he laughs reminds me of another place and time like I'm there in that other world where Theo and I are together, we're not quite happy but we might be again. "I know, right? And the fact that no one could make a decent Martini."

"But do you remember that trip we took to Stonehenge?" he pulls me out of my memory as if this is very important business.

"Stonehenge was amazing." Esther's trip to Stonehenge flashes across my mind. "The traffic getting out of London was insane. It took us almost an hour and a half just to leave the city. GPS sent us through Chiswick instead of just taking the M3."

"Yeah, that was terrible. And then, once we got there, we had to wait in line forever and they gave us a time to see the stones and it totally messed up our dinner plans."

"And so we went to lunch in a little town not far away and after we left Stonehenge we decided not to drive back to London."

"Because the traffic getting back into the city at six on a Sunday night would have been insane, something like four hours one of the tour guides said." We're finishing each other's sentences again.

"So we just decided, screw it, we'll drive in the other direction, and we drove to Cardiff . . . to Wales, to freaking Cardiff, and we sat on the water and had a nice dinner and wandered around." A small English town, Stonehenge, Cardiff, I hadn't put it together before, the trip had been too far from my memory and why is Theo thinking of this now? Why is Esther's life coming back to me? I didn't even think about that trip while I was reading the manuscript but now it makes perfect sense why it hit me so hard.

"And Cardiff wasn't that big but it had been built up, it was nice. I remember."

"Theo, what's wrong?" I ask him. "Why are you talking about Cardiff?"

"Did you like it? Being there? By the water and stuff? It was so different on the other side of the ocean. I know it wasn't London, but it was calm, peaceful, you know? I just wish . . ." His voice breaks and I hear tears in it. I want to ask him if he's okay again. I want to coax something out of him but Theo has never been the kind of man who is easily coaxed. "I think if I could go back to any other time or place, it would be then, that trip to Cardiff. If I had to live my life in one moment, just one moment, it would be then."

"Why's that?"

"Things weren't complicated. It was before . . . before . . . and you know it wasn't your fault, what happened. I tell myself I loved her but I don't know. All I can say to justify it is at least I loved her, you know?"

"I know, Theo, it's okay. Are *you* okay?"

"All of this is my fault." Theo's voice cracks and he stops. I don't hear anything for a while and assume he's put the phone down.

"Theo, let's not try to blame . . . I think the worst thing we can do right now is blame . . ." There's nothing. The phone is quiet. It's not dead, I don't hear the silence of a disconnected line. I can't make out his tears in the background or a television on in his living room. But there's rustling, there's movement, like the phone is still connected. "Theo, are you all right?" I ask again, my stomach sinking. "I'm coming over," I decide after a full minute has passed. "Do you want me to call someone? I'm coming over." Still there's nothing.

I consider calling Eamon for a ride, but the condo Theo is renting is only a mile and a half away. I clocked it once when he asked me to drive over to sign some divorce related document and I wanted to see how much gas and mileage I was wasting. Separation makes us petty. Sand scratches the arches of my feet as I slip into my sandals and march more purposefully toward the house. I consider going inside to get out of these beach clothes and maybe put some makeup on. Something is wrong but to say we have reached a state of emergency, that I should run out of here as if the house is on fire . . . this has only occurred at the very back of my mind, where things get stored and then thought better of.

I try calling again. Why isn't he answering? Is the line still active? Should I call the police? I wonder as I grab my keys from the table on the deck and walk more purposefully to my car. I don't want to blow this out of proportion. Still a terrible, sinking fear grabs the pit of my stomach and I'm almost shaking. Should I call Theo's neighbor? Do I know Theo's neighbors? Does he?

I call his number again once I'm in the car. I put the phone on speaker as I pull my seatbelt over my lap and prepare to drive. The phone rings and rings and rings. Did Theo even bother to hang up on me? I watch the road, yellow lines on whitening asphalt, and picture the waves a few miles away.

When I reach the condo he's renting nothing is amiss. It's a newer building with cream white siding and blue shutters. The condo sits in a set of row houses, one after another like in a city; it stands three stories tall with a garage at the bottom. It does not face the ocean but it does have a lot of space. The last time I was there I remember admiring the yard in back as I wondered why a single man needed so much room.

I park in the driveway, run to the door, and ring the bell several times. I knock. I pound on the door, first the wood, then the glass window. Something is wrong, it has to be, why isn't he answering? Nothing moves in the condo. No noise, no gestures. Still, I do not consider calling the police, that would be silly, it would open up a whole ordeal and what if he's just in the shower and forgot to hang up? I didn't call the police when Ashley came to the house and knocked over a planter and that had been the right decision. I run toward the garage to see if there's another way in, a side door, a way to lift the latch and go in through a back entrance. It's then that I make out the smoke, not a steady stream, just a murmur. It's not smoke like the place is on fire, more like exhaust fumes and the bitter fumes make my eyes water. I smell it, like rotten eggs and motor oil, like being at the back of a county fair when a bunch of old cars leak a little too much oil.

I cough as I pound on the garage door and of course, of course that doesn't help. I run to the pin-pad at the side of the garage. I have no idea what Theo would have used to open his door but then again, this is a rented condo, it might not even be his code. I press Theo's birthday, his mother's birthday, the day we got married. Finally I press 09171998, Heather's birthday. I know this only because it was on the funeral announcement. I got one in the mail, I don't even know why. Perhaps it was an accident, sending one out to us. When it came in the mail I stared at the announcement, the birthday, the death day, the picture of Heather, eyes big, her skin so smooth and young. Heather Larsen: September 17th 1998 to May 31st 2018. She was wearing a bright pink sweater and it was like she was dressed for a party. But the birthday struck me. Apparently it stuck with Theo as well and a green light flashes and the garage begins to open.

Smoke spews out like it's coming from everywhere. A giant cough escapes my lungs as I rush to the driver side door. Fumes spread from Theo's idling car and I wonder how long . . . had he called me from the car while this was happening? Was he sitting here while we were going on about our trip to Cardiff? He's in the car, his big shoulders hunched over the steering wheel. I see the back of his head, curly dark hair, a slight sliver of his neck. I want to hear the horn, like you do in the movies, when you know . . . that's how you know . . . but the car sits quiet as I pound on the window. I try the latch, it's locked, of course it's locked. I hunt around the car for a key, I try every door. I pound and pound, tears in my eyes as the urgency rises. Coughing, I feel light headed, in a second this is going to get to me and I'm going to have to sit down. I make one more loop around the car. And my mind, it's not working right, it's like I'm moving and not moving. Fuzzy, everything goes fuzzy. I pound once again at Theo's window. It's then that a piece of paper falls from the top of the car. I grab it hastily and turn back, away from the car as my eyes start to water.

It's not until I'm outside, gulping cool, crisp air, that I can think straight. Never in my life have I felt so free, so crisp, so alive as I do away from the gas. I can breathe, now I can breathe. I shove the paper in my pocket and dial 911. They say they're coming. I do not have to stay on the line. I can already hear a siren and wonder if it's for us, for Theo and I . . . for us. Now, in these moments, there is an us.

The police arrive within minutes.

"When he called he sounded funny." I replay the story to an officer while others work on breaking into the car in the garage. "I decided to come over and that's when I noticed smoke coming out of the garage. I got in using his code." (I do not tell him I only guessed it). "That's when I found him. The car's locked." I tear up, gasping the final word, as the officer looks down at me and diligently begins to write.

"It's okay. We'll get him out, we'll get him out," he says. "The ambulance will be here soon. They should check you for possible poisoning."

"Okay," I whisper. I feel fine, really, after all this, I feel physically fine.

I walk away from the driveway and into the yard. It's not until I'm far away, when the scene before me, the squad car and flashing lights, neighbors coming out of their houses, officers huddled around the car with masks on their faces, that I pull the paper from my pocket and start to read.

"Dear Life. Dear whoever finds this. Lorelei, dear Lorelei, I'm sure you'll be the one to find this letter, but if you're not, get this letter to Lorelei Bauer.

"You were a doer, Lorelei, that's what I liked about you. I was this law student at Harvard and you were a writer who hung out in cafes and still there was something about you. You weren't like your friends . . . or my friends for that matter. You went out and did things. Like Cardiff. Do you remember when we went to Cardiff? We were at Stonehenge and the traffic back to London would have been hell and you just said, 'Screw it, let's drive to Cardiff, have dinner there. Get back at one in the morning, who cares about a plan!' And so we did. You got us a reservation for dinner, you planned the route. I guess you call that spontaneous. But the only spontaneous thing I ever did was Heather.

"Don't ask me why I did it. I wasn't happy. You were pregnant and that was sapping our life. We weren't together as much and a lot of that was on me. I was cold, I was distant. You wanted me to go to the Red Sox game with you that one time when Sandy's sister was over and all I did was work. Then I met this girl. She was your student, I knew you liked her, I shouldn't have even talked to her. But she listened to me go on and on about my boring job all wide eyed. And you hadn't looked at me like that in years. You were busy promoting your book and worrying about how you were going to write the next one. You had these friends and this life and this girl, she just hung on me like I was her everything. And yes I took it too far and I never should have let it happen. I never should have let it hurt you. But here we are.

"But what happened to Heather, what we lost. I mean, I know I had an affair. I know I was bad, I was terrible, but the punishment, my god the karmic punishment. What did I do in a previous life to add up to that? She didn't deserve to be beaten the way he beat her and she sure as hell didn't deserve to die. And when I'm really angry I tell myself it's not my fault. Who could have foreseen *that*? An obsessed cousin beats her to death in a warehouse. Who could have seen that coming? But she told me she was worried about her cousin. That he was inappropriate with her as a child and he was still strangely clingy. She said he'd been violent with his last girlfriend and he was very old school about women. I don't know I just thought things would be okay. I was sure we wouldn't get caught. That was very, very stupid of me. They call that hubris, right? Isn't that a literary term? But how was I supposed to know, how was anyone supposed to know her cousin would do *that* to her? And then your mother died, she picked the pitch perfect time as usual. Right when you're dealing with all this shit Maggie kills herself. I'm sorry, I'm being callous, she was your mother, you still love her, but she was so selfish there, right when you needed her, don't you ever fault her for that?

"And the baby, on top of that to lose the baby. I was so mad at you, Lorelei, for not calling me. You didn't even let me be there for it or afterward. I could have helped. I could have at least seen my son before they . . . before they . . . That hurt. That really, really hurt. The fact that he was gone, that we lost him . . . and I still think that was my fault. Obviously if I had not done what I did to you you would have been in a better mental state and I'm sure that didn't help the baby. But to lose him. To lose you. All I had was my job and I should have just walked away from that.

"And so I'm here, about to get into my car. Why did I choose this way to die? I read once that gassing yourself to death is painless (that makes me a coward) but it also doesn't require a lot. You don't have to know how to do it. If I wanted to hang myself, I read up on it, it's really hard to hang yourself right. Most people do it wrong, the rope breaks and they end up with this scar around their neck. And slitting your wrists, you have to do that right too and then you have to wait to bleed out. I don't know how good I'm going to be about waiting. I was always practical, but I was also impatient. And a gun . . . I don't want to use a gun. Too much violence. Too messy. Pills? You need to get the pills, you need to know how much to take and how to do it right so you don't wake up days later and get locked away in some institution. That left this, a car. Easiest way in the world. Go figure I'd take the easy way out.

"But I want you to know that I love you, Lorelei. I love you and I would have loved our child. I would have loved Heather too if I'm telling you the truth. I really don't want this to hurt you. I've set everything up, all my money, everything, you can have it. I have a few debts, but once those are taken care of you're in the clear. But I think it would be nice if you sent an olive branch to that girl, her cousin, Ashley, the one we met the other day at your house. I didn't have time to call my lawyer, to set something up formally, that would have looked fishy. But she's a strong girl, she was rude to us, but I liked her. I think if she weren't attacking you you'd like her too. She's a strong modern girl as well, you saw that. You think she wants to be a journalist? Help pay for her journalism school with my money. They might not want to take the money right away but you'll find a way to convince them. Please, I didn't have time to add it to the Will but I'd really appreciate it and I know you'll do it, not just because I asked but because you want to help. I'm sure on some level you liked her. And don't blame yourself. The phone call, telling her mother. Her mother was going to find out. You were angry. For the longest time I was so mad at you for telling but now that I'm here I understand.

"Would it be too silly, writer wife, if I said good-bye cruel world? Too cliché, right? Anyway, good-bye. The world has not been all cruel, but the last two years have been. A lot of that is on me and it's time I take responsibility. If the world will not thoroughly punish me then I must punish myself. Take care of yourself, Lorelei. Be well. Do not follow me."

Do not follow me? As if he thinks I would, that I could. What is there to follow? I try to picture us all together somewhere else, the next life. I hold the letter, a single sheet of paper, his handwriting started out so neat and particular, just like Theo, but it grew messier the longer he wrote. The ink started to run and the writing became black and jagged like claw marks. Do not follow me? As if he and our unborn child, my mother and Theo's grandmother, Heather even and everyone else, how many people have I lost in my life? Does he think we'll all settle together? But I can't think about that. I can't.

I hold the note in my hand, sure I'll have to give it up. I've taken evidence I'm sure the officers will need. I've read it first, but the note is addressed to me and I'm sure the police will understand. I wipe the tears from my eyes before I realize I've been crying. I feel Theo then, an emptiness. He was a person, at one time I loved him, I really loved him. And I love him now, after everything of course I love him. But I know, I know before the officer approaches with his head down, it's over. I look up, wiping the tears from my checks with hard fists. If I can delay this moment, if the officer does not come up to me, it will be like it never happened. I can just pretend. Then again I already know. I never had a doubt, not once while reading the letter, not once while I was waiting, did I feel anything close to hope. If Theo was going to do this he'd do it right.

"Is he okay?" I ask. It's a natural question.

"Okay? No," the officer says, looking me in the eye. "We're going to take him in, but he wasn't breathing. The paramedics tried to perform CPR on him but he's not breathing."

"He's gone," I whisper and the officer nods. I'm sure he's not supposed to answer so definitely, that's the job of someone more qualified in grief management, someone on call at the hospital they'll take him to. Yet the officer knows how to be human that's why he told me. "Thank you. Can I see him?"

"They've taken him away, ma'am," the officer goes on, getting more formal. "You can see him at the hospital. But there's another ambulance and they'd like to check you out, make sure you didn't get poisoned by the air as well. We're checking everyone nearby, the neighbors also."

"The neighbors were home," I nearly gasp and the officer nods. They could have smelled something. They could have saved him. I could have come more quickly. So many things could have conspired to save him but they did not.

Sylvia
1963

SHE'D BEEN UP all night. There was no use denying it, the fact that she couldn't sleep, that the pills stopped working and now, now it was that dark hour, a sunless hour of artificial light, the one just before five and she could not take her medicine. But it was decided, had been decided before she was born, when Daddy met her mother, he a German professor and she his student and they'd both been so smart and so free and so German and so they had borne that stain of history. He'd kept bees, her father, he wrote whole books about them and she, little Sylvia, would sit outside while he wore that giant beekeeper's hat and sprayed that grey smoke that worked like magic on them. "Yes, they sting," Daddy used to say, "but it's because they've built a whole world in there, they have a queen, she controls them all and they have to protect her." The queen, always, always protect the queen. The queen controls the men. The Lorelei. Yes, the Lorelei and why had she not taken her cues from such a mystical creature-woman? Why had she let a man take her power? She could have been so free, so easy and then Ted had come along and snatched her up in a net and he'd been kind but he'd also pushed her and hit her and told her to kill herself, he'd slept with That Woman and who knew how many others. And she'd been under glass, under a spell, for the last seven years.

Sylvia had finished the papers and bound the manuscript. She placed it on her desk, out in the open, clearly marked so anyone would know what it was and what to do with it. She didn't think she had to spell things out, not so much and maybe they'd find her in time and she could explain. Then again maybe not and that would be okay too, she'd made her peace. She'd finished her letters and gone just down the block, walking in that early morning twilight when the air was still so cold and the snow crunched under her feet. But the promise of the sun was just coming up and Sylvia could feel it. Soon, soon it would be spring and the snow would melt and this horrid, horrid winter would be behind London. It was almost enough to make her lose her resolve. Only almost.

With the letters mailed Sylvia taped a note to the pram, which sat just inside the door, in the outer hall. A new girl would be coming in the morning. She had the right address; Sylvia had called the agency to verify. She would come in the morning and find the note and rush upstairs. She might not know what the note meant, but she didn't need to spell things out, "Call Doctor Horder." That would be enough.

Sylvia walked through the flat, the place where she had planned to start her new life. She saw the nicks in the wooden floor and the shabbily upholstered furniture, the wooden tables and shoddy chairs. It had all looked so nice but just under the surface it was cheap and unstable. There was a picture on the wall of the sea and she had decided, soon after she and the children moved in, that it was a sea in Ireland. This was Yeats' house after all. She walked back and forth, finding that movement was the best way to take it all in. She had not been a person to sit still, not ever. Sylvia had always wanted to get up and move, to walk the beach instead of simply staring out at the ocean, she wanted to bicycle all through Cambridge and London, moving, always moving as fast as she could. In school she'd always wanted to get up though she never did, she was not the kind of student who fidgets. Her teachers liked her, they thought she was brilliant and she always got A's and she tried so hard to keep it that way always. She'd never failed, not as bad as this. Sylvia paced and she could just see Mr. Thomas, her downstairs neighbor, if he was up, tossing and turning in bed, annoyed at her for all the noise she was making. He would wake up and want to knock on her door but she wasn't sure if anyone would answer. Then again that note on the pram would scare him. He'd get up and find it and come rushing, upset that he'd been so angry before.

Sylvia walked back to the window. She stared out at it, at the blue of the night, the way the sky emerged as if from a chrysalis at this time, the clouds would start to glow like stars, light shining through them as if God Himself were there and she could remember looking out at such a sky when she was a child and they lived by the ocean. Even with this constant London fog, the dreary cloudiness and all the tall buildings, the chimneys with their sooty smoke, still she could see the clouds and the sky and the sun would break through eventually.

Sylvia went into the kitchen and opened the refrigerator door. There wasn't much in it. The remnants of dinner, some potatoes, some baked beans now grown cold. But the British ate everything cold. She stuck her hand into that florescent light, as if into another dimension and grabbed first the milk and then the bread and butter. Setting it out on the counter she took two slices of bread and buttered them. The butter was hard and the bread not very thick and so she tore a piece and had to start over. She really didn't want to give the children torn bread even if, as her mother always used to say, "It all ends up in the same place anyway." And it did all end up in the same place, didn't it? Then again her poetry, would it go someplace better? It had to or what was the point?

She placed the buttered bread on a little china plate and then poured two mugs of milk. She carried them carefully, in both hands, like the expert waitress she had been that summer at the Cape in college. She pushed open the door to the children's room, it had not been fully closed earlier, Frieda grew scared at night and wanted it open at least a crack. Sylvia placed the buttered bread and mugs of milk on a table where the children could reach them. She looked long and hard at them, sleeping so sweetly, so peacefully, and then turned around. But she turned back, she watched little Nicholas with his baby head so soft, his hair billowy and Frieda, her hair straight and almost bobbed, her eyes so big when they were open. The way they lay there it was almost enough . . . almost enough. She'd said goodnight to them earlier, she'd hugged them and kissed them extra hard. But this was for the best, it really was, this was for the best, for everyone. Most of all the children. The children needed a better mother. A sane woman.

Sylvia closed the door behind her, making sure it was shut tight, she pulled on the handle and swallowed hard, tears in her throat as she grabbed the towels from the bathroom and placed them under the door, pushing hard so no air could get through. She then took the duct tape that had been in one of the drawers in her study and taped up the children's room, just to make sure no air from the apartment could get in.

The children, she knew, would be safe. Nothing could touch them.

Sylvia walked back into the living room. Ah, the life I've built, she thought to herself. The people, the things I have lost and the poetry I have written. And really, isn't that what it's been about, the children and the poetry? To create, to give, to put so much into this world. She thought about writing a little something, a note of some kind. Don't they always write a note? But she hadn't written a note before and they would know, they'd figure it out. And on the table, her manuscript, her final words, "Ariel" the manuscript read, "Poems by Sylvia Plath."

She'd never finished her latest novel. She didn't want to get to the end, that cold dark place just staring her in the face. And life . . . who knew, maybe it was better to have an unfinished novel hanging over you.

In her life there had been mother and Warren and her pen pal friend Eddie and Buddy and Richard and so many others. She had lived in New York and London and traveled to Spain and Paris and so many places. She'd been so far, seen so much and now she was here, living in Yeats' flat and she had wanted it and she'd gotten it. She could do things, Sylvia Plath, the straight A scholarship student got things done. There would always be that.

Sylvia walked into the kitchen. Her hair was combed and styled, she was dressed in a white robe. She closed the door to the kitchen making sure it was shut tight. She grabbed more towels and pushed them tight under the door. She tried to pull the handle again and it stuck. There, the towels were doing their job. She grabbed the duct tape and taped all the way around the door. One layer, she thought to herself, may not be enough and so she reached all the way to the top of the trim and taped the sides of the door around twice. It would be hard for someone to get to her, but measures like these would make sure all the gas stayed in, around her and away from the children or anyone else.

It was the oven then. That was the only thing left to do and Sylvia turned it on. She knew not to turn on the heat, just the gas. That was the thing, people always thought when it was mentioned "she stuck her head in an oven," that they burned themselves alive but who would ever want to do that? No. It was only the gas that would go on and she would breathe it, she'd breathe it and breathe it and breathe it until it put her to sleep.

Sylvia got to her knees, she opened the flue so the gas would keep coming. She then grabbed a little white towel. It had to be white, these things, so sacred, one must use white. The oven had been cleaned not too long ago and so the white towel wouldn't get soiled. She placed her head on the towel inside the oven and lay there.

The floor was hard and the gas had just been turned on but she could turn it off if she really wanted to. She could take it all back and no one would even notice. She could take the tape from the doors, make sure the children were okay. She could take them and leave the flat and even if the gas flooded everywhere they would all be safe. But she remained where she was, breathing deeply. The gas had a funny smell, putrid, yet, thick and sour like an egg cream gone just a little bit bad. But it was still so good. Maybe more like lemons, perfectly tart lemons.

Breathe, Sylvia thought to herself, taking a deep, deep breath. And then another. And then another. She closed her eyes and breathed and the smell, it went away very quickly, it became the fabric of her world, of everything. Breathe in, hold it, breathe in, hold it, Sylvia said to herself. Her knees were on the floor, it was a little uncomfortable but she'd get used to it.

And really, with the note and Trevor downstairs and the girl coming, there was a chance they'd find her. She'd been found before and patterns sometimes repeat themselves. But if they didn't . . . it would be okay if they didn't, she'd left her manuscript, she'd secured the children, that was all that mattered.

She pictured the manuscript lying on her desk. Her final words. *Ariel* Poems By Sylvia Plath. They would see the manuscript when they came in, after they got the children out, they would see the manuscript and Jillian at least would know what to do with it.

Breathe . . . just breathe . . . Sylvia thought and those worries, so inconsequential.

Breathe . . . just breathe . . . Sylvia felt the gas, but it wasn't gas anymore, it was a lightness, as if the darkness had gone and there was only weightlessness. So much like the sea. And when she was a child she used to stay with her grandparents on Cape Cod. Her mother had grown up by the ocean and so had she until she was older, but after Daddy died they moved inland for good. Landlocked forever. But it had been the blue of it all, how never ending it was. We would sit there, just looking out at the water, and . . .

I'd walk that tightrope where surf and sand meet and the little pinpricks of cold that used to start at my toes kissing them like a lover and then moving, the tingling up my leg and I could feel it everywhere, the ocean. It was so big, such a very, very big thing. And I would look out at it as the tide sucked and flowed and there would be a shoe sometimes or the little chips of china tea cups or I'd find a box or a broken toy, all gifts to the sea that had been thrown in and the sea had spat them right out. But I watched it all. And I wonder, I wonder what life I would have lived, what freedom I might have had if I had walked into the sea. If I had decided to be a mermaid instead of a human child, if I had lived that life, not simply beside, but inside the ocean. If only its bigness could swallow me. Then I never would have been so hollow. I would not have needed to be pulled or carved or cut up. They would not have sent electricity through my brain. With something so very, very big, with its arms around me, I never would have needed to look for something else. And there I was at the edge of it and I went inland when I should have gone out . . .

Lorelei

"YOU'RE SO BIG," I tell the ocean and I know, I know it can hear me. Poseidon with his rippling waves and the way Venus, his daughter, born from the sea, riding on a salmon colored shell like that Botticelli painting. Venus, his daughter, a flickering lighted planet in the sky. The waves hit the sand, pounding into the quiet earth, the once molten core we tread, cooled and bound into tiny, shifting rocks. The rock and the water, always the rock and the water. There used to be rocks here, great boulders a geological border but the sea has pounded them so much they are nothing but tiny grains. What is stronger the rock or the water? No wonder the sea is so very big.

I picture my mother, just as big, waiting by the water for her only daughter, her Lorelei, to be born. I see her years before, when she was only a child herself, not sitting, but shuttering by the sea as her greatest fears were realized and she didn't know what to do. She buried her child here, whatever was left. So much . . . she lived through so much, and there was suffering, right up until the end but there were also good times. There was happiness. One cannot sit by the sea and forget happiness.

I'm sitting by the water. Eamon is with me. I told him to go back inside, it's chilly out here, but he wouldn't hear of it. Knight in shining armor—he won't give up. I stare up at the stars, they're bright tonight, like the white rock of the moon. There are whole other worlds out there and what is this man, what is anyone, what is Theo and Heather, what is Joanne and her illness, what is every mistake I've ever made in my life and Sylvia Plath, compared to Venus and the unimaginable universes in the sky that we cannot touch, cannot know? The ocean pulls the shore and I grasp Eamon's hand as if he's all that's left, the last line of defense before I am pulled out to sea.

"I love Venus," I tell him and he looks over and sadly smiles. "The planet, right there, the blueish one. Ancient man named the planets because of the way they moved in the sky. Wanderers, that's what the ancient Greeks called them. But Venus, she's so beautiful, even with the naked eye look how bright she is."

"*Your loyalty is not to me / But to the stars above.*" Eamon repeats a Bob Dylan lyric and I remember that he's really into that. "Sorry, this isn't the time for Bob Dylan."

"It's always the time for Bob Dylan."

"It's okay, Lorelei," he says, draping his arm around me he grasps me tighter and I fall into him, holding him close he's just so big, so solid and kind and good and big.

"The Universe, it's just so, I don't even know. Does it end?"

"I don't know," Eamon replies, grasping me more tightly before I let go. "Is there anything . . . I mean, are you going to be okay?"

The house is full. Eamon came first, I called him from the hospital, after I identified the body. I saw Theo's face, cold, a winter-frosted glass blue; he was pale and vacant, like he wasn't even human anymore. Eamon offered to drive me home but I said I'd be okay and so he met me at the house. My aunt Sarah came right away. She wrapped her arms around me and I felt her, the great fuzzy sweater of the aunt I grew up with, and did not want to let her go. Amelia was already at the house, she's been staying all summer and Eamon must have told her when he arrived. When I returned from the hospital Tammy had also come, she stood in the kitchen making tea as Amelia rushed to put a fruit salad together. What is it about death, about tragedy, that makes everyone think of food? Is it really so elemental? When we're faced with the most human of conditions the most basic survival instinct kicks in on overdrive as if nourishing yet another body will make up for what we've lost. But it's like I'm his wife again, the woman in mourning, the way everyone rushes to me now that Theo is gone.

"You know, isn't there a Sylvia Plath story where a woman goes into the sea?" Eamon asks.

"'Sunday at the Mintons,'" I reply. "A brother and sister go out to look at the sea and the sister drops something as a wave comes in. The brother tries to fetch it and doesn't come back and so the sister goes in after him. But she doesn't go in to save him, that's obvious, she's not frantic or upset, she walks into the sea, very deliberately to join him. It seems it had always been her intention to join her brother in a watery grave. I read that in high school."

"That's dark. I think I was supposed to read it as well. Not in high school but at University."

"Really, they read Plath over in County Kerry?"

"My professor was a fan, loved anything from America, anything feminist like that. But how are you holding up?" he asks, patting my arm before I stand.

"I'm okay, thank you, really, thank you." I look over at him, so grateful he's here. I know by next month he'll be living in Boston, he'll be staying over more and more often until I finally pull that trigger and let him move in. "I think I'd just like to walk on my own right now. Just down the beach. I'll be fine."

"It's dark out there do you need a torch?" Eamon asks. He's never been so practical and it's as if he's channeling the spirit of Theo with his little worries.

"I'll be okay, enough of the houses have their lights on, I can tell. And there are a few hotels just over where the beach turns in."

"I'll be here," Eamon says and I believe him. The knight does not move from his post.

Walking so near the sea—it's not the same thing but it's just like my mother, immersing herself in water as the pills took her. She fell asleep and did not wake up. There was water in her lungs, water from the bath, but still, she drown. Yet my mother and I, our favorite thing was to stare out at the ocean. These very big things and those who worship them. We're always being eaten, these very big things constantly spit us back out, and yet we return for more, we let them pummel us. They are so much greater than us, so much stronger, they must have something to give us, to show us, and so we'll take their abuse because someday, maybe, they'll make us content. Someday, maybe, they'll show us the key to the universe. We keep diving back in time and time again. The sun and the stars and the sea. Our entire life, all of it, a thing we cannot conquer, we cannot control.

As I walk it starts to rain.

There are not many people out in this chilly, slanting rain. Only flecks like dust in the wind, a figure maybe a hundred feet off, another with a dog fifty feet in the other direction. I wonder how long it would take to reach them. I stand and stare at the ocean and feel Theo. He used to hold me tight when we were at the Cape and it started raining. I remember feeling so safe then. The sea changes, shifting on molten sand every few seconds, turning and turning, the water from one end having come up from Brazil. Did Sylvia Plath see this same ocean? Was it as gigantic to her? Did she see this same water when she looked out from the barren hills of England as a grown woman?

I pass a white lifeguard chair, painted red in places and sitting abandoned, a ghost of itself and wonder at the fruitlessness of a lifeguard in such a vast, such a dangerous, ocean. Would it even be worth it to dive in? Could a lifeguard have done anything for my mother and I if we went too far out? The ocean is always taking but somehow because it's so big, because it's not a mother swimming too far and scaring her daughter, it's not a cousin beating a girl to death for something that is done every day. It's not a mother struggling so many months out of the year, it's not a husband who strays. All this I can make a fist at, all this I can rage after, but this, this wine dark sea? I am no match for it. Best to simply submit.

It's difficult to walk by the ocean, the sand is hard, clumpy, it sticks to my bare feet as my toes sink further in. Rain falls sideways into my face and I close my eyes but then I can't see the water. I can only hear it and what's the point of all this if I cannot see the ocean? If I cannot look it in the eye and dare it, dare it. The ocean, I know, would take me up on that dare every time. The ocean would tangle me in its seaweed limbs and pummel me with underwater currents but isn't that the point? The specks of people have moved closer inland as the rain picks up. It had been calm for a moment, still raining but calm, but the further I walk from the house the worse the weather gets and still I walk away.

I saw the body. I lost a grandmother once, my mother, a few aunts and uncles, a friend from college who got cancer soon after graduating and I flew to Denver for the funeral. I have seen death but never this raw, this close. My father IDed my mother's body and then had her pumped with so much formaldehyde that she was unrecognizable in her casket. I was upset with him at the time, but after seeing a dead body, I'm grateful my father spared me my mother's. Theo hasn't been my husband in years—not really. I hadn't even seen him, heard from him, except to talk about money, in so long and still when I looked at his body he was so raw, naked, human. His eyes were closed but in his face there was something peaceful about him. And he was right; we should have gone back to Cardiff, to that place where we'd been happy and whole.

I called his mother. Someone had to do it and she shouldn't have to hear about his death from a doctor or the police. The phone rang for such a long time but even then I didn't want her to pick up. I wondered as the phone rang if I could just leave a message, maybe text her. It was a cowardly thought but I started shaking the moment she answered. "Oh hello, Lorelei," Theo's mother said. She's an older woman who knits and runs a book club, good New England stock. I believe she's a member of the DAR. "How is Teddy?" Teddy, she always called him Teddy.

"I'm afraid he's not okay, Mrs. Stonington," I stated, trying to be as focused and kind as possible. "It's just, Teddy was in an accident." I couldn't bring myself to tell her it was not an accident. She'll learn, it's obvious what happened, but just then the words wouldn't come out.

"Oh no, is he all right?" she asked but she knew. I could tell by the way her voice cracked. I have never had a great poker face. I'm sure it was in my voice the moment she picked up.

"I'm sorry," was all I needed to say and she was in tears. Her husband, Theo's father, picked up the phone and I explained in more detail. I told him exactly what had happened. He didn't cry, he only listened. He was shocked but he wasn't going to show any emotion with me on the phone. Perhaps later he'll cry quietly with his wife.

"Well, thank you, Lorelei, for letting us know. We're getting in the car now. We'll be down as soon as possible." It was as if there had been a minor fender bender, Theo's father was so calm. I can only imagine what they'll be like at the funeral.

I remember Theo and his parents as I look out to sea. The ocean, the universe, is trying to tell me something I can feel it as I walk beside it. I take my tennis shoes off and toss them aside. I don't care if I lose them, they weren't that nice and today I am the kind of woman who loses her shoes on the beach and doesn't think twice about it. I'm sure this is something Sylvia Plath would have done. She had a thing about all those discarded things she used to find by the sea. I walk a tightrope, between the land and water, feeling the chill of wetness and the sucking of the waves.

Seagulls stand in a flying V formation, four lines evenly spaced with one larger gull at the head, as if they're waiting to attack. I draw nearer and one of them flies out, assaulting the water, it does a great loop, a planned dive and flies back, the scout. Another flies out of formation and then another. Like a choreographed dance they all come back to the same spot. Always the same spot.

A little further down the shore tiny sandpipers, brown and white small boned birds, stand in the same formation like tin soldiers.

Finally the rain is too much. Time converges, under these rocks that have been pummeled, these stones that were once the earth's igneous core, mingling with this water that has been living, breathing since the dawn of (could it be, could it really be?) all of space and time. This water a product of great space gasses that once inhabited the outer reaches of our solar system and then our atmosphere came comingling together when the earth was molten and raw and newly formed. These gases fused from space into atoms their byproducts—hydrogen, hydrogen, oxygen. Water. Water from space what a concept.

But here it is, so very big, so dangerous. I turn around, I step slowly back toward the house, you cannot be quick here. The wind whips into my face and I see that before I had been going in the calm, wind-at-your-back direction and now I must stand and face the sea. I see Heather there, a great ghost of a girl, her hand raised in class ready to say something brilliant.

My feet are already in the water as I walk further in. The cuffs of my pants, then my waist, descend into wetness. It's always a shock, how cold the ocean is. Then you get used to it as you walk farther. Always, the farther you go the colder it gets but you get used to it. That's the thing about the ocean, about anything really, you always get used to it. No matter what pummels you, you adjust. I'm waist deep before I look back. The lights of the hotel nearby and the houses on the Cape shine yellow and homey, they are domestic, earthly lights unlike the alien whiteness of the full moon.

Someone shouts to me, I don't even know who it is, but I keep walking, walking until I am no longer walking but swimming. My feet cannot touch down and I picture the sea creatures that might be at my feet. The giant squid, the blue whales. Yes, I'm only a few feet from shore but the things that are down there human eyes have not seen.

I keep swimming. Whoever was shouting has stopped and I turn around and swim further. How far was my mother when she would just keep going, scaring everyone to death? How bad were the waves? But the sea is calm tonight, completely without fury, and Poseidon must know what I have been through. I need to wash this away with salt and spray before I can come back from this.

It all lies bare on my skin, I feel it in my muscles, as I swim out.

Of your ice-hearted calling-/Drunkenness of the great depths./O river, I see drifting . . .

The shore gets smaller and smaller the farther I swim and I look out. The ocean, a very big thing. The moon, white and full, a colossus so far away. It's only then, when I see, when I feel, how big it is, that I turn back.

Acknowledgements

I'd like to thank my family. My husband, Adam, thank you for the constant, unwavering support. To my children, Addison and Jacqueline, two amazing people who give and receive love so warmly. To my parents, David and Gina Stilling, who taught me the value of hard work. To my siblings, Stephanie and Ian, thanks for putting up with me. For listening to my outlandish stories and for playing ridiculous games with me as a kid. I'd like to thank my aunt Kerri Price, the librarian, for always giving me books. Thanks to Donald for all your help and support. Thanks to Karen Greenberg for the babysitting, the pep talks and the books you've sent me. Thanks to Claude and Katie, my brother-in-law and sister-in-law. And my nephews Jasper and Diego, you're great kids with great parents. And thanks to Ruth Savin Greenberg, my first and best copyeditor.

This book would not be the book it is if it weren't for my workshops. Thanks to Rob, Matt and Susan, who tirelessly workshopped this novel. And thanks to Michael, Denise, Alejandro, Andrea and Brad for workshopping some of my other stuff. I learn so much from you guys. Thanks to Laurie, my writing pen-pal, for keeping in touch like a character in a Victorian novel. Thank you to Adrienne for looking at so many pages of this and other things. Thanks so my good friend Brook for all her hospitality.

I'd like to thank Linsey Abrams from City College for teaching me how to write and think about writing like a grownup. And Collette Brooks from The New School for supporting my work. And of course Felicia Bonaparte who taught me about Rome. Who taught me about Greece. Your wisdom and confidence astounds me.

I have taught at The Gotham Writer's Workshop for many years and teaching there has made me a better writer and a better teacher. Thanks to all my students. You've all been great. Thanks to Alex, Kelly and Dana for keeping the place running.

Thanks to The Academy of Mount Saint Ursula, an all girl's school that has truly given me a professional home. Thank you to Sister Jeannie for her openness and kindness. To Carolyn and Jeannie D. for all your help and support. And to the rest of the faculty and staff, especially Amanda, Keri and Noreen, in the English Department.

I would like to thank Jodi and Melissa my dear friends from Illinois. In many ways you are my best and oldest friends.

I would also like to humbly thank Sylvia Plath and all who knew her. Her writing, her poetry, her words, inspired so much of this novel. Thank you, Sylvia, for guiding me with a novel and so many short stories, with the poetry and journal entries I read while researching this. I would also like to thank her biographers and achievers whose work I used to research many facts on many occasions especially Andrew Wilson's *Mad Girl's Love Song*, Elizabeth Winder's *Pain, Parties, Work*, Janet Malcolm's *The Silent Woman*, Paul Alexander's *Rough Magic* and Diane Middlebrook's *Her Husband: Ted Hughes*

Jessica Stilling is the recipient of the Bronx Council on the Arts Chapter One Award and she is the author of the critically acclaimed novel Betwixt and Between. She has studied writing and literature at The New School and holds an MFA from City College. Her short fiction and poetry have appeared in over forty literary journals including *Wasifiri, The Warwick Review* and *Caustic Frolic.* Her feminist nonfiction has appeared in various media outlets such as Tor.com and the Ms. Magazine Blog. She has taught writing and literature in New York City for many years. She lives in New York with her famil

The Beekeeper's Daughter

by Jessica Stilling   **ISBN 978-1-949290-19-6**

Lorelei Bauer is a modern day woman with a penchant for Sylvia Plath, a woman struggling with the injustices of the fifties with her marriage, her role and status as a poet, her "job" as a mother, and her mental illness.

Lorelei's own mother suffered from mental illness and when Lorelei learns of her mother's breakdown and illegal abortion, she goes on a quest to better understand her as a parent. Lorelei soon discovers her life is paralleling Plath's and she panics about her fate.

During her quest, she meets up with an old friend of her mother's, Joanne, who gives her a secret, unpublished manuscript that her college friend, Sylvia Plath, sent her before her death. It is a continuation of the story of Esther Greenwood, Plath's protagonist from The Bell Jar. Lorelei learns many secrets from the Plath manuscript which both hurt her and makes her hopeful for her own future.

From the author

This book was in me for a while. After I read *The Bell Jar* and learned that Plath had written another novel about Esther that she'd destroyed and that people thought there was at least another novel out there that Ted Hughes never let see the light of day, I started considering the idea of continuing Esther's story on my own. For the longest time that's all I knew, that I wanted to do some kind of continuation of *The Bell Jar* but I wasn't sure how it would work. Ideas come slowly sometimes. They percolate, they simmer, you have to wait for them to truly form. But I continued to think about this idea for years. And I knew someday the story would come to me and I would write it. I just wasn't sure how right away. Would it be an interlocking narrative like Cunningham's *The Hours* or a retelling or continuation like *The Wide Sargasso Sea*?

After a trip to Cape Cod the idea for Lorelei started to take shape. I did more research on Plath and her life there and as I was doing it Lorelei and her story started to come into focus and become a part of the novel. Then I decided that Plath should have a narrative voice in the book and I started to wonder about what time in Plath's life I'd like to write about. At first I thought maybe I'd write about when she was a child growing up near Cape Cod, like Lorelei, then I thought maybe her time in New York, like *The Bell Jar*. I read many different Plath biographies while writing this. When I got to the end of the biography, to the part when she moves into Yeats' house, something clicked. I knew that this was the time in her life I needed to write about— the horrible London winter after her divorce that led to her suicide. It was dark, but that time really spoke to me. The novel emerged from there. I saw it very clearly but at the same time it took about two years of just thinking about it, doing a little research but just thinking about it, before it became something clear I could start working on.

Discussion Questions

1. How does the theme of the role of mental illness in the life of a woman take shape in the novel? Does it show a change in the way women were treated from Plath's time (the 1950s) to the present when we are introduced to Joanne's character?

2. How does the ocean (or the sea) work as a metaphor throughout the story? How might the image of Stonehenge in Esther Greenwood's story accomplish the same things?

3. How are the various men in this novel portrayed? From Ted Hughes to Esther's Tom, to Lorelei's ex-husband Theo, to her boyfriend Eamon ,we meet many different kinds of men who have many kinds of relationships with women. Are there any consistent themes or personality traits portrayed? How might they influence the outcome of the novel?

4. During the final section of Esther Greenwood's story she narrates, "And what was art, any art, but a byproduct of damage, of pain and loss so unimaginable? . . . and what kind of pain had the creator of the ocean felt as He made the waves so violent they trekked across the sea pummeling rocks and sea creatures, entire mountain ranges in their wake? What kind of pain had the makers of Stonehenge felt? What were they looking for, what did they need to know so badly they had to pull stones from the sea and drag them hundreds of miles?" How is the role of art and the creative process shown to affect an artist's life in this novel?

5. How is the marriage of Ted Hughes and Sylvia Path portrayed in this novel?

6. What impact does seeing Stonehenge have upon Esther Greenwood's character? Can you pinpoint the moment when things start to change for her?

7. Can you pinpoint a moment when Lorelei's life goes wrong? What is it for you? Why?

8. Throughout the novel Lorelei has a close group of friends Amelia, Eamon, her aunt Sarah and Joanne, to fall back on. Sylvia Plath seems very much alone (though a few friends look in on her). What role does friendship and familial ties play in the mental health of a woman going through a trying time in this novel?

9. Lorelei learns of a secret, illegal abortion that her mother had before she was born when she reads her mother's journal. How does this impact the story? Why might the author have chosen to portray an abortion in this way?

10. At the end of the novel Lorelei walks into the sea. It is left ambiguous what happens next. Do you think she goes too far? Does she come back? Why do you think this?

CPSIA information can be obtained
at www.ICGtesting.com
Printed in the USA
LVHW042019021219
639194LV00002B/274